ONI
S T O R I E S
F R O M   D A R K N E S S   T O   L I G H T

TERESA ELIZABETH CURTIS

LifeRich Publishing is a registered trademark of The Reader's Digest Association, Inc.

LifeRich Publishing books may be ordered through booksellers or by contacting:

LifeRich Publishing
1663 Liberty Drive
Bloomington, IN 47403
www.liferichpublishing.com
844-686-9607

ISBN: 978-1-4897-4431-9 (sc)
ISBN: 978-1-4897-4762-4 (e)

Library of Congress Control Number: 2023908901

Print information available on the last page.

LifeRich Publishing rev. date: 05/18/2023

CONTENTS

CHAPTER 1
SCIENTIST TROUBLE

Rummaging through his supplies Aster was getting ready to do something he'd dreamed of for years. He would enter the Oni Realm and capture an oni. But experiencing the oni fog was dangerous to humans. He felt like he was safe from this because of an experiment his father did on him. The experiment altered him greatly. He now was blue in color because he was 99% water and only 1% human. Surely, he could handle the oni fog. His friends Nick and Zane were not so convinced.

"Guys, this is a bad idea." Zane sighed while holding a broom.

"Keep cleaning." Aster said.

"Ok." Zane mumbled. He continued cleaning the lab wondering why he even hung out with these guys. They were always getting into trouble and usually treated him like crap. He needed some money to help his mom out. Being a single mom isn't easy and he wanted to help however he could. So for now this job would have to do.

"It's getting really late guys. We should do the oni kidnaping tomorrow." Zane said hoping to deter them.

"You just don't want us to take an oni!" Nick yelled.

"Yeah!" Aster agreed.

For two years Aster had been inventing a teleporter gun in which to enter the oni realm. He worked endless hours and this morning finally put the finishing touches on it. Crossing his fingers, he hoped it would work. No body wants to be stuck in a realm with evil creatures.

Walking toward the foggy cliffs an oni thought about her life and how empty and dark it was. *I don't want to be evil anymore. I don't understand why we are so cruel to humans when they don't do anything to deserve it.* She thought. "What am I thinking, oni's can't be good or nice! "Savannah yelled out loud.

Entering the Oni Realm Aster heard someone screaming and his heart began beating fast. He never dreamed he'd find an oni so quickly. He snuck around some rocks and spotted what looked like a girl somewhat, but definitely wasn't human. It had pitch black skin, horns and a tail with purple hair. How should he introduce himself without startling it.

Clearing his throat, he slowly walked toward it, "Hello." He spoke

"Human!" Savannah yelled.

"Are you an oni?" Aster asked.

"Yes, are you a blue human?" Savannah cried, hiding behind a rock.

Wow, oni's are interesting beings, Aster thought.

"Get away or I will slaughter you!" Savannah yelled.

"Can you come here? I will not hurt you, I promise," Aster smiled.

"Do you really promise?" Savannah asked.

"Of course, I always keep my promises," Aster smiled slyly.

She walked up to Aster and as she got closer, he noticed fangs and purple eyes with skull shaped pupils. She also wore glasses which he thought was very odd.

"What is your name?" he asked.

"I'm Savannah."

"That's a cool name, Savannah," Aster smiled trying to gain her trust.

Savannah began to feel panic grip her. She knew if she didn't get home soon her father would come looking for her and slaughter this human on the spot and discipline her for not already doing so. She began walking backward toward her home.

"Wait!" Aster yelled.

"What is it?" Savannah asked.

"I have a gift for you."

Curious, Savannah stepped toward him to see what was in his hand wondering why a human would give her anything. Suddenly, he grabbed her arm and before she knew it, he poked her with a needle. She immediately felt sleepy. "What have you done? "She mumbled.

"Let's hope Aster didn't die from the oni fog," Nick said.

"Yeah, that would be sad," Zane said while dusting a desk.

A bright light caught their eyes and as they turned Aster appeared and threw Savannah on the floor in front of them. She was not moving and they wondered if he killed her. He explained how he found her and put her to sleep with a tranquilizer shot.

"It's really odd. Does it have a name? "Nick asked.

"I think it's a girl and her name is Savannah. "Aster replied.

"I like her name. "Zane said.

As they were observing the oni Nick remembered promising his dad he'd help fix the car and he was already late. "I gotta go guys. Let's wait until tomorrow to begin testing on her. She's still asleep anyway."

"Ok, I'll see you tomorrow then," Aster smiled.

"I'm going home as well," Zane said. He exited the lab through the back door which automatically locked when it shut. He put on his helmet and rode his bike through Science City thinking about Savannah and wondering if Aster was going to harm her. He knew she would be scared when she woke up and was concerned for her.

Back at Aster's lab Savannah finally woke up and realized she wasn't in the Oni Realm anymore. Her eyes were not used to light so she squinted and looked around the room. She noticed she was in a tube and she could not get out. There were many wires and glass objects sitting on metal tables. Where was she? Aster approached her with a big grin on his face. He was pumped he finally had an oni.

"Where am I? "Savannah asked.

"You are in my lab," Aster said while putting his hands on the tube.

"What do you want?" Savannah cried.

"I'm a scientist and I want to study you," Aster explained.

"Why?" Savannah asked.

"Just shut up you dumb oni!" Aster yelled.

"Don't call me dumb!" Savannah yelled back.

"I'm going to test on you tomorrow because it's getting really late so I'll see you then" Aster said.

As morning arrived Savannah struggled to get out of the tube wondering why her oni powers would not work. Normally she would could easily escape something like this using her power of darkness, but pushing against the tube and summoning her power was not working.

Aster walked in dressed in a white lab coat sipping coffee feeling great about the day to come. Finally, he had an oni and would soon begin testing on it. Noticing her struggling he laughed and said," trying to escape I see. You are in x-stone bracelets. It's a very rare metal that will keep your power from working. So, you may as well quit struggling and try to relax."

"Sup Aster?" Nick said

"Oh, hey," Aster said.

"Don't you think about testing it without me dude," Nick laughed.

"I just can't wait any longer," Aster said.

"Hello," Zane smiled.

Are those humans, Savannah thought

"I want to see the oni," Nick said while walking toward her.

"Get away from me human!" Savannah yelled feeling helpless.

"Wow, her horns, tail, and teeth are so cool, "Nick smiled.

"I know right, "Aster said.

"What are you going to do with her?" Zane asked.

"Don't worry about what we're doing. Just start cleaning," Aster snipped.

Zane hung his head down concerned for Savannah's safety. He watched as Aster prepared a needle in order to draw some of her blood knowing that was just the beginning of many hurtful procedures.

"Do we really need to do this to Savannah? "Zane asked.

"Yes," Nick smiled.

"So, you're just going to hurt this oni girl and test on her? She's probably never seen a human before. Can't you see she's terrified?" Zane explained.

"I don't care what you say. I'm the scientist here!" Aster yelled while up in his face.

"Look Zane, I would leave if you can't handle it and don't come back," Nick said.

"Fine, if you don't want me, I'm out of here," Zane sighed. Gathering his things, he mounted his bike and headed home. As he pedaled faster and faster his determination to help Savannah grew stronger. He was going to think of something.

Len was doing the dishes when he arrived and she could tell by the look on his face something was troubling him. "Are you ok dear?" Len asked. Drying her hands, she walked over and gave him a hug. Zane explained to his mom how Aster had kidnapped an oni and was going to test on her. Len was concerned about her son.

"Oni's aren't real Zane and tell me who does Aster even test on? "Len asked.

"Oni's are real mom," Zane said.

"Are you sure sweetie?" Len asked.

"Yes, Aster went to the oni realm and kidnapped one," Zane cried. "I never told you this but Aster tricks people into getting a vaccine saying it can make you live forever. Some people believe it and when they get to Aster's lab, he just takes them and gives them really bad shots that hurt them," Zane cried.

"Zane, why do you even hang out with a guy like that? "Len asked.

"It's hard for me to make friends. He at least gave me a job," Zane sighed.

Len and Zane said a prayer asking God to protect Savannah. Len wanted to call the police but Zane was afraid they would take Savannah and give her to science to test on which would be no better than Aster having her. They would continue to pray and ask God to show them what to do. Zane decided he would he would try to rescue her somehow.

"Stop please!" Savannah yelled.

"Hold still you little brat!" Aster yelled back while taking her blood.

Nick put a gun to Savannah's head.

"I wanna go home," Savannah cried.

"You aren't going anywhere," Nick said.

Aster took out the needle and said," wow, oni blood is purple."

"Do humans normally do this?" Savannah asked.

"Uhhhh," Nick stammered

"Sure," Aster smiled.

"Humans are weirder than I thought," Savannah sighed.

"Hey, I'm not weird!" Aster yelled.

"You kinda are dude," Nick laughed. "Ever since your dad did that crazy experiment on you, you're not a typical guy. Ninety nine percent water and one percent human is a little weird."

"Whatever, "Aster sighed.

As Zane entered the building her heard Savannah scream. Opening the door, he saw Nick kick her and he yelled, "Stop!"

"Why are you back?" Nick asked.

"To stop you from hurting the oni," Zane said.

"Haha, you think you're so tough," Aster laughed.

"Can I ask you a question?" Zane asked.

"Sure weirdo," Aster said.

"Would God want you to do this to the oni girl?" Zane asked

"Ugh, for the last time, we aren't Christians like you," Nick said.

"Psalm 11:5 says," *The Lord tests the righteous, but his soul hates the wicked and the one who loves violence"*, Zane said.

Aster slammed the tube door while Savannah was pounding on its walls and screaming. He teased her by saying "boo" and laughing in her face. "Nick, take care of Zane."

Nick pointed the gun at Zane.

"Easy with that," Zane said.

"Listen Zane, you can't tell us what to do!" Nick yelled.

I can do this, Zane thought as he ran to Nick and got ahold of his arm. Zane took the gun out of Nicks hand and thew it across the room.

"You're going to pay for that brat!" Nick yelled.

Nick always wins fights, Aster smiled with folded arms watching as the two stared each other down.

"I can do all things with Christ who gives me strength," Zane smiled.

"Haha, I hate your bible quotes," Aster laughed. Zane ran to Nick and hit him in the face.

"Dang bro," Nick sighed.

"Wow, he hit you," Aster said surprisingly.

"Don't make me hurt you, I just want to help the oni girl," Zane breathed.

"Never," Nick yelled.

"This would be a nice time for popcorn," Aster smiled.

"What's popcorn?" Savannah asked?

"It's a human thing, you wouldn't get it, "Aster said while leaning on the tube.

"Aster, help me!" Nick yelled.

"You got this," Aster said.

Zane kicked Nick in the leg than he fell down.

"Dude, get up!" Aster yelled.

Zane kicked him in the head and knocked him silly.

Crap, he's good, Aster thought.

"This is the last time I'm saying this. Let me take the oni and help her," Zane demanded.

"Never!" Aster yelled.

"I guess you want knocked out just like Nick?" Zane smiled.

"You know what, I'm just going to go before you call the cops," Aster laughed.

Zane crossed him arms and said," Taekwondo lessons sure paid off."

"Bye," Aster cried than ran out the door.

Wow, that was easier than I thought, Zane smiled. Zane walked to Savannah.

"I don't want to be a test subject, "Savannah cried.

Zane slowly walked toward the tube and pushed the red button. Savannah quickly ran and hid behind the desk. He took several minutes trying to convince her that he was there to help her and that he was going to rescue her from Aster and Nick. After smiling softly and speaking in a kind voice he reached for her. Still not ready to trust humans she pulled away deeper under the desk.

"Don't touch me!" Savannah yelled.

"My name is Zane and I'm a really nice human who wants to help you," Zane said.

Savannah hid her face and said," I'm scared."

I need to get her to a safe place and get her used to me so I can talk to her, Zane thought while on his knees.

Just then Savannah got closer to Zane and slowly reached out to touch his hair.

"Hi," Zane smiled.

"Where are your horns?" Savannah asked.

"I don't have any," Zane said while Savannah was feeling his hair.

"Would you like to come to my house? "Zane asked.

"I don't understand what that means," Savannah cried.

"I will let you come where I live to be safe from Aster and Nick," Zane smiled while Savannah was feeling his arm curiously.

She continued looking at Zane examining his face and teeth noticing all the things that were different about humans as well as things that were the same as her kind. *Should she trust him?* she wondered. She was taught her whole life that humans were the enemy. But this one seemed so kind. Finally, she agreed to go with Zane.

"My mom will be happy to meet you," Zane said.

Forty-five minutes had passed before Len realized Zane had left the house. It wasn't like him to not tell her where he was going. She was worried he had decided on an attempt at rescuing that oni on his own. She would give him fifteen minutes to get home then she would call the police. Suddenly, she heard the door close and hurried to the living room. What she saw shocked her and she almost had to sit down. In front of her was a girl like creature with horns and a tail standing next to Zane almost hiding behind him. Even though she looked a little scary she could see innocence and fear in her eyes.

"Mom, this is Savannah."

"So, Savannah, how did you get into this realm?" Len asked nervously.

"A human tricked me," Savannah said shyly.

"Hey, its ok Savannah," Zane said.

Savannah tried to hug Zane and, in the process, almost poked him in the eye with her horns. He warned her gently to be careful and she licked his arm. Glancing at his mom he shrugged his shoulders and said, "I guess we have a lot to teach her."

"I'm sure you are hungry Savannah," Len said.

"Do you have any human eyes to eat? "Savannah asked?

"Uh, we do not," Len said trying not to panic.

"Sorry Savannah we don't," Zane said.

"Do you have human blood?" Savannah asked.

"We don't," Len said casting a worried glance toward Zane.

"Oh," Savannah sighed.

"I might have something you will like, "Len said.

They followed Len into the kitchen and Zane pulled out a chair for Savannah to sit in. She looked really confused wondering if that is what she was suppose to eat. Zane laughed and showed her how to sit in the chair. Len had made pizza earlier so she put some slices on plates for them and set one in front of Savannah.

"What is that?' Savannah asked.

"It's called pizza," Zane smiled.

"What do you do with it?" Savannah asked.

"Its food," Len said.

"Zane, can I eat your mom?" Savannah asked.

"Um, why don't you try this," Zane said quickly.

"Please don't eat me sweetie," Len said nervously.

"Mom, I won't let her eat you," Zane laughed.

"Zane, can I talk to you?" Len asked.

"Sure," Zane said.

"In the living room please."

Len shared her concerns with Savannah being demonic, wanting to eat people, and how she would fit into the human realm. She had so much to learn. Zane assured his mom that he would teach Savannah about Jesus and the truth about God and His ways. He wanted to be a friend to her. Now that Aster and Nick wouldn't want him as a friend, he was hoping to be a friend to Savannah.

"Maybe God put Savannah in your life," Len smiled.

"I hope so," Zane sighed.

"We should go check on her to make sure she doesn't get into anything," Len laughed.

"Ok," Zane agreed.

Savannah was up against the fridge.

"What are you doing?" Zane asked,

"That pizza thingy is creeping me out," Savannah said.

"It's ok dear, its food and Zane loves it," Len said.

"Does It have blood in it?" Savannah asked.

"No, I'm sorry", Len sighed.

"Please try it," Zane said.

After much encouragement, Savannah opened her mouth, closed her eyes, and took a bite of the pizza. It had a strange taste but wasn't too bad. She was going to have to get used to eating human food. Evidently blood is not a common food item in the human realm but a necessity in hers.

Back at the lab Aster was fuming mad. How in the world did Zane kick Nick's butt and take the oni. He considered him a wimpy Christian. He had to come up with a plan to get rid of Zane so he could get his oni back. As he and Nick racked their brains, they remembered something about a Nether Realm. This was a place of nothingness if that is possible.

Endless ground where you just walked and walked but go nowhere. They continued making their plans well into the night and decided to wait until morning to trap Zane.

As night fell and Len and Zane began their bedtime routine Savannah was confused as to what "time for bed" meant. Zane gave her his bed and he put a mattress on the floor for him.

"I don't know who sleep is or what a bed is," Savannah cried.

"Is everything ok in here?" Len asked.

"She doesn't know how to sleep," Zane sighed.

"Savannah, would you like me to teach you to sleep?" Len asked.

"Are you a nice human?" Savannah asked.

Len went to Savannah and smiled," I will never hurt you and plus this is a safe place".

"I will try to sleep like you Len," Savannah smiled.

"Ok, let's go then," Len said as she led her into her bedroom.

Twelve o clock midnight came and Savannah was wide awake. Len woke and got her a glass of water which she thought tasted like nothing. What she craved was a drink of blood. Len explained to her that in the human realm you drink water or something else made with water. It is good for your body and refreshes you. Drinking blood was not appropriate or safe.

"I can't do this!" Savannah yelled." I can't do the sleep thingy like you and the human named Zane can."

"I need to get some sleep," Len yawned.

"But I can't sleep," Savannah sighed.

Len picked up a remote and said," I can put some music on for you"

"What is music?" Savannah asked.

"You will see. It will help you relax," Len smiled.

The next morning the smell of pancakes and bacon filled the house. They gathered in the kitchen to sit down and Savannah wondered if she should show them her human form. She definitely would blend in better.

"Can I ask you something?" Savannah asked,

"Sure thing," Len smiled.

"I have a human form if you would like me to be in it," Savannah explained.

"Yeah, I would love to see it," Zane said.

Savannah went into her human form which pretty much was like a human. She could hide her tail in her clothes and wear a hat to cover her horns.

"Wow, you're so pretty," Zane said quite stricken.

"I love your blue hair," Len smiled.

"Thank you," Savannah said.

"Breakfast will be ready in about ten minutes. I think you'll like bacon Savannah," Len said.

"Who doesn't like bacon," Zane said as he rubbed his tummy.

"Ha, that's called a gaming controller", Zane laughed as Savannah began chewing on the wires of his game system.

"What do you do with it? Savannah asked.

Zane pushed the console button and turned on the television. He began playing a superhero game and Savannah was wide eyed with wonder. Suddenly something caught her eye behind them. He turned to look and there was Aster standing in his living room. He had used his teleporter gun to show up and began pulling Zane into the portal. All of this was so confusing to Savannah she didn't know what to do.

"Wow, look at you," Aster smiled.

"What do you want with me?" Savannah cried.

"Nice hat oni," Aster said.

"Leave me be", Savannah sighed as he walked toward her.

"Shut up!" Aster yelled.

"What did you do with Zane?" Savannah asked.

"Don't worry about him", Aster smiled.

"I said what did you do with him!" Savannah yelled.

"Calm down oni, he is just in the Nether Realm," Aster sighed.

Zane stood up and looked around. *Where am I,* He wondered. As he turned around looking in every direction, he saw the same thing. *Aster has sent me to some other realm. How do I get out of here?* He began walking and walking making no progress at all.

Len walked in the room to announce breakfast was ready when she saw Aster reaching for Savannah.

Savannah blasted Aster with her darkness fog causing him to fall to the floor.

I had no idea oni's can do that, Len thought." Where's Zane?" she asked nervously.

"Aster sent Zane to the Nether Realm," Savannah cried.

"You little demonic oni, I will make you my test subject and I will make you mine!" Aster yelled.

Poor Savannah. Please God help her understand that you love her by protecting her, Len prayed.

Aster got up and jabbed her in the shoulder with a sleeping needle.

"What did you do to her and how can I get my boy back?" Len cried.

"Relax Len, its only gonna make her fall asleep. As for your boy he's going to get really bored walking for eternity," Aster laughed out loud.

"Please," Savannah sighed while on the floor.

"Goodnight oni," Aster laughed.

"Savannah is mine and mine forever," Aster mocked glaring at Len.

"You are a monster!" Len yelled.

"The oni is the monster," Aster grunted.

Len was crying and said," You make me sick."

Aster put on Savannah's hat and smiled," See ya later Len the loser."

"Leave her alone," Len cried as they teleported out of the house.

Aster teleported Savannah and himself to the lab.

Len ran to the door praying for God to protect Zane and Savannah.

This is a never-ending path, Zane thought. I hope Savannah is ok, Zane sighed. Zane knew Aster had sent him somewhere but had no idea how to get back home. He had to believe somehow God would help him even if he had no clue how. *I guess this is what faith is,* Zane thought.

Aster put X stone on Savannah so she couldn't use her oni powers.

"Wow, I never knew oni's had a human form," Nick said.

"I know, I was thinking the same thing, "Aster laughed.

As Nick put Savannah in the corner she began crying loudly. She had never been so terrified. Nick put a gun to her head and threatened to shoot her if she didn't shut up. Aster grabbed her arm and pulled her toward the examining table. She struggled and yelled as Nick chained her down.

'I would love to have power like an oni," Aster smiled.

"Yeah, but we can't dude," Nick sighed while hooking on the chains.

I'm so scared, Savannah thought while crying.

Nick thew her hat off so he could check out her horns.

"You will only feel a little pinch," Aster smiled while putting a sleeping needle in her arm.

"Let me go!" Savannah yelled.

"Nap time oni," Nick chuckled.

"I have an idea Nick," Aster smiled.

"Now what," Nick sighed wondering what bright idea Aster had now.

"I can take some of Savannah's blood and put it into me so I can get some of her power," Aster explained.

"I don't think that's a very good idea. It might hurt you or maybe even kill you," Nick said with concern.

"At least I can try bro," Aster smiled.

Please don't be an idiot, Nick thought while slapping his hand on his forehead.

"I can't wait to be powerful," Aster smiled, while feeling for a vein on Savannah's arm.

"Are you sure this is the best way to get powerful dude?" Nick asked.

"Shut up!" Aster yelled while Savannah's blood was flowing into the syringe.

Nick covered his face with both hands shaking his head.

"I'm ready for this Nick," Aster said.

"I'm not", Nick said fearfully.

"Quit being a baby. We're scientists," Aster said.

"Ok, I'll stop talking", Nick sighed.

Aster handed Nick the needle and sat down in the chair. He nodded at Nick and insisted he inject the blood into his vein. Nick rolled up Aster's sleeve and with shaky hands stuck the vein.

This is the best idea I ever had, Aster thought. Within a few minutes he began to feel different." This feels awesome", he said. His eyes began to turn purple.

"Dude, your eyes changed," Nick said.

"It's working then", Aster smiled.

"Oh my gosh, you are growing horns on your freaking head," Nick screamed.

"Just like an oni," Aster laughed.

"Be careful dude," Nick said.

"I feel like a god," Aster smiled.

"You already know oni darkness can kill humans and you put oni blood into you.

You might die or get sick," Nick sighed.

"You know what Nick?" Aster asked.

"Now what,"

"I think I will kill Zane so little Savannah and Len the loser can feel sad for the rest of their lives," Aster explained.

"This blood has made you even more cruel than you already were."

Aster was holding his teleporter gun and said," Stay here and watch Savannah for me."

"All by myself?"

"Dude, she is in X stone, she can't hurt you," Aster said.

Ok, I'll be here waiting, Nick said.

As Aster teleported to the Nether Realm, Len pulled into the parking lot of his lab. She didn't have any idea what she would do but her Mama Bear instinct had kicked in.

"Hello Zane," Aster smiled as he entered the Nether Realm and pulled out a gun aiming it at Zane.

"What happened to you?" Zane cried noticing his eyes and horns.

"I became a powerful person and no one will stand in my way", Aster laughed.

"Did you do something to Savannah to make you like this?" Zane asked.

"Oh, just a little oni blood in me did the trick," Aster smiled.

Back at the lab Savannah noticed Nick sleeping with a book and keys sitting on the table next to him. If she could get the keys maybe she could get away. She reached for them but the chains would not allow her to reach that far. She heard footsteps coming down the hall and suddenly Len opened the door.

"What?" Nick yawned as he was awakened.

"Dang it!" Savannah swore.

'Were you trying to escape? "Nick asked.

"Uh, no." Savannah lied.

"Hey!" Len yelled trying to distract him from Savannah.

"Well look who it is." Nick laughed.

"Let her go." Len grunted.

"Never old lady! "Nick yelled.

"I wanna go home." Savannah cried." You and your blue human friend act like my dad, someone who just cares about my power and not me." Savannah explained while crying.

"Ha, sad story freak." Nick laughed.

"Tell me more about your dad Savannah." Len asked hoping maybe Nick would have some compassion if he knew more about Savannah's life.

Savannah explained how her dad separated her and her brother so that he could torture her. Her brother tried to defend her so her dad sent him to the Human Realm to never return. She hadn't seen him for years. She tried to escape so her dad drugged her to diminish her power.

Giving in, Nick said, "Fine I'll take you to Zane as he let the oni girl out of the X stone." We have to go now because Aster is going to kill Zane." Nick said.

"Kill!" Len yelled.

Crap, Nick thought. Len got in Nick's face and began telling him what would happen if he didn't get her son away from that murderer. Spending the rest of his life in jail didn't sound like a good option to him. Nick unlocked the x-stone chains and Savannah ran to Len.

"It's ok," Len smiled while hugging Savannah.

"Here's your dumb hat back," Nick said.

"Uh, thanks," Savannah said reaching for it.

"Let's go," Nick said while holding the teleporter gun. Before he had a chance to explain where they were going, he teleported them to the Nether Realm and immediately heard Zane's voice.

"Aster, please," Zane sighed while running. Aster got a hold of Zane." Please, don't do this," Zane said while crying.

"Any last words Zaney?" Aster asked.

"Aster!" Len yelled.

Crap, Aster thought.

"Put him down dude," Nick sighed.

"Nick, why is the oni out of the chains?" Aster asked.

"If only you knew what Savannah has been though. She told me everything about her scary life. She's more like you than you know. She had a mean father too. "Nick explained.

"I don't care about the oni's life. I only care about her dang blood!" Aster yelled while having the gun on Zane's head.

"Why do you want my blood?" Savannah asked.

"For money," Aster smiled.

"Ugh, he wants to sell your blood to become richer than he already is." Nick sighed.

My head hurts, Aster thought.

"Just let Zane go. "Nick said.

Aster pushed Zane to the floor as he stumbled forward. He was holding his stomach and grimacing.

"Are you ok?" Nick asked.

"I don't know." Aster sighed.

"Why does the blue human have oni horns?" Savannah asked.

"Aster put your blood into him so he can be powerful." Nick explained.

"But I have oni blood and if he's a human he can die from it." Savannah said.

"I told you idiot!" Nick yelled.

Aster fell to the floor." Is he dying?" Len asked.

"Yes." Savannah said.

"Savannah, help him." Zane cried.

"Why should I? "Savannah asked.

"Killing is not right Savannah. You can be a good person and not be evil like the other oni's." Zane said.

"Sweetie, do you know who Jesus is?" Len asked.

"Yeah, he is a bad guy who wants to kill everyone in the universe." Savannah said.

Poor Savannah, Zane thought.

"Listen to me. Jesus is the good guy." Len said.

"But my dad told me Jesus is bad. "Savannah said.

"I'm, sorry to say this but, your dad was lying to you." Len sighed.

"Why?" Savannah asked.

John 3:16 says, "For God so loved the world, that he gave his one and only Son, that whoever believes in him should not perish but have eternal life." Len explained." Does that sound like God wants to kill everyone? It's the opposite."

"But I can't die." Savannah said.

"I know but you can choose where you spend eternity. Jesus loves you Savannah, please don't listen to your dad. You said he hurt you and you know fathers shouldn't treat their children that way. Trust us." Zane said.

"Help him." Nick begged while kneeling next to Aster.

"God is Jesus by the way." Zane smiled.

"But God hates oni's" Savannah cried.

"If you ask Jesus in your heart, he will forgive you of all the evil you've done." Len smiled.

"So, God loves me?" Savannah asked.

"So much that he died for you." Len smiled with tears in her eyes.

"My own dad lied to me?" Savannah asked.

"I'm sorry he did but we will tell you the truth." Zane said.

"Aster please don't die!" Nick yelled.

"You can be a good oni Savannah, you got this girl." Len smiled.

Dad told me to be selfish and mean to humans but I don't think that's right, Savannah thought." I'm going to do the right thing." Savannah smiled.

"Go Savannah!" Zane cheered her on.

Savannah went on her knees next to Aster. "The only way I can help him is if I use my power and…. never mind, you guys wouldn't understand what I was gonna say." Savannah said.

"Hurry oni!" Nick yelled.

Savannah put her hands on Aster's stomach. She went into her oni form and purple fog began forming around them and they were barely visible. She summoned a gold bag and when it appeared she shook some red dust out and wiped it on Aster. He still wasn't moving,

"Is he dead?" Nick asked in dread.

"Yes, but I'm resurrecting him." Savannah said.

Aster eyes opened but were bright red.

"Oh my gosh!" Nick yelled.

Savannah put her hands on Aster face and said," He's fine now. "His eyes returned to normal

Aster started to cough." What happened?" Aster asked.

"I just resurrected you." Savannah smiled.

"I never knew an oni would help a human. "Aster said.

"I guess I'm the first." Savannah said.

"Is God and the human Jesus proud of me?" Savannah asked.

"Ha, yes, He is." Len smiled. Savannah went out of her oni form.

"Aster, what do you say to Savannah?" Zane asked.

"Savannah, I'm sorry I scared and hurt you." Aster sighed.

"You said my name." Savannah smiled.

"I hope you can forgive me?" Aster asked.

"Oni's don't forgive but since I want to be a good person, I do forgive you." Savannah said.

"And me?" Nick asked.

"Yep." Savannah smiled

"I will give you and Nick a chance to be nice and not hurt or kill anyone." Len said.

"So, you won't call the cops?" Nick asked.

"Not this time." Len said.

"Wow." Aster said surprised at how forgiving they all were. He teleported them all back to the lab.

"I understand you guys were just curious about me. But no more kidnapping and testing." Savannah. said. "I don't want to have to go all Oni on you." She laughed.

Night had fallen and they all began to go their separate ways. Aster thanked Savannah once more for saving him. As they arrived back at Len's house Savannah felt a sense of belonging. She asked Len if she could sleep with her again. She felt safe here. Maybe the Human Realm wasn't so bad.

CHAPTER 2
THE MISSING SIBLING

"Ok kids, time for bed." Len smiled.

"It's really hard for me to sleep like humans and besides, oni's are not supposed to sleep." Savannah explained.

"You can stay up dear." Len said.

"Goodnight Savannah. If you need anything just wake me up." Zane said.

Savannah smiled at Zane.

Savannah was sitting down on a white couch with navy blue dots and holding a fluffy black pillow thinking about the new realm she was in. After sitting there for five minutes, she got bored and started to get curious about the human realm. She wanted to go outside and see what was different from her realm and this one. She threw the pillow on the ground and ran to the front door. She smiled and took a deep breath. She opened the door in excitement.

I hope Zane and Len don't mind me going out. Savannah thought while walking in the dark.

She looked at the moon.

Zane and Len tell me God made this realm and I think he did a great job, Savannah thought while looking at the moon.

"I love this place!" Savannah yelled while running around excitedly.

"No torturing and no screaming, just peace. "Savannah smiled.

Too much running, Savannah gasped while sitting on the ground near the woods.

In a nearby cave in some rocks a humanlike creature suddenly caught the scent of something. Being hungry he was excited to finally get something to eat. Since he had come to this realm food was not easy to come by. Humans don't take lightly to being eaten and put up a pretty good fight. He summoned his oni knife and quietly crawled out of the cave. He saw someone sitting on the ground and pounced on her. He suddenly had a fight going on he did not expect. Savannah yelled and went into her oni form in response to the attack. He jumped on her and was about to stab her with his knife and realized she was an oni. She bit him and blasted him with her power. Looking in her eyes he noticed something familiar. Before he could say anything she quickly got away. He ran back the cave and picked up a picture of him, his dad and his sister." It can't be her." he mumbled." I need to find that girl!" he cried.

Back at the house Len was getting ready for work while Zane was searching for Savannah not finding her anywhere in the house. Suddenly Savannah burst through the front door and ran to Zane shaking all over. She explained she couldn't sleep so went for a walk and some creepy guy tried to eat her. Len looked at Zane and rolled her eyes believing she had a great imagination. Worried about what Savannah might get into while she was gone, she told them to stay in the house and call her if they needed anything. She only worked half a day on Saturdays as a part time nurse so she wouldn't be gone long.

Laughing to herself, Len thought, *there better not be a cannibal on the loose, with all this craziness going on it wouldn't surprise me.*

"Savannah, let's eat some breakfast." Zane said.

"I'm scared.!" Savannah yelled.

"Relax, the person who tried to eat you doesn't even know where we live." Zane smiled.

Savannah sensed a presence and turning around saw a being with pale skin. He was dressed in a purple and neon green cloak standing there with a big creepy grin on his face. She screamed and Zane immediately jumped to his feet to defend her. Yelling at the creature to leave they faced off and pushed and shoved on another around the living room.

"Look, I just want to ask some questions." He sighed.

"No, get out!" Zane yelled.

"Let him talk." Savannah said noticing he looked more like an oni than a human.

"Ok, when is your birthday?" He asked.

"October thirty first. "Savannah said while hiding behind Zane,
"Your name?"

"Savannah." she said.

"Savannah it's me your older brother Drake! I knew it was you!" He smiled.

"If you don't believe me, I know you're the only being alive without a heartbeat." Drake said.

"I never told anyone that." Savannah cried.

Looking at the confusion on Zane's face they explained that it had been forty years since they saw each other. They were separated by their father and Drake was banished to the human realm. Even though Savannah looked like a teenager she was actually thousands of years old. Onis live forever and don't age quickly. Zane was still in disbelief.

"Drake, is it really you?" Savannah asked.

"Yes sis, the funniest oni in the world." Drake smiled.

A phone rang startling them all. Savannah had never heard a phone before. Zane pulled it out of his pocket and Aster was on the line. He asked to speak to Savannah. Still annoyed with this blue human she held the phone to her ear like Zane did and asked what he wanted. As he spoke, she looked at the phone wondering how he got in this little device. Zane laughed at her confusion. She had a lot to learn.

"I'm guessing you never seen a phone before." Aster laughed. "I just wanted to ask if I can have some of your blood, Aster smiled.

Savannah shouted no in the phone and asked why in the world he would want her blood. Hadn't he just almost died by using it to make himself feel powerful? This human is really not very smart. He explained to her that he ran a business and sold rare items and that her blood was so rare it would make him a lot of money. He truly was a very selfish human, not at all like Zane.

"Drake, break this idiotic phone!" Savannah yelled.

"Sure thing." Drake smiled.

"No don't, phones cost a lot of money." Zane said while grabbing the phone from Drake.

I really want to eat that human, Drake thought.

"Hey Aster, we are heading to your lab, see you in a little bit." Zane said.

"Why are we going to see Aster?" Savannah asked.

"Who is Aster, is he a human I can eat?" Drake asked.

"You don't eat people, "Zane said.

"Oni's do." Drake grinned.

Zane grabbed the teleporter gun Aster had given him to try out and immediately transported the three of them to Aster's lab. He wasn't convinced this was Savannah's brother. He will have Aster check him out to be sure. The only way to know would be a blood test. Savannah shuddered at being back at this lab. It scared her remembering how Aster treated her.

I hate this place, Savannah sighed.

"That Drake guy is creeping me out." Zane said.

"I barely remember him." Savannah confessed.

"That's why we can see if Aster is willing to get some of Drake's blood to make sure he is really your brother." Zane explained.

"But Zane, he kind of looks like my brother and the name is a little familiar." Savannah sighed really hoping it was him.

"Let's find out. "Zane smiled.

"Teehee, hello human, you look yummy." Drake laughed eying Aster.

Zane filled Aster in on Drake's story about being Savannah's brother. They wanted to be sure and a blood test would prove that. Getting a chance to get some oni blood Aster was delighted to help out. He told them all to wait in the lobby and took Drake to the exam room. He got several tubes ready. Maybe a few more than actually needed to do a DNA test and instructed Drake to sit in the chair. Drake was very nervous and began laughing and talking which went on the whole time. Aster was exhausted from all the wiggling and talking and sent Drake to wait with the others while he ran the test.

"Is that Savannah's blood? "Nick asked.

"Nope." Aster said.

"Then who's is it?" Nick asked.

"Zane wants me to do a DNA test on this weird guy who says he is Savannah's brother. "Aster explained.

"Oh, that's weird. Maybe there are more onis here than we realize." Nick said.

Sitting in the lobby waiting, Zane watched as Drake kept poking himself in the eye. *This guy sure is strange Zane* thought. Drake couldn't sit still and would not stop chattering.

"I think I know what type of being Drake is." Aster said while looking under a microscope.

"Tell me bro." Nick said.

After checking the results and double checking them Aster called everyone into the lab. Boy was this interesting. He explained that Drake was both oni and Simbyot. A Simbyot was a combination of a demon, alien, vampire, and spider. Savannah was half oni and half Simbyot. Even though they weren't exactly the same they were siblings. He continued by telling how he used some of Savannah's blood he had and put it in a memory machine that Nick had invented. It looked back at Savannah's history and found memories of Drake. The reason she could not remember him was because her father tried to erase the bonding with Drake and their mom.

"Savannah, I can get your memories back using my new brain invention if you want." Aster said.

"I guess. It's not going to hurt, is it?" Savannah said.

"Follow me." Aster smiled.

"Why do you have a knife, Drake?" Zane asked.

"Hehe." Drake smiled.

"Uh, never mind." Zane said rolling his eyes.

After a long hour of sitting with a contraption attached to her head Savannah finally had her memories restored. She was so excited to be able to remember Drake that she jumped up and ran to him hugging him with all her might. After some time of celebrating their reunion, the group decided to order some pizza and hang out watching a movie.

"Why can't I just eat you, Zane? I don't know what pizza is but oni's don't eat that. We eat humans." Drake said.

"Drake, these humans are my friends." Savannah said.

"Wow, never thought you would want a human friend." Drake laughed.

As Nick began to call and order pizza the lab alarm went off. No one knew about the lab except those that were there and maybe Len. The alarm stopped and assuming it was Zane's Mom they waited for the door to open. All of a sudden, a tall dark man with appeared and Aster's heart sank.

"Nice to see you again my son." Russell laughed.

Aster began to feel panic rising inside him. He knew what his father was capable of and what he was after. The others stared wondering if this really was Aster's dad. He never talked about him at all. All Nick knew was that his name was Russell. Getting up in Aster's face he asked the question Aster knew was coming.

"Did you find an oni yet my son?"

"No, I haven't and you can leave. You're not welcome here." He realized he would earn his fathers respect if he turned them over but deep down he knew they were his new friends and his father would never really love him.

Zane slowly slid Savannah behind him shielding her from Russell's view. The others were getting nervous but tried to remain calm so as to not alert him that they were lying. Russell noticed Savannah hiding and asked who she was. Zane said she was just very shy. He also noticed one was dressed extremely weird, had fangs and just stood there with a stupid smile on his face.

"What's up with this guy?" Russell asked.

"He's just a friend who is an oni wanna be. You know how weird teenagers can be." Nick said.

Not trusting them, Russell pulled out a device explaining it was an oni tracker. He would soon find out if they were hiding something. As he turned it on two red lights began to blink. His eyes widened in disbelief. He pushed Zane aside and saw Savannah's oni tail. He was angered that his son was lying to him and he grabbed Savannah. She bit his arm and drew blood. He threw her to the ground and pulled a gas mask out of his lab coat. The others immediately knew what was about to happen. He released sleeping gas into the room and waited.

"Night, night." Russell smiled.

Great, now I have to carry my son and one of the oni's to the car, Russell thought. *I didn't think this through.*

Zane, Nick, and Drake woke up on the floor of the lab. They were a little dizzy and it took them a few minutes to realize Aster and Savannah were missing. They knew Russell took them. But where?

"Oh my gosh, I can't believe I slept like a human, Hehe, it never happened before, I feel so relaxed now. Drake smiled.

"I am so hungry. Can I eat one of you guys?" Drake asked.

Nick and Zane yelled," No!"

"We need to find them." Zane sighed.

"I can read minds teehee. I can probably read Savannah's mind." Drake laughed.

Drake concentrated really hard but Savannah was too far away for him to connect with her.

"Let's just pray that God can help us find them." Zane said.

"Oh crap, I'm with a Christian." Drake said.

"What's the matter with being a Christian?" Zane asked.

"It's just that my dad is the King of the Oni and he hates Christians because oni's are satanic." Drake said.

"Look, you can be whatever you want to be. I asked Savannah about your dad and I could tell your dad was so mean to you both." Zane said.

"I can't be a Christian!" Drake yelled.

"Savannah is learning about Jesus and so can you." Zane smiled.

"My dad will hate me if I turn good. Even talking to a human without hurting them will get me hurt." Drake sighed. "If he only knew I was here with you all now I'd be toast."

"Jesus loves you, Drake." Zane smiled while putting his hand on Drake's shoulder.

Drake began crying.

"Dude it's ok." Nick said.

"I will get tortured." Drake said while crying.

"We wouldn't let that happen." Zane said.

"At least let Zane tell you about God." Nick said.

"Listen Drake, your sister is happy and feels so much better with Jesus." Zane said.

"I'm scared to be good." Drake sighed.

"God doesn't give you a spirt of fear, but love, power, and a sound mind." Zane said.

"Oni's fear every day in the oni realm." Drake said while crying.

"Jesus can take your fear away," Zane smiled.

"He can?" Drake asked.

"Yes." Zane smiled." When a person comes to understand how much God loves them, they won't fear anymore."

"You know what?" Drake said.

"What is it?" Zane asked.

"If Savannah was brave enough to become Christian, so can I." Drake smiled.

"Now, let's work on a plan to get our friends back." Nick said.

Aster and Savannah began waking from the sleeping gas and found themselves in a lab with Russell staring at them. He was examining Savannah's sharp teeth and wondered why she wasn't in oni form. He was getting ready to leave for a business trip and wanted to get a look at the oni before Scarlet, his boss, got a hold of her. She was a mad scientist who would do crazy experiments on this oni. It's hard to tell what kind of shape Savannah would be in when he returned.

"Since you lied to me and tried to hide the oni from me, son, I'll let Scarlet deal with you. "Russell sneered. Russel left the room knowing he may never see his son again and not really caring. He himself tried to end Aster's life but the experiment failed.

Thirty minutes later a female scientist entered the room carrying a knife. She had brown hair, black glasses, and blood all over her hands. Fear instantly gripped Aster because he knew what she was capable of. He feared not only for Savannah but for himself too.

"Well look who we have here." Scarlet smiled.

"Please don't hurt her." Aster cried.

"I can do what I want water boy!" Scarlet yelled.

"Why do you have blood on your hands?" Aster asked.

"I just got done killing your dad." Scarlet smiled.

Aster's heart dropped. Even though his dad was mean and evil he still hoped one day he would love him and be proud of him. Even though he was Scarlet's right-hand man and was a valuable asset to her he wasn't surprised Scarlet killed Russell. She was a lunatic and thought people were replaceable.

Scarlet approached Savannah with an evil grin on her face trying to scare her. She stroked her arm and Savannah pulled away from her. Scarlet couldn't wait to see the rest of Savannahs body. She was curious about all her body parts.

"Get away from her pervert. Leave her alone!" Aster shouted.

Savannah kicked Scarlet making her stumble. Scarlet punched Savannah in the nose causing it to bleed. She let the blood run onto her finger noticing that it was purple in color. This excited Scarlet. *I can't wait to test on this one* she thought. She decided to let Aster go because he was really annoying and would just be in the way. She could have killed him but decided to let him hurt over his father's death.

"I don't want to be alone." Savannah said while crying.

Aster hesitated to leave but knew he and the others would come up with a plan to save her.

"Oh, and don't call the police or else." Scarlet smiled while looking at her knife.

As Aster was running away, he yelled," I will save you Savannah!"

Savannah started to panic realizing that she was alone with this crazy human. She decided to cooperate hoping Scarlet would take it easy on her. Scarlet led her to a chair with x-stone straps and pushed her down hard and grabbed the scissors. Thinking she was going to stab her it was a relief to see that she was just cutting her hair so that it wouldn't be in the way of the experiments. She threw her hat on the floor commenting how dumb oni's look in hats. Much to Scarlet's surprise Savannah's hair instantly grew back. Another interesting thing to note.

"How about you let me go?" Savannah smiled.

"Fat chance oni, the fun is just beginning." Scarlet mocked.

Staying in the shadows, so as to not be noticed, Aster stayed along the edge of the woods of Science City making his way back toward his lab. Ever since his dad experimented on him his appearance embarrassed him and frightened others. He not only had blue skin color but his eyes were two different colors of blue with no pupils making him look creepy. His hair and tongue were also blue. After walking for over an hour in the dark windy city he finally arrived and darted through the door glad to see his friends were there.

"Savannah is trapped by the world's most evil scientist, named Scarlet, and she is going to do bad things to our friend; worse than what I did to her." Aster explained.

"How did you get away?' Zane asked.

"Scarlet let me go but threatened to hurt Savannah if we called the police."

"Savannah always had people coming for her, Drake sighed.

"What do you mean?" Aster asked.

Drake explained how Savannah was always being hunted down or targeted because she was the only one without a heartbeat. She never had privacy or could live a normal life. She felt like a freak.

"This Scarlet sounds like a freak!" Nick said.

"Surely one person would not be hard to take down." Zane commented.

"Teehee, how about I eat the human than boom, she is gone." Drake smiled.

"Killing isn't right." Zane said.

"Come on, I didn't eat that much today" Drake whined.

Zane felt in his heart that the group should stop and pray asking God for His help and a good plan. He needed to explain to them what prayer was, where should he start?

"Hey guys, you know I'm a Christian and you always give me a hard time about it but right now I need you to listen to me a minute. We are in a serious dangerous situation that is much bigger than us and we need help. So, we're going to pray and ask God for a plan."

"How do we pray?" Drake asked.

"First, I need to tell you about Jesus or praying makes no sense. You see Jesus came to earth so that we could have a personal relationship with God, the one who created the whole universe. God loves us and wants us to talk to Him anytime we need to. He's there anytime, any day, to listen and help. He cares and wants to help. But if you don't believe this much, prayer is useless. You have to believe that God is, that He exists. Do you believe this?"

They all shook their heads yes. In their hearts they knew God was real it's just they were never taught anything about God. But deep inside they knew it to be true. Zane continued to explain about Gods great love for them and how Jesus died on the cross for them. All three friends were moved to asked Jesus in their hearts and receive forgiveness for their sins. After this Zane prayed "God, we need your help. Savannah is in danger and we need to help her. Show us a plan to rescue her. Thank you for loving us and for your help. In Jesus name we pray, Amen"

"I have an idea." Nick smiled.

"What is it bro?" Aster asked.

"How about we sneak into Scarlets' lab and go undercover as her scientist assistants." Nick explained.

"Good idea." Zane smiled.

"It might work. Hopefully she's gullible." Aster said.

"We have to try." Zane said.

"Drake, you can distract Scarlet while we try to find Savannah." Nick smiled.

"Oh yeah, I'm the best at distracting people." Drake laughed.

"Let's do this.", Aster smiled.

"Three versus one teehee and also one captured, so that's actually four versus one." Drake smiled.

"Come on silly." Zane laughed.

Back at Scarlet's lab the poking and prodding continued. It was difficult to find a vein so Scarlet was getting very frustrated. She continued throwing insults at Savannah as if she were some stupid satanic freak. Along with drawing her blood to analyze it, Scarlet was curious about the reproductive part of Savannah's body. Even oni's have some modesty and Savannah was offended at Scarlet for invading her privacy. Lastly, she made her go into her oni form so she could compare the anatomy between humans and onis.

"Now that's what I want to see." Scarlet smiled.

Savannah was crying than said," Zane says God doesn't give me a spirit of fear."

"You are the spirit of fear!" Scarlet yelled.

"Jesus, Zane said that you listen to me and I want you to know that I want you to be in my heart and I want to give you my life." Savannah prayed quietly while crying.

Becoming annoyed at Savannah's crying and whining, Scarlet put a knife to her chest threatening to stab her if she didn't shut up. She felt like being brutal with her but decided to wait until after she was done testing on her. There would be time for that later.

The three guys jumped in Nick's black sports car and headed to Scarlet's lab which was a part of the League of Science Hospital. In her facility they tested on humans and did experiments that were ethically questionable. This would be a safe place to test on onis and no one would suspect a thing. When they arrived, they all put on lab coats they brought from Aster's lab

"Why are you saying sneaky out loud when you're not supposed to talk when you're sneaking? "Nick whispered.

"Oh, was I saying that out loud… sneaky sneak?" Drake smiled.

"You little …" Nick sighed.

"Guys focus." Zane whispered.

"Crap, the door's locked." Nick grunted.

"I know the code." Aster said.

"How do you know it?" Drake asked.

"Because I'm mostly water, Scarlet used to test on me. When my dad brought me here, I would watch him type in the code. "Aster explained.

"A human drink teehee. Drake smiled.

"Will you cut it out!" Aster yelled.

"Guys, be quiet." Zane whispered.

Nick yawned looking at his watch. He didn't realize it was midnight. No wonder he was tired. Hopefully they would be able to get into the lab this late. Aster told them how Scarlet would work late because she didn't want to get caught doing illegal experiments. She was an evil person obsessed with onis for many years. She finally had one and they were all very worried what she would do to Savannah.

Having studied onis for years Scarlet understood that they could not die. So, removing Savannah's internal organs and examining them sounded like fun to her. Should she put her to sleep first or do it awake? She didn't want to listen to Savannah cry like a baby so she pulled out a needle and gave her a sedative.

Drake's job was to distract Scarlet so the others could search for Savannah. He brought a frozen microwave pizza he found in Aster's freezer thinking that he would dress like a pizza delivery boy and trick Scarlet. The others rolled their eyes realizing they shouldn't have left the planning up to him. They all headed off in different directions of the hospital to try to find Savannah agreeing to meet back in the lobby when she was found.

"Someone ordered frozen pizza, it's me the delivery man.!" Drake yelled as he jumped into action.

"Who the heck is that?" Scarlet mumbled to herself while wiping blood off her hands. She walked to the door wondering who would be in the lab at this hour.

"Hello, someone ordered pizza!" Drake yelled.

She threw open the door impatiently to find a weird, chubby pizza boy standing there with a stupid grin on his face.

"Hello human, I mean girl." Drake smiled.

"What do you want? "Scarlet asked.

Wow, she has oni blood on her, she must have hurt my sister, Drake thought.

Scarlet crossed her arms and said," I don't have all day."

"You ordered frozen pizza." Drake laughed.

"No, I didn't. "Scarlet said.

"Yes, you did." Drake smiled.

"Who orders frozen pizza? No one does that. It always comes hot." Scarlet said.

"But you did." Drake insisted.

Scarlet kicked Drake and he fell down." I have work to do, get out of my lab!" Scarlet yelled.

"She hit me in the wiener." Drake cried while on the floor.

As Zane, Nick, and Aster continued searching for Savannah they felt like they were looking for a needle in a haystack in this huge facility. They heard Drake running toward them and saw him holding his privates and whining. Oh no. What kind of trouble did he get himself into. As he was explaining the dangers of this human woman, Scarlet rounded the corner and spotted them. She thought something was fishy about a pizza boy delivering a frozen pizza. He was standing near three guys in lab coats that did not look familiar.

"Who are you guys and I thought I told you to leave pizza boy?" Scarlet glared.

They immediately began trying to convince her that they were interns sent to help at the lab. They stumbled over each other's words until Scarlet had no more patience left. Drake finally blurted out that she had his sister and they wanted her back.

"She's, our friend." Zane said.

"Why would you have an oni as your friend? Oni's are just satanic freaks who only want power." Scarlet said.

"Not Savannah and her brother." Nick said.

"Yeah, Savannah and Drake want to become Christians." Zane said.

"I hate Christians and I don't care what you say." Scarlet said.

Scarlet got her knife and yelled," follow me or you all die." She grabbed Nick putting the knife to his neck causing them all to cooperate and follow her to the testing room made of x stone. Drake found out quickly x stone did not allow him to use his power as he tried to stop Scarlet. She ran out and locked the door.

"Great now we are trapped. "Aster sighed.

"Hope you like your new home. You will stay here until you die from starvation. "Scarlet laughed.

Scarlet returned to the testing room to find Savannah waking and out of her oni form.

"Didn't I say if you went out of your oni form, I would hurt you?" Scarlet grunted

"Wait, please, I'm sorry, I won't do it again." Savannah cried.

Being the cruel person she was, Scarlet pinned Savannah to the wall putting a knife to her chest. She began taking pictures of her body on her phone once again invading Savannah's personal space. She felt around on her stomach and attached wires to her chest so she could check out her heart. It was very odd to her that the Holter monitor was not picking up a heartbeat. Savannah told her she didn't have a heartbeat and Scarlet was in disbelief. Maybe she was lying and her monitor was faulty. This oni was definitely more interesting and unique than she could have ever imagined. One thing she know for sure firsthand was that onis were evil and she would pay for all the pain they caused her friend.

"What are we going to do?" Nick asked.

"Why doesn't my power work!" Drake yelled.

Aster explained that x stone was an element that prevented onis from using their powers. Whether it was hand cuffs, chains, or a room lined with it, x stone stopped the flow of powers.

Drake whined about being there so long when in reality it had only been twenty-five minutes. He was hungry as usual and Zane was also getting concerned about his mom worrying about him. At that very moment she was talking to the police describing his appearance so they could look for him.

"He has brown hair and likes to wear his white hoodie; he is 20 years old."

"We will try our best to find Zane mam." the officer said.

"He also has a friend with him named Savannah. She has blue hair and she looks a little different but she's a real sweetheart. "Len said.

The officers left stating they would call her with any information they had. Len had already been to Nick and Asters houses and they were not home either. She tried to calm herself by doing the only thing she knew to do; by praying for God to bring them home safely.

Savannah began crying that she wanted to go back to Zane and Len's house. Scarlet taunted her with the fact that her brother and friends were actually right there in the building, captured, and she'd never see them again. Deciding to kill them she grabbed her keys and headed for the door saying "I think I'll kill them just for fun." As she slammed the door her keys dropped to the floor.

Savannah quickly grabbed the keys not sure what they were. She licked them and tried to chew them. She remembered seeing Scarlet put them in a hole in the door so she tried several times before being successful.

Wow, it opened, Savannah smiled proud of herself.

"Savannah doesn't deserve to be hurt; she is the nicest person I know." Zane said while Scarlet was pining him to the wall.

"Don't you dare kill him!" Aster yelled.

"Shut up water boy!" Scarlet yelled.

Savannah was running in the hallway following the loud voices.

"Any last words?" Scarlet smiled.

"Listen to me, Savannah is good and not evil!" Zane yelled while crying.

"Goodbye." Scarlet smiled raising her knife.

"Wait!" Savannah yelled. She attacked Scarlet pinning her to the floor. Scarlet knew she was in trouble as Savannah was showing her strength. She punched her in the nose causing her to loosen her grip on Scarlet enough for her to stand up quickly. Scarlet reached for her gun in her belt but Drake attacked her from behind knocking her to floor. He grabbed the gun and Savannah grabbed Scarlet's shirt getting in her face.

"You don't understand. All of my life I've been bullied because I want to be a human and be good. Other oni's want to kidnap me because I'm the only one without a heartbeat and now you are hurting me as much as my dad did. Yes, I was satanic and did evil things to humans, but now I'm a Christian and have the best human friends." Savannah explained backing away from Scarlet.

"That was deep," Nick said.

"Just forget it. I am a satanic freak." Savannah yelled while darkness fog was forming around her.

"No, you're not. "Zane smiled.

"Just look at me." Savannah cried.

"Savannah, its ok" Aster said.

"I just want to be loved." Savannah said while crying.

"I had no idea." Scarlet said.

"Savannah is trying really hard to be a child of God." Zane said while Savannah was hugging him.

"Ha, God is not real, "Scarlet laughed.

"Yes, he is, he helps people in the darkness like you. All you need to do is believe that Jesus is God's son and loved you so much He died to pay for your sins. Ask Jesus into your heart than he will make your life awesome." Zane said.

Scarlet walked up to Savannah.

"Get away from her." Nick yelled.

"I'm sorry Savannah, I never knew oni's could be nice and please explain how God is real, Scarlet sighed.

Jesus said *"The thief comes only to steal, kill and destroy but I have come that you may have life to the full in abundance until is overflows"*, Zane explained.

"Ha, Jesus is a killer." Scarlet said.

"No, he is the opposite of a killer. He's the one who gives abundant life. The thief is Satan." Aster smiled.

"Jesus died on the cross for your sins." Zane said.

"Why would he do that? "Scarlet asked.

"Because he loves you and wants you to have an eternal life and go to heaven." Savannah said while hiding behind Zane.

John 3:16 says," *For God so loved the world that he gave his one and only son that whosoever would believe in him would not perish but have everlasting life*", Zane said.

"Then why did Jesus kill my husband's parents!" Scarlet yelled while crying.

"He didn't. There is a devil." Aster said.

"The devil is my uncle." Drake smiled.

"What! "Zane yelled.

"Please don't hate me Zane." Savannah cried.

"You can't help who your relatives are. I don't hate you; I still love you." Zane said.

They continued sharing about God's love with Scarlet but she couldn't comprehend how God could love her after all she had done to Savannah. There was even much more than that. She had been odd much of her life enjoying the sight of blood with tendencies toward cruelty. Something inside her wanted to know more so she decided to let the group go if they agreed to come back and share more the next day. She apologized to Savannah and was surprised when it was accepted. There's something different about these friends.

"Matthew 4:16 says *"if you don't forgive people their sins, God will not forgive your sins. It may take a while for me to trust you but I forgive you Scarlet.* "Savannah said.

"Your moms are probably so worried about you. I'll take you home. "Scarlet said.

"Satan is bad at air hockey. "Drake said.

"Where did that come from." Nick laughed?

"He watched me on the weekends." Drake said.

"Uh, that's cool to know I guess." Zane laughed.

They all piled in Scarlet's car and she drove them to Zane's house. Savannah, Drake and Zane got out of the car. Scarlet once again felt shame for what she had done and apologized to Zane. She was shocked at how readily he forgave her. Drake was on the sidewalk looking at Len. Len was so relieved to have them home.

Savannah introduced her brother to Len telling of how they found him. Drake acted very uncomfortable around Len. This world of humans was a bit overwhelming. With everything they had just been through, trust was a big issue with him. Len spoke softly and calmly to Drake offering for he and Savannah to stay with her and Zane. He leaned over and licked her arm.

"Oh my!" Len cried quite surprised.

"Thanks for letting us stay." Drake smiled.

"You're welcome, but please don't lick me," Len said.

"it's a nice way to say friend or I love you." Savannah said.

Len led them inside to make some homemade mac and cheese. Drake wasn't sure what that was but he was starved and would try anything at this point.

Zane approached Scarlet's car promising to come see her the next day to finish their discussion about God. She waved and pulled away taking the others home. Her husband sent her a crying emoji saying he was hungry. She'd stop to get a pizza but not a frozen one. The thought made her laugh out loud.

CHAPTER 3
SCARLET'S SPECIAL DAY

The next morning Savannah woke feeling nauseated and very irritable. It had been several days since she had eaten human blood. Oni's, particularly girls, get really sick when they haven't had blood for a while. It is very important to their nutrition. Len explained that it was inappropriate to kill humans so they needed to come up with another alternative. Zane offered to let them have his blood but of course this horrified his mother. He cared so much about Savannah he was willing to help her however he could. They decided to head to the grocery store to check out the meat section to see if anything else would do. Zane remembered that they needed to go see Scarlet and wondered if she had any blood in her lab she could spare.

Heading to Scarlet's lab was the last place Savannah wanted to be going. She and Drake tried to explain to Len how mean Scarlet was. It was so unbelievable to Len anyone could be that cruel she thought they just had some over active imaginations. They were going as Zane promised so they could answerer Scarlet's questions about God.

"Joshua 1:9 says, *"be strong and courageous do not be afraid or discouraged for the Lord your God is with you wherever you go."* So, don't be scared of Scarlet, I think God is calling me to help her." Zane explained.

First, they would stop at the store for their first experience shopping for food. As they pulled into the parking lot Drake and Savannah were shocked to see many driving thingies, as Savannah called them, all lined up and lots of humans. After her experience with Scarlet, Savannah was terrified another human would take her and hurt her. She grabbed Zane, shaking, and insisted they not go in the store. He grabbed her hand and

37

assured her she would be fine. As Len was looking in the meat section Drake wandered off.

"What is this? Drake asked a man who was standing nearby.

"It's called beer." he said.

"Is it good?" Drake asked.

"Well, how old are you?"

"I stopped counting when I hit a billion years old." Drake smiled.

"Uh, how about you find something that will not make you crazier than you already are." the man suggested walking away.

Realizing Drake was missing Len searched the store and finally spotted him licking a beer cooler. She was so embarrassed and quickly took him to Zane and told him to head to the car while she checked out. These oni's have so much to learn.

As Seth was relaxing on the couch Scarlet appeared in the doorway. She looked pale and was holding her stomach. She sat down on the couch and gave him some surprising news. She was pregnant. Seth was really excited and rubbed her tummy. She smiled and then quickly ran to the bathroom to puke.

"Are you ok?" Seth asked as he stood outside the bathroom door. "I'm glad I don't have to feel the pain. They say giving birth is like pooping a telephone pole." Seth laughed.

"Did you really have to say that!" Scarlet yelled.

"I was just trying to be funny." Seth said. "Hurry Scarlet. I have to pee!"

"We have more than ten bathrooms Seth!" Scarlet yelled.

Zane motioned for his mom to turn left into a parking lot. As they pulled up to the building Len was surprised to see how large it was. They all got out of the car and rang the doorbell. A man with a red shirt and black stripes answered the door. His appearance took them by surprise as he was human but also had traits of a wolf. Drake explained that he was called an alpha as he was part human, part wolf.

They asked to see Scarlet so Seth, not knowing who they were, asked them to wait outside until he checked with Scarlet. She told him to let them in and she brushed her teeth to freshen her breath. She hoped she could get through their visit without puking again. Drake was fascinated with Seth. He had heard of the Alphas but had never seen one in person. He followed closely behind Seth trying to touch his tail Seth didn't appreciate it and told him to back off. Drake had personal space issues. At least that's what everyone tells him.

"This is a lovely place you have." Len smiled.

"Thanks, now I will take you all to Scarlet." Seth said.

"What's your name?" Zane asked

"I'm Seth."

"Nice to meet you. "Zane smiled.

"I hate this place." Savannah said while hanging back from the group crying.

"Is that girl, ok?" Seth asked.

"Well, she is a little scared of Scarlet." Zane said.

"She can get scary, anyway follow me." Seth laughed.

He led them to a living room where Scarlet was sitting on the couch trying to drink a cup of coffee. She smiled at them and motioned for them to have a seat. Just as she began to introduce everyone to Seth a wave of nausea hit her.

"Hold this oni." Scarlet said while handing Drake the coffee.

"Wait, did you call him an oni?" Seth asked.

"I don't wanna talk about it!" Scarlet yelled while running down the hallway.

"So, is Scarlet your wife? "Len asked.

"Yes, she is." Seth smiled.

"Are you a scientist like Scarlet?" Savannah asked.

"I'm not a scientist."

"Thank God." Savannah said.

"Is Scarlet sick?" Zane asked.

"Not really, she's just pregnant." Seth said.

"Congrats to you both. "Zane said.

"Seth, help me, my lab coat is covered in puke!" Scarlet yelled.

Seth left the room to go help Scarlet. Zane asked if they should come back another time but Scarlet insisted, they stay. Len had to go to work so she left them there and headed home to put the groceries away. She would return to get them later and bring something back to help Scarlet's nausea.

While Zane and his friends were waiting for Scarlet and Seth to come back something was stirring in another realm. An oni named Arlo was scheming on how to overthrow the King of the Onis, King Chen. Arlo felt he would be a better king. King Chen didn't even care about his own kids and preparing them for the throne. So, he would find a way to take it from him. For now, he had an itch to disrupt the human world a little; maybe just have a little fun to blow off steam. He summoned his staff and created a portal.

"Uh guys, why is there a portal in here?" Zane asked.

"Hehe, it kinda looks like an oni portal. Drake laughed.

"Drake, don't laugh. If an oni is trying to come here that means Zane and Scarlet can get killed." Savannah cried.

"Right." Drake sighed.

"Is Seth considered a human when it comes to oni food?" Zane asked.

"Yes, an alpha is part wolf and part human." Savannah said.

At that moment Arlo stepped through the portal. Drake immediately recognized him as Arlo, one of the meanest onis who always threatened to take over the kingdom. Drake read his mind to see Arlo was there to cause some suffering and pain to humans. Arlo was pleasantly surprised to find King Chen's kids here. Since their father sent Drake away maybe he could convince them to be on his side to overthrow their father. The siblings of course refused causing fury to burn in Arlo's heart. He looked around the room to see if there were any humans to eat. If they wanted to stay here in the human realm then they would suffer while he ate their so-called friends. Drake lunged at him with his knife stabbing Arlo in the chest.

"Why would you do that, you are onis?" Arlo yelled while blood was coming out of his chest.

"No, we are not evil anymore." Savannah sighed.

"What happened to you two? You're supposed to be evil. We are oni's who kill and make suffering to all humans!" Arlo yelled.

"You can't tell us how to live." Drake grunted.

Arlo kicked Drake and he fell down. Arlo was about to stab Drake but Savannah went into her oni form and got a hold of Arlo's sword and threw it far from him. He got furious and darkness began forming around him. Zane ran and jumped in front of Savannah as Arlo blasted him with his darkness. He fell to his knees and Arlo approached him thankful for a human to eat. Savannah ran to Zane to defend him against Arlo.

"Are you literally trying to save a human?" Arlo asked.

"Yep." Savannah smiled.

"Ugh, I'll show you how an oni is supposed to act!" Arlo yelled while darkness was forming around him.

"I don't feel good." Zane sighed while his hand began turning black.

Drake pushed Arlo to the floor pinning him down while Savannah tried to move Zane. At least Arlo hadn't frozen Zane in darkness completely. Zane was passed out so Savannah kept calling his name and slapping his face. Arlo threw Drake off him into a desk. He decided to leave Zane alone because he smelled other humans and would hunt them down while they were distracted. Savannah looked up to see Arlo head down the hallway toward Seth and Scarlet. Her heart fell because she knew what he would do.

"No, don't eat anyone!" Savannah yelled while on the floor crying.

"Bye suckers." Arlo smiled while running.

Seth had put a bean bag chair outside the bathroom door so he could comfort Scarlet while she was throwing up. This could be a long night so he might as well get as comfortable as possible. He heard a laugh behind him and all of a sudden was being picked up and launched against the wall. A tall dark creature-like form had him by the neck and stabbed him in the chest. He was in shock and felt such horrible pain that he didn't have time to fight back. He noticed horns, a tail and a purple eye patch. He had never seen anything like this before. Arlo laughed in his face mocking his weak alpha abilities. He sliced his throat and Seth immediately died.

"Hey Arlo, I will not let you kill anyone!" Savannah yelled.

"It's too late Savannah." Arlo smiled while blood was on his face and hands.

"Why would you do that to him, he was going to be a dad?" Savannah cried.

"Like I care." Arlo laughed.

"You are so evil." Savannah sighed while crying.

"Oh Savannah, you're not acting like an oni should act and also, you're the daughter of the oni king. Wait until I tell your dad." Arlo said.

"Get out of this realm now!" Savannah yelled.

"Just because you're the oni princess, that doesn't mean you can tell me what to do." Arlo laughed.

"I don't even want to be an oni." Savannah sighed.

"You are acting so weird." Arlo said.

Savannah went out of her oni form and said," Oni's are so mean and evil, I don't want to be like that."

"Ugh, I got what I wanted anyway." Arlo said while holding his staff and teleporting he and Seth away.

Scarlet had turned on the sound proofing in the bathroom so no one would hear her puking. She had not heard anything that was taking place out side her door. Savannah was so heartbroken that she would have to give her such bad news. She was finding it hard to believe that Arlo had done what he did. Scarlet came out of the bathroom apologizing for taking so long. Savannah stood so that Scarlet would not see the blood on the floor. She didn't want her to freak out without being seated. Scarlet noticed Savannah had been crying and asked her what was up. Savannah told her to come sit in the living room and she would explain.

Drake continued to yell and shake Zane trying to get him to awake. Zane began to cough which made them all happy. He woke feeling dizzy and disoriented but at least he was moving. Drake moved him to the couch and gave him a blanket to warm up in. The warmer he got the better he'd feel. Savannah and Scarlet walked into the room and everyone could tell by the look on Savannah's face that something was terribly wrong.

"Well, we have to tell you something about your husband." Savannah sighed.

"Where is he?" Scarlet asked." He said he was waiting for me outside the door."

Savannah explained that an oni named Arlo had teleported into her lab and that they tried to fight him off. He had hurt Zane which was why he didn't look so good and was freezing. He smelled humans and ran down the hall and found Seth sitting outside her door. Savannah broke down and couldn't finish so Drake told her that Arlo had killed and taken her husband. Scarlet was in disbelief and thought they were teasing her. Looking around the room at all their faces she could tell it was true. Savannah tried to hug and comfort her as she cried hysterically but Scarlet pushed her away.

"I knew oni's are evil!" Scarlet yelled as she got up and backed away.

"Scarlet, wait." Drake said.

Scarlet ran to her bedroom and slammed the door. Savannah felt so bad for her that she wanted to do something, but what? Scarlet laid across her bed crying. She went from disbelief, to anger, to panic, and back to crying. She was an emotional mess. Savannah quietly knocked on her door. This woman who once tortured her was now in pain and Savannah wanted to comfort her. It's amazing what having God's love in your heart helps you do. She had forgiven Scarlet and now she actually cared about her.

"What do you want?" Scarlet yelled.

Savannah sat down on the bed beside Scarlet and said," I'm so sorry he did that."

"Just go away." Scarlet cried.

"Why did it have to be him? He did nothing wrong!" Scarlet yelled while crying.

"I never would have thought an oni would be nice, especially after all I did to you. "Scarlet said.

"I don't like sad humans." Savannah said.

Zane and Drake were peeking in the room and Scarlet motioned them to come in.

"Why didn't you rat me out to your mom when you had the chance?" Scarlet asked?

"Because God says to give people second chances and to forgive." Zane smiled.

"Again, I'm so sorry. Maybe God is punishing me by taking Seth away." Scarlet cried.

"God is not like that, Scarlet. God is love. Jesus came so we don't have to pay for our sins. Evil comes from Satan. He likes to mess us up. Just always remember, God is good and the devil is bad. "Zane explained.

They decided it was not good to leave Scarlet alone after all she had been through. Zane called his mom and explained all that had happened. Len said they could stay and she would bring clothes and food in the morning. Savannah promised that she would never leave Scarlet's side and that she would always be there for her baby. Scarlet appreciated how kind hearted and sincere Savannah sounded. She didn't know if she could really follow through. They stayed up until about three in the morning until Scarlet was finally exhausted enough to fall asleep. The boys had all crashed about midnight. Drake had been in the human realm for years so he slept easily. Savannah still had not learned to sleep so staying awake was no problem for her.

"Good morning everyone." Zane smiled.

"I still can't sleep like you can Zane. "Savannah cried.

"It's ok, you will get the hang of it soon." Zane smiled.

Scarlet was in the kitchen cooking breakfast when Drake and Savannah walked in. They began asking question after question about the food which was really getting on her nerves. Between her grief, hormones from pregnancy, and lack of coffee and sleep, she was a grouch.

"What are eggs and bacon?" Savannah asked?

"Its food dummies!" Scarlet yelled.

Zane told Savannah and Drake to give Scarlet some space. They all knew she was sad and thought they could help by taking her mind off Seth. But the grieving process is something you have to *go through* in order to *get through* .

Zane tried to comfort her with a scripture. She really needed to know how much God loved her. He was hoping he could help her realize that. "Matthew 5:4 says, blessed are those who mourn, for they shall be comforted." Zane smiled.

"I don't feel blessed." Scarlet sighed while crying.

"You are so blessed, God died a sad and brutal death for you, He loves you so much." Zane said.

"Maybe someday I'll believe that. Not to change the subject but, can I ask you something?" Scarlet asked.

"Sure thing." Zane said.

"How did you even get an oni? I've been trying almost my whole life to get one, "Scarlet asked.

"My friend went to the oni realm to get an oni and he kidnapped Savannah for testing just like you did to her. I was there when he abused her so I wanted to free her from Aster and I did. Now, Savannah and I are really good friends." Zane explained.

"Oh, that water boy got Savannah." Scarlet sighed.

"Yeah, I'm glad he did because now I have friends." Zane smiled.

Scarlet suddenly had the urge to vomit and ran to the bathroom. Zane was really grateful that he was a guy. Puking during pregnancy didn't sound like fun to him. He went into the living room to find Savannah curled up in a chair deep in thought. Arlo had said something to her that made her wonder if onis could really change or if she truly was a satanic freak as Scarlet once called her. Zane encouraged her that anybody can change with God's help. God does an inner work in our hearts to change us. She already was growing in God. The ability to forgive Scarlet was evidence of that.

"Listen Savannah, we aren't bad anymore so don't let Arlo mess with your head." Drake smiled.

"But I still crave blood." Savannah said while crying.

"Even if we do bad stuff on accident, it's not our fault because we were raised different. "Drake said.

"It's ok Savannah, I will be your friend no matter what." Zane said.

"Thank you."

Scarlet came out of the bathroom looking like a mess. Her hormones were so wacky that she felt like she could either cry or kill someone. She would have loved to have a glass of wine but drinking alcohol while pregnant could cause Fetal Alcohol Syndrome. She didn't want to harm her baby. She decided to go back to bed. Originally, they were going to go to church if Scarlet felt up to it but instead Zane suggested they do a Bible study at home. Scarlet was curious about this Jesus but was unsure how she could be forgiven of all the junk from her past. She was crying in her pillow wishing Seth were there when they all walked in and piled on her bed. Zane had his bible and they began to read and talk.

Scarlet began to feel some peace in her heart and they left the room so she could get some rest.

"Hey Sav, where is Drake?" Zane asked.

"What did you call me?

"I just gave you a nickname." Zane smiled.

"What is a nickname?"

"Oh, it's just a name that a friend or a family member gives you for fun." Zane said.

"Oh ok. I like it."

"So Sav, where is Drake?" Zane asked again.

"Drake went to Aster's lab to see if he can use his teleporter gun to go into the oni realm to get a chi stick." Savannah explained.

A chi stick is a device that onis smoke to get energy up so they can use their powers. After their experience with Arlo, they may need to keep their energy up to help protect their new friends. She likened it to a Vapor that humans use but a chi stick is healthy and vaping is not. All of a sudden Drake came running into the room and tackled Savannah down to the floor overly excited to have gotten them some chi sticks.

"Get off me please." Savannah said.

"Teehee, sorry sis." Drake laughed.

Drake decided to smoke a chi stick. Savannah forgot how good they smelled but that was a matter of opinion. Zane said they were gross and smelled like blood encouraging them to smoke them outside. The smell may make Scarlet even more nauseated, at least it did him.

Zane went to check on Scarlet. She was sitting on the side of the bed holding her stomach. Much to her surprise she able to feel the baby moving already. She was feeling some pain and wondered if they were contractions. Her water broke and she began to panic. She told Zane to call his mom so she could take them to the hospital. Something was wrong. She was not very far along but felt like she was in labor.

"This can't be happening. A baby can't come out the day after you found out." Zane said.

"Are you sure you're in labor?" Drake asked.

"Yeah!" Scarlet cried.

Zane never plays pranks on me, Len thought while driving. She couldn't help but drive faster and faster wondering if Scarlet was losing the baby. They needed to get her to the hospital fast. She arrived at the lab and pounded on the door. Zane and Drake helped Scarlet to car. Everyone piled in and Savannah sat next to Scarlet holding her hand. Len knew now that they were not pranking her. Scarlet was breathing hard and could barley walk. Scarlet began crying wishing that Seth was there. The ride seemed to take forever as they tried to keep Scarlet calm.

When they arrived at the Emergency Room the receptionist got Scarlet a wheel chair and when they said she was in labor they took her straight upstairs to labor and delivery. Dr. Lee came in the room and introduced himself to everyone. Savannah immediately felt panic because he was in a lab coat and there were bright lights everywhere. It gave her flashbacks. He asked everyone to leave the room while he examined Scarlet. Savannah insisted on staying with Scarlet because she made a promise to never leave her. The dr. agreed that one person could stay in the room with her.

"Listen human with the lab coat, you will not do anything hurtful to her or I'll go oni mode on you." Savannah said while in Dr lee's face.

"I promise I won't hurt your friend." Dr Lee said.

The nurse came in to put an iv in Scarlet's arm and Savannah almost fainted. Scarlet had to say that Savannah was her daughter in order for her to stay. This nurse was a stickler for the rules. Family members were the only ones allowed to stay in the room during delivery. Scarlet spent more time trying to keep Savannah calm and wondered if she made a mistake allowing her to stay. It was sweet of Savannah to want to help her but right now she really wished her husband was there. The nurse eyed Savannah closely. She commented on her sharp teeth and skull shaped pupils. Scarlet told her she had a rare disease. She didn't want to lie but saying she was an oni would not go over very well.

"I'm hungry." Drake whined.

"Let's go to the vending machine to get a snack." Zane said.

"What's a vending machine?" Drake asked.

"Come on, I'll show you.?" Zane smiled.

"What is that?" Drake asked.

"It's money." Len smiled while handing Zane some quarters.

"Some human objects confuse me." Drake said.

"Wait until you get older and do taxes Drake." Len laughed.

As they approached the vending machine Drake's eyes grew wide. He had never seen anything like it before; all these snacks behind this glass. He pressed his face against the glass trying to smell the food. Zane laughed and explained how to use quarters to get what you wanted.

"Do you have any idea why Scarlets' baby is coming so early? Maybe alphas come early?" Zane asked.

"Maybe. "Drake said as he pulled out a chi stick.

"No wait, not here", Zane said.

"Why?" Drake asked.

"First of all, it has a strong blood smell and second, we can't bring any suspicion that you're not a human." Zane explained while hiding Drake behind him.

"Right." Drake sighed.

"You can do it outside at Aster's lab or Scarlets' lab." Zane smiled.

"Ok Zane. "Drake said.

Len came to tell them that they could go see Scarlet before she had the baby. It was still so crazy that she was delivering so soon but the dr. said everything seemed fine with the baby. Len was learning to just go with it. Since these onis came into their lives nothing seemed normal. Just to prove her point she turned around to find Drake with his head in the trash can. She got him a few more snacks from the machine and directed him to Scarlet's room. As they were walking down the hall, he asked her if she thought a demonic being could become a Christian.

"If you believe Jesus is Gods son who died for your sins and you ask him into your heart you can become a Christian. As you change you will want to leave your evil ways behind you. "Len explained.

"Savannah and I asked Jesus in our hearts but I get theses voices in my head making me question God and its bothering me." Drake sighed.

"We will pray for you sweetie." Len said.

"Let's go see Scarlet now," Zane said.

Savannah was trying to be a support to Scarlet but the sight of needles was freaking her out. She sat in the chair still and quiet. Every time the nurse came in to give Scarlet a shot or give her medicine Savannah would turn white and feel nauseated. Scarlet was more worried about Savannah than herself. She was concerned that she was having a baby so early in her pregnancy. Her belly wasn't even big but she could already feel the baby kicking. She felt like she was losing her mind.

Zane, Len, and Drake entered the room to see how things were going. Scarlet was tired and said she felt like poop. It wasn't long before she felt like she needed to push so the nurse made them all leave and called Dr. Lee to come quickly. Savannah wanted to stay because of her promise to never leave Scarlet. There was no way the nurse would let her stay and she had a meltdown. Len led her out the door explaining that there were rules and they had to follow them.

An hour went by and the doctor came out to tell them that all went well and they could go see Scarlet. Savannah ran down the hall before Len could remind her to walk. Zane followed behind her laughing.

"It's a boy." Scarlet smiled while holding him.

"And it's an alpha." Drake said.

The doctor told Scarlet that he thought the baby had a birth defect because of his unusual ears and butt. Drake laughed because he knew why he was different. Evidently the doctor had never seen an alpha before. Scarlet didn't care how he looked. She knew God made him special.

"Do you have a name for him?" Dr. Lee asked.

"I kinda like the name Kaden. "Scarlet said.

"That's a cool name. "Zane said.

"OK, Welcome to the world little Kaden Jones." Dr. Lee smiled.

They all gathered around to congratulate Scarlet and look at Kaden. He was so cute. He had a lot of hair and wagged his tail. The doctor was still concerned that something might be wrong. He seemed very alert for just being born. He sure was an unusual baby boy but at least he was healthy. The family wasn't concerned so he'd give it some time.

"Are you happy about your new brother?" the nurse asked.

"For the last time, Scarlet isn't my mom!" Savannah yelled.

"Calm down Sav." Zane said.

"Scarlet, I will protect Kaden with all of my oni power and I will not let him get hurt." Savannah smiled.

"Thanks." Scarlet laughed. "Thank you for forgiving me even after all I did to you. Also, you're not a satanic freak, you are a good girl." Scarlet smiled.

Savannah hugged her and the baby. This was a good day.

CHAPTER 4
QUEEN OF BROKEN HEARTS

Scarlet and Len were enjoying a cup of coffee and getting to know one another better. They talked about every thing from, husbands, babies, and work as well as God and Jesus. Len shared about being a single mom and how hard it was to make ends meet. She worked part time as nurse so she could also be there for Zane. Realizing she needed help with Kaden and that she had plenty of room in her lab, Scarlet offered for Len, Zane and the others to live with her. She had several floors that weren't being used so there would be room enough for everyone to have their own space. It took about a week of moving but in no time they were all settled in.

"What stinks? That smells worse than me." Drake laughed.

"The kid pooped again." Scarlet said carrying Kaden to her bedroom.

Zane offered to help and followed her. He wondered where Savannah was. She was being way to quiet. He'd have to go find her when he finished helping Scarlet. He got a diaper and was trying to keep Kaden distracted while he was being changed. He was very wiggly. Sort of like trying to change a flopping fish. Scarlet screamed that he pooped like a gorilla.

"Yeah, I'm out." Zane laughed.

Zane heard knocking on the door and let Aster in. He came by to see the new baby. Len offered him some breakfast and of course he never turned down home cooking. He followed her to the kitchen while Zane went to check on Savannah.

Finding her in his room he was surprised to see her trying to put his clothes on. She struggled to get the shirt over her head and cried in frustration. Len walked in and saw her in her bra with her head stuck in the arm hole. She asked what was going on and Zane explained she wanted to look human so she was trying to wear his clothes. She asked Zane to leave and explained to Savannah that she needed to be more modest, especially around boys. She encouraged her to be herself and wear her own clothes. A cool thing about onis is that they change their clothes by using their powers. Len wished she had that super power. It would save a lot of time digging through her closet.

"Sweetie, I know you want to be a human, but I want you to be yourself and not something you're not." Len said.

"But I'm an oni and oni's are evil, "Savannah cried.

"You're not evil. You are an awesome Christian girl." Len smiled. She grabbed Zane's bible from his night stand and looked up Psalm 139 and read verses 14-16. It read "I am fearfully and wonderfully made, wonderful are your works, my soul knows it very well, my frame was not hidden from you, when I was being made in secret, intricately woven in the depths of the earth, your eyes saw my unformed substance, in your book written, every one of them, the days that were formed for me, when as yet there was none of them. Len wanted Savannah to know that God was there when she was formed and has a plan for her life.

"What I am getting out of this is that God knew me before I was even born and he has a book about me?" Savannah asked.

"Yes, He does." Len laughed.

Somewhere, in another realm, Luna, was feeling very bored. She smoked a chi stick as she sat and thought about what she might get into. If only she knew how to use her dad's staff she could go to another realm and create some mischief. Hurting a few humans sounded like fun. She snuck into her dad's room and found his staff. Grabbing it, she tried to make it work. She shook it, banged it and yelled at it. Soon dark fog began to form around her as the staff glowed purple. She wasn't sure what was happening but she hoping to teleport somewhere.

Drake had become very fond of human food. You might even say he loved it. Junk food was his favorite of all, especially cookies. He headed to the kitchen once again for some cookies and milk. As he was pouring the milk something or someone fell from the ceiling and landed on him spilling his snack all over the floor. He summoned his oni sword which alerted Luna to the fact he was not a human. She was not sure where she had teleported. Drake threatened to read her mind if she didn't explain who she was and why she was there.

"Wait, you're a Simbyot like me?" Luna asked.

"Yes, I'm a Simbyot ." Drake said while helping her up.

"What's your name?" Drake asked.

"I'm Luna. Where am I?"

"This is my human friend's lab." Drake said.

"Your friends with a human!" Luna yelled?

"Yeah, her name is Scarlet."

"Wow,. "Luna said

As Drake looked at Luna he noticed how cute she was and began blushing. She reminded him that she was simbyot and could read minds also. That made him blush even more. They talked some more and Drake became an open book telling her that he was the son of the King of the Onis and that his sister, the princess, was also here in the human realm. Luna saw an opportunity to gain Drake's favor and try to gain some power for herself. She was very selfish and always looking for ways to prove she was evil. She came up with a plan to win Drake's heart. She already knew he would be easy to fool.

"So, are you powerful like your dad?" Luna asked.

"Yes." Drake said proudly trying to impress her.

"Don't look in my mind then I'll be your girlfriend." Luna said while tickling his neck.

Savannah came into the kitchen to keep Drake from eating all the cookies and stopped in her tracks. She wasn't expecting to see Drake and a girl smiling and flirting with each other. Drake introduced Luna to his sister. He explained how Luna teleported there and that they were dating. Savannah had never seen Luna before and didn't realize Drake had a girlfriend. Something wasn't right and she would figure it out. Drake continued to eat up all the attention Luna was giving him and was acting like a stupid love struck boy.

Drake and Luna went to the living room to sit on the couch. She put her star shaped sunglasses on because the brightness of the human realm hurt her eyes. She also liked wearing them because they were a gift from her mother before she died. A full blooded Simbyot could die but being part oni Luna would live forever and live with the pain of loosing her mom.

Luna continued getting information from Drake and asked him what kind of powers he had.

He rambled on saying, "I have oni power that's darkness and summoning a sword. My Simbyot side of me can make webs. I also can make black goo and blast it on people. I can summon a knife; I can spray out a white colored venom that can stop a person's body from working if it gets into the blood stream. I can possess people, and I have a very good nose to track my prey."

"Anything else?" Luna asked sounding impressed.

"Well, oni's can't die, but you knew that." Drake smiled.

"I'm part oni." Luna said.

"Nice." Drake said.

Luna could tell he was holding back and probably could do more than he said. She decided to turn up her flirting to the next level. She kissed him and convinced him he could trust her and he willingly spilled his guts.

"Well, because Satan is my uncle, my sister and I have the power to curse a human and teleport to hell when we want." Drake said.

"Wow." Luna said.

"But now my sister and I are Christian's and we don't want to do that." Drake sighed.

"Wait, you are a Christian?" Luna yelled.

Normally Luna would hate Drake for leaving the dark side and choosing the light but she must keep up her plan. She would have plenty of time to make him suffer for being a traitor. This made her more determined to take his power. She asked where the bathroom was so she could think about how to convince Savannah she cared about Drake.

Savannah saw Luna walking toward her and noticed she was dressed like a ho. She normally wouldn't use that word but she really distrusted her for some reason. She asked Luna when she met Drake and when she replied, today, that made her more suspicious. You don't get a girlfriend in a day. Luna gave Savannah attitude and Savannah pushed her. *It was definitely going to be difficult to win her trust*, Luna thought.

A scream from Scarlet's bedroom interrupted the girls' conversation. Savannah turned to see Kaden, who was only a week-old walking in front of Scarlet who was freaking out. This may explain why he came so early in the pregnancy. He grew super-fast . Not only could he walk but he was saying their names randomly. Scarlet was so shocked by all this she felt like she was losing her mind. She handed Kaden to Savannah and headed to her office. She needed some place where she could go crazy by herself. Zane and Aster came to help Savannah and get a better look at Kaden. This was unbelievable!

This is a weird house hold. Luna thought.

Hearing all the yelling and excitement from the other room, Drake came to see what was going on. As he walked in Kaden looked at him and said his name. Drake picked him up and went and sat next to Luna who had lit up a chi stick. Before they could tell her to smoke it outside, she blew smoke in Kaden's face. This made Savannah so mad. Kaden was part human and blowing darkness on him could harm or even kill him.

I don't trust this Luna girl at all, Savannah thought while crossing her arms. Drake defended Luna's actions saying she didn't know that the darkness smoke could hurt Kaden. Savannah wasn't buying the excuses. All satanic beings know darkness harms humans. Luna laid her head on Drake's shoulder giving Savannah a side way glance. Savannah was definitely keeping her eye on Luna.

Aster went to check on Scarlet who was sitting at her desk, crying. He handed her a tissue and assured her everything would be alright. Just because Kaden is different doesn't mean anything is wrong with him. He suggested she go shopping or do something for herself. Kaden needed clothes anyway and maybe a new pair of shoes would make her feel better; *at least it did for Cinderella,* Scarlet thought.

While Scarlet went shopping Zane was playing with Kaden on the floor. Savannah came in with a worried look on her face and began telling Zane about her suspicions about Luna. She was really concerned she was up to something evil but she knew Luna would never tell her. Maybe Zane could find out. He's easy to talk to and people open up to him. Savannah played with Kaden so Zane could find Luna. He found her sitting in the bean bag chair listening to music.

Zane was covering his ears and yelled," Hey Luna, I want to talk about something!"

I love this human rock music, Luna thought while shaking her head and wearing her sunglasses.

"Luna!" Zane yelled.

Who's saying my name, Luna thought?

"I want to have a talk." Zane said.

Zane tried to get Luna to talk about herself saying that since she came, he hadn't had a chance to really meet her. She told him she was part Simbyot and part oni which he already knew. He asked about her family and if she had any siblings. She was very closed mouth about her life which caused him to have suspicions as well. When he pushed her for answers, she told him that was all he was getting out of her and to leave so she could go back to listening to music. She was quite rude and made herself at home for someone who just showed up recently. He sure hoped Drake knew what he was doing getting involved with her.

When Zane came back to the living room Aster was chasing Savannah with a needle trying to draw her blood. He had discovered he could sell rare items, like oni blood, and make money. He was already involved in this type of business and was trying to convince Savannah to let him sell hers. When he wouldn't quit pestering her, Savannah went into her oni form and just smiled at Aster daring him to come closer. As he stepped forward, she blasted him with her power and he hit the floor. He got up with his hands in surrender and limped off to the lab.

Luna was still sitting in the bean bag chair listening to music while smoking a chi stick when Drake walked in. He smiled at her and commented on how often she was smoking. Normally you smoke three times a day. But Luna was smoking every hour as if she were getting ready to fight someone. It gives you extra strength in battle. She made an excuse that she needed to get stronger because Savannah insulted her saying she was small and weak. That sounded unlike Savannah to Drake. Maybe she was just being protective of him but she never had mistrust issues before. Luna distracted Drake by cuddling and kissing him hoping he wouldn't become suspicious of her like Savannah. She couldn't believe how easy it was to fool Drake. He was so dumb, playing right into her hands. Savannah came in and saw them kissing and said they missed supper. Drake jumped up and ran to the kitchen. He never missed a good meal.

"You must really like my brother." Savannah commented.

"Yeah." Luna said.

"You met in day and you are acting like you've been dating for like a year." Savannah grunted while crossing her arms.

"Can I not kiss my boyfriend?" Luna laughed.

"It's a bit much don't you think?"

Luna changed the subject and asked if she could have something to eat. Savannah turned and walked toward the kitchen and she followed. Drake was there stuffing his face with a human food called pizza. Luna had never eaten it before and really didn't want it but she was hungry. While she tried to choke down a piece Kaden came into the room.

"Hi poopa." Kaden smiled.

"What did you call me?" Luna asked.

"Poopa." Kaden laughed.

"No, it's Luna not poopa." Luna grunted.

"Poopa." Kaden repeated.

"My name is Luna you dumb alpha! "Luna yelled.

Savannah gave Drake the eye telling him he better shut his girlfriend up before she did. There was no need for her to be so mean to Kaden. As Drake led Luna out of the kitchen, she started flirting with him again. Savannah thought she might puke.

Scarlet would have normally got in Luna's face for treating Kaden like that but she was so distracted with trying to figure out why he was growing and maturing so quickly that you could have set off a bomb in the lab and she wouldn't have noticed. She grabbed a cup of coffee and sat down on the couch saying she felt like she was going crazy. Luna jumped into the conversation saying Scarlet was already crazy. Scarlet had enough of this new girl and blurted back that Luna was inappropriate. The way she dressed and flirted with Drake was over the top in her opinion. Scarlet walked into the kitchen and sat down next to Len.

"Hello Scarlet. Are you ok?" Len asked.

"No. My son is walking and talking and he's only a week old. I tried to give him a bottle, he took it out of my hand and drank without my help." Scarlet cried.

While Scarlet was dumping all her emotions on Len Aster came in holding Kaden's hand saying he was getting taller. Scarlet didn't know if she could take anymore. Len comforted her reminding her that Kaden was special and that different was ok. Kaden climbed up on his mom's lap and hugged her. As she stroked his hair, she realized that no matter what she would love this boy. He was hers and even though Seth was gone, he had given her a son and she would always be thankful for that.

"Thanks for helping me out. "Scarlet smiled.

"No problem. You know we're all here for you." Len said.

As everyone was focusing on Kaden and his issues, Luna thought this would be a good time to start her evil plan. She had been searching for an abandoned building in the forest so she could lure Drake and Savannah there. She would invite the humans as well so she could kill them and take Drake's powers. The icing on the cake would be to make Savannah her slave. She would wait for the right time.

Zane and Drake were hanging out in Zane's room. They were reading and discussing the bible. There was so much to learn and Drake had a lot of questions. Zane tried his best to answer them and if he didn't know he asked his mom.

"What are you doing?" Luna asked.

"Zane is reading me some pages in the bible. "Drake said.

"But aren't oni's against Christianity?" Luna grunted.

"Listen Luna. Satan is the bad one who wants to kill and make suffering and yes, oni's love that; but we can get out of the darkness by letting Jesus in our hearts. Then, we don't have to be forced to do evil things. We can make our own choice to do good." Drake smiled.

This guy is stupid, Luna thought.

"All you have to do is let Jesus help you and you won't have such a hard life." Drake said.

"He's right." Zane agreed.

It took everything within her not to give her opinion of Jesus and all this Christian stuff. She bit her tongue and just nodded. "Anyway, I would like to show you my little place where I like to hang out and also, Zane can come too." Luna said.

Drake followed Luna and Zane began to search for his phone. Luna hurried him along telling him he wouldn't need it. She surely didn't want him to be able to call for help. Finding her reaction, a little suspicious, Zane secretly grabbed his phone off his bed and slid it into his hoodie pocket. Thinking they were going to need a car Zane suggested Aster drive them since he didn't have his license yet. Yes, he was twenty but he had always been a little afraid to get his license since he and his mom were in a car accident years ago. He knew that pretty soon he would face his fear. God had been dealing with him about this lately.

Zane was surprised to see Luna standing there with a staff that look ancient. Drake asked to invite the others to come hang out too. She informed them that she would teleport them and then come back for the others since it was difficult to teleport a large group. This didn't sound right to Drake but he didn't say anything. His father had teleported a large group of people before but maybe Luna's staff was different. Purple flames began forming around them as they teleported. It felt really weird to Zane. It was almost like getting car sick.

When they finally arrived, he immediately noticed how dark and scary it was. The building before them seemed so old and broken down that he didn't know if it was safe to go inside. It looked like an abandoned jail. As they walked Luna could barley contain her excitement that her plan was unfolding. Even though Drake was an oni this place scared him too. She encouraged them that it was nicer inside and that she was going to do some repairs on the outside soon. She began being all lovey to Drake so he'd get distracted.

"Oh Drake. No need to be afraid. Nothing bad is going to happen to you." Luna laughed while tickling him.

"This looks like a jail with the bars on the windows. "Zane said.

"Yeah. It looks like one, but I'd never trap someone in there." Luna laughed.

"Why are you laughing?" Drake asked.

"Oh, it's just that I'm super happy about having friends like you and Zane." Luna lied.

"I'm happy to be your friend." Zane said.

"Me too." Drake added.

As they were standing there, rain began to fall. Neither Drake or Luna had every experienced rain before. They didn't like the way it felt on their skin. Luna welcomed the rain though because it caused them to run for cover into the building. As they entered, Luna told Zane she had something cool to show him and that Drake should wait there for her to come back. She winked at Drake leading him to think there may be some more kissing in store for him.

Placing her hand on Zane's arm she led him into a room with a large jail cell. She rubbed Zane's arm making him uncomfortable and he pulled away. He commented on how big and creepy the cell was and at that moment Luna pulled out a knife saying the cell was big enough for all his friends. She forced him into the cell and pinned him to the wall. He was shocked that Luna was turning on him and he fought back causing her to kick him in the crotch. She leaned over him whispering in his ear that she never loved Drake. She tricked him so she could take his power. Zane couldn't believe how evil she was to use Drake and lie to all of them. He should have listened to Savannah. She's a better judge of character than he thought. As Luna headed to find Drake, she shouted back that after she took his power, she would be back to eat Zane. He sat in the corner of the cell trying to stop his arm from bleeding. She had sliced him when he was fighting back. How was he going to escape? Drake was wondering what was taking Luna so long. This place was creeping him out sitting there alone.

Aster walked into the living room and found Savannah sitting on the couch. He had searched around and could not find Zane, Drake and Luna. She was concerned as well since Zane didn't tell her where he was going. He always told her if he was going to be away from the lab. She began to worry that her suspicions about Luna were true. She didn't want to believe it but her oni sense had been right. She and Aster began to look around to see if they could find any clues about what Luna was up to or where they all may have gone. The fact that Luna made Drake promise not to read her mind should have warned them all. Savannah continued to tell Aster about a time in the oni realm where this guy befriended her dad so he could get to Savannah and try to sell her to science. Since she didn't have a heartbeat, he felt he could get some big money out of it. She tried to tell her dad she was suspicious of the guy but he wouldn't believe her. Now Luna was pulling the same thing on them. She didn't have trust issues like her dad thought. She had good oni sense. What she sensed now was very disturbing. Luna was pure evil.

As they were searching Drake's room for some clues, Scarlet came in holding Kaden. She looked really tired and told them about Kaden's latest stepping stone. Now he was going potty by himself. If there was one thing good about his quick growth it was getting to skip the potty training. Aster and Savannah shared their concerns about Luna with Scarlet. She agreed Luna was iffy and inappropriate and hoped they were wrong about her taking Zane and Drake somewhere. Maybe they just went out to get pizza or something. Savannah was sure Luna was up to something. They had to just figure out what.

Apologizing for taking so long, Luna wrapped her arms around Drake acting like she was going to kiss him. Instead, she asked him if he thought she was evil. He laughed answering no and when he did, Luna pulled out her knife and stabbed him in the chest. He cried out in pain questioning why she would do that to him. She explained how she never loved him but just wanted his power. She called him pathetic and ugly saying he could never get a real girlfriend. She not only wounded him with the knife but her words cut deeper. He had truly thought they loved each other. His heart was broken. She put the knife up to his mouth and dared him to cry like a baby. She stabbed him again the chest screaming hateful words in his face. *This can't be real*, he thought.

"I had fun messing around with you but you're not for me," Luna laughed.

"So, you lied to me?" Drake asked.

"Oh, and you're not the first I played girlfriend with." Luna smiled.

"But I loved you!" Drake yelled while crying and trying to push out of her grasp.

Luna got up and grabbed his shirt threatening to take his power. She had stolen X stone hand cuffs from Scarlet's lab and put them on Drake. She stabbed him a couple more times for the fun of it and then went to check on Zane.

"Dang it! No phone service." Zane sighed while on his phone.

"Hello Zaney." Luna smiled. "I just wanted to see what you were up to. No cell service, huh?"

"Don't call me that." Zane grunted. "What have you done to Drake? You better not hurt him."

"Ha! A human can't tell me what to do." Luna laughed. She opened up the cell and grabbed Zane by his hurt arm. He growled in pain as she continued to squeeze hard. She threatened to put a knife down his throat if he didn't shut his mouth. Sniffing Zane, she decided to save him for later. He would be a good eat. Right now, she was going to head back and gather his friends and his little Oni Princess, Savannah. She had plans for her. She decided to pay Drake a little visit first.

Drake laid on the floor still not believing that Luna betrayed him. He heard her footsteps and looked up to see her coming at him with a knife. She got him in the eye and he began bleeding badly. He cried for help. She laughed at him because of course no one was there to help him. She told him her plan was to take all his power and lock him up for eternity, make Savannah her slave, and eat his human friends; and she said all this with a smile on her face.

Picking up a board lying on the ground, Luna swung it like a bat hitting Drake. She was so angry that he had become a Christian. Onis are suppose to be satanic, not Christian. She loved being bad and evil like onis and Simbyot's were supposed to be. He was a traitor. As she was hitting him, he kept telling her that she could become "a new creature in Christ" and could change if she just trusted in Jesus. She didn't want to hear any Jesus crap. Maybe it was true Jesus could change people and could lift burdens and heal depression. She was fine just the way she was. She didn't want to change. Besides, she liked tricking guys into liking her and hurting them. She was the Queen of the Broken Hearts!

Savannah gave Scarlet the sample she asked for hoping to help Scarlet get back to some sort of normal by working in the lab. Since Kaden was born Scarlet had been so stressed out over his quick development and not knowing why. Savannah noticed some empty wine bottles in the trash can and asked Scarlet about it. She encouraged her to pray to God instead of using other ways to try to get peace. Humans resorted to alcohol, drugs, sex, smoking, and who know what else. Savannah said a prayer right then and there for God to help Scarlet figure out what was up with Kaden and to help her relax. Scarlet was surprised at the peace that short little prayer gave her. She had struggled with using alcohol for several years maybe it was time to give that up and let God help her.

Aster peeked into the lab looking for Savannah. He needed some more of her blood and as soon as she saw the needle and tubes in his hand she ran. She screamed threatening to blast him if he came near her. Aster was persistent and chased after her. Scarlet just shook her head and put on her googles to test on Savannah's sample.

Back at Luna's hideout she was preparing to go back and get the others.

She hoped she could use the staff. She wasn't very experienced with it yet. She shook it and it started glowing purple.

While preparing the slides in the microscope Scarlet was very surprised when Luna fell onto the table in front of her. They both screamed. Scarlet because she was scared and Luna because she was covered in a stinky liquid.

"What is this liquid all over my arm? "Luna asked in disgust.

"Well, I don't use Savannah's blood because she hates me sticking her with needles so I was trying out some different DNA solutions, and what fell on you was Savannah's urine sample." Scarlet said.

Luna looked at her with daggers in her eyes and took a deep breath to control herself. She needed to get Scarlet and the others to her place in the woods even though she wanted to hurt someone right now. Savannah's pee on her, how gross!

"Anyway, would you like to go hang out at my place?" Luna asked.

"Ok sure. "Scarlet said while holding a towel.

"I'm so sorry this happened." Scarlet sighed while wiping the pee off Luna.

"Its fine. I would never kill you for that." Luna laughed.

Scarlet sure hoped she was kidding. Kaden came into the room informing his mom that he had grown some more. He apologized because he knew this stressed out his mom. Scarlet hugged him and told him it was going to be ok. Luna once again asked Scarlet to go to her house and bring Kaden too. She didn't want to get distracted from her plan. She walked down the hall to try and find Savannah and Aster and when she did, she found Aster holding Savannah down trying to take her blood.

"I need your blood to make some of that good money. "Aster smiled while pining her down.

"Get off me idiot!" Savannah yelled.

Savannah kicked Aster off her and took off running. He followed behind shouting about how he made 50,000.00 off her blood when he first sold it. He wanted to be the richest man in the world. Savannah was glad that onis regenerate their blood very quickly. Aster took so much the first time she would have died, if onis could die. He caught up with her and sat on her pleading for her to let him have some blood. Luna tried to interrupt and invite them but they were too distracted. She would come back tomorrow for them. This blue guy was crazy. She didn't understand why Savannah didn't just blast him. That's what she would do.

Kids are very observant. Kaden realized his mom was upset about his growth and he took it personal. He felt like she hated him because he wasn't normal. Scarlet held Kaden assuring him that she loved him no matter what. Luna walked in to them hugging and was disgusted by the show of love. She never knew that feeling.

"Are you two ready?" Luna asked.

"Did you ask if Sav and Aster can come?"

"Well, they are having a moment." Luna said.

"Let me guess, Aster is trying to get Savannah's blood?"

"I think so. They can come another time." Luna said as she grabbed the staff. Scarlet was a little nervous about teleporting with the staff. Kaden thought it looked cool as it glowed purple. The next moment they were standing outside an old abandoned shack. Scarlet began to feel a bit panicky.

Getting tired of scuffling around with Savannah to get some blood Aster walked around Scarlets' lab looking for a sleeping needle and found one mixed in with Scarlet's other serums. As he approached Savannah waving the needle around and grinning, she became extremely irate.

"You are messing with me while I really believe Luna is up to no good. Zane and Drake are missing and all you care about is money. They could be in danger so back off!" she screamed. As she turned to walk away, she suddenly felt a prick in her arm. Aster had successfully given her a sleeping shot. At least he thought he did.

Scarlet noticed that the building had bars on it like an old prison. It had ivy growing up the walls covering most of the building. It almost blended into the forest itself. Kaden was afraid and grabbed his mom's hand squeezing it tight. She tried to smile and reassure him. Luna told him it was cool inside. As they approached the building Scarlet reached for the door and Luna grabbed her arm. She insisted they go in the back door. As soon as the door shut behind them, they heard a voice yelling for help. Kaden immediately recognized Zane's voice. As they took a few more steps into the dark room they could see Zane in a cell behind bars.

"Zane, why are you in a cell? "Scarlet asked.

"She is evil!" Zane cried.

"Who is evil?" Scarlet said.

Luna pulled a knife out and pushed Scarlet to the floor. Kaden ran to his mom with an instinct to protect her. Luna laughed at him making him even more angry.

"She has been hurting me and Drake." Zane cried.

Luna put a knife up to Scarlet's' face threatening that if she didn't get in the cell, she would hurt Kaden. A few options quickly went through her mind. She could run and try to get help but really how was she even going to get help. They were in the middle of a forest somewhere and Luna teleported them there. If she went into the cell what would happen to Kaden and the rest of them. Her only hope was to do what Luna said and hope Savannah and Aster figured out where they were. She stepped into the cell begging Luna not to hurt Kaden. Luna grabbed him by the neck and shoved him in the cell behind her. At least they were together.

"This God of yours isn't doing a thing to help you, so I would get ready for death. "Luna mocked.

"Deuteronomy 31:6 says," Be strong and courageous. Do not be afraid or terrified because of them, for the Lord your God goes with you; he will never leave you or forsake you," Zane quoted.

"Jesus is faithful." Scarlet smiled.

"I hate Jesus!" Luna yelled.

"Zane told me God loves everybody. He even loves you right now. "Scarlet smiled.

"Just shut up before I rip out your organs!"

"Even if we do die, we will go to heaven." Zane smiled.

"I'll be taking Drake's power, so see you later suckers." Luna had heard enough about God and Jesus and love. She was going to do what she was taught to do, be evil.

"We are doomed, "Scarlet sighed as her faith wavered.

Trying not to panic, Aster realized he put the wrong shot into Savannah's arm. He thought he gave her a sedative so he could draw her blood without her squirming around. This definitely was not a sedative. She was talking crazy. Where was Scarlet when he needed her.

"Wow, look at you blue, you are the most boot full blue person I ever meet." Savannah smiled while holding Aster's shirt and slurring her words.

"My hair so soft." Savannah smiled while playing with her hair.

"BLUE" Savannah smiled while poking Aster's tummy.

"Yes, I'm blue."

"Why did you break that wall, it was fine a second ago!"

Picking up a bat, Savannah hit Aster with it expecting water to spray out from him. She was frustrated that it did not happen. He grabbed her trying to get her to snap out of it. She took off her hat, which she never did, and threw it across the room saying she hated it. She reached up and was rubbing her horns. She usually wanted to hide them from others. Aster helped her off the floor and headed to the lab to find Scarlet. Hopefully she could reverse this with a different shot.

"Come on, let's go to Scarlet, "Aster said

"Who is Scarlet, is she a puppy?"

"Scarlet are you in here?" Aster called out.

Huh, she was here an hour ago. Aster thought

"I want macaroni !" Savannah yelled.

Can this girl shut up? Aster thought.

"Ow, I bit my tail." Savannah cried.

"Hey Scarlet!"

He continued searching room to room and could find no one. Where could they all be? He got on his phone and tracked Zane's phone. It was two hours away. Something strange is going on. Zane would never have left without telling Savannah where he was going. Savannah was right. Luna was up to something. He had this crazy girl to deal with while trying to figure out where everyone was. He needed help. He whispered a prayer, "God help me"

Walking into the living room he found Savannah licking the tv.

"Hey Savannah, check out this."

"Why do I need a hammer?" Savannah asked while touching the tv.

"You were right about Luna having an evil plan."

"I always right." Savannah said while picking her nose.

"I tracked Zane's phone and he is two hours away from the lab."

"Cool." Savannah smiled.

"Not cool, they all might be in danger! "Aster yelled getting frustrated with her nonsense.

"I'm sexy and I know it," Savannah sang. "Omg, your eye balls are blue also."

"Savannah, we are going on a road trip to save our friends." Aster said.

Aster buckled Savannah in the car hoping she would fall asleep on their drive. She was making him crazy with her talking and poking. Whatever was in this shot made her hyper and silly. His hopes were dashed when she unbuckled and climbed in the front seat. She must have listened to every radio station there was. Not only listened but sang, loudly.

Back at the forest hide out Luna focused on trying to get Drakes power. Not only did Luna torture Drake physically but she enjoyed breaking his heart with her words. He begged for her to let him go home. He just wanted to get away from her. She broke him in every way.

"You can't escape from me." Luna smiled.

"Luna, I loved you." Drake sighed.

"You are nothing. You're just an idiotic oni who is alone and will never be loved."

"Just stop."

"You are too dumb to have a girlfriend." Luna laughed.

"I'm not alone, I have Jesus, my sister, and my human friends."

"Jesus is nothing and he doesn't love you. The devil is better." Luna smiled while in Drake's face.

"John 8:44 says," you are of your father the devil, and your will is to do your father's desires, He was a murderer from the beginning, and has nothing to do with the truth, because there is no truth in him. When he lies, he speaks out of his own character, for he is a liar and the father of lies," Drake said looking her straight in the eyes.

"You learn way too much from your human friends." Luna smirked while pining Drake to the floor.

"They teach me truth." Drake sighed.

"What did you say? I think you gave me attitude!"

"I said they taught me truth!"

Drake pushed Luna off him and he stood to his feet facing her on. She summoned her knife and lunged at him missing him as he stepped aside. This made her angry and she charged him stabbing him in the chest. He pulled the knife out of his chest not only feeling the pain of the wound but feeling the pain of betrayal. They spent so much time together and she totally had him thinking she loved him. She came at him again and he punched her in the nose. As it bled, he noticed her blood was green and glowing. *What the heck?* Luna pushed Drake into the wall and sliced open his stomach with her knife.

"Stop." Drake cried while on the floor.

"Nice try Drake, you can never defeat me." Luna smiled while wiping the blood off her nose.

Jesus, I can't take this anymore, I need your help, Drake thought while crying.

As Aster drove, he promised Savannah, he would get her back to normal. She begged him for a drink and he tried to hold her off so they could get to their friends. She continued crazy talk which was a little funny but annoying too.

"Hold me fluffy hair blue poo." Savannah smiled while climbing to Aster's lap.

"Savannah, I'm driving in the dark and rain, so please sit down before I wreck the car!" Aster yelled.

"Stay in that seat and I might get you a drink from the gas station."

"You would make a good carpet."

She's getting more and more crazier, Aster thought. "For the last time, quit chewing on the arm rest of my dang car!" Aster yelled.

"You smell like a jelly fish." Savannah said.

What the heck was in that shot, Aster thought.

"Where are we going?"

"To find our friends." Aster grunted.

"Is my friend an alligator?"

They finally arrived where the tracker led them. As Aster opened the door, he noticed how creepy this place was. It looked abandoned to him but the tracker led them here. They had to be here.

"Meow, I'm a cow." Savannah smiled.

"Let's go check this place out and see if the others are here." Aster said while dragging Savannah.

"Man, it's getting windy out." Aster sighed.

"Wow, what is that?"

"It's lightning."

"It looks like bright human veins."

"Whatever. "Aster said while trying to open the door. He jerked the door and tried kicking it open. Between Savannah's craziness and being in this dark forest with a storm brewing trying to find his friends, he had just about reached his limit. He felt like he was going to lose it. He had to stay calm. His friends' lives were in danger.

"Come on, why isn't it opening!" Aster yelled while kicking it." Savannah, blast the door with your power."

"Otay." she said while slurring her words. She accidently blasted Aster. "Not me, the door!"

Savannah blasted the door than it reflected back to her. "The door hates me." she cried.

"It must be X stone if it didn't break." Aster said.

Inside the cell Zane tried to keep Kaden calm with a game of "I Spy". After a few rounds everyone got bored with it. There was not much color in this dark, cold stone building. When everyone's clothing color had been used, they stopped the game. Scarlet pulled Kaden close trying to comfort not only him but herself as well. She wondered if they'd ever escape.

"Do you know how to pick a lock?" Aster asked.

"Yeah, I'm doing it right now." Savannah said while picking her nose.

"Not picking your nose! I said pick a lock!

Savannah began giggling and walking toward something in the dark. As Aster turned around, he saw her squatted down trying to get a skunk to come to her. He yelled for her to step back away from her furry friend and before he barely got the words out the skunk sprayed them both. Savannah thought it was funny but the smell made Aster sick. He ran behind a bush and puked. After several minutes he stomped out from behind the bushes. He was furious. This was the last straw. He dragged Savannah to the car and headed to Nick's house. He lived in the next town over. Aster needed help and hopefully Nick could give him some ideas.

Crap, I burnt my popcorn, Nick thought. *I guess I'll make more.*

Twenty minutes had passed and they finally pulled into Nicks driveway. He lived in a small town outside Science City. Nick always said if you blink you might miss it. It was a quiet place but the people were friendly. His parents said it was a great place to raise kids. He recently got his own place. It was a 2-bedroom brick house with a basement which he called his man cave. He had a pool table and video games set up down there. It was small but it was all he needed. As he was popping corn, he heard a knock at the door. He was surprised to see Aster standing there but the smell was even more of a surprise.

"Dang, you smell disgusting." Nick said while holding his nose.

"Sorry about that." Aster laughed.

"Did a skunk spray you?"

"Yeah, and Savannah too." Aster said.

"Where is she?"

"In your dumpster."

"This place is cool!" Savannah yelled.

"Is she ok?"

Aster explained how he meant to give her a sedative and accidently injected her with something else that made her act and talk crazy. He continued the story explaining who Luna was and that she may have taken his friends and locked them in an abandoned jail. He needed Nick's expertise in picking the lock to try to rescue them. So much for a quiet evening watching a movie. They walked to their cars almost forgetting Savannah was dumpster diving. Aster pulled her out. Now she not only smelled like skunk but garbage as well. His car would never be the same. Nick followed them in his grey pick up truck. It had some tools in it if they would need them. As they arrived Nick looked around feeling a little creeped out.

"Wow, this place looks scary Aster." Nick said.

"I know. Right?"

Savannah jumped on Nick's back startling him. He squirmed trying to get her off but she held tight. Aster had to pull her off. She was stronger than they all realized. She still was pretty out of it acting so out of character. They laughed at how silly she was acting. She would be so embarrassed if she only knew.

Aster explained that Savannah couldn't blast the door down because it was made of x-stone. Nick got out a tool from his truck and it took about three minutes for him to get the door open. Not wanting to put another friend in danger, Aster told him he could go. He told Nick to send the police if he did not hear from him by midnight.

They slowly opened the door and creeped in. Keeping Savannah quiet was going to be a challenge and to prove that point it didn't take long before she knocked over an old lamp. They walked carefully down a hallway listening for anything that sounded like their friends.

We need to get out of here, Zane thought.

"Mommy, I'm scared of this house." Kaden cried.

"Please don't cry," Scarlet whispered.

"I wanna go home."

"Relax Kaden, we will find a way out." Scarlet smiled.

"It's ok bud, your mom and I are right here.' Zane encouraged.

As they continued weaving their way through many hall ways and rooms Aster and Savannah discovered jars of blood, only because Savannah knocked one over. They realized that this definitely was Luna's hideout.

Listening carefully, Zane thought he heard Aster and Savannah's voices. He tried calling Aster on his phone hoping Luna would not hear it. He was so relieved when Aster answered very quickly. He explained that Luna had locked them in a cell toward the back of the building and that she was evil. Scarlet and Kaden were relieved that help was coming. Their prayers were answered.

Aster could see a dim light ahead and they moved quietly toward it. He pushed the door back and found his friends locked in a jail cell but all smiling at him with relief. They told him that Luna had Drake somewhere in the building and was trying to take his power.

"Savannah was right. We should have listened to her." Zane sighed.

"Where is she? "Scarlet asked.

"Sav, come on." Aster said as he went back to pull her into the room with them.

"I'm so sorry I didn't believe you." Zane said.

"Otay." Savannah said.

"Why is she acting weird?" Scarlet asked.

Aster laughed nervously as he explained he gave her a shot of an unknown substance instead of a sedative so he could draw her blood. He told of her crazy behavior and her attempt to tame a skunk. He apologized to them all and he hoped they would all laugh about this later.

Scarlet immediately knew what substance Aster injected in Savannah. When she was in the early stages of testing on onis she created a serum to use to make onis do whatever she told them to. She did not finish tweaking the serum because she realized what she was doing was wrong. She also forgot to dispose of the serum so that this would never happen. She felt so bad that this accidental injection had harmed Savannah making her go crazy. Hopefully when they return to the lab, she can develop something to help get her back to normal. Scarlet knew Jesus had forgiven her for her past but sometimes things like this come back to remind her how wicked she was. She bowed her head and once again prayed "God forgive me.

"Why are you crying mommy?" Kaden asked.

"Scarlet, that was your old life. God says old things have passed away and all things become new. That's what's cool about God. He doesn't hold anything against us. When He says you're forgiven, it's forgotten. "Zane said.

"Yeah." Aster said.

"Yesh." Savannah smiled.

"Hi Zane, I like you." Savannah smiled.

"Wait, you" like" like me? "Zane asked

"Yesh, not just your blood smell, I like your human body looks." Savannah smiled.

Zane blushed a bright red and they all laughed at Savannah because they knew if she were in her right state of mind, she would never have said those things. She would be much to shy.

Aster picked the lock with a tool Nick gave him and released his friends. They still needed to find Drake and figure out how to get out of this place. They were discussing a plan when Savannah ran off saying something crazy about her plan. Zane ran after her but she was quickly out of sight.

In the darkest part of the prison Luna continued tormenting Drake with her hurtful words. She told him how ugly he was without his hood and playfully pulled at his hair. Drake's heart was breaking as he poured out his feelings for Luna. He had loved everything about her; her raspy voice, bold personality, cool hair, even her being a little edgy. Now he realized a little edgy was her toning down her down right evilness. Despite it all, he still loved her.

"Luna, I wanted to teach you about Jesus and have a life together." Drake cried while on the floor.

Luna jumped on Drake stabbing him in the chest and smiled," just keep dreaming Drake."

"Get off me, I had it." Drake cried.

"Cry baby." Luna smiled while stoking his hair.

As Savannah drew closer to the voices, she could tell it was Luna and Drake. She quickly barged into the room." Hello Luna and Drakey." Savannah smiled.

"Well look who finally showed up." Luna laughed.

"Sis, help me!" Drake cried while Luna was putting a knife to his neck.

"Whoop." Savannah smiled.

"Uh, are you ok?" Luna asked.

"Hey Luna, you wanna see meh oni look?" Savannah smiled.

"Huh?" Luna said.

"Sis, are you drunk?" Drake asked.

"I haz chemicals in meh body." Savannah smiled while in her oni form and holding her tail.

Luna thew Drake to the floor and began approaching Savannah.

"Look at dis guys." Savannah smiled while darkness was coming out of her hands.

Crap, Luna thought.

Savannah blasted Luna with her power and she fell next to Drake on the floor hitting her head.

"Your nose is using the bathroom." Savannah smiled while blood was dripping out of his nose.

"What happened to you?" Drake asked.

"Your hair so soft." Savannah said while playing with it.

"Oh my gosh. Who has made you go crazy?"

They could hear footsteps coming their way and it was such a relief to see Zane, Scarlet, Aster and Kaden fly through the door.

"Thank you, Jesus!" Zane panted as he bent down to catch his breath.

"Are you ok?" Kaden asked.

"Yeah, I'm ok." Drake sighed while crying.

Kaden ran to Drake and gave him a hug also crying. Scarlet immediately began to check out his wounds hoping he was well enough for them to get out of there quickly.

"I'm so sorry Luna broke your heart." Aster said.

Drake put his hood back on.

"You don't have to hide who you are." Aster said.

"I'm ugly anyway." Drake sighed.

"No, you're not." Scarlet said.

"Shut up, you hate us oni's. I looked in your mind when I first met you and you thought me and my sister were ugly!" Drake yelled.

"Drake, that was the past." Zane said.

"I'm sorry. I now know everyone has worth and value. I hope you can one day forgive me." Scarlet said with tears in her eyes.

Drake was so angry that he hadn't seen through the real Luna. He so badly wanted a girlfriend. He thought he could teach her about Jesus and they would have a great life together. He felt stupid and embarrassed right now. His friends gathered around him reminding him that no matter what, they had each other. Zane sat beside Drake and said, John 14:27 says," Peace I leave with you, my peace I give you, I do not give to you as the world gives, do not let your hearts be troubled and do not be afraid". This scripture helped him when his dad passed away and he was so hurt. It would take awhile but Drake would find peace and joy again.

"Guys, we better go before Luna wakes up." Scarlet said.

"Come on." Zane smiled while helping Drake up.

"I love you my brother and why are your eyes peeing?" Savannah asked.

"Can someone tell me what's up with her?" Drake asked.

"So, where should I start?" Aster laughed.

They all loaded in Aster's car and headed back to Science City. They hoped Luna wouldn't wake up until they got her secured in a lock down room. Aster and Zane carried her into the lab and put her in a testing room. It was securely locked and they all went to get cleaned up, eat, and figure out what to do with Luna.

"You freaking idiots!" Luna yelled while banging the testing room door.

"Hush it." Scarlet said while in a chair with her coffee.

"Let me out now!"

"No, we cannot trust you, Luna. You betrayed all of us let alone how you physically and mentally hurt Drake. When Savannah gets back to herself, she will send you back to the oni realm." Scarlet said.

"I freaking hate you!"

Luna continued throwing threats and insults at Scarlet. She didn't want to go home to do chores or whatever else her father would have her do. She was a selfish, lazy, Simbyot teenager who wanted things her way.

Scarlet continued working on the serum to give Savannah. Hopefully it would bring her back to normal. When she walked into the living room, she found Savannah sitting on Drake trying to comfort him when actually she was hurting his wounds. She meant well but poor Drake was not only physically hurt but emotionally a mess. Aster and Zane helped Scarlet get Savannah to the lab so she could give her the serum. Savannah, of course did not want to have anything to do with it so they had to strap her to the chair.

"I hope this works." Aster sighed. "You will only feel a little pinch." As Aster put the needle in her arm she began crying. Zane held her hand to comfort her. She cried out for help then fainted. They put a band aid on her arm and laid her on the examining table. Forty minutes passed and she woke up. As they discussed what happened that day Savannah had no memories of any of it. She was surprised to know that she saved Drake. She realized her hat was missing and began freaking out when Aster handed it to her along with an apology for his actions. He promised he would not try to draw her blood without her permission anymore. She hugged Aster and ran to check on her brother.

"Hey sis, I'm sorry I didn't believe you that Luna was evil." Drake said while grabbing her hand.

"It's ok. I'm just glad you're ok."

Scarlet had heard enough of Lunas cursing and threats. The sooner she was gone the better. "Just send Luna home now!" Scarlet said.

"I'm on it, with pleasure." Savannah smiled. She grabbed Luna's dads' staff and went to the testing room. As she looked at Luna she seemed like a caged animal. She was yelling and threatening to come back for revenge. Savannah knew they would always have to be on guard. The thing that bothered her most was the pain Luna caused Drake. She squeezed the staff and darkness formed and just like that, Luna was gone.

Running up the stairs in the lab Len had to stop to catch her breath. She had been searching all night for Zane. He didn't answer his phone, all his friends were gone, including Scarlet, so she thought the worst. She normally was a calm person but fear had taken over and she frantically drove all over town trying to find them. As she stood there, she heard voices and burst through the door.

"Where in the world have you all been?" she yelled.

"Calm down mom." Zane said.

"Why didn't you tell me where you were going?" Len cried.

"I took care of him Len. "Scarlet said.

"You took care of him, did you? Just look at him. There's blood all over his hoodie. Clearly, he's hurt. I don't know if I'm cut out for this crazy kind of life with oni's, Simbyot's, and all this violence. I don't know if I'm willing to risk Zane's or my life for all this. I thought you all were dead and I'd never even know how or where to find you."

"Look Len, I know you were scared as I would be also. Honestly, we were in a dangerous situation but thankfully God came through and used Savannah to rescue us. You'll have to decide if you can handle this crazy family we've created here. If you choose to go, I understand but I will always make a home here for these kids. If I don't protect them, science will get to them; and we all know what that means."

"You know I love all of you. Scarlet, you're only twenty-three yourself and I know you need help. We will stay. I was just so scared. I guess you guys are going to keep me on my knees." She laughed.

"Luna's back where she belongs and I guess I'm back to normal." Savannah smiled.

"So, do you all mind telling me what happened?" Len asked.

"Where do we even start." Zane laughed.

CHAPTER 5
THE LEAGUE OF SCIENCE

Scarlet was in a really foul mood after talking with her boss on the phone. Mya fired her for refusing to test on the oni who now seemed to have somehow moved in with her. She was growing fond of these kids being there even though they could be quite annoying at times. She refused to hurt Savannah any more. In the past she felt all oni's were evil but she now realized they can change. Maybe being a Christian did make the difference. She realized that she herself had some evil within to deal with. She was going to church for the first time today. She was a little nervous but curious as well.

Zane and Drake were trying to wake Savannah to get ready for church. Zane had to teach her how to sleep when she first came to the human realm. Maybe he taught her too well. She was so hard to wake up. Drake tried jumping on her, giving her a wet willy and finally came up with the idea of banging a pot with a spoon. Drake was asking for it. Savannah just might blast him if he went to far. He came up by the head of the bed and began hitting the pot with a wooden spoon. Savannah shot straight up out of bed with eyes as round as baseballs holding her ears.

"That ought to do it." Drake laughed. Even though he was still depressed about Luna, it still made him laugh to aggravate his sister. It was his duty.

Savannah whined and pulled herself out of bed wondering why church was so early. She got dressed and wondered into the living room. Scarlet walked in saying she and Kaden were ready. She was still wearing her lab coat and Zane mentioned not wearing it to church. Her statement was *if I can't wear it, I'm not going.* He dropped it because God doesn't care what you wear to church. She must love that lab coat. Come to think of it he has never seen her without it.

"You can wear it, no problem." Zane said.

"Zane, did you get your bible?" Len asked.

"Yes." he smiled.

"So, what do you do in church?" Savannah asked.

"Well, you sit in a big auditorium and a person called a pastor teaches about things in the bible and some churches like ours, sing Christian music." Zane explained.

"I love music. "Drake said banging the table like a drum.

"Let's go guys, we don't want to be late." Len said.

Realizing that Scarlet didn't have a car seat for Kaden, Len quickly went to the storage area in the lab to find Zane's old one. She saved everything and this time her being a pack rat came in handy .

They all piled in Len's SUV and were off for their first experience at church. Drake looked a little sad because he wished Luna was going to. He had hopes of her turning her life around from dark to light as he had. Savannah comforted him with words of encouragement and overhearing their conversation Len joined in by saying that a lot people find healing for their broken hearts at church. It's not church that heals you, it the presence of God. "Just ask God to heal your heart Drake and see what happens."

"God hears everyone and He cares what you're going through." Drake, Zane added.

As they entered the church, a little late, Pastor Dan had already begun his sermon." Hebrews 11:6 says," without faith it is impossible to please God, because anyone who comes to him must believe that he exists and that he rewards those who earnestly seek him," he said.

"I have a question?" Savannah yelled out.

"Don't make a scene please." Len whispered.

"What does God give for a reward?"

"Well, eternal life." Pastor Dan said.

"But oni's have that already, we can't die. "Savannah said.

"Eternal life with God is different than eternal life with Satan. God offers forgiveness of sin, freedom from guilt and shame, and a blessed life here where you can have peace no matter what. God doesn't bring torment like Satan but peace and joy. Bottom line, God operates out of His love for us and has nothing but good in store for us." Pastor Dan smiled.

"Well then, why do bad things happen?" Savannah asked curiously.

"People have a will and sometimes our choices or choices of others can cause bad things to happen. The good news is that God can take bad things and turn them around for good. I don't know how He does it but it's pretty cool." He responded.

"Savannah, I can't believe our dad would lie to us about God." Drake whispered.

"I know." Savannah sighed.

Pastor Dan finished his sermon and they all listened closely. Savannah said she learned a lot and wanted to come back again.

Scarlet had tears in her eyes and Savannah noticed. "Are you crying?"

"It's just that all of my life I've been doing my own thing and I feel terrible l for what I've done." Scarlet cried.

"Do you want to give your heart to Jesus?" Zane asked. "He takes away all our guilt and shame."

"Yeah, I really do." Scarlet cried.

"Let's go talk to Pastor Dan. I know he would love to pray for you." Zane said.

As they approached Pastor Dan, Scarlet noticed he was tall with red hair and very kind green eyes. Zane introduced them to one another and Pastor Dan was happy to pray with Scarlet. She asked Jesus to come into her heart and lead her life. She was truly sorry for her sins and was amazed that God loved her no matter what. She had never felt love like that before. She had a bounce in her step and for the first time in a long time she had hope that her life was going to be a good one. *I guess this is what they call peace*, she thought.

Len had gone to the nursery to pick up Kaden while Scarlet was praying with Pastor Dan. The nursery worker commented on how sweet Kaden was and that he played nicely with the other kids. He had a paper in his hand he had colored and was excited to show his mom.

"Mommy, I had so much fun." Kaden smiled.

"What did you learn? "Scarlet asked.

"About Mary and she had to go on a donkey to Bethlehem."

"Tell us why dear." Len encouraged.

"To have God's son Jesus, he picked Mary to have Jesus." Kaden smiled.

As they were talking about Mary and Jesus Drake had some flashbacks into the past. Since he was over a billion years old, he was around during the time of Jesus birth. Satan's plan was to kill Jesus so he sent out many oni's and evil beings to find the baby. Jesus was a big threat to Satan's kingdom. Such a threat, that Jesus would one day destroy it forever. Drake was one of those oni's. He came vey close to killing Jesus. Now he knows he was fighting a loosing battle. God was never going to let that happen. And here he was now a converted oni. God really is amazing!

He explained all this to his friends and they all were shocked. His age was a big surprise and what was most amazing to them all is that once he tried to kill Jesus, God forgave him, and now, he served God.

"Yeah, now that I know Satan was the evil one, I will always be Gods follower." Savannah smiled.

"Same with me." Drake said.

"Today was fun Len, thanks for letting me go with you." Scarlet said.

"I'm so happy for you Scarlet." Len smiled.

As usual Drake began complaining about being hungry. He had eaten Scarlet's ice-cream before church but that didn't fill him up. Wait until she went to the freezer and realizes it's gone. He'll blame Savannah. They decided to stop at the gas station to pick up some pizzas. While they were waiting Kaden got a headache so Scarlet took him to the car. Since he was growing so fast his hormones were wacked out and he got headaches. Len went to the car as well instructing Zane to keep and eye on the others. Being out in public was tricky at times. Savannah was still not very comfortable with a lot of people in a small space.

"Remember, humans are nice and won't hurt you." Zane said as he stood next to Savannah.

"Ok, I trust you." Savannah said.

"Look at all this food." Drake smiled while walking the aisles.

"What is this?" Savannah asked.

"It's a human snack called chips." Zane said.

Zane picked up a couple different kinds of chips for Savannah to try. She began to experience an overwhelming fear as people were filing in the store. A man pointed at her hat to compliment her but she thought he was going to take it so she yelled out, "don't hurt me!"

"You are weird." the man said.

"Help me, Zane. I can't take this anymore." Savannah cried while running.

Zane calmed her down so they could wait for the pizzas. He had to use the restroom so he told Drake and Savannah to stand together and wait for him.

Crap, I'm craving human blood, Drake thought.

Savannah reached for Drakes' hand.

"We need to leave soon." Drake sighed.

"Are you craving humans?" Savannah asked.

"A little bit."

Len parked in the parking lot of the city bank across from the gas station. Savannah and Drake decided to get out of the store before Drake lost control. Zane could catch up later. They crossed the street and headed to the back parking lot.

Being a scientist in Science City wasn't always easy. There were so many of them that sometimes you felt like competitors. The one who made the discovery first was the best. Mya always felt that push to be the first. She had been trying for years to capture an oni with no luck. She was so close. Her best friend had found one but chose not to tell her and let it go. She felt so betrayed that she fired her. She didn't need her. She would get an oni on her own and do all the tests she wanted to. No one was going to stop her. Her assistant James insisted they drive around the city with an oni tracker and try to find onis. Mya knew they just wouldn't be walking around town. She felt like they were wasting their time.

"Um, Mya." James said while looking at his phone.

"What!" Mya snapped.

"The oni tracker is working." James said.

"What do you mean?"

"The tracker is detecting two oni's nearby." James smiled.

"Ha, nice prank." Mya laughed.

"I'm not pranking Mya!" James yelled.

Mya snatched the phone out of his hand and her eyes grew wide. "I can't believe it."

"See." James smiled

"All these years the league of science has been trying to find an oni and now I'm going to be the first one." Mya smiled while walking.

"But Scarlet found an oni before you, "James said.

"Shut up James!" Mya yelled. "She doesn't count."

"Let's head to the van and find them before they get away from us." James said.

"No duh stupid." Mya said rudely.

As Savannah and Drake walked to the parking lot, they discussed liking the human realm but still not being used to a lot of things. Getting around in a car or truck was unusual to them.

"Look at that." Savannah said.

"Human car things are weird. "Drake said while looking at a white van.

"Why can't humans ride dragons like us oni's?"

"Yeah, dragons are better." he smiled.

As Mya and James approached the van, they noticed the tracker lighting up. They couldn't believe their eyes. Could two onis be walking right near their van?

"Let's get them." James said.

"Do you have the sedatives ready?" Mya asked.

"Heck yes." James smiled.

"Hurry." Mya hissed.

"Hi humans." Drake said to a man and woman approaching them. They seemed friendly to him. The man was stocky wearing ripped jeans and a red t-shirt. His black hair stuck out from underneath a ball cap. The lady was dressed as casual wearing jeans and a peach-colored sweatshirt. She was about as tall as Zane but a little heavier. She had a nose ring and glasses.

"Drake, I want to go." Savannah cried feeling uneasy.

"Well, theses humans want something I'd say." Drake said.

"Here." James whispered while handing Mya a syringe.

"What do you need humans?" Drake asked.

"You guys must be new to this city because we never saw you two before. "James smiled.

"What are you doing?" Mya whispered.

"Watch and learn Mya."

"Yeah, we are new." Drake said.

"Let's leave Drake." Savannah said pulling on his arm noticing there was a lab coat hanging in the window of the van.

Drake asked them for directions to the bank to find his friends saying they were lost. James offered to give them a ride which sent Savannah into a panic. She was not getting into that van. One of her brothers' weaknesses was trusting people he didn't know. You'd think after Luna hurt him; he'd be a little more careful but he wasn't. She pulled on his arm trying to get away from these humans.

Realizing Savannah was getting suspicious, Mya decided to jump into action. She was getting impatient and wanted to get these oni's into the van before someone came along and saw them. James grabbed her arm trying to stop her so he could calmly get near them but Mya pulled away from him lunging toward Drake. Mya told Savannah not to scream or she'd hurt Drake. Right now, he was just falling asleep since they gave him a sedative, but if she drew attention to them Drake would suffer. Savannah went into her oni form hoping it would scare them into letting them go.

"Listen oni, I can do this the easy way or the hard way." Mya said.

"How did you know I'm an oni?" Savannah asked.

"You have a tail and humans don't call each other humans." James laughed.

Still in her oni from she yelled," what do you want with us?"

Mya had enough. Pulling out a gun she shot Savannah in the stomach making her fall to the ground. Overwhelming fear caused her to go back into her human form and James quickly grabbed her and gave her a sedative. He loaded her in the van as she tried to yell for Zane, but the words wouldn't 't come out.

At the convenience store a man entered saying there was a gun shot down the street. Zane quickly began yelling and searching for Drake and Savannah. He asked several people if they saw someone in a purple hoodie with a girl with blue hair. That shouldn't be hard to remember. A woman said she saw them leave five minutes earlier. Panic filled Zane as he dashed out side yelling for them. He quickly ran to the bank parking lot where his mother said she would be hoping they were waiting for him there. As he ran to the car noticing they weren't there he tried not to freak out. He explained to his mom and Scarlet that he had gone to the bathroom telling them to wait for him.

"If they aren't with us, that means they are out in the city somewhere." Scarlet said.

"A man said a gunshot was heard. I sure hope it doesn't have anything to do with them. I'm sorry mom, I shouldn't have left them." Zane said feeling responsible.

"They may have gone back to the lab without us. It's not that far from here and if they couldn't find us, they could have walked home. "Len said.

As they were driving home Scarlet's phone rang and the caller id said "League of Science". She was not in the mood to talk to Mya. She had fired her recently and Scarlet was too mad to even talk to her. She told Kaden to ignore it. There's no way she'd let Kaden answer and have to listen to Mya's foul mouth.

"Who are you trying to call?" Jeff asked.

"I want Scarlet to know I have 2 oni's and rub it in her face, but she isn't picking up." Mya said.

As they opened the van doors, Jeff a long-time employee of the League of Science and Andy, an intern working with Mya, approached wanting to see what the oni's looked like. Mya started shouting orders to get them unloaded before they woke up. She was rude and bossy.

Rushing upstairs to the living quarters, with Kaden right behind him, Zane began yelling for Savannah and Drake. *Please let them be here* he thought. They searched all the bedrooms, game room, kitchen and bathrooms. They were not there.

Scarlets' phone rang again irritating her but Kaden told her it might be important. She grabbed the phone out of her purse and answered ready to give Mya a piece of her mind.

"What do you want?" Scarlet asked.

"Well, I have some news." Mya laughed.

"I'm not in the mood for this, so just get it over with." Scarlet grunted.

"I found two oni's and it was so easy. "Mya taunted.

"What!" Scarlet yelled.

"I can tell you are jealous." Mya smiled.

"Um, does one of the oni's have blue hair and the other wear a hood?" Scarlet asked.

"Yeah, why? "Mya said.

"You little…." Scarlet bit her tongue trying to control herself.

"How did you know that?" Mya asked. "Aww, poor Scarlet want's my oni's I captured."

"Mya, they are my friends. They were the oni's I refused to torture. Don't hurt them!" Scarlet yelled.

When Zane and Len looked at Scarlet's face, they could tell something was seriously wrong. Mya had hung up on her and now she felt dread come over her. She knew what Mya was capable of and her friends were in real danger. As she sunk into the couch she explained to Len and Zane that the League of Science had their friends and that she at one time was among a group of scientists that were testing on oni's. She refused to continue testing on Savannah and Drake so she was fired. Her boss now had them and she knew what Mya was capable of doing. Torture was the mild word for it.

"What will Mya do to them, Zane cried?

"The same thing I did to Savannah when I was evil but Mya is a pervert and is a little too curious." Scarlet said not wanting to say much more with Kaden in the room. "We need to come up with a plan to rescue them."

"The first thing we need to do is pray." Len said. They asked God for protection and a plan.

Finding it hard to wake up, Drake sat up and tried to focus his eyes. It was very bright, almost like he needed sunglasses. As he squinted, he saw Savannah across from him and heard a strange voice.

"Ugh, what's going on?" Drake sighed.

"Well look who finally woke up." Mya laughed.

"What am I wearing?" Savannah asked looking down at a white tank top and shorts.

"By the way, your lower body is really fascinating to me." Mya smiled while holding her phone.

"Did you take pictures of us while we were passed out?" Savannah cried.

"Yep," Mya said.

"Did you look at my, you know?" Drake asked.

"Yeah, but Jeff did the examination. We're scientists. We do research on things, all things. "She laughed.

"You are a bit of a pervert. "Jeff laughed while walking in on the conversation.

"Only to oni's. They're not human!" Mya yelled.

"They still are like us humans in some ways. "Jeff said.

"Just shut up!" Mya said rudely.

"Can someone tell me what's going on?" Drake asked.

Jeff explained to them that they were at the League of Science lab and were to be test subjects. He and Mya kidnapped them and they just found out that they were the onis that Scarlet had been testing on. How crazy is it to have captured the very onis that Scarlet had refused to give to Mya. Scarlet lost her job over the whole thing and their friendship turned to hatred. Savannah started to panic remembering the torture she went through the first time. She began to cry.

"Boss, do you want me to bring the testing equipment?" James asked.

"Yes, and be quick because I've been waiting my whole life for this." Mya smiled.

We know you have, Jeff thought rolling his eyes. Mya has been obsessed with finding an oni for as long as he has known her. He didn't know what it was all about but she sure hated them. He hurried along getting things set up. You didn't want to get Mya mad if she was in bad mood.

Savannah continued crying while hugging Drake. Andy commented on her being a crybaby. He thought onis were supposed to be evil, scary, and mean. She seemed more like a scared girl to him.

"What are you going to do with me and my sister!" Drake yelled.

"To make you feel like you're dead." Mya laughed.

"We can't die, human." Drake smiled.

"You can still feel pain." Mya said.

With that being said Savannah lost it and Drake got mad. He stood up ready to fight back. He wasn't going to let them hurt his sister. Mya yelled for Andy to get her knife and syringes to draw blood. She was going to make these onis suffer the way they made her suffer. Mya took the knife from Jeff and walked toward Savannah. She put the knife near her face threatening Drake to back off. The first thing they were going to do was draw their blood. Jeff and Andy held Savannah down. Drake didn't know what to think about this. He was getting worried for his sister. She had been through so much already at the hands of evil scientist. Savannah had tears running down her face while Mya laughed at her. All the scientists put on their lab coats while Drake was getting ticked off.

"Don't lay a hand on my sister!" Drake yelled.

"Shut up before I cut your head off!" Mya yelled back.

"Teehee, I can tell you are mad." Drake smiled.

Mya just about had it with the boy oni. She took a deep breath and before she could calm down, Drake hugged her and he told her that he was glad to be here with new humans. Drake was trying to tease Mya so they wouldn't focus on Savannah. While Drake was poking and hugging her, Mya instantly went into a panic. She quickly pushed Drake off her. Mya yelled at Jeff to take the dumb fatty oni to a testing tube in a different room so she could have time with Savannah alone. Jeff grabbed a hold of Drake. James gave Drake a sedative than he and Jeff took Drake away.

"Don't take my brother away from me." Savannah cried.

Mya threated Savannah to go into her oni form, so out of panic and stress she listened to her. Mya was amazed to see her oni form. She wondered what she would look like without clothes on. Andy saw her perverted face and told her not to be weird when he's around.

While Mya and Andy were getting ready to draw Savannah's blood, Jeff and James put Drake into a tube. Andy was still new to the Scientist thing. He was glad to have a cool job like this. He thought he would be doing things like helping sick people. This hospital was different from a normal one. What they were doing was illegal, but he found it interesting. Drake started to wake up. The bright room was making his eyes hurt. He got up and looked around. Jeff and James looked at Drake's worried face and James began to tease him about how ugly he was.

Mya had Savannah strapped to a hospital bed. Andy was trying to find a vein for Mya but he couldn't find one. Mya pushed Andy off the chair and took the syringe out of his hand. Andy suggested that they could use the vein finder. Mya didn't want to do that. She told him that she would keep sticking the oni until she found a good vein. Andy sighed and went to grab a cherry soda out of the mini fringe. Savannah started to feel nauseous and her face got pale. Mya kept sticking her and sticking her. Savannah couldn't take it any longer and she puked all over herself and on Mya's arm. Mya got mad and she thew the syringe on the floor and it shattered.

She started to cuss up a storm. Andy tried to calm her down. He got a new syringe for her and told her that it would be ok.

Back at Scarlet's hospital, Kaden told his mom that he didn't feel good. Scarlet patted him on the back. She went to her desk to get her coffee and as she turned to get it, Kaden turned back into a baby. Scarlet looked at Kaden in shock. Kaden was crying and blabbering. Scarlet was so confused. She began to panic. She ran to the left side of the testing room that they were in and she opened up a white cabinet and took out a stethoscope. When she turned back at Kaden, he looked like a five-year-old again. She wondered if she drank too much alcohol last night.

"Hey Scarlet, what are you doing?" Zane asked.

"Give me a sec." Scarlet said fumbling through her cabinets.

Zane could tell something was bothering her. She explained that Kaden had some kind of power that let him change into a baby and back to a five-year-old. She had to do some tests to see if he had some kind of disease. She grabbed a syringe to draw blood, a cup to collect his pee and a measuring tape. She began measuring his legs. This was really freaking her out and she had no idea where to even start. She had never heard of anyone who could do what Kaden could do. Zane calmed Scarlet down and talked her into testing on Kaden later. They needed to come up with a plan to rescue their friends.

Drake didn't realize it, but when he got nervous, he talked; a lot. He kept annoying Jeff by asking for pizza and ice cream. Those were his comfort foods, and boy did he need them now. He was more worried about Savannah than himself. Drake talked so much that Jeff wanted to put him to sleep to shut him up.

Mya put a shock collar on Savannah in order to control her. The next thing she was going to do was pull one of her sharp teeth, without any numbing medicine. She threatened Savannah not to bite her or she'd hurt Drake. Savannah had to listen to Mya. She didn't want her brother to get hurt, all though, biting Mya might make her feel better. That would be dumb of Savannah to make Mya furious,so she decided against it. Andy went to the hospital bed where Savannah was strapped and told her that this was going to hurt her a lot. Him saying that made her even more scared. She never had teeth pulled but in the oni realm, oni's pull out human teeth to torture them and it made the humans scream. Savannah knew it would hurt very bad. Andy strapped her even tighter so she couldn't wiggle around. He made it so tight it was hard for her to breathe. Mya put on gloves and fixed her dirty blonde hair out of her face and put it in a ponytail. James came in and put dentist equipment next to the hospital bed. After five minutes of getting everything ready for the tooth pull, Mya sat down in a grey chair and gave Savannah a smirk. Savannah yelled at the top of her lungs to let her and her brother go. She began to cry as Mya was putting a sharp tool into her mouth. Mya put the tool on one of Savannah's middle teeth and was ripping it out. Savannah screamed so much her face was red. Blood began to come out of her mouth and onto Mya's gloves. Savannah prayed for help. God was all she had. *God is with you wherever you go. He can never leave you and he won't,* she said to herself. If Savannah didn't have Jesus by her side, it would have been so much worse. Mya got the tooth out and laid it on a tray next to her.

"It hurts so bad. Make the pain stop!" Savannah cried while blood was dripping from her mouth.

"Now you know what it feels like to be tortured." Mya smiled.

"What do you mean?" Savannah asked while wiping tears off her face.

"You oni's only care about yourself and hurting humans. Now you get to feel how the humans feel." Mya said.

"I'm sorry for what my kind has done to humans. I am really sorry for all I did in the past. A human that loves me taught me how to be nice and loving and you're nothing but a perverted evil human!" Savannah yelled.

"Humans will never love oni's." Mya yelled.

Savannah had her feelings hurt, badly. She was trying to be a good oni. She hoped Mya would see good in her, but for some reason, she hated her.

"I think it's a good time to examine your oni body." Mya smiled while putting her hand on Savannah's leg.

"You're a creep!" Savannah cried.

Down the hall in another exam room James and Andy were teasing Drake. All Drake wanted was to go home. Not the oni realm but his new home here in the human realm. He had found a place where he was accepted and he never wanted to see his Uncle Satan or his dad again. He was done with being evil. James and Andy didn't believe he was a Christian because of his relatives. There's no way an evil oni could be good. Drake kept trying to explain but they just joked and made fun of him. He buried his head in his arms praying for God's help.

Scarlet still had her computer from the League of Science so part of the plan was to hack their cameras. This sounded like fun to Aster and got right at it. While he began working on this Scarlet found a lab coat for Zane to wear. They were going to sneak in and pretend to be employees at the lab. Aster gave them his teleporter gun explaining how to use it. Len was a little nervous about Zane going with Scarlet but he insisted on helping to rescue his friends. Aster gave them all ear coms so they could communicate with each other. Hopefully no one would realize Scarlet had been fired and shouldn't be there. She tucked a small gun in her pocket in case of an emergency and pushed the button on the teleporter.

"We made it." Scarlet said.

"How are we even going to get in?" Zane asked.

"I have an ID card but I'm fired. Let's hope that they forgot take me out of the system." Scarlet said.

"I'm kinda scared." Zane sighed.

"Like you say," God doesn't give you a spirt of fear, but love, power, and a sound mind." Scarlet smiled.

"You're right." Zane said.

Scarlet put her ID into a card reader. "We're in." she said.

Carrying a black metal bracelet with spikes on it, Mya returned from her lunch break ready to get back to Savannah. She teased her saying she had made a gift for her which Savannah knew was a lie. She slid the bracelet on Savannahs' arm explaining that if she tried to escape this room the spikes would heat up and jab her wrist. It was already poking her. She hated to think of what it could feel like when it turned on.

"My friends will find me." Savannah grunted.

"What friends?" Mya laughed "An oni like you shouldn't even have friends. Oni's only care about power." Mya said.

Part of the experiment was to put oni blood into a human and see if they would die. Savannah tried to tell her that a human would get power for about an hour but then die. Mya was willing to take the chance. After all, she was a scientist and if people had to die to get answers, she could live with that. I guess she lived up to the name "mad scientist." Her real hatred was toward onis.

Why do you hate oni's?" Savannah asked.

Mya's face turned red as she began her story. "My parents were killed by you awful beings. They were scientists just like me and they studied Oni's. Then one day they decided to go into the oni realm by doing evil sorcery and they both were slaughtered by an oni."

"They aren't the only ones that my kind has killed." Savannah sighed sadly.

Mya got her knife and said," it's all your fault." She kept walking toward Savannah and talking.

"I was watching them get slaughtered through the portal of which they went into the realm."

"I'm so sorry my kind did that." Savannah cried.

"Yeah right." Mya grunted. "I was a little kid and can you imagine a kid watching their parents get stabbed and eaten by a scary creature at the age of six!"

"I'm sorry."

"Ever since that day, I wanted to do the same to oni's that they did to my parents. Anyway, now you know why I hate you." Mya said.

"You are letting your anger control you." Savannah said.

"Shut up!"

"Don't let the devil mess with your head. Jesus can help you through your pain and can heal your heart." Savannah smiled. She had experienced this for herself and now she was different.

"I'm satanic dummy!"

As Aster searched the cameras, he could see Drake in testing room #12 on the second floor. Len was impressed with the technology as she leaned over Aster's shoulder to watch. She had to turn away when she saw Drake getting shocked by a scientist. She decided the best thing she could do to help was pray them all through this ordeal.

Scarlet and Zane tried to hurry to the second floor when they heard someone coming. They went in the closest door which was a stinky bathroom. Being a neat freak, Zane noticed they needed someone to do a better job at cleaning. Scarlet looked through the crack and noticed Andy passing by. She was glad it was the weekend and hardly any employees were there. It would be impossible not to be spotted by someone she knew on a regular work day. Scarlet led the way to the stairwell and as they came to the top, they could hear Drake screaming. They peeked through the small window and saw Jeff shocking Drake, mainly because he wouldn't shut up. Scarlet was to distract Jeff while Zane got the red key hanging on the wall. If their plan worked, they could have Drake out of the testing tube in no time.

"Um, hello," Scarlet smiled.

"Scarlet, I didn't know you were here," Jeff said.

"Um, is that an oni you have,"

"Yes. "Jeff said.

"Wow, that's nice." Scarlet smiled while Zane was sneaking to get the key.

"Wait, I thought Mya fired you." Jeff said.

"Well, she kinda did."

"You can't be here!" Jeff yelled.

"Scarlet, save me, "Drake cried.

"Dang it Drake, you blew it." Scarlet yelled.

"Wait, you know this oni?" Jeff asked.

"No, I have no clue who he is." Scarlet laughed.

"Scarlet, I live in your lab, you know who I am." Drake cried once again opening his big mouth.

At the same moment Zane reached the key, Jeff pulled out a gun. He was not going to let them take this oni. Mya would kill him if they got away. Scarlet punched Jeff in the face knocking him out and giving him a nose bleed. She was quite proud of herself even if it did hurt like heck. Zane quickly let Drake out and they hurried out the door to continue their search for Savannah. Aster kept scanning all the cameras to try and find her. After what seemed like forever, he located her.

"Sav is in something called a punishment room on the third floor, room 304." Aster said.

"Crap, we have to go now." Scarlet said.

"Better hurry guys, some girl is doing inappropriate things to Savannah, this scientist is disgusting and doesn't know personal space." Aster said.

"Who would do that to her?" Zane said becoming furious.

"Mya would." Scarlet sighed.

"What is a punishment room?" Zane asked.

"It's a place where you get tortured." Scarlet explained.

When they found the elevator, they couldn't get Drake to go in. He was just in a testing tube and this sort of reminded him of that. Zane once again had to give him a pep talk.

"Come on Drake, it won't hurt you. Get in." Zane smiled." Be brave, God is with you wherever you go."

"Even when I was in that tube thingy?" Drake asked.

"Right beside you." Zane smiled.

Drake stepped into the elevator and found it to be a fun experience. He noticed all the buttons and began reaching for them when Scarlet grabbed his arm and said," don't you even think about it."

With every insult Mya hurled at Savannah she also swung a bat and hit her causing much pain. As Scarlet, Drake and Zane approached the door they heard Savannah scream. Drake ran into the room without thinking, which is common for him. So, sneaking in was no longer an option. Mya's assistant, James, pulled a gun from his belt and shot Drake without hesitation. Mya wondered how he escaped until she saw Scarlet and Zane come in behind him.

Mya should have figured Scarlet would come after the onis, her so called friends. While Drake lay there bleeding, Zane comforted him, reminding him that onis can't die. Mya and Scarlet began arguing. Scarlet tried to explain that Savannah and Drake were not evil and that they actually were Christians. Mya had such hatred in her heart for them that nothing Scarlet said mattered. James had his gun pointed at Scarlet and Zane picked up a pipe and knocked James out . He got out his phone to call the police when Mya pulled out a gun and shot Savannah. Scarlet told Zane to get an instrument hanging on the wall that would release Drake from the chains. She distracted Mya while he got it and released Drake. They needed Drake to use his power to help them get away from Mya. Savannah was to hurt to be any help at this point but Drake had enough energy to blast Mya. She hit the wall knocking her out. They quickly helped Savannah up and as they walked toward the door Savannah remembered the bracelet on her arm. She couldn't leave the room without activating the bracelet. Scarlet recognized it as something she and Mya were working on together. She had a key to it but wasn't sure if Mya had updated it or changed it in any way. Savannah was going to have to put up with some pain until they got to the lab and tried the key. As soon as they began to teleport she spikes on the bracelet heated up and began poking in and out of her skin. She screamed as Scarlet quickly ran to her office to find the key. Scarlet dug through a bin and finally found it. Savannahs arm began to swell as well as bleed. She began to get nauseous and throw up from the pain. Zane comforted her while Len, Drake and Aster prayed.

"He gives power to the weak and strength to the powerless, Isaiah 40:29", Zane quoted in Savanah's ear.

"Here." Aster said while putting a trash can near her.

Savannah not only was sick and in pain but she was panicking thinking they would never get the bracelet off. She couldn't take one more minute. She felt like she was going to pass out when Scarlet ran into the room holding the key. Hopeful that it would work, she quickly ran to Savannah and put the key in the hole. It wouldn't turn so she turned the key around and it released the lock. Relief came over all of them and at this time Savannah did pass out. They carried her to an exam room so Scarlet could clean her up. She bandaged her arm and gave her some smelling salts to wake her up. She of course needed a hug from everyone. She spent the rest of the evening cuddled with Zane. She never wanted to leave this lab again. Zane got a phone call letting them know that Mya and all her assistants were in jail. Let's hope they stayed there for a long time. Scarlet knew better. Mya always found a way to get what she wanted.

CHAPTER 6
THE GATHERING

While Savannah and her friends were recovering from their ordeal with Mya there was something else going on in another realm far away. In the Wizard Realm two teenage wizards become aware that there were others who have powers besides themselves.

"Hey Talon. Have you heard the news? it's really interesting. "Wizzy asked.

"I don't watch the news. I'm trying to learn a new trick I found in the wizard's book." Talon said.

"Your conspiracy about people having powers other than wizards was right." Wizzy smiled.

"No way!" Talon said.

They listened closely as the news anchor told about Mya and her assistants going to jail for torturing the onis. The onis said they were not here to hurt anyone but wanted to live a peaceful life in the human realm.

"Wow, oni's are in the human realm." Talon said as he shut off the tv. They immediately began talking about using Onis to mine for the Power Stone. They had been searching for the stone for years. It had the power to resurrect their Master. Talon also was hopeful that an oni could resurrect his mother who had died sixteen years ago. Wizzy thought Talon should just let his mother rest in peace but Talon was determined to bring her back. Wizzy didn't agree with Talon to use the onis in the mines. Talon got mad and decided to go to the human realm on his own.

Drake was still having a hard time getting over Luna. He missed her even if she was a creepy, boy hunting, psycho dummy. Those were words Savannah used to describe Luna and she was right. It still hurt to remember the mean words Luna called him. Maybe he was ugly and would never find someone to love him. He was so depressed he ate two tubs of ice-cream in the middle of the night and when Scarlet said breakfast was ready he decided to go back to bed. He needed to be alone. Zane gave him a pat on the shoulder as he walked by. He felt so bad for him.

Zane had something important to talk to Savannah about. He couldn't believe how nervous he was. He told her she looked pretty making her blush. Even though he was a human and she was an oni he wanted to be more than friends. Savannah misunderstood thinking he didn't want to be friends anymore. He explained he wanted to be her boyfriend. She was new to this dating thing. She was so excited that Zane liked her because she felt the same way about him. She went skipping into the kitchen telling everyone that Zane was her boyfriend now. It was no surprise. Everyone knew they liked each other. Len was going to have to keep her eye on those two.

Aster talked Drake into coming out of his room and introduced him the world of video gaming. The next two hours the boys challenged, dissed, and teased one another through game after game. Drake got pretty good at it and actually won a few. It was amazing how Luna never entered his mind while he was preoccupied. All of a sudden something caught their eye.

"Why is there a portal in front of the tv?" Drake asked.

"I have no idea dude." Aster said.

After two hours of searching Science City, Talon finally found himself standing in the living room of two guys playing some sort of game. One looked strange so he assumed he was an oni. Talon introduced himself as a wizard. He began moving toward Drake and Aster jumped up standing between them.

"Listen here. You can't just welcome yourself into someone's home bro!" Aster yelled.

"You're not my boss blue pants." Talon grunted.

Aster was getting really ticked at this guy just popping in and insulting him. He was ready to physically show him to the door when Drake asked Talon if he was a scientist who came to get he and his sister.

"No. I'm not a scientist." Talon said.

"Then what do you want?" Aster asked.

Savannah walked in carrying a movie to watch and stopped in her tracks when she saw a stranger standing there. She immediately freaked thinking it was a scientist. Zane came in right behind her asking what was going on.

"This random guy just welcomed himself into the hospital!" Aster yelled while pointing to Talon.

Drake was not in the mood for this guy and moved toward him. Talon wacked Drake on the head with his green staff causing Drake to grab his head in pain.

"Now that I have all of your attention. I want slaves in the mines and I think powerful oni people will fit in just right." Talon smiled.

Savannah knew that onis were more powerful than wizards and went into her oni form to blast Talon. As she released her power Talon put Drake in front of him and Drake hit the floor. Savannah was quite scary looking but somehow, he knew she didn't want to hurt anyone. She would be easy to control in the mines.

"Why is green stuff forming around me?" Drake asked.

"It's doing it to me as well." Savannah cried.

"You are not very smart. I'm teleporting you trashy oni freaks." Talon said.

"Rude." Drake said.

"Where are you taking them?" Zane yelled. What are you going to do with our friends?"

"Well. I will make the oni's work in my mines to find an ancient crystal to bring back my master to take over the world." Talon explained.

"Ugh, bad guys always want to take over the world." Aster said.

"It's just the battle between good and evil." Zane sighed.

"Can you two shut up so I can do my evil biding!" Talon yelled.

Zane and Aster began laughing at Talon's attempt to do his "evil biding". Their teasing frustrated Talon and distracted him some while they were trying to figure out what to do. Len, Scarlet and Kaden came into the room asking questions causing Talon to get more irritated. He insulted Len calling her an old lady and when Zane defended his mom Aster punched Talon in the face. He was done messing with these people. He began chanting some words and waving his staff around. A wind began to fill the room which freaked them all out. He did a spell and sent them all to different realms. Now that they were out of the way he would return to the wizard realm and get back to his plan.

Arriving at the mine, Talon went to check on the two oni's. He was met by the mine supervisor who complained at how dumb the boy oni was. Drake had been so hungry that he started chewing on the pick axe. He didn't know what it was and thought maybe it was food of some kind. They decided they didn't want Drake thinking he'd be more of a problem than a help so Talon sent him to another realm alone. They kept Savannah in x-stone chains so she couldn't go into her oni form. Once again, she felt helpless, alone, and afraid. Talon thew down a pickaxe next to her.

"Start mining princess." Talon smiled.

"How did you know I was the Princess of the Oni?" Savannah asked.

"Um, I didn't know that. I just call girls princess." Talon said.

Savannah thew the pickaxe at Talon's face causing a nose bleed. She really wished she could have some of that blood. It had been so long since she had any.

"Can I lick your nose bleed?" Savannah asked.

"Eww, your disgusting!" Talon yelled. "I knew it, oni's are sickos."

"What do you want with me?" Savannah yelled.

Many years ago, the Master of the Good Wizards killed Talon's mom in a battle of good and evil. Talon has been seeking revenge in his mind hoping one day to avenge her death and resurrect her. He's hoping an Oni has the ability to help him so he strikes a deal with Savannah.

"If you help me resurrect my mom, I will give you back your friends and send you back to the human realm. "Talon offered.

Savannah explained that she could resurrect someone unless they were a Christian. Her power was evil and had no power over Christians. Talon assured her his mom was not a believer in Christ, just the opposite. She was a wizard as well as he and their faith was not in God. Talon added another condition to the deal. He wanted her to kill the Master of the Good Wizards. She agreed in order to save her friends. Savannah realized that the thought of killing someone really bothered her. Her relationship with God was bringing about changes in her heart. She must think of another way to help Talon and release her friends but for now she will play along and trust God to show her a way out.

Since Talon sent her friends to different realms and forgot which ones, they would need to get the realm maps from the Map Protectors. This wasn't going to be easy because their job was to prevent anyone from getting the maps. She would possibly need to use her powers so Talon took off the x-stone chains reminding her of her promise to kill the Master of the Good Wizards.

"We have been walking forever." Savannah sighed.

"It's only been an hour of walking oni." Talon said.

"An hour!" Savannah yelled.

"If you're getting tired, I can teleport us to the temple." Talon said.

"All this time, we could have teleported to the temple!"

Savannah's frustration rose. Working with this guy was going to take patience. He wasn't the smartest wizard around. He teleported them and they arrived at the good masters home.

Killing is super bad. what did get myself into, Savannah thought while walking in.

As they entered the temple, they saw an old man with a green wizard hat and a grey cloak. His pupils looked like snake eyes and he was very tall. The old wizard was sitting on a purple throne and holding a green staff. Talon pushed Savannah towards the old wizard. Savannah gave Talon a mean face.

"Nice to see you again Lance. Remember me?" Talon smiled.

"Why are you here. This place is for good wizards only. I command you to leave!" Lance yelled.

Lance stood up from his throne and Talon yelled at Savannah to kill him. Savannah looked at Lance and he asked who she was. Talon told him that she was an oni and would kill him for killing his mom. Lance knew Talon would one day try to and take revenge. He knew he should have killed the son too.

"Savannah, kill this murder for killing my mom!" Talon yelled.

"I'll hurt, not kill." Savannah smiled.

"Oni's kill, what the heck Savannah!" Talon grunted.

"You will be punished because you two walked into a restricted area and were attempting to kill me!" Lance said.

As Talon and Savannah were arguing, Lance was saying a spell to his staff. The staff shot out a ball of wind and it thew them into the wall. He told them an oni couldn't defeat him. Savannah needed to get her friends back. She took a deep breath and got up went into her oni form and ran to Lance and blasted him with darkness. As she hit him, he lost his balance and fell to the ground. He started to feel nauseated and his body began to shake. Savannah had shed a tear knowing her power was really dangerous to humans. She didn't use full power on Lance so that he couldn't die from the darkness entering into his blood system. Talon wondered why Lance wouldn't have died already.

"You will feel better soon." Savannah whispered in his ear.

"You are nice for demonic being"

Savannah, why isn't he dying?" Talon asked in a rude way.

"I would never kill a person no matter what they did to me. God wants us to forgive people and not take revenge." Savannah sighed.

"But Lance killed my mom. He deserves it!" Talon yelled.

"I was sexually, mentally, and physically abuse by a women named Mya. She deserves to die and I want to kill her for what she did to me but I'm not going to because God hates killing and wants us to forgive. Not killing is one of the Ten Commandments." Savannah explained while crying.

"What's the Ten Commandments?" Talon asked.

"You shall have no other gods before him, you shall make no idols, you shall not take the name of the Lord your God in vain, Keep the Sabbath day holy, honor your father and your mother, you shall not murder, you shall not commit adultery, you shall not steal, you shall not bear false witness against your neighbor, and lastly, you shall not covet." Savannah quoted from memory.

"Too bad." Talon laughed.

Talon ran to a case of display swords and used his staff to break it open. He grabbed a sword and ran back to Savannah and Lance. Savannah yelled for him to not kill the poor human. Talon stuck is tongue out her and stabbed Lance in the heart. Savannah was really mad at Talon for what he did. She told him that she was disappointed in him. Talon didn't care what Savannah said to him. He wanted the master of the good wizard's dead for years and he finally got his revenge.

"You're so bad." Savannah cried while getting out of her oni form

"I know and I love being bad." Talon laughed.

"Please can you get my friends back now?" Savannah sighed.

Talon looked at Savannah knowing she was upset so he agreed to get them back for her. He didn't want to but after hearing her story about her getting abused, he wanted to make her happy.

"We need to get the maps from the map protectors and the closest protector from here is Quickster." Talon explained.

"Ok then, let's go to this human and get the map." Savannah smiled.

"One more thing." Talon said.

"What?"

"Quickster has the power of speed."

"And I have the power of darkness so this will be an easy fight."

Talon teleported them to a home that was made in a rock. Savannah never saw a house like this before. It didn't look a house like Zane and Len used to live before moving into Scarlet's hospital. Talon told her Quickster was a very skilled fighter. Savannah nodded and told him she could summon an oni sword If she needed it.

"You go inside Quicksters home and distract him while I find the map." Talon said.

"Ok"

Savannah was searching around for Quickster. As she entered a room, she saw a middle-aged man in an orange medieval outfit with white dreadlocks, black eyes, and burn marks on his face. He looked a little creepy for a human. She walked up to him and told him that she was a wizard who wanted to learn some new spells. The man looked at her and asked who she was. She smiled and told him that her name was Savannah Overlord. He told her that he was Quickster. Savannah now knew this was the guy. She needed to act like a wizard so she wouldn't get into any trouble. Quickster was looking at Savannah's tail and thought, *this can't be a wizard. She has a demon tail and sharp fangs.*

"Let me guess, you want to steal my map of the realm, Hell?" Quickster asked.

"Hell!" Savannah gasped.

"Look, I don't want to deal with trespassers today."

Quickster got his staff from a wooden table and was saying weird words that Savannah couldn't understand. The staff began to glow. Savannah knew she was in a bad situation. The staff shot out a lightning ball. It hit Savannah's face and she fell to the floor and her hat and glasses fell off her.

Quickster saw her horns. Savannah picked up her hat and put it on. Her nose started to bleed as she was reaching for her glasses. Savannah was coughing and breathing heavily. She looked up at Quickster and put her glasses on. He told her that she was weak. She got up and started to cry.

"I am not weak. I have God on my side!" Savannah cried.

"Show me then. Show me your power. Hit me as hard as you can!"

"If you say so."

Savannah went into her oni form and she had darkness forming around her. Soon afterward the Satan's pentagram was under her feet. It was glowing red. Savannah had her full power and blasted Quickster all the way to a different room. Savannah lost her balance and went to the floor. She was breathing heavily. Quicksters stomach was oozing blood and a black substance. He was throwing up black goo. Savannah walked up to him and told him that she only uses her satanic power for good. She told him that she was sorry and that she didn't mean to hurt him that badly.

"You're satanic. That's what an oni is and nothing can change that"

"I said I'm sorry. I'm a Christian and trying to be good."

"You can't be good. Look what you did to me. If I didn't have my healing orb in my house I would have died because of your demonic power!"

"It's not my fault my power is like the way it is. I am not like my father. I don't use my power for evil and the only reason I used my power on you because you asked for it dummy!"

Savannah was crying and was thinking that maybe she couldn't be good because she is an evil being. Demons and oni's can't get into heaven anyway. What was she thinking. Savannah's mind was all over the place. She was trying to be the best Christian oni she could be. A soft voice came into Savannah's mind and told her that she was his child. She was a child of God. Savannah's heart felt warm. Quickster was throwing insults about her being a demon and God hates them. Savannah got up in his face.

"I am a child of God. He loves me even though Satan is my uncle and I'm a oni!"

Quickster didn't believe her no matter what she said to him. As Savannah was asking for the map, Talon comes in with a proud smile on his face. Quickster saw his map in Talon's hand. Savannah ran to Talon and gave him a hug. Talon didn't want to hug her so he pushed her off him. Savannah was glad to see he got the map. Quickster was trying to get up but the darkness in his body paralyzed him. Savannah asked Talon if he could use his staff to heal Quickster. Talon yelled at her saying that he would never heal him because he was a good wizard. Savannah sighed and grabbed Talon's staff out of his hands.

"What do you think you're doing!" Talon yelled.

"If you're not going to heal him. I will!" Savannah said.

Savannah shook the staff around. She didn't know how to use a wizard staff. Talon sighed and took the staff from her and did it himself. Quicksters hand began to move and black goo was dripping out of his body. Savannah knew the darkness was coming out of the wizard human. She was very proud that Talon would help Quickster. Talon was in disgust. He never knew what an oni's power could do. Savannah thanked him for letting Quickster live. The only reason Talon saved his life is because he wanted to show Savannah his skills. Talon tied Quickster up in a rope so that he can't follow them. He knew Quickster would be after them if he didn't. Savannah was crying and Talon noticed. He asked what was wrong and Savannah told him she wishes she was a human so she wouldn't be called a demonic being. It offended her. Talon patted her on the back and told her that it's the way she was.

"So, you got the map?" Savannah asked.

"Yep. The realm that we are going to first is, Hell aka, the underworld."

"I need a word with my uncle anyway, let's head to the underworld."

"Is the devil your uncle?"

"Yes, and I hate that he is."

"I thought you were a Christian!"

"I'm a Christian but I'm not evil like him and also, most humans don't know this but, all oni's have the 666 marks, also know as the mark of the beast somewhere on our bodies. Me and my brother have 777 and that means we are Christians. Jesus rested on the 7th day after he made the earth. So that's his number."

Talon asked if he could see her mark. Savannah showed him her right wrist. Her mark was like a tattoo to Talon. He thought it was dope. As Talon was examining her mark, Savannah asked if they could go save her friends now. Talon got his staff from the ground and started to say some words. Again, Savannah had no clue what he was saying. Just in a blink of a second, they made it into Hell. Savannah shed a tear. She hated his place after since she became a Christian. Talon was sweating and his body was staring to get really hot. Talon herd so much screaming and pain going on.

"This is what happens when you mess around with evil things." Savannah sighed.

"I'm guessing bad people live in hell." Talon laughed.

"Talon, People who aren't Christians go here when they die."

"Why"

"You have a choice of living for God and going to heaven or reject God and go to this place. In heaven, there will be no suffering but if you don't ask Jesus in your heart, you will end up here for eternity and be tortured"

"How do you become a Christian?"

"You have to believe that Jesus is Gods son and died on the cross to pay for your sins and ask Him to come into your heart. God will give you His Holy Spirit to be your helper. He will help you live a clean, good, life that is pleasing to God and will always remind you that when you mess up, or sin, God still loves you, forgives you, and wants a relationship with you. He is your Heavenly Father"

As Savannah was talking to Talon. A creepy black shadow came around both of them. Talon was in so much fear. Savannah knew what was about to happen. Talon ran to hide behind a big black rock. The shadow was circling around Savannah.

"Show off." Savannah sighed.

"I haven't seen you in a while, my evil niece"

"Show yourself Uncle!"

"*That's one creepy voice,*" Talon thought.

The shadow was forming a person. Savannah crossed her arms at her uncle. Talon peeked to see Satan and when he did, it traumatized him. He had black hair, glowing red eyes, red horns and a red tail. All of his teeth were sharp and he was about nine feet tall. As Savannah was giving Satan a mean face, he saw that her mark was not red and it was different numbers. At first, he thought this was a big prank but by the look of Savannah's face, he knew something was up.

"One of my friends got sent here by accident. Can you please let me take them back to the human realm?" Savannah sighed.

"I wanna know why your mark isn't normal"! Satan yelled.

Savannah began to panic. She didn't want Satan to know she was a Christian. She mumbled telling him that she didn't want to talk to him. Satan grabbed Savannah's right arm and squeezed it tight. Savannah grimaced from the pain.

"Tell me the truth. Did you become a Christian!"

"Um, maybe"

"This has to be a prank. You would never be good. You and I hate God!"

Savannah tried to get out of Satan's hold but he was holding her arm super tight. Savannah cried for Talon to help her. Talon too was scared to move. Satan thew Savannah to the hot ground and he kicked her in the ribs. Savannah was crying for help.

"Are you a Christian!" Satan yelled.

"Yes!" Savannah cried.

"Is your brother one as well?" Satan yelled.

Savannah nodded. Satan was furious. He summoned his big metal axe.

"Savannah!" Talon yelled.

Savannah dodged the axe and told Talon to find her friend. Talon knew what they all looked like so he told her he'd be back. Savannah went into her oni form than a demon knocked her down. Satan grabbed her and thew her into some ashes. Savannah's knees started to bleed. She got up and prayed for God to help her.

"You and Drake are a disgrace to our family and you both will be punished." Satan yelled.

"I love God and nothing will change that." Savannah said proudly.

Talon was walking around. He turned his head because he heard people screaming and when he looked, he saw a demon stabbing an old woman. Lots of demons were hurting people. All the people had no clothes on and their faces were burning off. His face was starting to get very hot and it started to burn. He screamed then summoned his wizard staff and put a healing spell on himself. As he got his self together, he heard a familiar voice. It sounded like Aster but he wasn't sure. He started to walk to the voice. It was hard to hear because of the sound of people suffering. Talon thought to himself that he hoped he would never come here when he dies. He began looking for Savannah's friend. As he turned his head to the left, he saw Aster. Aster was chained above lava. His face looked traumatized. He kept yelling that he was a Christian and that he shouldn't been in hell. He didn't realize that the fact he was a Christian, kept him from being tortured by demons. Talon walked to the lava pit. Aster looked at Talon with a mean face knowing it was his fault he was even in hell. Talon apologized for his actions. Aster yelled for him to get him down. He used his staff to take off the chains and teleported him to the floor. Aster was relived. He kissed the floor and told Talon that he was free.

"Let's go, your oni friend is fighting the devil." Talon said,

"What!"

"Savannah needs our help before he does any damage to her!" Talon yelled.

As Talon and Aster were running to save Savannah, Satan had a sword in her chest. Blood started to come out of Savannah's mouth. She felt like she was going to pass out from the pain. Satan pulled the sword out of her and she fell to the floor. Aster saw Savannah and started to run towards her but Talon grabbed his arm and told him that Satan would kill him if he tried to help Savannah. Aster told Talon that Jesus wouldn't let anything happen to him. Aster pushed Talon away and ran to Savannah.

"Are you ok!" Aster cried.

Savannah tried to talk to Aster but the blood from her mouth was choking her. Satan was about to slice Aster with a sword but Talon ran to Satan and but a blind spell on him so he couldn't see.

"What the heck"! Satan yelled as he was rubbing his eyes.

"Savannah, we will get you out of here." Aster smiled.

Talon teleported Satan to the other side of hell. Savannah was breathing heavily than passed out into Aster's arms. Aster began to panic. He pushed the hair out of her eyes. He prayed for God to heal her. Talon went on his knees next to Aster and told him that she was fine because oni's couldn't die. His words made Aster mad. He laid Savannah on the ground and got up into Talon's face.

"What's with that face?" Talon asked.

"yeah, oni's can't die but, they feel pain like us humans. She's been through so much trauma in her life and this made it ten times worse!" Aster yelled.

"So what, she has a family and I can tell her friends have given her a good life. I have nothing, my mom and dad are dead and I have no one!"

"Her dad killed her mother!"

"Oni's can't die dude."

"Her mom was full blooded Simbyot!"

"Well, I don't care. My mom died from the master of the good wizards only because she was an evil sorcerer, so that's why I killed him!"

"Dude, you're letting anger get control of you. I have a bible verse for you but it's too late if you killed him. I'm just gonna say in case you want to kill someone else!"

"Whatever."

"Luke 6:27 says, love your enemies, do good to those who hate you, bless those who curse you, pray for those who hurt you and Matthew 5:21, you shall not murder, anyone who murders will be subject to judgment.

As Aster and Talon were yelling at each other, Savannah opened her eyes. She started to cough out blood and Aster ran to her. Aster told her it would be alright. She gave Aster a hug and Talon reminded her that they needed to get the next map. Aster helped her up and he thanked her for saving him. Talon picked up Savannah's hat from the ground and handed it to her. She put it on and told them that she was ready to save the rest of her friends. Talon used his staff to heal Savannah than he teleported them all to an old green house. Aster asked where they were. Talon answered to them that the house was the Arrow Master's home and he had the next map. Savannah was still shaken from her fight with her uncle and was dreading having to face another enemy to get the next map. As Talon opened the door, it was dark in the old looking home. Aster got out his phone and turned the flashlight on. He told them that the home was very creepy. Savannah was hanging onto Talon's shoulder. Talon remembered that Arrow Master was executed by the evil wizard. He ran to see if the map was still in the home. They looked for about ten minutes and found nothing but spider webs and dusty furniture. While Savannah was sitting on a love seat and Talon was batting spider webs from his face, Aster realized he had his teleporter gun at Scarlet's hospital. He ran to Savannah and told her his idea. He was feeling really stupid for not thinking of it sooner. It will be much easier to rescue the rest of his friends rather than having to fight for the maps. When you enter someone's name it tracks them and teleports them to the location you choose. He explained everything to Talon. He summoned his staff and asked where the hospital was. Aster responded where it was. It was located in the middle of Science City. When they got there, Aster, Talon, and Savannah went into the elevator.

"This is a cool place you guys got." Talon smiled.

"I know. Scarlet let me and Sav live here. My little lab I lived in before this lit place, sucked"

"I still don't understand your human slang words." Savannah said.

"It's a cool way of saying it's nice"

When they got out of the elevator, Aster ran to his room and grabbed his teleporter gun. Savannah and Talon followed. Aster quickly typed Zane and then Len's name into the teleporter gun. While Talon was looking at Aster's gaming computer, he heard Savannah yell the name Zane. Len and Zane looked like they been in a fight. Zane had a scratch near his eye and it was bleeding. Len's shirt was ripped a little. Savannah asked what happened to them. Zane told them all that he and his mom were in a realm that had rock monsters, flying rock creatures, and a big volcano. Len added that a monster almost killed her and Zane. Talon went up to Zane and told him that he was sorry for what he done to all of them. Zane and Len forgave Talon. God loves when people forgive. No matter what a person has done to someone, you should forgive them. If you think of the worst thing someone could have done to you, you still need to forgive. God doesn't forgive you for your sins if you don't forgive others. Savannah licked Zane's blood off him and Len grabbed Savannah. She reminded her to not lick anyone. Zane told Savannah that he was ok. She was so happy to have her human boyfriend back. Now they needed to save the others. Aster typed Scarlet and Kaden's names into the gun and when he did Kaden was crying and Scarlet... looked like she'd had some trouble in the jungle. Scarlet was covered in mud from head to toe and was very traumatized. She explained that she was getting chased by wolves and thought she was going to die and then, fell into the mud and a large snake landed on her head which terrified her. She stomped off to the kitchen leaving muddy footprints behind her yelling, "I need alcohol and a shower!"

Kaden ran to his mom telling her that he liked the nice elves that help his mom live. When Kaden said that, Savannah knew that he and Scarlet were in the Elf and Dragon Realm.

"Yikes." Talon said

"She has so many problems." Aster laughed.

"I heard that!" Scarlet yelled.

"Now all we need is Drake." Aster smiled.

"Hurry, I miss my brother!" Savannah cried.

Aster let Savannah type Drake's name into the teleporter gun. She didn't know her letters so Zane helped her spell her brother's name. Aster told her to press the green button. When she pushed it, Drake was on the floor picking his nose.

"Where am I now, am I back?" Drake asked.

"You're back." Savannah smiled.

Savannah helped Drake up and she gave him a big hug. Len asked why Savannah had scars all over her body. Savannah didn't know what to say to Len so she started crying and told Aster to tell her. He explained that she had to fight her uncle who is the devil. Talon told them that Satan hurt her very bad. Drake was calming Savannah down and Zane gave her a tissue. As Scarlet was walking back to Aster's room, she heard Aster talking about Satan hurting Savannah. Scarlet went up to her and asked if she could check to see if any bacteria went into her wounds. Savannah nodded at them and told them she was scared.

"Remember that God doesn't give you a spirt of fear but, love, power, and a sound mind." Drake smiled.

"It's midnight, we all need some rest. After I take a look at your scars, I can tuck you into bed". Scarlet said.

"I love all of you guys and I love this realm so much. You guys make me happy." Savannah explained.

Zane gave Savannah a kiss and Savannah started to blush. Talon said his goodbyes and told everyone that if they ever needed help just ask. He grabbed his staff, and like that he was gone.

CHAPTER 7
AN OLD ENEMY

Scarlet and Aster were in the lobby talking about Mya. Scarlet was upset that she had fired her. They were friends since Scarlet was born. Aster took a drink of his coffee and went and sat at the front desk. Early in the morning, Aster had hacked into the League of Science computers to see what plans they had for Savannah.

"I did what you asked. And yes, some of the League of Science members are still looking for Savannah." Aster sighed.

"Again, thank you for hacking into their system for me." Scarlet said.

"So, should we tell Sav?" Aster asked.

"It's probably best if everyone knows for their safety."

"She is still recovering from what happened yesterday so it would be best if we waited and tell her at dinner." Aster suggested.

"Good idea."

When It became dinner time, Savannah ran to Zane showing him a picture she had drawn. He looked at it and asked what it was. Savannah had been trying to draw humans. She told him that she drew him. Zane smiled at her and said that he loved it… even though it was just scribbles. Len gathered everyone to the kitchen and they all thanked Jesus for their food. Aster and Scarlet looked at each other and Scarlet began to explain everything. While she was telling them that the League of Science wants the oni's, Savannah was trying not to cry and asked why scientists want her so bad. Aster didn't want to offend her but he told her that oni's are very different and weird to humans. Drake rubbed Savannah's back and told her that he loved her. Scarlet added that not all scientist were evil and that most scientist want to help people. Savannah asked why she was different.

All of them didn't know how to explain. Drake sighed and mumbled that Savannah had autism and she'd probably didn't understand them. Savannah gave Drake a mean face knowing that Drake said he wouldn't tell anyone.

"Wait, she has autism!" Aster yelled.

"I didn't know oni's could have that." Zane said.

"Don't say it, self. They will hate you" Scarlet thought.

"It's ok Savannah, we still love you no matter what" Len smiled.

"But people think I'm weird." Savannah cried.

Zane held Savannah's hand and said that God made everyone different. God loves everyone and everyone is perfect to him. Scarlet's leg was shaking and Len asked what was wrong. Scarlet was chewing on her lab coat trying to calm down.

"Savannah, you're not the only one with autism." Scarlet smiled.

"But you guys don't have it!" Savannah cried.

Scarlet smiled at Savannah and told her she had it too. She has very high functioning autism but she still had it. When Scarlet said that, they all were in shock. Savannah didn't know humans could have it. Savannah gave Scarlet a hug. *"Maybe saying it wasn't that bad"* Scarlet smiled to herself.

As they were eating. Aster asked them to think of a plan to keep Savannah safe. After an hour of thinking. Zane had an idea.

"We can let Sav stay with Talon while we figure out a plan." Zane smiled.

"Not him!" Savannah yelled.

"I think that's a good idea. He was very sweet when he took us out of the realms" Len said.

"Why!"

"The league of science can't teleport to realms and Talon lives in a different realm." Scarlet said.

"Awesome. let's do it." Aster smiled.

Zane texted Talon on his phone about the idea and Talon agreed to letting Savannah stay at his house. When the next day arrived, Len was trying to wake up Savannah. Savannah loved to sleep and it was very hard to wake her up every morning. Zane started shaking her back. She grunted and pushed his hands off her. She asked for five more minutes but Len and Zane couldn't let her sleep any longer. She had to be a Talon's by eight and it was seven-fifty. Drake told Savannah that they let her sleep in a little bit. She got up and yawned. Len helped her with her clothes while Zane was tying her shoes for her. Savannah couldn't get dressed like a human yet and she wished that she could. Zane told her that he helped Drake with putting his clothing on. Len put Savannah's hat on her head and told her that she was pretty. Savannah thanked Len and Zane for helping her. Everyone went to the lobby and Savannah told them that she was scared. Aster explained that she was only going to be there for a three days. He teleported her to the wizard realm. As she got their Talon was right in front of her sipping sweet tea. He told her that he made a cinnamon roll for her to eat. She never had one before and she was confused if it was food or a person. Talon and Savannah walked into his home. It was a small stone house that had a mushroom garden to the right of it and a statue of a wizard on the left. The grass was greener than the human realm. The grass in the wizard realm was more of a neon green. Talon opened the door for her and she smelled something sweet. Talon took Savannah to his kitchen and she sat down in a chair. he gave her some milk and a cinnamon roll. It smelled good to Savannah. All the food in the oni realm smelled like rotten flesh. Savannah grabbed a fork and tried it. She loved it and told Talon that he was a good human that was a cook. Talon laughed at her and told her that he tried. As Savannah was taking another bite, she and Talon heard someone knocking on the door. Talon told her not to be frightened. He said that it was probably his best friend Wizzy. When he opened the door Savannah saw a young man with a green wizard hat on and a brown sweater with a wizard cape. He also had yellow eyes and black hair. He went inside and Savannah asked who he was. He said that his name was Wizzy, a wizard that wanted to be a scientist. Savannah looked at him with a traumatized face. Wizzy grabbed a soda from the fringe and sat down beside her. Savannah quickly ran to Talon and gave him a hug.

"Do you want to take a walk around Wizard town?" Talon asked.

"No, I don't wanna be here or go on a walk!"

"Fine. I'm going on a walk while Wizzy and you can stay here."

"Heck no. Not with a scientist!"

"Hey. I'm a scientist that loves to make frogs fly."

"*Oh. That's not harmful. Maybe he's a nice scientist like Scarlet said some are.*"

"See ya!"

While Talon was walking out the door Savannah looked at Wizzy picking his nose. He remined her of Drake a lot. Wizzy told her that he was going to take a nap and if she needed anything to ask him. Savannah went to finish her breakfast and while that was happening, an oni from the oni realm was not very happy. In that realm there was a big scary mansion and an oni named Arlo had just stabbed a human in the chest. He was very ticked off and killing humans was one way he let his anger out. All of his life he wanted to be the oni king but an oni named King Chen was currently on the throne.

"I will show the oni's of this realm who their new leader is. I just need to take the throne and the only way to become the new king is to make the human realm into darkness"

As Arlo leaned his back on the wall, he knew the only way to make the human realm into darkness was with King Chen's daughter Savannah who had no heartbeat. If Chen tried to make the human realm into darkness all by himself, he would have lost all of his power because he had a heartbeat. Oni's power comes from the devil and the strength of their own heartbeat. If their heartbeat isn't strong then their power isn't strong. But even though Chen's daughter had no heartbeat at all she somehow had super strong power. King Chen once used her and her power to take over the human realm and put it in darkness but Jesus kicked their butts and the realm went back to normal.

"I will capture Chen's daughter to make the human realm into darkness. I'm so glad my daughter got close to Savannah and Drake and I made her put a tracking device on Savannah"

Talon had been gone for about two hours and Savannah was getting bored so she got up from the couch and ran to the door. She was going to go find Talon because she was scared of Wizzy being a scientist. She couldn't trust him. What if he was part of the League of Science. It was a hot summer day in wizard town and Savannah was really hot so she went to sit on a sidewalk in the shade. She was looking up at the blue sky and thinking how cool it looked. In the oni realm there wasn't any light, just darkness. After five minutes of relaxing, Arlo walked up to her. He had used his oni staff to teleport to the realm where she was at and it took him right to her. Arlo was right behind Savannah and he pulled her into an alleyway. He pushed her into a dumpster. As she looked at Arlo rubbing her head, she remembered who he was. He killed Scarlet's husband and almost got Zane frozen into darkness.

"Remember me Savannah?"

"What do you want!"

As Savannah got up from the ground, she summoned her oni sword ready to fight him if she had to. Arlo laughed at her knowing she was weak. She was only five foot three and he was seven foot tall. He walked to her, grabbed her by the shirt, and pinned her to the wall. When Savannah was about to go into her oni form to try to get out from Arlo's hold, He used his oni staff to knock her out. She fell into Arlo and he told her that he had a fun time planned for her. A teenage wizard saw everything and was yelling at him to leave the girl alone. Arlo blasted the wizard with his darkness and the poor guy died a slow and painful death. Arlo laughed at him and used his staff to send he and Savannah to his mansion in the oni realm. When Savannah was opening her eyes, she found herself in X stone and was lying down next to a machine. She got up and looked around. She didn't know where she was and she was scared. She yelled for help and began to walk around. As she got to the hallway, she saw Arlo. She started to panic as he saw her. Arlo ran to her and pushed her to the floor and he got on top of her. He weighed a lot and was hurting Savannah. She begged him to stop and he punched her in the nose. She started to cry as her nose was bleeding. Arlo grabbed her shirt and he dragged her to a machine.

"What is that!"

"Listen Savannah. You will obey me and do everything I say or you'll get punished. Do you understand?"

"No. I will never listen to you!"

Arlo made her look at a machine. She didn't know what it was or what he was going to make her do with it. It was a glass tube with black wires sticking out of it. The wires were connected to a satanic symbol on the wall. She asked what he wanted from her. He thew her into the machine and chained her arms into a slot in the tube. Arlo wiped the blood from Savannah's nose and picked up a helmet that had needles inside it. The top had little tubes that would be attached to the top of the machine. He firmly put the helmet on her head and blood began to seep out of it onto Savannah's face. She was crying and yelling for help but only she and Arlo were there. Arlo also added iv's into Savannah's right and left arm. She was breathing heavily and her face got pale. She had hated needles after what Mya did to her. It made her think of the trauma Mya had given her. Arlo was laughing at the fact Savannah was crying. All oni's were taught not to get scared but she had so much fear in her. He closed the door of the tube and locked it.

"I'll explained how this machine works." Arlo said.

"*I don't think I wanna know.*"

"I need you to go into your oni form and summon your power. When you do that, your dark energy will flow into the tubes and out onto the satanic symbol and when you do, it will open up a portal to the human realm. Your power with go into the realm and turn it into darkness. When a human breathes your oni power, they will get frozen into darkness and a demonic entity from your power will make the human become paralyzed."

Savannah didn't want to do that. If she did, her friends would be in so much danger. Arlo yelled at her to go into her oni form. She told him that she wouldn't do that. She told him that she was a good oni and that she would never do anything to hurt humans. Arlo was shocked an oni would say that. Oni's were evil and powerful beings and when Savannah told him that she wanted to be good, he got so angry that he broke a purple lamp on a desk and a picture on the wall. Arlo yelled again for Savannah to go into her oni form. She got scared so she listened and did what he said. Arlo was excited to become the King of the Oni's. That was his dream for years. Savannah began to cry and pray for her friends to save her. Savannah remembered what Zane had told her. God is with you wherever you may go. Even in the darkest times, he is still with you.

"Say goodbye to your human friends Savannah. Summon your power or I'll force you!"

"They will come for me!"

"They don't even know where you are!"

Savannah felt hopeless. If she wouldn't listen to Arlo, he would hurt her. She summoned her power. Black goo was flowing though the helmet and the iv's. It was hurting her. She screamed and cried for help. Arlo was laughing at her. He never would have thought an oni would be this scared of something. While that was happening, Talon was searching for Savannah for an hour. Wizzy was looking all over the Talon's home but couldn't find her either. He suggested that Talon call her friends. Talon yelled at him that this was his fault. Wizzy told him that he was napping and didn't know she left. Talon summoned his staff and teleported to Scarlet's hospital. At the hospital, Aster and Scarlet were playing cards in Scarlet's room when they herd Talon yelling that he was sorry. Talon opened Scarlet's door and his face was worried.

"Are you ok dude?" Aster asked while putting down a card.

"I'm so sorry!" Talon cried.

"What happened?" Scarlet asked while taking a sip of sweet tea.

"I lost Savannah." Talon sighed.

"What!" Scarlet yelled.

Talon explained that he let her friend Wizzy watch Savannah so he could take a walk. She didn't want to do anything with Talon so he left her at his home while he could have some peace. Aster got up in Talon's face and yelled at him. Savannah had been so traumatized by Mya that something like this could send her over the edge. . She had trust issues and she would run away if she didn't feel safe. Drake and Zane walked in asking why Aster was yelling. Aster explained what Talon did. Drake became furious.

"I can try to track her." Scarlet said.

"How?" Zane asked.

"I gave Savannah my autism tracker. My mom made me wear it when I was little because I liked to run away from her. I thought it would been a good idea to let Savannah wear it in case the League of Science would find her and we know where she was. I made Len put in on her leg this morning just in case something like this would happen." Scarlet explained.

They all went into the lobby and Scarlet went on a computer at the front desk. She opened the app, Find My Autistic Kid. She hoped that Savannah wasn't in danger. She clicked a button and it said it was loading. After a minute, it said there was an error. Scarlet was confused.

"Is everything ok Scarlet?" Zane asked.

"This is weird." Scarlet mumbled.

"Why does it say error?" Aster asked.

"I don't know." Scarlet said.

"Maybe realms wont work for the tracker." Drake said.

"It still should have worked." Scarlet sighed.

"Should we look around the Wizard realm?" Drake asked?

"Guys, I just used my magic to find her but my staff says she isn't in the Wizard or human realm!" Talon yelled.

"I don't trust magic." Zane mumbled.

"Dude, magic is awesome." Talon smiled.

"How could Sav even get out of the Wizard realm without a teleportation device!" Zane yelled.

"I don't know." Talon sighed.

"Maybe your friend brought her back here." Drake smiled.

"But my magic says she isn't in this realm or my realm."

"What if you have her locked up!" Zane yelled.

"Take a chill pill Zane." Aster said.

"What if Sav is in danger!" Zane cried.

"We can try to look around science city a little bit if that makes you feel better." Scarlet said.

"Yes, let's do that." Zane said as he hurried to the door.

"I'll get my car." Aster said as he put his shoes on.

Len came running in asked why Zane was yelling. Zane shed a tear and told her that Savannah was missing. Len was in shock and gave Zane a kiss and calmed him down. Zane knew Savannah hated being alone and it scared her to be without him. He loved her and wanted to make the human realm feel safe for her. Len gave Zane a glass cup of water to calm him down. While they were heading to the car, Savannah was going through a lot.

"Why do you want to hurt me?" Savannah asked.

"Oh, that's right, you don't know." Arlo laughed.

"Quit laughing like that"

"My daughter says she knows you."

Savannah had no idea he had a daughter. She didn't know his child and she had no clue what she looked like. When she asked what her name was, Savannah was shocked. Arlo told her that her name was Luna. Savannah gave him a mean face while remembering what she had done to her brother.

"Luna is your daughter!"

"Yes. You made her really mad."

"Your child is a ho!"

"I know that. Don't remind me!"

"Why would you let her do that to boys. Drake thinks about her everyday and everytime we go to church, he prays that he would get to see her again!"

"Oni's are supposed to sin Savannah."

"My dad is telling lies about Jesus to all of the oni's. Jesus loves you so much and he doesn't like people sinning!"

"Shup up!"

"*I tried.*"

"I just wished my wife could see how much she's grown."

"Who is your wife and also quit trying to make me feel guilty when I did nothing to Luna"

"Her name was Lilly but she left us and went off with some other oni but she got killed by him, that's all I know."

"I had a mom named Lilly."

Arlo looked at Savannah with a confused face. Savannah began to cry and told Arlo that her dad killed her mom and that her name was Lilly. She told him that she had purplish pink hair like Drake and her mom's face looked like hers. She had Black eyes and her power was webs like a Simbyot. She loved wearing a bracelet made out of human teeth that was made by Drake when he was little.

"Stop talking for a second!" Arlo yelled.

"I miss my mom so much." Savannah cried.

"*This can't be true. Everything that Savannah said matches Lilly. Could Drake and Savannah be half siblings to Luna?*"

"Was Lilly full blooded Simbyot," Arlo asked.

"Yeah. How do you know that?"

"You and your brother are half siblings to Luna…"

"What!"

"My ex wife was Lilly but she left me for some other guy, that I'm guessing is your dad. You said that your dad killed your mom. Someone told me that Lilly was killed. Luna has eyes like your mom and I remember what Lilly looked like and everything that you described matches Lilly's appearance.

"*Welp. Drake is gonna feel uncomfortable.*"

The others had been looking for Savannah for over two hours. It was a hot summer day in Science City and they all were tired. Drake dropped down on the grass and was sweating. Aster helped Drake up and blasted him with some water. That felt so good to Drake. Everyone decided to take a rest. They all sat down in a parking lot at a mall. While they all sat down and grabbed some water to drink, Kaden got up and his ears began to hurt. Scarlet asked him if he was good. Kaden was staring in the distance. Scarlet poked his shoulder and asked again if he was ok. Kaden looked at his mom and told her he was hearing people screaming. Scarlet had to remind herself that Alphas had good hearing and they could hear things from far away. Len asked Kaden if he wanted a pack of gummies. Kaden started to stare in the distance again. While everyone was worried about Kaden, Drake's oni sense went crazy; He knew something evil was near them.

"I hear people yelling mommy!"

"Calm down Kaden." Scarlet said.

"I know why people are yelling!" Drake cried.

"Huh. Are you ok dude?" Aster asked.

"It can't be!" Drake cried.

"Drake. Talk to us buddy." Zane said.

"I feel a dark presence nearby."

"What does that mean?" Aster asked.

"Mommy, what is that?" Kaden asked while pointing to black fog.

"That's what I mean!"

"What is that thing?" Scarlet yelled.

"Darkness fog…"

"Can you please explain sweety?" Len asked.

"Some oni is making this happen but no oni has enough strength to do that!"

"Whatever it is, it's getting closer." Scarlet said.

"Savannah is the only one who can do this. I know where she's at. She's in the oni realm. Somebody is making her turn the human realm into darkness!"

"It's scary!" Kaden cried.

Scarlet picked Kaden up and asked Drake if the darkness hurts humans. Drake nodded and told them that they needed to get everyone to safety. As Drake explained what oni darkness could do to a human, the fog was right behind Len. Drake wiped his tears and told them that his sister is in danger and she doesn't mean to do what she's doing. She would never want to hurt humans. The darkness shot into Len's face and made her fall to the ground. Zane saw what happened and he began to ran to her. Scarlet grabbed a hold of Zane and told him not to get near the darkness. Zane was screaming for Len. The darkness was all over her and it made her skin turn pitch black. Zane was trying to get out of Scarlet's hold.

"Zane. It's not worth it!" Scarlet yelled.

"But my mom is in danger!" Zane cried.

"We have to leave before what happen to Len happens to us!" Aster yelled.

"Zane. It's too late for her." Scarlet sighed.

"Scarlet let me go!"

"I'm sorry Zane. We can't do anything to save her."

"Mom please!" Zane cried.

Drake was trying to get Len out but the darkness already got to her body. Drake ran out of the darkness and told them that he couldn't save Len in time. The darkness was everywhere and was surrounding them. Aster opened the car door and grabbed his teleporter gun. Everyone but Len was teleported to the hospital.

Savannah was getting sick from all of her power going into a portal. It was making her tired. Arlo shut off the machine and told her that she needed a break to get her energy to rise back up. Arlo took everything off her and thew her to the hard cold floor. She couldn't get up. She was very exhausted and it was hard for her to breathe. Savannah had an idea pop into her head. She got up and smiled at Arlo. He looked at her wondering why she was smiling after what he had done to her.

"To be honest, I don't like being a good person. I can't have any fun." Savannah smiled.

"I thought you became a Christian?" Arlo said.

"I miss eating humans and I can't kill anyone and what I really want to do now, is kill my boyfriend Zane because he's a human. I hate humans!'

"Wow. I never have thought you would say that."

"I want to kill all of my friends; I want to kill them right now and I want to make the human realm into darkness!"

"You know what? I'll let you go kill your friends and I can't believe that you would act evil again."

My idea Is working.

Arlo undid the x stone bracelets and Savannah asked where Luna was. Arlo didn't know why she wanted to see Luna. Savannah explained that she wanted Luna to help kill her human friends. Arlo laughed at her and told her Luna was at the abandoned subway next to the oni restaurant called "Flesh and Fluids" Savannah knew where that was at so she said she will be back to turn the human realm into darkness. Arlo smiled at Savannah while she was walking down the stairs.

"But! If you are lying to me just to escape, you will be punished!"

"I know…"

As Savannah was walking in the oni realm, she thought to herself that maybe she could get Luna to help her save the humans and stop Arlo's evil plan. When she got to the subway, she went out of her oni form and started to walk down the subway stairs. As she was walking down, she heard a familiar voice. It was raspy and she knew it was Luna. When she got down, she saw Luna messing around with an oni guy. *Little pervert.* Savannah thought.

"Hey Luna. Remember me!" Savannah smiled.

Luna stopped kissing the oni guy and gave Savannah a mean face. She walked up to Savannah and asked what she wanted in a rude way. Luna summoned her knife and was very alert in case Savannah would try to hurt her.

"Don't even try to threaten me shorty."

"Aww. Does Drakey miss me that much that he wanted his little sister to come find his old girlfriend to try to get me back?" Luna laughed.

"No. I have something to tell you."

"Let me guess. You want me to unbreak his heart but I can't. A broken heart is a broken heart."

"This might sound weird to you but you are mine and Drake's half sibling!"

"Quit your lying dumb butt!"

"I'm serious. I talked to your dad!"

When Savannah brought up her dad, Luna was shocked she knew she had a dad. She was thinking that maybe Savannah was telling the truth, but thinking about being half siblings to Drake, made her feel weirded out.

"How are we even half siblings. I wanna know if you are lying or not!"

"We have the same mom. If you don't believe me, look into my mind."

Luna was reading her mind and she saw Savannah and Arlo talking about Lilly. Luna was in shock and got out of her mind and shook her head. She looked at Savannah with a embarrassed face and unsummoned her knife. She hated the face that Savannah and Drake were her siblings. She messed around and kissed with her half-brother. It made he feel disgusted. Luna asked if Drake knew about it. Savannah responded that he didn't know and that she and Arlo just found out about an hour ago. Luna laid on the floor feeling sick about what she had done to Drake.

"Are you ok?"

"Let me drown in my sorrows!"

"It's kinda funny that you and Drake were boyfriend and girlfriend."

"I hate you!"

"I hate you too."

As Savannah's friends made it to the hospital, Zane ran to Scarlet's room and slammed the door shut. Aster, Drake, and Scarlet were very worried for Zane. Scarlet knocked on her door and asked him to get out of her room. Zane was crying so loud that his face was blood red.

"Zane. Your mom will be ok." Drake smiled.

"How. She's dead!" Zane cried while wiping his snot on Scarlet's bed sheets.

"Your mom isn't dead. She's just frozen into darkness. She's just in a coma right now." Drake explained.

"God has her back bro." Aster smiled.

"You better not have gotten snot on my bed!" Scarlet yelled.

'Sorry!"

"Come on out. We need to come up with a plan" Aster said.

"I'm staying in here…"

"Ok, I guess. If you need us, we will be in the living room." Scarlet sighed.

"I learned this bible verse in Sunday school and it will help you Zane. Put on the full armor of God, so that you can take your stand against the devil's schemes. For our struggle is not against flesh and blood, but against the rulers, against the authorities, against the powers of this dark world and against the spiritual forces of evil in the heavenly realms. Therefore, put on the full armor of God, so that when the day of evil comes, you may be able to stand your ground, and after you have done everything, to stand." Kaden smiled proudly.

"This is freaking crazy. It would have taken me weeks to remember that bible verse. He is only a year old and he's a genius!" Scarlet yelled.

"Thanks Kaden, that helped me a lot." Zane smiled while wiping tears form his face.

'Yay! I love helping people that are sad. God wants all of us to be happy!" Kaden smiled.

Drake had an idea. He leaned his back to Scarlet's door so Zane could hear it too. He told them that he was the only one in this realm who can go into the darkness fog. He said that he would see if any humans were not frozen and try to help them and try to find Savannah in the oni realm. They all agreed to his plan. Aster told Drake to be careful.

"Are you ok Scarlet?" Aster asked.

"My son floored me." Scarlet cried.

Back in the oni realm, Luna was trying to process all that Savannah had told her. She felt disgusted and didn't know what to think.

"Your dad is forcing me to make the human realm into darkness"

"I cannot believe I am related to an idiot; Drake was an idiot!"

"Let me finish talking and quit whining!"

"Nope."

"So, I guess you're stuck in this boring realm and can't have any fun in the human realm."

"I will help you only because I have nothing else to do!"

"Come on Luna, we need to hurry."

"Fine."

Luna and Savannah walked out of the subway. While they were walking Savannah explained that they needed to get Luna's dads staff to teleport into the human realm to see what the darkness had already caused. She also added that they needed to get Drake to help them. Luna did not like the idea of seeing Drake again but she wanted something to do. It was boring to live with her dad, so getting out of her realm was the best thing she had heard all day.

"Does Drake know we are half siblings?" Luna asked while following behind Savannah.

"No"

"How is my dad even making the world into darkness?"

Savannah stopped and looked at Luna and told her that it was Savannah that was making the human realm into darkness. Luna didn't believe her and told her that she was lying because she was weak. Savannah explained about herself not having a heart beat and if an oni with a heart beat tries to make that realm into darkness they couldn't. Luna was confused but she walked in front of her and told her that she was dumb. Savannah gave Luna a mean face and Luna smiled at her.

"I looked in your mind and yes, I will give you a long day by harassing you all day."

"Shut up."

"I don't wanna be siblings to you!"

"Me neither. I don't like what you did to my brother. I forgive you but that doesn't mean I like you!"

While Luna and Savannah were fighting, Drake was in the oni realm looking for Savannah. He had been searching for over an hour and was getting tired. He kept yelling Savannah's name but never heard a response. He didn't want to give up so he began to run and started yelling for her name again. The oni realm was dark and had little lighting. It was hard to see. As he started to lose hope, he heard two voices yelling at each other. He summoned his oni sword just in case the oni's didn't want to be bothered. He knew oni's didn't like to be interrupted. He walked towards the voices and he saw Savannah. He yelled her name and she ran to him and gave him a hug. She started to cry and she said that she was scared. Luna began to laugh and walked up to Drake. Drake's heart dropped and he stopped hugging Savannah.

"What is she doing here!" Drake yelled.

"Did you miss me." Luna smiled.

"Guys listen!" Savannah yelled.

"Sis. What is she doing here?"

"She's going to help us fight Arlo and get the human realm out of darkness."

"Arlo?"

"Yes. Arlo is the one who took me."

"Quit being a baby Drake."

"You be quiet!" Drake yelled.

"I have to tell you something Drake. It's very weird but I must tell you."

"I puked when she told me this so you better not. If someone pukes, I'll puke!" Luna cried.

"Why does her face look uncomfortable?" Drake asked.

"Both of you SIT!" Savannah yelled.

Drake never knew Savannah would be firm like that so he listened and sat down on the cold black grass. Luna sat down and stuck her tongue out at her. Savannah took a deep breath and told them that they were all siblings. She explained everything that she and Arlo had found out. Drake stood up and began to remember Luna making out with him. He stared at Savannah with his face all pale. Luna could tell from inside his purple hood he was thinking about what she did to him. His pink hair was covering up his eyes but she could tell he was embarrassed. Savannah was patting Drake's back and trying not to laugh. She did think it was a little funny that Luna and Drake kissed each other.

"Are you sure we all have the same mom?" Drake cried.

"Yes. I told you that and we need to quit talking. We have a realm to save." Savannah said.

"We don't even look the same!" Luna yelled.

"I dyed my hair blue; I had the color of your hair when I was little. "Savannah smiled.

"Whatever."

"So, Luna is helping us?" Drake asked.

"Only because I want to go to the human realm dimwits, I will never be good!"

"Blah blah blah!" Savannah said.

"What's the deal with the portal under us?" Drake asked dumbly.

"An oni portal you dumb butt!"

"Oh crap. That's probably Arlo's portal. He is trying to find me!"

As Savannah was finishing her sentence, All three of them landed inside Arlo's mansion. Drake and Savannah were on top of Luna. Her skinny body was about to crack from the weight from both. She yelled for them to get off her and Savannah got off her and helped Drake up. Arlo yelled Luna's name. he didn't know she was coming though the portal.

"Sup Dad." Luna smiled.

"Luna, get your X-boyfriend into X stone... I mean your half sibling." Arlo demanded.

"Ok Dad." Luna said.

"That's my girl."

"Luna! I thought you were going to help us!" Savannah cried.

"I can't believe you would think I would help you. I hate you and your bother so much. If you guys were human, I would have killed you already!"

"Luna. Maybe God put us into your life. We can be good to each other and be a happy family." Savannah cried.

Luna walked away to get X stone for her dad. She hated Drake so much she wouldn't care what her dad would do to them. Arlo blasted Drake with his darkness and it made Drake pass out. Savannah began to cry. She didn't know what to do. She wanted Luna to be good and give her a chance but Luna didn't want a chance she guessed. Savannah wiped her tears from her eyes and when she opened them, she saw Arlo about to stab her with his oni sword. Savannah quickly dodged it and told him she was sorry. Arlo lifted her up by the shirt. She was in the air with Arlo holding her up. Savannah was trying to get out from his hold but he was too strong. He knocked her out and dropped her to the floor. After two hours Drake and Savannah were starting to wake up. As Drake was catching his breath and putting his hood back on, Arlo grabbed him and thew him into the wall. Savannah was coughing and feeling light headed. Luna asked what he was going to do with then. Arlo locked Savannah back in the machine. She was banging on the door begging Luna to let her out. Arlo told Luna to follow him as he picked up Drake. He was too weak to fight so he let Arlo take him. As Arlo was walking Drake mumbled that he wanted food. Luna remembered that he loved food and tried to get her to try pizza. She smiled and laughed. Arlo thew Drake on the floor. Drake could barely move. As he looked up, he saw Luna with an upset face. Drake's stomach was beginning to growl. He smiled at Arlo to give him food. He thought to himself if he was screwed, at least give him some food. Arlo was getting mad at Drake's annoying mouth.

"How about instead of food, I'll burn you with a lighter!" Arlo yelled.

"Wait what!" Luna asked.

Arlo grabbed a black lighter from a rusty desk made of human bones and pinned Drake to the wall. As Arlo turned on the lighter. Drake begged him not to do it. He told him that he wouldn't talk about food again. Arlo was burning Drake's nose off. Drake was screaming at the top of his lungs and crying. His nose was burning off. As Arlo was hurting him, Luna was remembering all the time she and Drake had. She remembered Drake teaching her how to tie her shoes, play video games, eat with her mouth closed, and much more. She felt guilty of what she had done to him. She looked at Drake with his nose burnt off and bleeding all over himself. He was crying and she could tell by looking into his mind he wanted her to be good. He missed her a lot and would think about her every day.

"Please Arlo. Stop!" Drake cried.

"This is a way to get you to shut your dumb mouth!" Arlo yelled.

"*Why am I feeling bad for Drake. Why would he forgive me. Why does he still care?*" Luna thought while looking into his mind.

Luna summoned her knife and took a deep breath. She walked to her dad and stabbed him in the hip. Arlo pushed her away.

"What the heck Luna!" Arlo yelled.

"Don't hurt him!" Luna cried.

"Why would you care if I hurt him. You hate him!"

Drake fell to the floor in pain. Arlo summoned his staff and was about to hit Luna with it than she grabbed the staff and kicked Arlo in the crotch. Arlo was grimacing and demanded his staff back. Luna used her dad's staff to make Arlo fall to the floor. Luna hit Arlo in the head and he passed out. Luna ran to Drake. She saw his nose was gone and that she could see some of his teeth from his cheek. Luna helped him up. Drake was in shock. Drake took his hood off and began to cough out blood. Luna patted his back and told him that he was ok. She took the x stone bracelets off him and got him to stand up. Arlo was starting to move his arm.

"We need to go!" Luna yelled.

"Why did you save me? Drake asked.

"Luna!" Arlo coughed.

Luna pushed Drake to the door and yelled that they needed to leave before Arlo hurt them. They began to run while Arlo grabbed his staff off the floor. As they were running, they heard Arlo yelled very evil words at them. When They ran down the stairs, they saw Savannah.

"*Abcdefghjklmnop.*" Savannah sang while fidgeting with the tubes on the machine.

"Sis!" Drake smiled.

"Drake what happened do you!" Savannah cried.

Luna explained what her dad had done to him. She unlocked the tube and helped Savannah out. As Savannah asked why Luna saved them, Arlo blasted Luna with his power and made her fall to the floor.

"Why would you do that Luna!" Arlo yelled.

"I'm sorry." Luna cried.

"You are the worst daughter ever. You should know not to mess with me!" Arlo yelled.

Savannah helped Luna up as Arlo was throwing insults at them. Arlo told Luna if she could die, he would have killed her. Drake could tell Luna was upset. No father should be that way to their kids.

Drake blasted Arlo with all the strength he had left, Arlo fell down hard on the floor and his nose started to bleed. Luna ran to her dad and grabbed his staff and ran back to Drake.

"Can we just stop this freaking darkness?" Luna asked.

"Let's do this!" Drake smiled.

"I'm ready to see my human boyfriend." Savannah smiled.

"You will not get way this this!" Arlo yelled.

"Teleport us. Hurry!" Drake yelled.

Luna used her dad's staff to make Arlo pass out and she teleported the three to Scarlet's hospital. As they got there, Luna ran to the door and went on her knees and started to cry. Drake and Savannah looked at each other. They were both thinking the same thing.

"We need to forgive Luna." Savannah sighed.

"Definitely. She saved me from my face burning off." Drake said.

"Maybe we can help her become good and we can be together because we are family."

"We can try."

"We need to forgive her; God says to forgive and forget what a person has done to you."

Drake and Savannah sat down beside Luna. Luna was trying to cover up crying but they knew that she was very upset.

"We care about you so much Luna and Jesus cares about you too." Savannah smiled while hugging her.

"How could Jesus care about me when I've been so evil!" Luna cried.

"John 3:16 says, For God so loved the world that he gave his one and only Son, that whoever believes in him shall not perish but have eternal life." Savannah smiled.

"Jesus loves you so much. Can you believe that Luna?" Drake asked while putting his hand on her shoulder.

"I'll think about it…" Luna sighed while wiping the tears from her eyes.

"Let's go. I wanna see Zane!" Savannah smiled while running into the lobby.

Drake helped Luna up and smiled at her. Luna opened the door and walked inside. While Savannah was looking for Zane, Scarlet and Aster were trying to get Zane calmed down. Scarlet kept asking for him to get out of her bedroom. Zane was so depressed he couldn't move. He told her that when Sav comes back, then he will get up. Luna, Drake, and Savannah were walking in the hallway trying to find the others.

"Why is this realm so bright?" Luna whined while putting on her sunglasses.

"We are used to only darkness but this realm has something called day." Savannah said.

"Day?"

"Yeah, it's really confusing." Drake said.

"I'm gonna stay here. None of your friends want to see my face again"

"They will forgive you." Savannah smiled.

"I doubt it." Luna sighed.

"We will be back." Drake smiled.

Savannah and Drake ran to where the sleeping rooms were and they found Scarlet and Aster. Savannah ran to Scarlet and gave her a big hug. She asked where Zane was. Aster answered that Zane was crying like a baby in Scarlet's room. Drake was trying to hide his face.

"What's the matter bro?" Aster asked.

"Arlo… Arlo burned my nose and mouth." Drake stuttered.

"Let me take a look." Scarlet said.

Scarlet took Drake's hood off and they all saw his face. Aster was freaked out. He asked if oni's can grow their body parts back. Savannah nodded yes at Aster. Scarlet told Drake that she will get him cleaned up when she had the chance. Savannah knocked on Scarlet's door than she heard Zane saying that he wasn't coming out. Savannah opened the door and smiled at him.

"Savannah!" Zane smiled.

They both hugged and kissed. Savannah was blushing and told him that she had a sister. Zane asked who it was so she grabbed his arm and dragged him to the hallway. Aster asked where they were going. Drake explained that he and Savannah had a sister and that they might know who it is. Savannah pointed to Luna. Zane, Aster, and Scarlet were in shock.

"Wait. How is Luna here!" Aster yelled.

"How did she get past the security!" Scarlet added.

"Guys, it's ok." Drake smiled.

No dude, it's not ok, she doesn't love you. I know you miss her but you didn't need to bring her back. You know what will happen bro!" Aster yelled

"I can tell you don't want me here, so I'll leave…" Luna sighed.

Luna was running out of the lab and crying. When she got out she fell to the ground with many tears coming down her face. Drake gave Aster a mean face than started to run to find Luna. Savannah explained that Luna saved her and Drake. She told them what happened and that they all needed to forgive her. Zane was in on forgiving her. He knew that God loves when you forgive. Aster didn't want to forgive Luna but he thought that Luna would be a cool friend. Scarlet smiled at them and told them that they forgave her so she will forgive Luna. Savannah smiled at her friends thankful that they could forgive. They all went to see if Luna was ok. Luna and Drake were hugging. Savannah smiled and gave them a hug.

"I'm so sorry Drake!" Luna cried.

"It's ok. I forgive you."

"We all forgive you." Zane added.

"You do?"

"I was a very evil person. I did worse things than you. Savannah forgave me, so I forgive you. So does everyone else." Scarlet smiled.

"I want to be a Christian." Luna said.

"That's awesome Luna!" Drake smiled.

"But how do I become one?"

Savannah explained that you must tell Jesus that you are sorry for your sins and that you want a life with him. You need to repent and lay your sins down for him and love him. The last step is to believe that Jesus died on the cross for you. Luna wanted to believe so she prayed that her sins would be taken away and that she would try her best to do good for him. As she prayed that prayer, Luna was grimacing. Drake asked what was wrong. Savannah asked to show Luna her mark. She asked why. Savannah explained that when an oni becomes a Christian, the mark of the beast turns into three sevens. Luna flipped her purple hair out of her face and it showed what Savannah had explained. Everyone was proud of Luna. She was evil but she tuned to the good side and she was ready for her life to be a good one. As Drake gave Luna a high five, darkness began to surround the hospital.

"The darkness is getting worse guys!" Aster yelled.

"It's all my fault!" Savannah cried.

"No, it's not. Arlo was forcing you." Zane said.

"Everyone get in the hospital. The darkness is very close to us!" Drake demanded.

"Let's go." Zane said.

As they got into the hospital, darkness had covered the whole outside. Savannah hugged Zane and started to cry. She didn't want humans to be frozen into darkness. It was a terrible feeling for a human. Scarlet asked everyone if they had a plan to stop it. No one knew what to do. After five minutes of thinking of a plan, Drake had a good one. His idea was for he and his siblings to go back into the oni realm so Savannah could get back onto the machine that was making the human realm into darkness. She would try to reverse the darkness with the power of God. She will pray for help from Jesus and use her power for God to take control. Scarlet added that she had ear coms for them to wear so the others could hear what's going on. Zane told her that was a great idea.

"Let's get them. Follow me." Scarlet smiled.

They all ran up the stairs to the third floor. Scarlet opened a hospital room door and they all ran inside. She opened a white cabinet and grabbed the ear coms. Savannah saw human teeth and blood samples in the cabinet and asked what she got them. Scarlet was laughing and told them she was a mad scientist and they didn't want to know what she did with the samples. She gave Luna, Drake, and Savannah ear coms and they put them into their ears.

"Does the ear coms fit?" Scarlet asked.

"Yeah, but it feels weird. I never wore one before." Luna smiled.

"It's mine and my sister's first time too. I mean our sister." Drake laughed.

"It's bothering my sensory!" Savannah cried.

"Guys. We need to hurry. I want my mom back." Zane sighed.

"We will get your mom back Zane. I promise." Savannah smiled.

"And Luna, we don't need your dad's staff. I have a teleporter gun!" Aster smiled.

"A what?"

"Watch and learn cutie." Aster smiled.

"What did you call me!" Luna yelled.

"Sorry. I didn't mean to. It just came out of my mouth.!"

As the three oni's go into the oni realm. Scarlet asked from the ear coms if they could hear them. Luna replied with a yes. Drake told Savannah and Luna that they all needed to be alert and stealthy. Zane told them to be careful. Savannah told him that they would be ok.

"Hey Luna. I've been looking for you all day!"

"Who is that?" Drake asked.

"Um. My boyfriend…"

"Luna!" Savannah yelled.

"Ok, Ok. Look, I never loved you. You are nothing to me. It was fun making out with you but, I'm a Christian now so I'm not going to fornicate because God doesn't like that." Luna smiled.

"*Welp. She's trying.*" Savannah thought.

"Leave and I never wanna see your face again and if I do, I'll stab you!" Luna yelled.

"*She's learning…*" Savannah thought.

"I did good right?" Luna smiled.

"You did fine. It just takes some time to learn how act." Drake smiled.

"Come on guys. We need to go before Arlo finds us." Savannah cried.

Zane told them that they couldn't risk Sav getting captured again. As the three walked into Arlo's home, Drake told the others that they made it in and found no signs of Arlo nearby. Aster replied with a response they didn't know. He said 10-4 to them and the oni's were confused. Scarlet sighed and told them it meant the word, ok. Savannah went into her oni form and told them she'd be in the machine. Drake told Luna that they had to distract Arlo so Savannah could do her thing. Savannah ran down to Arlo's basement and told herself to be brave because God was with her. As she was about to go inside the machine, a little human girl started to cry. Savannah looked at the little girl and her dad. The two looked all beat up. The dad had a big gash on his stomach and head and the little girl had a black eye and a nose bleed.

"Daddy. I'm scared!"

"It's going to be ok my daughter. Be a brave girl for me."

Savannah walked up to them and told her what her name was. The dad grabbed her kid and began to yell at Savannah. He told her that she would pay for what oni's did to him and his daughter. Savannah was confused. The little girl told her that she didn't do anything bad.

"You little demon brats killed my wife in front of me and my girl. You will not hurt anyone else from my family!"

"But I didn't do anything!" Savannah cried.

"You black scary creatures kidnapped us. I can barely breath. I have a big scar on my forehead and I'm bleeding!"

"I didn't do that. Arlo must have done that!"

"Don't hurt me. Please!" The little girl screamed.

"I won't. I'm nice and I will get you and your dad out of here." Savannah smiled.

"Someone like you ate my wife in front of my little girl. She is traumatized and I will never trust someone like that evil demonic being!"

"I don't wanna be food!"

"Don't talk sweetie. The other thing said if you talk there would be consequences."

Savannah walked up to the girl and asked what her name was. She replied that her name was Grace and that she and her daddy were sad. Savannah put her hand on Grace's shoulder and told her that she would get her and her dad out of the realm. The dad thanked Savannah for not hurting them. She told them that she wasn't like the others oni's. Back at the lab, Scarlet was trying to get Savannah to speak. She asked if she could hear her but they got no response. Zane asked if Savannah was ok, but nothing. Drake replied with his ear com that Savannah was in Arlo's basement so she probably didn't have a good signal.

"Do you hear me anyone!" Savannah cried.

"I think Sav is trying to tell us something." Scarlet said while fixing her headphones.

"Zane, I'm scared and hurting bad. I'm trying to reverse it. It's just that I'm part demon and demons can't be around the power of God. I'm trying!"

"You can do this Savannah! I believe in you!" Aster smiled.

"Isaiah 40:31 says, but those who hope in the Lord, will renew their strength, they will soar on wings like eagles, they will run and not grow weary, they will walk and not be faint!" Zane smiled.

"I needed that. I'll keep trying."

Luna and Drake were trying to find Arlo. Luna suggested that they go in the vents to be stealthier. Drake used his webs to take he and Luna to the vents. Drake could barely fit with his overweight body. Luna pushed him into the vent and told him to be quiet. Luna climbed in the vents and they both began to crawl.

"Your butt is in my freaking face." Luna whispered.

"I have to fart." Drake cried.

"You better not dimwit."

Luna pushed Drake than he fell though the vents and landed right in front of Arlo. Drake gave Luna a mean face.

"You were gonna fart on me dumb butt!" Luna yelled.

"Well, well, well, look who we got here." Arlo laughed.

"Crap!" Drake yelled.

"This is all your fault Drake!"

"You're the one who pushed me!"

Arlo summoned his sword and sliced Drake's stomach. Drake was grimacing and told Luna to help him. Luna was scared to fight her dad. She didn't know what to do. Drake dogged Arlo's sword and summoned his. Drake told Luna to summon her oni sword. She told him that she was only part oni and didn't have one. All she could summon was a Simbyot knife. Arlo told her not to summon it and that she was weak.

"Do you really want to hurt your own dad!"

"Luna, don't let him mess with you!"

Luna slid down her black webs and landed on her knees. Arlo told her that she was weak and she meant nothing to him. Luna was trying not to cry. Arlo picked Luna up and thew her into Drake and they both fell down. Drake got up and he and Arlo started to fight.

"I can't fight my father. I'm too afraid. He is my dad!"

"This is Zane from the ear com. Remember that God has your back and you can do all things with Christ who gives you strength," Zane smiled.

Luna got up and summoned her knife and took a deep breath. She needed to save the human realm. She ran to Arlo and stabbed him in the leg. Arlo pushed Luna to the floor and was about to stab her. Drake ran to Arlo blocking his sword with his own. Luna got off the floor and thanked Drake.

"I wish you were full Simbyot so I can kill you!' Arlo laughed.

That's how you feel about me. You want me dead!" Luna cried.

"I hate you for becoming a Christian. You know oni's are evil beings and look what you became Luna. When you stabbed me, I saw that your mark was different." Arlo yelled.

"I know this might have some static but, we all love and care about you so don't let your dad keep you down." Savannah said.

"Thanks Savannah. You are a great sister."

Back at the hospital, Kaden was getting tired. Scarlet asked Zane to take Kaden to bed. Zane told Scarlet that he would. Kaden ran to his bedroom and got into his race car bed. Zane tucked him in and went to shut the blinds. As he looked outside, he could see the darkness going away.

"Hey. It's not black outside anymore!" Kaden smiled.

"Sav is doing it." Zane said.

"Go tell my mommy that the black is gone."

Zane ran to his friends and told them that he and Kaden saw that the darkness was fading away. They all smiled at each other. Zane was going to get his mom back and the human realm would be back to normal. Aster told Savannah though his ear com that she was doing it. The darkness was fading away and that made Savannah happy. She kept trying and trying. She took a deep breath and let God take control. Her mark turned gold and bright. She felt a relaxing feeling inside her body. She closed her eyes and smiled as she used her power to get rid of the darkness. While Savannah was doing her job, Luna and Drake were trying to get Arlo to stop his evil plan. Drake stabbed Arlo in the chest and told him that he was doing a bad thing to humans and he would be stopped. Arlo began to shed blood from his chest. Drake got him bad. He was catching his breath and grabbed his sword off the floor. He ran to Drake and stabbed him in the heart. Drake fell down in pain and he started to get dizzy. He was holding his heart as blood was dripping onto his hands. Luna ran to Drake asking if he was ok. Drake got up and told Luna that he was fine. As Arlo was getting ready to fight them, Drake had an idea. He told Aster to teleport a sedative for Arlo. Aster told Zane to get one from down the hallway in a metal cabinet. As Zane was getting the sedative, Savannah told Aster to teleport two humans that Arlo had kidnapped. Aster smiled and told her that he would. When Savannah got out of the machine, she went out of her oni form and ran to Grace. She told her that she and her dad would be safe. As Drake dodged Arlo's power, a syringe appeared right next to Drake. He picked it up and ran to Arlo and jabbed it into his arm. Arlo pushed Drake to the floor and Luna ran to him and helped him up.

"I got a notification from the news on my phone that people are tuning back to normal and the darkness fog is gone." Aster smiled.

"Thank the Lord!" Savannah smiled.

Aster teleported Savannah, Drake, and Luna back to the hospital. They were relived as Savannah ran to give Zane a hug. Hugs made Savannah feel safe and Zane knew that, so he hugged her back.

"So, the little girl just had a wrist fracture and a bad nose bleed and the dad is in the hospital bed because he lost a lot of blood. I'm giving him some blood and more oxygen." Scarlet explained while holding her coffee cup.

"Wait, you have blood to give to people?" Zane asked.

"What do you think people do with donated blood?"

"Doctors and Scientist?"

"Yep!"

"We can finally rest." Drake smiled.

"It's dark again!" Luna yelled.

"It's night time." Aster laughed.

"What does that mean and also who is rest?" Luna asked.

"I'll explain." Scarlet laughed.

"Zane!" Len cried as she ran into the room.

Zane ran to his mom and started to cry. Len told him that she was ok and that it didn't kill her. They all surrounded Len. Scarlet was checking Len's pulse. It was low so she told Len to come follow her into testing room 302. After Scarlet gave Len a checkup, Zane gave his mom a hug again. Len kissed him on the forehead. They all gave Savannah a high five for doing her part of saving the human realm. She was glad she could do it. She loved humans and wanted to protected them.

CHAPTER 8
GREEN GLOWING BLOOD

After having saved the human realm the day before Savannah was totally exhausted. It was Sunday and they needed to get ready for church. Drake asked Zane if he could wake Luna up. He didn't want to wake her up because she could get violent with him. Zane agreed to help him out. They both walked to a spare hospital room and Zane turned on the light. Luna was drooling on her pillow and her hair was a mess. Zane walked up to the bed and poked her. She wouldn't get up so he started to shake her. He yelled her name and she mumbled that if he screamed one more time, she would stab him. Drake jumped on Luna yelling her name to make her mad. Luna opened her eyes and pushed Drake off her. She got up and summoned her knife and thew it at him. He dodged it and apologized. As Luna was yelling insults at Drake, Zane told them that he would be waking Savannah up. Drake yelled for Zane not to leave him. Luna was ticked off at him and he didn't want to deal with Luna's scary behavior. Zane walked to Savannah's room. Scarlet just had painted her room teal for her and bought her a zebra pattern bed spread. He opened her door and said her name. He laughed at her because her horns were poking into her pillow. He tapped her shoulder and took the blanket off her.

"No, I don't wanna get up." Savannah whined.

"We don't want to be late for church. Come on Sav, my Mom made us a human breakfast meal called pancakes and bacon." Zane smiled.

"Five more minutes."

"Come on silly."

Luna walked into Savannah's room and told them not to go into her room. Zane looked at Luna because she didn't want people in her room.

He knew people needed privacy, but her face looked like she was up to something. Scarlet walked in with her coffee cup and asked Zane if he got Savannah up. Zane sighed and told her that she was a very sleepy oni. Luna gave Scarlet an ornery smirk. She snatched Scarlet's coffee and ran to Savannah and dumped it onto her back. She instantly got up and screamed.

"Luna!" Scarlet yelled.

"That wasn't very nice." Zane sighed.

"What the heck!" Savannah cried.

"I got her up" Luna smiled.

"Now Luna. Say you are sorry and you will help clean the bed." Zane said.

"I'm sorry I guess." Luna whined.

Savannah gave Zane a hug and told Luna that she forgave her, but to never do that again. As Scarlet was about to walk out of Savannah's room to wake Kaden up, they all heard Drake screaming. They all stared at Luna knowing that she did something. Luna smiled and ran to her room. As they ran to Luna's room, they saw Drake on the ceiling stuck to sticky black webs. Luna laughed and told them that she was sorry, but she really wasn't.

"I shouldn't have mad her mad." Drake cried.

"I knew something like this would happen buddy." Zane laughed.

"Get me down!"

"Ok!" Luna smiled while using her webs to hang on the ceiling.

She summoned her knife and cut the webs and Drake fell onto her bed. Len walked up to Zane and told him that they needed to leave soon. He told everyone to get dressed and head to the car. Zane and Len helped Savannah get dressed while Scarlet helped Drake and Luna. After they all got ready, they all walked to the car. Scarlet put Kaden into his car seat while Luna was trying to opened the car door. Zane showed her how to open it. He looked at Luna's outfit, knowing it inappropriate for church. She had a purple crop top on and a mini skirt with fishnet tights. Luna put her sunglass on her head like she always did. She told Zane that she was her gothic self and she wasn't going to change her look for some human. Savannah asked Luna if she was excited for church. Luna was a little nervous and told her that she was kind of scared. Oni's are not supposed to be Christians and they shouldn't even be messing around with the bible.

Luna really wanted to be a good person but it was very hard for her. Her dad taught her to be evil and demonic. Her dad told her to hate God and so did Drake and Savannah's dad. As Len was about to drive off, they heard Aster yelling. They all looked at Aster running in his camouflage underwear and having no shirt on. His blue dreads looked a mess and he looked tired.

"Put some clothes on!" Scarlet yelled.

"Why didn't you wake me up for church?" Aster asked.

"Sweety. You slept in the bathroom last night." Len said.

"I poop at midnight. Ok!" Aster whined.

"Get dressed and hop in the car." Zane smiled.

"Hey Luna. Do you like my abs?" Aster smiled.

"Eww!" Luna yelled.

When they got to the church, Luna was shocked it was so big. Savannah took Luna's hand and walked her inside. She looked around and saw lots of humans. She started to crave human blood. She took a deep breath knowing that she couldn't eat them anymore.

"Geez. Why are there so many humans here?" Luna asked.

"It's called the human realm. No oni's live here." Aster said.

"I know that dummy!"

"Guys, don't make a scene please." Len said.

Scarlet took Kaden into the nursery. Kaden waved goodbye to his mom. He sat down in a yellow chair and a women gave him a coloring book and some crayons. Scarlet walked to grab some water and Pastor Dan said hello to her. She told him that she liked coming to church. She told him it changed her life a lot. He smiled as Savannah and Drake ran to him. Luna followed behind them. He was glad to see the oni's came back to church. Savannah introduced Luna to the pastor.

"Nice to meet you Luna" Paster Dan said.

"What does nice to meet you mean?" Luna asked.

"Sorry Pastor Dan. We haven't taught them manners yet." Zane laughed.

"It's ok Zane. I understand."

"This is called a sanctuary; you sit down and listen to the pastor talk about God and the wonderful things He did." Savannah explained.

"Cool!" Luna smiled.

While Pastor Dan was preaching his lesson, Luna was having a hard time following his words. It was hard to understand. When she told Scarlet that she didn't get what the pastor was waying, Scarlet told Luna to follow her. She asked where they were going.

"I'm going to send you to the nursery with Kaden so you can have an easier lesson." Scarlet said.

"Ok. I guess I can try that." Luna said.

"Have fun!"

"Geez, so many little humans."

After church was over, Luna and Kaden ran to the others. They were both excited about something. Drake asked what Luna had in her hand. She told them that she drew a very bad butt picture of Jesus. She told them that she learned Jesus was a real bad butt and that he was a very cool master. They all laughed at Luna for calling Jesus a bad butt. Savannah asked Luna to show the drawing. She showed them with pride. It was an outline of Jesus with cool sunglasses and yellow scribbles for his body and hair. Zane told her that she did awesome. He smiled knowing she didn't know how to stay in the liens yet.

"That was a really good lesson today." Zane smiled.

"Hey Zane, how could all the animals fit in the ark? Savannah asked.

"It was a really big ark I guess." Zane laughed

"What did you and Kaden learn today?" Len asked.

"About Adam and Eve, now I know how sin first started." Luna said.

"That's nice." Len smiled.

When they got home, they ate pizza and drank sweet tea. After that, they played board games and played basketball. It had become night time and they were all ready to sleep. Savannah yawned and asked Scarlet if she could sleep with her. Scarlet told her it was fine. She helped her put on her panda pj's. Savannah put her hat on Scarlet's night stand. She took a sip of water and hopped into bed. Scarlet yawned and tucked Savannah in. She put her glasses next to Savannah's and laid in bed and got under the covers and Savannah's tail rubbed her legs. Scarlet told her to keep her tail on her own side of the bed. It was very pointy and she didn't want to wake up wounded. Luna ran to her bed and jumped on it. She loved her fluffy cage as she called it. As they all fell asleep, someone with black hair and a lab coat was creeping around outside the hospital. On his lab coat it had the logo of the League of Science. He was about five foot six and his skin was tan. He had a black beard and a mustache. He smiled and thought to himself that he would make Mya one proud scientist. He wanted to kidnap an oni for Mya even though she was in jail. Mya told him that her old friend was taking care of the oni's. He knew Scarlet was Mya's friend so he went to her hospital to see if she had the oni's. He walked up to the front entrance and tired to open the door. He knew it would have been locked but he just wanted to make sure. He went to his van and got out a taser. He ran to the door and looked at a key pad. He thought maybe if he used a taser, it would break the key pad. He used it and it blew up. After he wiped the smoke from his face he tried to open the door again. It opened it and it worked. He laughed to himself and walked in. He started to get scared. He didn't want to die from an oni. He told himself that he would just get some oni blood instead of kidnapping one. Mya was in jail anyway so she couldn't really test on an oni. He walked up some stairs and pulled out his oni tracker. He saw three dots. He was in shock that three oni's were in the human realm. He walked to the closest dot. He quietly opened the door and found a purple haired woman who was snoring and drooling all over herself. She had one side of her hair shaved off and she had a black choker on her neck. He tiptoed to her and took a closer look at the oni. She had sharp fangs and she was very skinny for a powerful being. He felt her hair. It was soft to touch. He traced his fingers on Luna's arm. She moved her arm and she mumbled who touched her. He took out a syringe with a light pink liquid inside it. He told her that she was going for a ride in his van. She opened her eyes finding a scientist about to jab her with a syringe. Luna shot her webs on the wall and pulled herself off her bed. She yelled asking who the guy was. He laughed and told her he was a friend of Mya. Luna remembered Savannah telling her that a human named Mya touched her inappropriately and stabbed her with knives. She also told her Mya would put bad chemicals in her body with a syringe. She guessed that the sharp thing that guy had in his hand was one of the bad chemicals. Luna summoned her Simbyot knife and told him that he wouldn't hurt her or her siblings. He ran to Luna kicking her down. She was on the floor holding her side. She yelled for help as the guy jabbed the pink liquid into Luna's leg. She screamed for help while the guy put her back on the bed. He told Luna that his name was Sam. Luna was looking a him and started to get dizzy. She started to breath heavily and yelled for Drake. Sam told her that he wanted her blood.

"Relax little oni. It will just make you fall asleep." Sam laughed.

How does he know about my blood? Luna thought as she closed her eyes and passed out.

Sam got out an empty syringe and laid Luna on her back. He put Luna's right arm on a pillow and started to look for a vein. As he found one, he poked her and something glowing came out. Green glowing blood was coming out of Luna's arm. He was confused. Mya told him oni's blood was purple. As he was getting the last bit of her blood, the syringe started to feel warm. He took the needle out of her arm and stared at the blood. The syringe started to get really hot. It shattered onto the floor and on Sam's face and arms. Glass had sliced his legs open. He screamed because the blood was burning him. it felt like lava was pouring on him. He ran out of Luna's room and ran into a closet hoping not to wake anyone. He dropped to the floor in pain. His eyes glowed green and his hair started to fade into a neon green color. He began to puke out glowing green goo. He yelled for help but no one heard him. As he was trying to get up, there was a black shadow with red eyes standing before him. He asked who was there. The shadow laughed at him. His laugh was evil and deep. The shadow walked to Sam. He was scared for his life. The shadow explained to him that he couldn't fully manifest in that realm. Sam got up off the floor and stood face to face with the shadow man. The shadow told him that his new name was Poison. He was confused and asked the shadow what was going on.

"You got that Simbyot's blood on you. Her blood is powerful and you are the first one to be exposed to her blood therefore you have become a powerful new creation. Anyone else after you who encounters it, will die."

"I thought oni and Simbyot's blood was purple. Not glowing and green." Sam cried.

"She is the only being with blood like that. It can kill any being. Even oni's who can't die. Even me."

"Who are you?"

"I go by many names. The devil. King of the underworld, Satan, god of this world. Call me whatever you want."

"I'm so ugly!"

"Yes, you are but something happened to you. When you got her blood on you, it made you green but also you have been given a power. You can poison people with a green toxic substance, you now have a power of a Simbyot. You can use gooey webs and look into people's minds."

"I feel weak and sick."

"Oh. I forget to mention that you can't live without the Simbyot's blood or you'll die."

"Huh. I'm confused. How can I die and how do I keep myself alive?"

"The Simbyot woman is named Luna Omagon. You need to eat her blood to live. You can cut her or draw blood like you scientists do all the time. You just have to feed off it or there will be consequences."

"I am starting to crave blood."

"I must go now. God's power is in this hospital. There must be a bible and some believers in his place. Goodbye for now Poison."

Poison watched Satan fade away. He thought to himself about his new life change. He wasn't really an evil scientist like Mya. He walked out of the closet and looked out the window. There was a sunrise and Poison was surprised that he had talked to the devil all night. He saw a knife sitting on a table that had a note that said that if there was an emergency to use it. He laughed and grabbed it and ran to Luna's room. Poison sneaked up to Luna and climbed on top of her. He wouldn't get on top of a lady like that but he needed her. Luna started to groan and Poison was lifting up her shirt. He put the knife on Luna's belly and cut it open. Luna jumped and started to scream at the top of her lungs. She pushed Poison off her and got out of bed. She was holding her side while blood was oozing out of her stomach. She was crying and yelled asking who he was. He told her that they met last night. Poison ran to Luna and knocked her down to the floor. He got on top of her and sliced her arm open. He licked it and his eyes started to glow. He felt something he had never felt before. He felt so powerful. Luna cried out for Drake as Poison was squeezing blood out of her arm. Kaden woke up to the screams of Luna. He ran to his mom's room and opened the door and woke her up. Scarlet yawned and asked Kaden what he needed. Kaden cried that Luna was screaming for help. Scarlet got out of bed and Kaden took her hand. She stopped and told Kaden to stay in her room. She got out her gun from her dresser and put some bullets into it. She put on her glasses and walked to Luna's room. As she walked closer to Luna's room, she heard her scream. She ran to the noise and she saw something she had never seen before. A green skinned guy with neon green hair and glowing green eyes was stabbing Luna. Luna looked at Scarlet and yelled at her to help her. Scarlet instantly pointed her gun at poison and asked who he was. He laughed at her and licked the knife with blood on it. She asked again who he was and why he was hurting Luna. Poison had an idea to get Scarlet out of the room. He swiped his hand around trying to use his new toxic power. As he did, he blasted Scarlet with a green and stinky green fog. She fell to the floor in pain. She was about to shoot him but she was too weak. Scarlet asked Luna what was going on. Luna cried that the green guy was eating her blood.

"Why is your blood glowing and green. That's not your beings color of blood?" Scarlet asked.

"I was born with it!" Luna cried while wiping blood off her face.

As Luna was crying, Poison saw another note on Luna's desk. It said that if you need to teleport fast to a place, use that. He smiled and grabbed Aster's teleporter gun. As Scarlet was getting up, Poison grabbed a hold of Luna and looked at the note to see how to use it. Scarlet was breathing heavily and got her gun from the floor. As she was about to try and shoot Poison again, he used the teleporter gun to teleport he and Luna to an abandoned house. Scarlet was mad at herself for not getting Luna help in time. She ran down the stairs to the lobby and turned on the speakers. She yelled for everyone to come to the lobby because Luna had been kidnapped. As she was speaking into the microphone, Drake got up and ran to Savannah. He woke her up and told her that there was a problem. She yawned and asked what happened. He grabbed her arm as Len was walking into Savannah's room.

"Sweetheart. We need to get up. Your sister is in trouble." Len cried.

"What happened!" Savannah yelled.

"Guys. Calm down. Scarlet will tell us when we get to the lobby." Zane said as he and Aster were walking to the elevator.

As they all got to the lobby, Scarlet was drinking alcohol. Aster asked Scarlet what was wrong. She stopped drinking and told them that she failed. Len walked up to her and rubbed her back and asked where Luna was. Savannah began to cry from the drama while Len was asking questions.

"I didn't get Luna in time. Some green man took her with Aster's teleporter gun and he was cutting her up and eating her blood!" Scarlet yelled than starting to drink again.

"Please don't drink that sweety. Let's just calm down a different way and ask God to help Luna. This bottle of whiskey you have isn't what God wants. I know you didn't get her before that guy took Luna and I know you're very upset but alcohol isn't going to help. Please Scarlet, trust God to help." Len smiled.

As Poison and Luna got to the abandoned home, he dragged Luna to a bed room. The home where Poison teleported them to was his college house. He pushed Luna onto the bed and he walked to the closet. He got out X stone chains. Luna was trying to get up but she was losing a lot of blood and she felt light headed. Green glowing blood was dripping onto the bed while Poison was walking up to her. She saw his face clearly. She couldn't see him clearly when they were in her room because the lights were off. He was ugly. He had warts and tiny holes everywhere on his body. He looked disgusting and definitely didn't look like a human. He got out a gun and told Luna if she didn't do as he said, she would get shot. Luna laughed at him and told him that she couldn't die. He grabbed her arm and was squeezing it tight. He thew her to the floor and kicked her in the ribs. Poison told Luna that he had paper work to get done. He walked out of the room and told her to stay there or else. Luna tired to get up but her side was hurting her. She prayed for Jesus to help her for the first time. She didn't really know what God could do to help her in that kind of situation. She hoped for the best and sighed. Back at the hospital Aster was very ticked off. As Scarlet was telling the story of what happened, Aster kicked a trash can over. He was mad about the guy who took his teleporter gun. Zane asked if Scarlet knew the man's name and Scarlet didn't know. She told them that she had never seen a green guy in her life.

"That guy will pay for stealing my teleporter gun." Aster grunted.

"I don't understand..." Scarlet sighed.

"What don't you understand dear?" Len asked?

"It's just that I have never seen blood like Luna's. Sav and Drake say that no being has blood like that, Scarlet sighed."

"Guys!" Drake cried.

"What is it dude?" Aster asked.

"I just now realized something. When I was in that abandoned jail when Luna was evil, I punched her in the nose and glowing green blood was coming out of it. At the time I was trying not to get hurt so I didn't think about it." Drake explained.

"Hey, at least I'm not the one captured this time!" Savannah smiled.

"Really Savannah..." Zane said.

"What?"

"How about we look for clues, maybe find fingerprints or something to know who that guy was." Scarlet said.

"Good idea." Zane smiled.

"Mommy, can I help?" Kaden asked.

"Sure, you can follow Savannah around." Scarlet said.

"Ok!"

"Me and Kaden can look in Luna's room." Savannah smiled.

"Ok. That's a good start." Scarlet said.

"I will check the front door to see how the dude came in." Aster said.

"Ok. when you guys find something, come and get me. I will run some tests if you find anything." Scarlet explained.

Savannah and Kaden walked to the elevator while Aster was opening the front door. Savannah ran to Luna's room and turned on the lights. She was in shock of what she found. She went down on her knees. She found shattered glass and glowing blood on the floor. Kaden ran in and asked If she found anything. Savannah told Kaden to come to her. He looked at the green glowing blood and smiled and told her that it looked like the slime that he and Savannah played with. She laughed and said that it wasn't slime. He walked up to the blood and was about to touch it. Savannah grabbed his hand and told him that it might be dangerous. He nodded his head and gave her a hug. Kaden asked if he needed to get his mommy. Savannah told him that it would be a good idea. Kaden ran down the stairs fast and ran to his mom. Scarlet looked at him while he was poking her. She asked what he needed. Kaden told her that Savannah had found a clue. Scarlet told him to show her. As Savannah was looking at the clue, the green glowing blood started to bubble. She backed away from it as Scarlet asked what they found. She pointed to the clue. Scarlet walked up to it and was examining it. She got out blue rubber gloves and told them that she would take a piece of glass to see if she could find any fingerprints. Scarlet put on the gloves and she put a piece of glass into a biohazard bag and zipped it up. She told them that she would run some tests. While Scarlet headed to her lab, Luna was having the worst time in her life. Poison had put her into a basement and chained her up. She begged Poison to let her go. He cut open Luna's lip and licked the blood off. She cried for help but no one was there to save her.

"Why are you doing this to me!" Luna yelled.

"You don't understand what I have to do because of you! I need to eat your powerful blood to stay alive. All I wanted from you was a blood sample but your blood got on me. The syringe shattered on me." Poison cried.

"You don't have to torture me!" Luna yelled.

"Shut up! I like that I'm powerful. I'm not the dumb Sam anymore!" Poison yelled back.

"My friend is a scientist; maybe she can get you back to a normal human."

"No, I love my power!"

"Listen, I once was a bad guy. I thought no one would defeat me but I was wrong. Power does feel good but it's not ok to use it for evil. People don't even need power, the only person who needs power is God. God is power!" Luna explained.

"I don't give a crap about what you say. You have no hope. You are mine forever!"

"I have hope. God is with me; he will get me out of this bad situation. I have so much hope that God is probably gonna make a social media post about how much hope I got!"

Back at the hospital, everyone was making a plan to save Luna.

"Me and the boys will work on making a new teleporter gun." Aster said.

"Sav and I will find out who took Luna." Scarlet added.

"Or I can watch Kaden while you test out the evidence so you don't get interrupted." Savannah smiled.

"You said that in a really suspicious way..." Aster said.

"I guess you can watch him. Len can help too." Scarlet said.

"Scarlet, I won't go into your room." Savannah laughed.

"Uh ok..."

"Bye!"

"You forgot Kaden." Zane laughed.

"Oh right!"

"You dudes ready?" Aster asked.

"Let's do this!" Zane smiled.

"Dang bro. Why do you always act like a cheerleader?" Aster asked.

"Hey!"

"I'm just saying."

"I don't know what a cheerleader is but I can tell it's funny." Drake laughed.

It had been an hour of Aster, Drake, and Zane working on the new teleporter gun. Aster grabbed some wires and put it into the space looking gun that was made out of metal. Zane asked if he needed some more gun powder and he shook his head no. Aster got out a welding torch and used it to close up the wires in the gun. He typed some numbers into a computer and the new teleporter gun's button lit up green. They were so happy that they got it to work. Zane and Drake gave each other a fist bump. Aster grabbed the teleporter gun and told himself that he was proud of his work. Scarlet was using a fingerprint brush on the piece of glass. She took a picture of it and went to her computer and hooked up the image onto her computer.

All I need to do is put the image into my computer and find a match.

After a few minutes, the computer showed a match of a guy named Sam Gibbs. Scarlet knew who he was. She took off her gloves and ran to the others. She explained that the guy who took Luna was named Sam Gibbs and that he was part of the League of Science. She added that he was never green and something must had happened to him.

"Let's find Sav and tell her that this Sam guy took Luna." Zane said.

"Where is she anyway?" Drake asked.

"Let's teleport to her." Aster said.

"Yeah. let's test the gun out!" Zane smiled.

Aster teleported them to Savannah to find her in a pool on a raft and in Scarlet's bathing suit with Kaden playing in the water. They all looked at each other than stared at Savannah. Savannah smiled and said that this was the life. Drake asked what she was doing.

"What are you doing in the back yard swimming in my pool and in my bathing suit?" Scarlet asked.

"Are you ok Sav...?" Zane asked.

"Finally. I'm not the one captured this time!" Savannah smiled.

"But why are you in a pool?" Zane asked.

"I think her getting captured all time is getting to her head." Aster laughed.

"We need to take Savannah to therapy..." Scarlet sighed.

"I looked up things to do after you have been tortured and abused in your life and swimming in a human pool was one of them." Savannah smiled.

"Anyway, Scarlet found out who took Luna, his name is Sam Gibbs." Zane said.

"Who in the world is that?" Savannah asked.

"One of the League of Science members." Scarlet said.

"Those guys make me sick!" Savannah yelled while drinking sweet tea and laying back on the raft.

"Yep, Sav needs a therapist." Zane laughed.

"Now that we have the teleporter gun, we can save Luna!" Aster smiled.

"Me and Aster can go get Luna. The rest of you guys get inside." Scarlet explained.

"Be careful, we don't know how dangerous Sam is." Zane said.

"We will be fine." Aster smiled.

As Zane was trying to get Savannah to come inside, Aster teleported himself and Scarlet to where Luna was. When they got there, they heard Luna screaming. They ran to the noise and peaked their head into the room. Poison was putting a blue liquid into Luna's mouth. Poison told her that it would make her fall asleep so he could get her blood without her squirming. Luna starting to get dizzy and passed out into Poison's arms. Aster whispered to Scarlet that they needed to do something quick. Aster had a blue and green backpack on with tools in it. Scarlet zipped open the backpack and got out a sleeping bomb. Scarlet thew the sleeping bomb into the room and closed the door. They waited three minutes and Aster opened the door. They ran to Luna and looked at her all beaten up. They both sighed than Aster found the other teleporter gun laying on the floor. Scarlet grabbed it and told him that they needed to go before Sam would wake up. Aster teleported the three of them to the hospital. Drake looked at Luna and ran up to her and yelled what happened to her. Scarlet pulled out a wheelchair and Aster put Luna in it. Aster took off Luna's shirt and they all saw that she had cuts and wounds all over her body. After Scarlet put her on a hospital bed and hooked her up to an oxygen tank, they all started to feel bad for Luna. Two hours later, she woke up. Scarlet took the oxygen mask off her face. They all were relieved that she was ok. Luna had banges on both of her arms, stomach, legs, forehead, and hip. Savannah gave Luna hug and started to cry. Luna patted her on the back.

"A guy was eating my blood and wouldn't stop hurting me!" Luna cried.

"God protected you. You are safe now." Len smiled.

"My body hurts so much!"

"We love you Luna. It will be ok." Drake smiled while putting her sunglasses on her face

Luna laughed and Drake gave her a fist bump.

"Friends stay together, we never leave each other's side." Savannah smiled.

CHAPTER 9
LUNAR DESTRUCTION

"I lost the human card game again!" Savannah cried.

"It's ok Savannah. You're new to this game." Zane smiled.

"Can I try one more time please." Savannah asked

"Yes, one more round than I have to use the bathroom."

"Human cleaning wipe thingies are different than an oni wipe thingy."

"What does oni toilet paper look like?"

"A rock."

"Oh gosh!"

"Human's paper is not painful."

"Yeah, I would never ever want use a rock."

"Can we play now?"

"Sure!"

"I hope I can do this like you can."

"I was never good at card games until I practiced."

"I will practice like you then."

Zane was trying to teach Savannah how to play a card game but she didn't understand. He had an idea. He was just going to let her win. Zane asked if she could get him a soda while he would get the cards ready. Savannah smiled and said that she would be right back. She ran to the kitchen that was down the hallway from the living room. When she opened the fridge, she saw Drake eating a whole pack of chocolate chip cookies. Drake stared at Savannah licking his fingers and told her to not tell Scarlet. Savannah sighed and told Drake that he eats too much. He was already over two hundreds pounds and he didn't care about his weight. He loved food so much. It was the best thing he liked in the human realm.

Luna walked in and told Savannah and Drake that Aster asked her out. They both looked at Luna blushing. Drake laughed at Luna and told her that he was just probably teasing her. Luna yelled that she looked into Aster's mind and he wanted to kiss her. Savannah was trying not to laugh. She quickly grabbed a cherry cola from the fridge and told her siblings that she was playing a human card game with Zane. As Savannah left, Luna walked up to Drake with an upset face. He asked what was wrong. She told him that she wasn't feeling good. Drake asked if she had a fever or that her stomach hurt. She told him that her body felt numb and her eyes were burning. Drake patted Luna on the back and said it was probably from what happened yesterday with Poison. She laid her head on Drake and said that she was going to go take a nap. Drake smiled and asked if she wanted to play video games with him later. Luna didn't know how to play one but she said she would. As Luna was about to go down for a nap, she heard Savannah yelling from the living room that she won the human card game. Luna yelled good job to her than walked to her room. After an hour, Drake went to check up on Luna. He knocked on her door than heard Luna crying. He opened the door and went to lay beside her on her bed. He asked if she was ok. Luna yelled that she was not ok. She laid on Drake crying and telling him that she was scared. Drake asked again what was wrong. She blew her nose on Drake's purple and green cloak. Drake sighed and kissed her on the head.

"This is a safe place." Drake smiled.

"Almost every time I close my eyes, I just see red. Also, last night I had this creepy voice nonstop telling me, get ready for the blood moon!" Luna cried.

"Listen, that voice was just part of a dream."

"But when I close my eyes…"

"I think you getting taken by Poison is making you like Savannah. When she got taken by Mya, she had hallucinations and she got loppy a little bit."

"Ok, I'll just try to stop thinking about it."

As Drake and Luna were talking. Scarlet walked in and asked if Luna could come to her. Luna got up from her bed and asked what she wanted. Scarlet explained that she needed to run some tests on her blood. She told her she was sorry for asking but they needed to know if it was deadly or not, She added that they also needed to know for their safety after what happened to Sam Gibbs. She told her that she would need to draw some her blood. Drake asked if it was safe for Scarlet to get near her blood. She didn't know if it could harm her but they needed to do it soon to help out Luna. After Luna got into testing room four-one -two, she heard a voice in her head that said the word blood moon. She shook her head and sat down in a big chair.

"Now Luna, this will not hurt. You will just feel a little pinch." Aster smiled.

As Aster was getting the syringe and Scarlet was getting her gloves on, Luna was starting to breath heavily. Her mind went dark and she couldn't see anything. All she would see was darkness. She asked what was happening. Everyone stared at Luna with her eyes closed and crying. Drake tired to wake her up. Zane asked if she was ok. Scarlet asked Luna if she could hear them. In her mind there was a shadow with red eyes walking up to her. She yelled who was there. The shadow just kept saying the words blood moon. As soon as Aster yelled her name, Luna got up and started yelling for help. Drake ran up to Luna and said that she was passed out. Luna looked out the door seeing the shadow waving at her. She used her webs on it but when she did it was gone.

"what the heck Luna." Aster asked.

"didn't you see that shadow!" Luna cried while pointing to the door.

"Um…no." Savannah said.

"Luna. Look at me. Are you ok?" Scarlet asked.

"I don't know!" Luna cried.

"Luna. Please don't cry. I don't like that you are crying." Savannah cried.

"Guys, what's a blood moon." Luna asked.

A blood moon happens every month in Science City and the sky and moon is red, Aster said.

"Yeah, and it really creepy and no one knows why." Scarlet added.

As Aster was explaining a blood moon, Luna's eyes glowed red. They all looked at her. Zane started to freak out and asked if oni's eyes turn red sometimes. Drake shook his head no and held Luna's hand. She mumbled that she wasn't ok than she passed out.

"Drake, would you please look into Luna's mind to see what's up with her?" Scarlet asked.

"Sure."

Drake used his power to look into her mind. Her mind was in a dark place. Drake explained that she might be having a vision. Aster asked Drake to explain. He explained that Luna was using her blood to kill people. He saw a throne made of human bone and Luna sitting In it. She had red clothing on with three sixes on her head. Drake stooped looking in her mind and he fell to the floor with his eyes wide open. Zane ran to him asking what he saw. Drake began to cry while they all were asking what the vison was, He explained that Luna was going to be an evil demic queen. They were all confused than Scarlet asked if he could look and see if Luna was dreaming or not. Drake told them that it was no dream. It was going to happen. He yelled that Luna could kill oni's even though they couldn't die. He told them in the vision that all of them died from Luna's blood. All of them were in shock.

"God will protect us. 1st Corinthians 16:13 says, be on your guard, stand firm in the faith, be courageous and be strong." Zane smiled.

"Yeah, if Luna does go crazy on us don't worry. God is with us wherever we go!" Savannah smiled.

Two hours later. Luna woke up in her bed with a band aid on her arm. She thought to self that Scarlet must had drew her blood in her sleep. Drake walked to Luna and told her that she was sleepy head. She said that her head was hurting and asked why everyone was in her room. When Luna got up Savannah ran to her and gave her a hug. She asked why she needed a hug.

"I love you no matter what you are going to do tonight!" Savannah smiled.

"What does she mean by that?" Luna asked.

"Ummm…" Zane cried.

"She's just worried about Mya trying to take her. She says random things when she's scared!" Scarlet laughed.

"No I don't!"

Drake grabbed Luna hand and told her that they needed to play video games. Luna sighed and followed him. She really didn't want to play but it was her brother so she agreed to spending time with him.

Why aren't we telling her, Savannah asked?

"Because we don't want to trigger it by saying that she's going to go evil on us tonight. Scarlet said.

"Yeah Sav, we don't wanna scare her either.", Zane added.

"And why are you talking about Mya." Savannah grunted.

"Because you do get loppy when you think about her." Aster laughed.

"Leave me alone!" Savannah whined.

Hours later went by and it was getting late. Luna was confused why everyone wanted to do thing with her. She liked the attention but it was getting a little weird.

"I don't want to put her in a testing room and lock her up." Scarlet sighed.

"But that might be the best option. "Aster said.

"Who wants to be caged up in a white scary looking room but I don't have anything else to keep her safe." Scarlet sighed.

"Ok, putting Luna in a testing room is the plan then." Aster said.

"What are you two talking about?" Luna asked.

"I thought you were going to watch tv with Zane!" Aster yelled.

"Why are you yelling?" Luna asked.

"Sorry!"

"Are you ok. you both seem upset?" Luna asked

"We are fine,." Scarlet sighed.

"I had a really bad nightmare about me going insane on a blood moon and Zane was right, some dreams can be weird." Luna said.

"Let's hope it's a dream…" Aster mumbled.

"What did you say?" Luna asked.

"Nothing,!" Aster yelled.

"He said that he has weird dream too." Scarlet smiled while having her hands on his mouth.

As she was about to question Scarlet holding Aster's mouth closed. She felt dizzy. Her eyes glowed red again. Scarlet and Aster were scared of what was happening. Scarlet yelled for Aster to get the others. Red fog was forming around Luna. Her clothes change red and she had Satan's symbol under her feet. She had a crown of human teeth on her head with a pendant filled with human's blood in the middle of it. As everyone came into the lob part of the hospital. They all saw Luna looking like some demonic queen.

"Who wants to die first.?" Luna laughed."

"Not me!" Aster cried.

"Oh Aster, you don't know this yet but, you will be my slave and everyone but you will die." Luna smiled.

"Aye. I'm special." Aster laughed.

"Luna don't kill us my awesome half-sister!" Drake cried.

"Ha, I have no family. "Luna laughed.

"You do have family. You are mine and Drake's sibling." Savannah said.

Luna blasted Savannah with a red fog kind of power. It made Savannah weak. She screamed from the pain. Drake ran to Savannah helping her up but she was too weak. Luna grabbed Zane and was using her power to force him onto the floor. His body was glowing red. Luna sued her new power to make Zane's nerves in his body to tight up. He yelled for help and he was crying. Drake used his oni darkness to make Luna fall down.

"You have to calm down. This isn't you!" Drake yelled.

Luna summoned her knife and sliced her finger. Drake explained that was part of the vision. Luna pushed Drake to the floor and Luna put her bloody finger on Drake's cheek and told him that this was is last day on earth. Scarlet got out a sedative from a meatal carpet and ran to Luna and jabbed it into her arm. Luna fell to the floor and passed out.

"what is this feeling…" Drake sighed why his body was failing.

"Drake!" Savannah cried.

"I'll try to save him. Aster, please put Luna into testing room 403." Scarlet cried.

"I feel weak." Drake sighed while crying.

Drake dropped to the floor in pain. An oni never had felt like it was dying. Scarlet was checking his pulse while Savannah was yelling for Drake. Len gabbed Savannah and was calming her down. Drake's face was getting pale and he was losing his conscience. Scarlet grabbed Aster's teleporter gun and teleported she and Drake to a hospital bed. An hour had passed by and everyone was waiting for Drake in the waiting room. Scarlet walked in and told everyone to come follow her. When they all go there. They saw Drake with stitches on his cheek and hooked up to an IV. Savannah ran to Drake calling out his name. Zane asked if he was alive. Scarlet explained that she surgically removed part of Drake's cheek to try and remove the blood. If she waited any longer, he would have died. They all thanked God while Drake was waking up.

"I'm going to check up on Luna." Aster said.

"Ok, I'll meet you there when I'm done putting my equipment away I used for Drake." Scarlet said.

As Aster was walking down the hallway. He saw an oni laughing at him. His heart dropped and the oni said hello to him. Aster yelled for everyone to come to him. He told them that it was urgent.

"We have an unwanted guest!" Aster cried.

'hello human..'' Arlo laughed.

"How in the world is he here." Drake sighed while Len was helping him walk.

"Now humans, I'm only here to see my daughter but… she's passed out in a room." Arlo said.

"Luna went evil on us. This must have been you who made her like that!" Aster yelled.

"No, I did absolutely nothing to her." Arlo said.

"Then why all a sudden she's like that?" Zane asked

"All I'm going to say is that, you all are doomed." Arlo laughed.

"Why?" Scarlet asked.

"Fine, I'll tell you dumb humans. You all probably know that today is a blood moon." Arlo said.

"Yes, we know, we aren't idiots!" Aster grunted.

"Luna doesn't know what she's the Lunar Destruction." Arlo said

"What is the Lunar Destruction? "Savannah asked while hiding behind Drake.

"I'll tell you only because I want all of you to hate Luna." Arlo smiled.

"We don't hate anyone!" Scarlet yelled.

"Me and Luna's mom Lilly doesn't have green glowing blood like her, we didn't know why her blood was like that until Satan Aka Savannah and Drake's uncle told us about it." Arlo explained.

"And what did my uncle say to you?" Drake asked

All the oni's in here know that God doesn't create oni's like humans, Satan creates oni's. When Satan created Luna in the womb, he messed up big time. He anciently gave Luna power that she doesn't need to have. Luna is more power than Satan himself. Her blood can kill any being, even me.

Luna will not stop until she eats and kills all the beings in every realm expect her king that I have no idea who it is." Arlo said.

"I'm the king baby." Aster smiled.

"Whatever." Arlo sighed.

"I don't get the blood moon thing." Zane said.

"Every blood moon from now on she will be like she is now; you guys have no chance of stopping her." Arlo smiled.

"But with the power of God, she will fight this evil in her!" Zane smiled

"I hate your dumb butt Christians!" Arlo sighed.

As Arlo was about to go back into he oni realm with his staff. Scarlet got her gun from her blet and shoot Arlo's staff. Arlo dropped it and it blew up into purple flames. He yelled why she would do that. His body had purple flames forming around him. he got teleported back to the oni realm and the staff turned to dust. As they all calmed down. Zane explained that it was kind of a good thing Arlo got out of the human realm to tell them about what happened to Luna. They all ran to where Luna was at. When they got there they saw that Luna had escaped.

"I thought X stone could hold power!" Savannah yelled.

"You really think that I couldn't be kept captive?" Luna yelled.

"Luna please. We need the real you back. We love you." Drake cried.

Luna's eyes were chaining back to black as Drake said that. She shook her head and the eyes went back to glowing red. Zane had an idea. He told them to say nice things to her and maybe the power of God could help her get back to herself. Aster sighed and ran to Luna and was holding her tight. Luna was about to blast him with red fog. Before she did, Aster kissed her on the lips. Luna stooped and just shood still and started to cry.

"In Jesus name, the evilness that is inside you Luna will be gone. No demon should have a hold of a Christian, so in Jesus name the evil will be gone!" Zane yelled.

Luna feel to the floor as her normal clothing was changing back. The crown went up into red dust and she was yelling for help. Aster went on his knees next to Luna and said that he loved her and that she could control it. It was sunrise and the blood moon faded away. Aster helped Luna up and she gave him a hug.

"Zane! You and Aster saved Luna." Savannah smiled.

"It was God's power. My words." Zama smiled.

"Oh mu gosh. You are you." Aster cried.

"Why do you care so much. Why do you all care!" Luna cried.

"It was not your fault!" Drake yelled.

"I almost killed you!" Lina cried.

As they all calmed Luna down. They told her that they loved her. aster also asked Luna to be her girlfriend. She laughed and told him that he was kinda cute for being water. As the morning hit. Luna and Savannah gave each other a hug. Savannah told Luna that she would always love her no matter what.

CHAPTER 10
HOTEL DISASTER

It's been five months of Mya being in prison. She wanted to escape. She wanted to get Savannah back and hurt Scarlet for what she had done. Mya had a plan to escape but it would be hard. She had to try. She wanted to abuse Savannah even more than she did the first time. But she needed to wait for the right time to escape. She met up with James and Andy to help with the plan. As the officers was taking Mya, Andy, and James to their cell, James asked one of the officers to use the bathroom. The officer told a guy named Randy to come to him. He was new guy so the job of taking an inmate to use the bathroom wouldn't be hard for him. Randy grabbed James and took him to the men's bathroom. He told James to hurry up. When James got into the bathroom he pretended to cry and asked Randy to come see him. He told him that he wanted to talk to someone about his daughter. Randy sighed and went into the bathroom and asked what he wanted. He walked up to James. James kicked him in the crotch and kicked his head to knock him out. He grabbed his gun and a key card and ran out of the bathroom. He headed to Mya's cell. When Mya saw James she let out an evil laugh. James scanned the key card into a slot next to Mya's cell and it opened. She ran out and snatched the gun out of his hands. She thew him into the cell and locked it. She smiled at him and told him he was so dumb. He begged her to let him go. He told her that he was a good assistant to her. Mya told him to suck it up as she ran out to escape. As she was about to head out, an officer pointed a gun at Mya. Mya gave the woman a mean look than shot her in the leg. The officer got out her walkie talkie and told everyone that there was a code red. Mya shot another officer in the chest and ran to the main entrance of the Science City Jail. As Mya ran out of the jail she shot an innocent visitor in the hip that was in her way and dove off with the lady's car. It's been three days since her escape.

Zane was looking for Scarlet and asked Aster where she was. Aster told him that she was in the meeting room looking at the mail. Zane thanked him and walked upstairs to the meeting room. As he went inside, he saw lots of envelopes and paper on the floor and on the table. He saw Scarlet was stressed so he walked up to her and asked if she needed help or anything. Scarlet took a sip of her wine and told him that she wished she had never been a scientist. Zane asked why she would say that. Scarlet handed him a paper. He skimmed though it and it was a terrible message about Scarlet. It said that Scarlet was fired and she sucked. It was from the League of Science.

"All of these papers are from the league of science telling me I'm fired and saying very bad things about me!" Scarlet yelled.

"Like what?" Zane asked.

"Words that make me wanna leave this place and move to Hawaii." Scarlet sighed.

"Why are there wine bottles on the floor?"

"These letters are making me depressed..."

"What did our pastor tell you about drinking?"

Scarlet took a drink of her wine and just stared at him as he was about to give her another life lesson like he always did.

"Provers 20:1 says, Wine is a mocker and beer a brawler, whoever goes astray by them is not wise."

"Isn't communion wine?"

"First of all, grape juice and second, are you drunk?"

"Yeah." Scarlet laughed while laying back in her chair.

"Let me help you with your mail problem."

"It's probably from the league of Science." Scarlet sighed while Zane took a letter out of her hand.

As Zane was reading he said, "this one isn't from them."

"Who is it from?"

"The mayor of Science City!"

"Oh no, are they wanting me to go to a mental hospital!"

"No, it's about Savannah.."

"Huh, why would Sav get something from the mayor?" Scarlet asked while looking at the letter with Zane.

"It says, Dear Savannah the Oni, You and your friends who helped save Science City are invited to a luxury hotel for a week as a thank you reward. You are the first people to be invited to this 50 yr old newly renovated hotel. We would love all of you to come and have a blast, and plus IT'S FREE, we will see you soon. Sincerely Mayor Connor."

Zane asked if they could go. Scarlet told him to ask Savannah. She didn't know if she would want to go to a hotel around other humans. While Zane was looking for Savannah, she was on her bed holding a stuffed animal of a panda bear. She was upset and didn't know what to do about it. Zane knocked on her door and he walked inside. He saw that Savannah was crying so he went up on the bed with her and asked what was wrong. She asked Zane if God still cared about her because she was sexually abused. Mya told her that God would hate her when she saw doing evil things to her. Zane patted her on the back and told her no matter what someone had been though, God always cares and loves. Zane told her that in the bible Isaiah 61:3 says that God will make beauty for ashes which means that He will bring healing to us for the bad things that happen. Zane explained that Mya shouldn't have abused her but she needed to forgive her. Savannah told him that it was the worst thing in her life and she didn't know how to handle it. Zane encouraged her to let God help her forgive. Forgiveness is a choice and the feelings come after the healing. Savannah gave him a hug and told him that he was the best human boyfriend in the world. Zane smiled and asked her to relax because he had something to ask to her.

"So, whatcha ya need?" Savannah smiled.

"Well, we got invited to stay at a hotel for a week and I was wondering if you wanted to go." Zane asked.

"It is safe and no scientist?"

"It's safe. I'm sure of it."

"I wanna go and try to be a big oni."

"Let's tell the others then."

Savannah put down her stuffed animal and she and Zane walked to the living room. Luna and Drake were fighting about who was the better oni. Zane laughed and told them that they both were awesome. Luna put on her sunglass and asked what they wanted. Scarlet was on the couch asking Zane if Savannah said yes. Savannah smiled and said that she really wanted to go. Zane asked his mom if they could go to the hotel. Len explained that they all could go and she could watch Kaden and stay and get somethings done while they had some fun. Aster was pumped and ran to his room to pack. He loved luxury places. Scarlet thanked Len for watching Kaden. Len told her that she would love to take care of him. After they all packed up, they headed to Scarlet's work van. Scarlet put the address into her car and it told her that the hotel was two hours ways. After an hour, Drake started to get hungry. He had been whining for food the whole drive. Zane asked Scarlet if they could go to the Burger Building. It was a fast food restaurant that was very popular in Science City. She asked what they wanted from there. Drake smiled and asked for five large fries and two lime sodas. Scarlet sighed and said that he needed to pick one meal, not a ton of fries. Zane told Drake that they had the best sweet tea in the world. Savannah wanted chicken nuggets and a root beer. When Scarlet pulled up to the drive though, a lady asked what would they like. Savannah, Drake, and Luna were shocked a voice came out of the speaker.

"My gosh. How is that talking?" Savannah asked.

"How does that human fit in that box?" Luna asked.

"I guess really tiny humans work here." Savannah said.

"Luna could work here!" Drake laughed.

"Shut up!" Luna yelled.

"It's called a speaker." Zane laughed.

"Wow, a speaker!" Luna smiled.

"Oh lord." Aster laughed.

After they got their food and ate it, Scarlet put on some music and they were having a blast. Another hour had pasted and they made it to the hotel. Scarlet parked the car in the parking lot and they all got out of the van and grabbed their things. Aster explained that only rich people could afford a hotel like that. When they all were about to go inside, Savannah yelled for everyone to come to her. Zane asked what was wrong. She pointed to a hospital on a hill. Scarlet sighed and put her hand on her shoulder and explained that most hospitals are there to help people who need it, not a place to get hurt.

"Out of all the places to be a hospital, it just had to be here!" Savannah cried.

"Trust me Savannah. No scientist in that hospital wants to abuse you." Scarlet smiled.

Zane kissed Savannah and told her that they all would keep her safe. She hugged him then they all walked to the front entrance. Aster was about to open the door but a guy with blonde hair and a suit walked out and said hello to them. Savannah asked if he was a scientist. He laughed and told her that he worked at the hotel. He explained that he wasn't smart enough to be one. He told them that his name was Gunner. Zane introduced everyone while Savannah was giving Gunner a mean face. Drake was about to go into the door but Gunner pushed him away from it. Drake asked why he pushed him. Gunner explained that they had a strict rule of no weapons, power, or yelling. Luna asked why they couldn't use their power.

"Because all of the workers here took a vow to never use violence." Gunner smiled.

"Explain the science lab human!" Savannah yelled while in her oni form. Scarlet stepped between them.

"Sav, calm down. He isn't a scientist so don't kill him." Scarlet sighed.

"I hate hospitals!" Savannah yelled.

"If I let you go, you have to calm down and get out of your oni form. "Scarlet said.

She got out of her oni form and cried for Zane.

"It's ok kid, that lab is a hospital. People go there who need care, and the reason why it's close to the hotel is because we donate to that hospital. We let them build one near our hotel." Gunner explained.

"I'm so sorry about that. She's been though a lot of illegal tests by evil scientist." Scarlet sighed.

"Oh, I'm sorry she had to deal with that." Gunner said.

Drake asked if they could go in the hotel. He welcomed everyone in and explained that the fountain inside the middle of the lobby was made out of real gold. He also explained that all the paintings in the hotel were made by famous painters.

"Hey Luna, where is your bag?" Zane asked.

"My bag was full of weapons…" Luna sighed.

"Wow.."

"Savannah and I shared a suitcase for clothes.".

"Oh ok."

"Remember guys. No powers or weapon." Gunner smiled.

"Where do we sleep at?" Drake asked.

"I'll show you all to your room!" Gunner smiled.

Everyone followed Gunner up to the elevator. He pushed floor ten. Aster was excited to have the room that was the highest. When they got to the room, Aster was amazed of how enormous the room looked. He asked Gunner if it was a suite. He nodded his head and told them that the left side of the room is a room for the boys and the other side of the room was for the girls and the middle was the kitchen and living room. Drake and Aster quickly ran to the boy's room. It was awesome. It had blue walls and a bean bag chair of a soccer ball. It had light green bed sheets and a painting of a knight. It had three beds. Drake jumped on the middle on and called dibs. His smiled as he laid his head on the pillow. He grabbed the tv remote and put on a basketball game. Gunner explained once more not to use powers or weapons than he left. Zane walked in and was shocked of how nice the room was. He took off his hoodie and put on an orange sports brand tee shirt and white shorts. While the boys were putting comfy clothes on, the girls was doing the same thing. Scarlet helped Savannah with her jean shorts and her teal tank top that had a yellow flower on it. Savannah put her hat on and asked why Scarlet always wore her lab coat. Scarlet sighed and told her that autistic people get stuck on things. Savannah knew that and told her that she was stuck with her stuffed animal. Scarlet took off her lab coat for a second while she put a pink and blue tie dye shirt on. As always she put her lab coat back on her.

"I'm going to call Kaden." Scarlet said while holding her phone and sitting on the bed.

"Cool, they have a tv in our room!" Luna smiled.

"Let's watch a movie!" Savannah said.

"Huh, that's odd." Scarlet mumbled.

"Is everything ok?" Luna asked.

"It says that there is no phone signal." Scarlet explained.

"That is weird." Savannah said.

"Do you guys think something is a bit weird about Gunner?" Luna asked.

"I don't like him!" Savannah yelled.

"Savannah, try to stay calm." Scarlet said.

"Ugh!" Savannah sighed while laying on her belly on the bed.

"I want to look into his mind so bad but he said no powers..." Luna sighed.

"Yeah, I would listen to him. We got invited so we need to obey the hotel rules even if we don't want to." Scarlet said.

Savannah walked to the boy's room and told Zane that she was hungry. He told her that they had a restaurant in the hotel. Savannah begged Zane if they could go. Zane laughed and told her that they could go. As they were about to leave for dinner, Scarlet yelled that she hated her phone. Drake asked what was wrong as Scarlet was hitting her finger on her phone. She explained that she had no phone signal and that she really wanted to talk to her son. Aster took her phone out of her hand and told her to get ready for dinner. She sighed as she fixed her glasses.

As they got to the restaurant, there was a lady with brown hair with pink highlights wearing a suit. She was about in her late twenty's and had her hair in a ponytail standing at the front with a menu. Zane introduced himself as the lady was getting out more menus. She smiled and told them that her name was Kate. She welcomed them in and thanked them for saving her realm from the evil oni.

"Are you a scientist?" Savannah asked.

"Why would you think I'm a scientist?" Kate said.

"Don't mind her." Scarlet sighed.

"I smell pizza cooking." Drake smiled.

"Make sure not to use your powers and please don't have any weapons with you!" Kate smiled.

"We know!" Aster yelled.

"I'm sorry sir, I had to tell you that." Kate sighed.

"Don't be rude Aster." Zane said.

"It's just annoying bro." Aster said.

"Can we be seated now. I can smell the yummy food and I need it badly or I'll go insane." Drake whined.

"Yes, right this way." Kate smiled.

As they got to their table, Zane quickly told Aster to hide the champagne menu from Scarlet. Aster smiled and thew it on the floor and told him that he had it under control. Kate explained that a guy named Bryan would be with them shortly. After five minutes of the friends talking about how nice the hotel was, a guy with black curly long hair wearing a cream colored suit walked up to them and told them that he was their waiter for today. Savannah was confused and asked what he was waiting on her for. All but the oni's laughed and Zane explained that he was going to serve them their dinner.

"Why does he talk funny?" Luna asked.

"It's called an accent." Aster said.

"But I though his name was Bryan not accent!" Drake cried.

"Wait... I thought there was only two oni's." Bryan mumbled

"Huh?" Zane asked.

"Oh uh! What's this one's name?" Bryan laughed while putting his hands on Luna's shoulder.

"None of your human business!" Savannah yelled.

"My name is Luna."

Are you an oni? You look a little different from a human?"

"Space!"

"Sorry. My boss told me that only two oni's were coming."

"Who is your boss. I want to see if he or she is a scientist!" Savannah said.

"I can't, I'm sorry."

"It's ok, we don't have to know." Aster smiled.

"Hey Luna. Can I please see your oni form?" Bryan asked.

"I don't have one. I'm only part oni but mostly Simbyot."

"Oh ok."

"I want cheese fries, chips, cake, root beer, pizza, and a hotdog." Drake smiled.

"Wow, that's a lot." Bryan laughed.

"Give me it!" Scarlet yelled while reaching over to Zane while he had a menu of adult drinks in his hand.

"You don't need wine!" Zane said.

"Ok fine! Only because God doesn't like it..." Scarlet whined while leaning her back in the chair and crossing her arms.

"I'm getting scared." Savannah cried.

"What's wrong?" Zane asked.

"My oni sense is telling me that evil is nearby." Savannah cried.

"Sis, sometimes our oni sense messes up." Drake explained.

"I just want to go to our room and eat." Savannah said.

"You guys may eat in your room. I don't know much about oni's but I can tell she needs some quiet." Bryan said.

"Thank you." Zane smiled.

"No problem."

After going back with their food, Drake began to eat before grace. Zane stopped Drake as he reminded him that they needed to thank God for their food. After they ate, Scarlet tired to call Kaden again but she still didn't have any signal. She thew her phone on the bed and rubbed her eyes as she was getting mad. Luna went to get her star sunglass out of Savannah's bag. She saw a knife in her bag. As Savannah saw that Luna found out that she brought a knife, she quicky ran to Luna and explained that she didn't trust that place and that the knife was for emergencies only. Luna nodded her head as Savannah was zipping the bag back up and smiling at her. When It became nighttime, Zane prayed for everyone and they all went to bed.

It was the middle of the night and it was raining outside. At midnight a woman named Genny sneaked into the friend's room. She tiptoed into the boy's side of the room and walked up to Drake and smiled at him. She didn't understand how a being that isn't an animal or a human could be in the human realm. She had a black suit on with red hair. She whispered to Drake to wake up. Drake turned his body the other way. She tapped his shoulder and he woke up. He yawned and asked who she was.

"Are you the oni named Drake?" Genny asked.

"Yeah?"

These creatures are so weird to me. Genny thought.

"Wait a second. Who are you and why are you in my room?" Drake asked.

"I'm Genny."

"And what do you want?"

"I'm sorry for waking you up."

"I've been woken up by my sister's lots of times so I don't care anymore."

"I would like to show you and your siblings around the hotel. Bryan told me that he thinks you three might be scared of this place so I would like to show you that there's nothing to fear here."

"Yeah, my sister Savannah is scared the most out of the three of us."

"So, what do you say, you want me to give you a tour?"

"Sure, let me put on my clothes and I'll get my sisters."

"Ok, I'll be waiting out in the hall."

This is so wrong. even if they are demonic creatures or not, Genny thought while crying.

As Drake woke up Savannah and Luna, they were mad at him for waking them up out of a dead sleep. Drake grabbed both of his sibling's hands and dragged them to the hallway. They were so groggy they couldn't think straight. Genny introduced herself as they were walking In the hallway. She showed them a picture of a man on a house working and she explained that that was made by a famous artist. Drake smiled and told her that whoever made it was a good painter. After ten minutes of Genny showing things to the oni's around the hotel, she lead them into a room that had nothing in it. Luna asked what the room was. She explained that they could hang out in there while she went to get something. Savannah asked what she was getting as Genny picked up a gun. She aimed the gun at Savannah and Luna yelled that the human lady had a gun. Drake asked what she was doing as she pulled the trigger and shot Savannah in the chest. Luna quickly ran to help Savannah up.

"Savannah, you asked lots of workers today if we were scientist. Let's just say, I work with one. "Genny said.

"I knew it!"

Drake tried to blast her with his oni power but he couldn't. Genny explained that the walls were made out of X stone. She sighed and told them that she was forced to harm them. She quickly ran out of the room and locked the door and pushed a green button that said sleeping gas. Luna tried to break the door open as Savannah was crying. Drake looked up and he saw a green gas was coming out of a vent. All three of the oni's started to cough then they all passed out on top of each other. Genny was crying outside of the room as Bryan walked up to her. He calmed her down as he explained that they had get the oni's or they would die.

"I don't want the oni's to get hurt." Bryan sighed.

"Me neither!" Genny cried.

"Relax, our families will live if we do this." Bryan smiled.

"I guess…"

"Come on, we need to hurry before she gets mad."

"Let's get the oni's into the truck and bring them to the abandoned hospital."

As they made it to the hospital. Bryan grabbed Luna and asked Genny for some help. When they got inside they saw a woman that had a grey crop top and a lab coat on. She had a nose ring and rose gold circle shaped glasses with dirty blond hair. Genny asked what her name was. She told them her name was Mya as she grabbed her gun from her belt. Bryan asked what she was going to do with the oni's. Mya sighed and told them that they better not ask questions. Bryan and Genny were afraid of this lady. Mya walked up to the oni's that were lying on the floor. She moved Savannah's hair out of her face and smiled at her.

"Are you going to be staying here mam?" Bryan asked while shaking.

"Nah. This is a temporarily lab for now. I will be leaving tomorrow morning to get back to The League of Science." Mya smiled.

"Mam, what are these things I had to put on the poor oni's?" Bryan asked.

"It's x stone. It holds any type of power."

Mya told them to put Savannah, Drake, and Luna to on hospital beds. When they did that, Bryan asked why she wanted to hurt the oni's. He told her that they didn't do anything wrong. Genny explained that they were nice and kind. Mya took a deep breath and aimed the gun at Genny. Mya explained that the oni's were not nice beings. She explained that oni's killed and ate her parents right in front of her. Mya walked up to her and put the gun on her head. She begged for mercy. Mya laughed and said she didn't believe in mercy. Bryan yelled for Mya to not kill her. He told her that she didn't do anything. Mya shot Bryan in the head and said that he shouldn't have spoken a word. Genny cried as Mya smiled at her. She explained that she helped her and she would do anything that she would say. Mya pushed her down and shot her in the chest. Mya sighed and grabbed a chair and sat beside Savannah's hospital bed. When an hour had passed, the oni's started to wake up. Savannah opened her eyes to find Mya standing close to her . She yelled at Mya and kicked her away. Mya backed up and explained that she wasn't doing anything. Savannah gave her a mean face as Luna asked what was going on. Mya introduced herself to Luna. She walked up to her and asked If she was an oni. Luna growled at her as Mya was looking at Luna's body. The oni's had a x stone hand cuff attached to the hospital beds. Drake tried to get free from it and yelled at Mya not to hurt them. Mya got out a black mini flashlight and shined in into Luna's eyes. Luna yelled for Mya to quit.

"You dimwit. You will pay for hurting my sister. She told me what you did to her!"

"Savannah. What did I say about telling people…"

"I'm sorry. Don't hurt me!"

"I hate you. You are an evil scientist who gets pleasure out of hurting others!"

"Shut up!"

Mya shot Luna in the arm. Green glowing blood was dripping onto the white hospital sheets. Mya was amazed. Luna called Mya a dimwit and started to cry in pain.

"Go touch it Mya. It will kill you." Drake smiled.

"Drake you idiot!" Luna yelled.

"Care to explain the blood?" Mya smiled.

"No!" Luna yelled.

"Tell me or I'll rip Savannah's guts out." Mya smiled.

"Please don't!" Luna cried.

"Then tell me what being you are to have such weird blood like that. I have studied almost every creature's blood type and color and I have no idea what being you are!" Mya yelled.

"Just tell her Luna. I don't want Savannah getting hurt anymore." Drake sighed.

"That's the only reason I'm going to tell her." Luna sighed.

"Tell me!" Mya yelled.

It was morning back at the hotel. Scarlet opened her eyes and yawned. She sat up in the bed and put on her glasses. She turned her head to see if Luna and Savannah were still asleep. When she looked she was very surprised that Savannah would be up that early. Normally they would have a hard time getting her up. She went to the bathroom to brush her teeth. As soon as she was about to put tooth paste in her brush, Zane yelled her name. She opened the door and asked what he needed. Zane's face looked worried and so did Aster's. As Scarlet was brushing her teeth she asked Zane if he was ok. Zane sighed and told Scarlet that the oni's were missing. Scarlet was drinking water then spit it out from shock. She yelled that if they were pranking her, that was a good one. Aster explained that Drake wasn't in his bed and Zane added that when they came to find Scarlet, Savannah and Luna were missing as well. Scarlet had an idea. They all walked down to the lobby and she asked Gunner if they saw three oni's come out of their room that morning. Gunner stopped typing on his laptop and asked what they needed. Aster yelled that his oni dudes are missing. Gunner smiled and told them that they left. Zane asked where they went. Gunner sighed and said that he didn't know. Zane was confused and asked him that if he was sure that he didn't know.

"Can we please look at the security cameras?" Scarlet asked.

"No, you can't!" Gunner yelled.

"You didn't have to yell." Aster said

"Just please leave me alone!" Gunner cried nervously.

"Yo, calm down." Aster said.

"Is everything ok?" Zane asked.

"Quit asking me things!" Gunner cried

"Are you sure you're ok?" Scarlet asked.

"She's going to kill me. No more talking to me!" Gunner cried while shaking.

"What's going on." Aster asked.

"Genny and Bryan died last night. I don't want to end up like them!" Gunner yelled.

"Wait. How did they die?" Scarlet asked.

Gunner explained that a scientist killed them and that she had the oni's. Zane asked who the scientist was. Gunner started to cry and yelled that he couldn't tell them. Aster slapped his hand on the front desk and yelled for him to tell them. Gunner took a deep breath and mumbled the name Mya. They all were in shock. Zane explained to Gunner that Mya was in jail. Scarlet got out her phone and found a picture of her and Mya together from three years ago. Scarlet showed Gunner the picture. Gunner nodded and told them that it was her.

"So, is the letter we got in the mail a lure to get us here so Mya could kidnap the oni's?" Scarlet grunted.

"Yes!"

"Is the lab on the hill where they are?" Aster yelled.

"Yes, I'm sorry!."

"But that's not the League Of Science lab." Scarlet said.

"It's an abandoned hospital and also, Mya is leaving with the oni's sometime this morning."

"Crap, we need to save them now!" Scarlet said

"Let's think of a plan fast!" Zane cried.

At the hospital on the hill, Mya was making Savannah go into her oni form. She cried and explained that she hated to look like an oni. Mya laughed and told her that Savannah's body was ugly and could just be used for fun, like an animal. Drake gave Mya a mean face and told her that she wouldn't get away with her evil doings. Mya smiled and explained that in ten minutes, they would head to the League of Science. Savannah started to cry. She hated that place with all of her life. She started to remember the evil things of that happened with Mya and her in the lab and all the mean things she said to her. Mya yelled for her to shut up as she was pushing on her shoulder.

At the hotel, everyone was stressed and mad. Aster pounded the wall in anger. That letter was fake and he wasn't happy about it. He hated Mya and he wanted her to stay in jail forever. Zane was getting everyone's things into the suitcases. As Zane was about to put Savannah's stuffed animal in the bag, he saw a black knife and yelled for Scarlet. She ran to him as he pulled out the knife. Scarlet grabbed it and told him that Savannah was very protective. She was looking at the knife and told Zane to finish packing because she had a plan. After Zane and Aster got everyone's things and put the bags into the van, they saw that Scarlet was upset. Aster asked what was wrong with her. She told everyone to hop in the van. When they all got into the van, Scarlet quickly drove up to the hospital on the hill. She got out Savannah's knife and told Zane and Aster to stay in the car. Zane was confused and asked where she was going. She pointed the knife toward Zane's face and yelled that she could save Savannah and her siblings alone and she don't need any help. She slammed the van door shut and went inside. Zane and Aster looked at each other in shock. Aster was about to get out but Zane grabbed his arm and told him that Scarlet wanted to save the oni's alone. Aster explained that she was no match for Mya. Zane calmed him down and told him to let God help her. Scarlet was walking in the hallway. She was watching her back at all times and had the knife ready. She left her gun at her hospital because she thought going to a hotel wouldn't have any need for one. Mya walked out of a bathroom and was looking at pictures of Savannah on her phone. She wasn't paying attention and hit her head on the wall. She yelled out a cuss word as Scarlet was hiding behind a trash can right in front of her. As Mya was rubbing her head, Scarlet ran down the hallway. Mya heard footsteps so she followed them. She found Scarlet looking in a testing room. Mya yelled her name and asked what she was doing there. Scarlet looked at Mya with tears in her eyes. Mya walked up to her.

"Scarlet, what are you doing here?"

"Give me back my friends!"

"Ha, you think a little knife can protect you?"

"It's been a while…"

"Shut up!"

"We used to be good friends."

"Not anymore since you didn't bring the oni's after I said to bring them to my lab!"

"You said you would be with me every day and you promised you would always be my friend no matter what. You said you would help me with making my life the best, even with my autism!" Scarlet said.

Mya ran to Scarlet and grabbed the knife away from her and thew it to the other side of the room as she kicked her to the floor. She fixed her glasses and got up and yelled for her to not hurt the oni's. Mya was about to reach for her gun but Scarlet pushed her down to the floor. She went on her knees and was trying to take the gun from her. Scarlet was on top of her trying to get Mya to stop her from getting her gun. Mya kicked Scarlet's stomach and pushed her off her. As Mya was about to get up, Scarlet took the gun from her and took all the bullets out and thew them to the floor. Mya cussed at Scarlet and ran to the knife. Scarlet grabbed her arm as Mya picked up the knife. She begged her to not hurt the oni's. Mya elbowed Scarlet in the ribs and stabbed her in the chest with the knife. Scarlet fell to the floor in pain. She was holding her chest as blood was dripping out of it. She felt dizzy as she was losing lots of blood. Mya pushed her down to the floor on her back. She stabbed her in the arm than the legs. Scarlet cried for help. Mya kept stabbing her as Scarlet was slowly dying. Mya was about to stab her in the heart, but she got off Scarlet and stood up. She wiped the blood off her hands onto her lab coat. She was covered in Scarlet's blood and kicked her in the shoulder as she walked past her. Scarlet had blood dripping down her mouth as she told her that evil never wins. Mya laughed at her seeing that she was hopeless. She thought to herself that if Scarlet was trying to find the oni's, her other friends would be looking for them as well. She ran back to the testing room where Savannah, Drake, and Luna were and locked the door. She grabbed a different gun as Luna asked why she had blood on her. Scarlet was breathing heavily as it was getting hard to breath. She was losing lots of blood and was dizzy. As her arm was shaking, she pushed a button on her ear com. Everyone was wearing one for the hotel trip just in case something bad happened.

"Wait, I hear one of our ear coms beeping." Zane said while putting in his ear com.

"Guys, I need your help. I'm losing lots of blood and I can't do this on my own. I was just mad. Please help me. I can't walk right now." Scarlet cried

"Ok, we are on our way in!" Zane gasped.

"What's going on?" Aster asked.

"Scarlet is in danger. She could be dying!" Zane cried.

"Let's hurry then!"

Mya put bullets into the gun and walked out to try to kill Scarlet. Scarlet's ears were ringing and she couldn't think straight. She was on the floor on her back holding her stomach as Mya was walking towards her. She went on top of Scarlet and put the gun to her head and asked if she had any last words. Zane and Aster ran and saw Mya was about to kill her. Aster ran to Mya and grabbed her arm and thew her into a wall while pinning her tight against it. Zane ran to Scarlet and was trying to help Scarlet up. Aster punched Mya in the nose and told her that she would pay for what she had did. Mya wiped the blood off her nose as it was bleeding and kicked Aster in the crotch. Aster fell down and let out a little tear. Mya kicked Aster again than ran out of the hospital. Aster got up and yelled that Mya was getting away. Zane sighed and told him that it's to late to get Mya. Zane walked Scarlet to a desk. She laid her arms and head on the desk. Aster kicked a wall and yelled that he was mad. Scarlet told Zane to find the oni's. Zane nodded and ran to the hallway. Aster got some paper towels from a wooden stand in the lobby and walked to Scarlet. He was wiping blood off her and praying for her to heal quick. As Zane was walking, he heard a voice that sounded like Drake. He ran to the voice finding the oni's chained onto hospital beds. Zane yelled Savannah's name as he smiled. Savannah yelled for him to help them. Zane ran to Savannah and gave her a kiss on the head. He explained that Mya got away and that Scarlet was beaten up bad. Luna asked if she was ok. Zane sighed and told them that he didn't know. Savannah started to cry and yelled that she didn't want Scarlet hurt. Zane patted her on the shoulder and told her that God would help her. Drake smiled and told Savannah that God could heal anything.

"Can you please get us out of these beds?" Luna asked.

"Sure thing." Zane smiled.

"The key is over there on the white desk." Drake explained.

Zane picked up the key and walked to Luna and unchained her. Luna got up and thanked Zane. He gave Luna a fist bump and took off Drake's chains.

"I'm scared Zane. I wanna go home now. I never want to go to a human hotel ever again!" Savannah cried.

"Did she touch you?" Zane sighed.

"No. I'm glad she didn't." Savannah smiled.

"That's good." Zane said.

Zane got Savannah out of the chains and she gave Zane a hug. He explained that they needed to see if Scarlet was ok. All four of them ran to the lobby. They saw that Aster was putting rubbing alcohol on Scarlet's arm. Scarlet grimaced and told Aster that she really wanted her lab coat on. Aster sighed and pointed at her lab coat with blood all over it. After they all got Scarlet calmed down, they helped her in the car. Aster told her that he would drive them home. When they got home they saw Len and Kaden drawing chalk in the parking lot of the hospital. As they parked the car, Kaden ran to it and smiled as Aster got out. Zane helped Scarlet out and she sat down on the ground. Kaden looked at his mom covered in scars and blood all over her.

"Is my mommy ok?" Kaden cried.

"I'm fine." Scarlet sighed.

"What the heck happened!" Len cried.

"I need my other lab coat." Scarlet sighed.

After Zane explained what happened, they took Scarlet to a testing room and gave her medicine to help with the pain. Len made dinner for them as the others were making Scarlet laugh to get her mind off Mya. It had been one heck of a trip for the friends. Savannah explained that she hated hotels as she was sitting next to Scarlet in the hospital bed. Scarlet laid her head on Savannah and smiled at her. She told Savannah that she hated hotels as well.

CHAPTER 11
LOVE YOUR ENEMIES

It's been a while since Poison had Luna's blood. He was getting sick and tired. He was lying down on the floor for days. He cried for someone to help him. He got up and walked to the kitchen and opened up the fridge. There was nothing to eat or drink. He started to cry as a shadow was behind him. The shadow said hello to him as Poison's face looked worried. He remembered that voice. It was Satan again. Poison looked up at him and asked why he was there. Satan laughed and told him that he didn't have much longer until he would die. Poison cried for Satan to help him. He told Poison to go back to his home with his wife. He explained that he was too ugly to go home. Satan demanded him to go home or he wouldn't help him. Poison sighed and told Satan that we would head to his wife. Satan laughed and disappeared. He walked to his car and put on his seatbelt and drove off to his home. At the League of science, Mya was shaking a jar of Savannah's urine. She was going to test it. As Mya was doing that, one of her employers was in the lobby at the front desk typing notes on a computer. As she was typing, she heard a banging sound coming from the hospitals entrance. She looked out the glass door and saw a green creature and began yelling Mya's name. She was in shock. She got up out of her chair and ran to the lab to get Mya. Poison was trying to get in but it was locked. He begged for someone to let him in. The worker ran to the lab finding Mya looking at her phone.

"Mya!"

"What is it Molly." Mya asked.

"A green person is banging at the front entrance and yelling out your name!"

'Yeah right."

"I'm being serious!"

"I will go see who this green thing is but if you're pranking me, I will kill you!"

"It's not a prank and also what are looking at on your phone that you've been yelling about all day?"

"First of all, I was yelling because I want the oni's and second, I was not looking at pics of Savannah's lower body so don't think that!"

"You are disgusting and a pervert ok. I know they aren't human but they have a body similar to us humans so that's why me and the others made you a day with a therapist to get rid of your perverted mind and brutalness."

"You what!"

"You need to talk about your problems."

"It is the oni's fault that I have problems!"

"We'll just talk about this later because a green ugly thing is outside."

"Fine. I'll check it out."

"Thank you Mya."

"You're still not making me go to a therapist!"

Mya walked to down the stairs to the lobby. She looked down at her gun on her belt wondering if she would need it. She laughed and thought to herself that Molly was probably pranking her. She turned her head towards the glass door and screamed. Poison yelled for her name. He started to cry and begged her to let him in. Mya pulled out her gun and walked up to the door. Mya asked who he was as Poison was banging hard on the door. He explained that he was her husband Sam Gibbs and that something bad happened to him. He told her that he needed help. Mya opened the door and lifted up his shirt. Mya saw that his stomach had warts and holes everywhere on his body. She was trying not to gag and asked him if he was really her husband. As Mya was examining his body, he grabbed her arm and yelled that he needed help and he was scared.

"Well. I'm scared too!"

"Please Mya. It's me Sam.

"I'm not buying it!"

"Look at my wedding ring then!"

"Sam! How in the heck did you get like that?"

Poison started to cough and fell into Mya's arms. She was so confused and asked what was wrong with him. He yelled that an oni did that to him.

"An oni did this to you!"

"Help!"

"Do you know the name of the oni?

"I think her name was Luna…"

"That little twit!"

Poison's eyes closed and he was breathing heavy. He mumbled that the pain hurt him. Mya laughed and yelled that that wasn't funny. Mya looked at Poison in pain wondering if he was teasing her.

"It's too late Mya. The pain is hurting…"

"No, I'm not letting you die!"

"There is nothing you can do."

"We are going to the hospital. I don't know what's going on. My team will have no clue what to do."

"But you're the only one who has studied oni creatures and their blood!"

"I don't know what to do. Maybe other scientist can help. I would try to do some test on you but my mind is just processing the fact that you look green and about to die of an unknown reason."

Mya was thinking about what to do. She wasn't the type of person who cared for people but he helped her when her parents died so that's why they got married. She took a deep breath and mumbled that she had an idea but she hated the idea she had. Mya ran inside her hospital and quickly took a phone from the front desk.

Savannah and her siblings had a great snack for Zane to try. Scarlet asked what Savannah was holding. Zane told her that it looked like a bag of chips. Savannah laughed and explained that it was oni chips and that Luna got it from the oni realm. Zane sighed and told Savannah that she doesn't need to be eating oni things anymore. Savannah cried and told him that because he let her try human food, she wanted him to try oni food. Zane and Scarlet looked at each other thinking the same thing. It was probably made out of something that was made out of the human body. Luna stepped in front of the two and laughed and told them that she read their mind. Scarlet asked Luna if what they were thinking was true. She gave them a smirk and said that they would have to find out. Savannah handed

Zane the black bag of oni chips then he asked her what the flavor was. She smiled and told them that is was blood favored and it was made out of human skin. Zane's face got pale and looked at Scarlet with her coffee in her hand giggling at him. He sighed and opened the bag. The smell was terrible. It looked like the human chips that are flavored barbeque. He sighed and thought to himself that Savannah really wanted him to try it because she tired human food. Zane gagged than held his nose and took a bite of the chip. Drake grabbed the bag out of his hands and started to snack on it. Zane ran to the bathroom and puked it up as Savannah was looking at him. She asked if he liked it. Zane lifted his head out of the toilet and explained that he loved it but really just saying that to make her happy. She helped Zane up and gave him a hug. As they walked back to the kitchen. Aster ran and gave Scarlet her phone. She took her phone and walked to the hallway. She answered the phone and asked who it was.

"I need some help.." Mya sighed.

"Mya?"

"I need to come to your hospital."

"Ha. After you tired to kill me. That's not happening!"

Poison told Mya that he loved her as he was dying. Mya yelled for Scarlet to help her. Scarlet heard Mya crying. She asked what was wrong and why she needed her. Mya explained that her husband was dying and she didn't know what to do. Scarlet told her that she didn't trust her. She begged her to help. She cried for Poison to wake up. Scarlet sighed and asked if she was near a hospital. Mya answered that she was at the League of Science and she didn't think her workers could help. Scarlet didn't know if she could trust her but hearing Mya cry was very rare. She told Mya that she would use Aster's teleporter gun to send her and Sam to her place. Mya smiled and thanked her. Scarlet hung up the phone and ran to the living room. Drake asked why she looked worried as Scarlet was pacing around the room. She stopped and told Drake, Luna, and Savannah to go into her bed room and lock the door. Luna asked why they needed to do that.

"I have a tv that is also used for security cameras. You don't come out no matter what."

"Why?" Drake asked

"Because I'm going to teleport Mya to the lab and help her husband."

"You are going to do what!" Aster yelled.

"Please no!" Savannah cried.

"What's the matter with her husband?" Drake asked.

"He's dying."

"Just let him die. Mya means nothing to us!" Aster yelled.

"Guys. God says to love our enemies." Zane sighed.

"Why dude?" Aster whined.

"Because loving everyone is making this world a better place." Zane smiled.

"Are you sure you can trust her?" Drake asked.

"I think I can." Scarlet smiled.

"Think doesn't mean yes!" Aster yelled

"We can't let him die just because we all don't like Mya. God wants us to help people not let him suffer like Mya's husband is doing. We can try to help him." Zane cried.

"He's right." Savannah sighed

"Are you kidding Savannah? You hate Mya and you want Scarlet to help her husband! "Aster yelled.

"Calm down dumbo." Luna sighed.

"I guess we can help this dude." Aster grunted as Luna was stoking his arm.

"Me and my sisters will be in your room, I guess."

"Only come out if it's an emergency." Scarlet explained.

"Ok." Drake smiled.

After the oni siblings ran to Scarlet's room, Aster handed Scarlet his teleporter gun and gave her a mean face. She put Mya's name into the gun than a second later she and Poison fell right in front of them. They were in shock that Poison was there. Aster yelled to Mya because Poison was next to her. She mumbled that that was her husband. As Scarlet saw Poison dying, she thought to herself that she didn't know how to help. Mya walked in front of Scarlet and Mya put a gun to her head.

"Hey!" Aster yelled

"Don't hurt her!" Zane cried.

"You're oni friend Luna did this to him!" Mya yelled while having the gun on Scarlet's forehead.

Savannah was looking at the cameras in Scarlet's room. As she saw

Mya putting a gun to Scarlet's head, she yelled for Drake and Luna. Drake looked at the cameras and yelled that they have to save Scarlet.

"Scarlet, I really need you. You're the only other scientist I know that can help!" Mya cried.

"Hey Mya, if you try to hurt Scarlet again, you will pay,!" Drake yelled as he walked in the living room.

"I told you guys to stay in my room!" Scarlet yelled.

"Are you ok Scarlet?" Savannah cried.

"I'm fine. Mya just wants me to help Sam this very moment and I don't know how to help him." Scarlet grunted while looking at Mya.

Scarlet walked to Poison and checked his pulse and she felt nothing. She sighed and told them all that he was dead. Mya yelled that it was all Luna's fault. She ran to Poison and went down on her knees next to him. Zane told Mya that he was sorry for her loss. Mya gave Zane a mean face as she was crying. Luna stared at Poison on the floor. She sighed and ran to Mya and snatched the gun from her hand. Mya was about to take it back but Luna used her webs on Mya's face to shut her up. Mya gaged and wiped the goo off her.

"Luna! What are you doing,!" Scarlet asked.

"Why do you have Mya's gun and crying?" Aster cried.

Luna's hands were shaking as she lifted up her shirt and put the gun on her ribs. Aster was yelling for Luna to stop. Luna shot herself in the ribs and yelled that Zane said even if they were an enemy don't kill them. She thew the gun away and let the blood drip from her side onto her hand. Mya yelled that she was disgusting. Savannah yelled to Mya that she was disgusting and a murder. As Mya and Savannah were throwing insults at each other, Luna put her blood into Poison's mouth. After two minutes had past, Poison began to breath again. He woke up and started to cough. Mya scooted over to Poison and asked if he was ok. He smiled and thanked her for loving him. He got up in Mya's face and whispered in her ear that he needed Luna to live so they needed to kidnap her. Mya nodded and stood up and walked to Scarlet.

"Now that your husband is fine, get out of my home and never come back!" Luna yelled.

"Back up Mya!" Scarlet grunted.

"I have something to say to you." Mya smiled.

"What is it? Do you want to be my friend again?" Scarlet asked.

"I was really surprised that you let me come to your lab to save Sam's life." Mya smiled.

"God says to love your enemies." Scarlet smiled

"I have one more thing to say." Mya smiled.

"What do you want to say to me?" Scarlet asked.

Mya gave her an evil laugh and used her gun to punched Scarlet in the nose. She kicked her down, as blood was dripping off her nose. Drake quickly summoned his oni sword and was about to run to her but Poison blasted him with a toxic blast and it made him dizzy. He fell down as Zane walked up to him to make sire he was ok. Len had Kaden in her grasp as she was running to make sure everyone one was ok. Kaden saw his mom's nose bleeding and in pain. He cried out her name and told her that he was scared of her getting hurt all the time. Mya looked at Kaden wondering who the little wolf boy was.

"Luna just saved your husband and you should be thankful!" Zane yelled.

"Shut up or I'll shoot you!" Mya yelled.

"Son!" Len cried.

"Let me go!" Luna yelled while Poison was pulling Luna by her hair.

"Listen Luna, I feed off you and I need your blood or else I die." Poison yelled.

"Stop squeezing my arm so tight!" Luna cried.

Poison thew Luna to the floor and knocked her out. He took Luna's sunglasses off her forehead and threw them to the other side of the room and thought that the sunglass made he look even more ugly. Drake demanded Poison to stop hurting his sister as Savannah was holding his arm in fear. Mya shot Drake in the chest and Savannah caught him. Savannah laid him down because he was heavy. Drake was grimacing and asked Jesus to help Luna be strong as he knew they were losing the battle. Aster yelled for Savannah go into her oni from. As she was about to do it, Mya reminded Savannah that her oni body was ugly and that her body was just a toy. Aster ran to Savannah and told her that it was not true and that God loves her body. She started to cry and laid her head on Aster's chest. Zane helped Scarlet up as she was getting her head together. She grabbed her gun from her belt and pointed the gun at Mya. Poison used his power to knock out Scarlet. She fell to the floor and Kaden ran to her shaking her. Zane rubbed Kaden's back and told him that she was just sleeping. Len explained to Mya that Kaden didn't need to see his mother like that. Mya laughed and told her that she couldn't believe Seth really wanted a kid with her. Poison told Mya to find and take the water boy's teleporter gun. Mya nodded and ran to the hallway. Aster was following her trying to stop her. He grabbed her lab coat than Mya elbowed him in the chest. He put his back against the wall in pain. She was searching for the teleporter gun. As she was running, she found it lying on a beanbag chair in a game room. She smiled and grabbed it. She put Poison, Luna, and her name into the gun than teleported them to the League of Science. As Mya was teleporting away, Aster tired to stop her, but it was too late. Aster yelled that he hated Mya as he starting running to the others. He quickly ran to them and cried that Mya won. Scarlet kicked a trash can over and walked to her room. Savannah followed her as Scarlet slammed her door shut. The others ran to Scarlet's door and Zane asked if she was ok. She opened up a closet and grabbed out a tiny bottle of alcohol. She opened it up and began to drink it. Aster was knocking on her door asking what she was doing.

"I looked in your mind Scarlet. Getting drunk is not the way to handle things!" Drake yelled.

"It's all my fault. If I didn't bring Mya and Poison here, Luna would be safe!" Scarlet cried.

"It's not your fault sweetie." Len smiled.

"I was the one who let Mya come here!"

"You're just very trusting and want to help people. God likes when your kind. Even though we all make mistakes, you are still cared about." Zane explained.

"I hate Mya so much. I can't take it anymore. She's a perverted brat!" Aster yelled.

"I hate her as well!" Savannah cried.

"Luke 6:27 says, but those that are listening I say to love your enemies, do good to those who hate you, bless those who curse you, pray for people who mistreats you." Zane quoted.

"What if Mya finds out about Luna's blood, she'll probably use it for evil." Scarlet sighed.

"Welp, she already knows." Drake laughed.

"She knows!" Aster yelled.

"And it's your fault Drake!" Savannah yelled.

Luna was on a gurney and she had needles with tubes on the end in her head, arms, belly, legs, and hands. She only had her bra and underwear on. Poison put her clothes in a bright orange biohazard bag. Mya walked up to Luna and yelled for her to wake up. Luna jumped and was looking around the lab. She asked where she was and what was in her skin. Mya laughed and told her that she was at the League of Science. Luna gave Mya a mean face. Poison laid Luna back down. She was looking around the room seeing lots of tools and equipment.

"When you and your siblings were captured by me from that little hotel trip, your brother said your blood can kill any being so I've decided to kidnap people in the city to be my test subjects. I'll put your blood into the people I kidnap and see what will happen." Mya explained.

"And I will be eating your blood." Poison smiled.

"You guys are monsters!" Luna yelled.

"You are a monster!" Mya yelled back.

"You're probably wondering why you have needles hooked into your body?" Poison asked.

"No duh!" Luna yelled

"Care to explain Mya?" Poison laughed.

"You will pay for this!" Luna cried

"Shut up and listen to my wife!" Poison yelled.

"That machine over there looks like an MRI scan but you'll be closed inside it." Mya smiled.

"It will be pitch dark in that machine." Poison laughed

"Let me talk Sam!" Mya grunted

"Sorry Hun…"

"Anyway, the needles inside you are going to be hooked up to tubes inside that machine. Your blood will flow into the tubes and out into a container. This is an easier and faster way than to keep drawing your blood for like for three hours." Mya explained.

"Why do you want to do this to me." Luna cried.

"I need your blood idiot and also my wife needles lots of blood to put in people!" Poison yelled.

"Put her into the machine." Mya laughed.

"Wait, wait, wait, please don't!" Luna yelled as Poison was pushing her into the machine.

"All we need now is some test subjects." Mya smiled.

Poison locked the machine as Luna was yelling to let her out. Luna was in darkness. She couldn't see anything. Mya pushed a green button on the machine and it started to beep. Luna was getting scared and cried for help. As the beeps were getting louder, Luna's blood was flowing out her body into the tubes. As it was flowing, she could see her green glowing blood going into the tubes. At least she had a little light in the machine. When she tried to move, the needles were digging deeper into her skin. She cried and prayed for Jesus to save her. After an hour had past, they had taken a gallon of her blood. Mya shut the machine off as Poison was looking in the plastic container where the blood was held. He smelled it and put his finger in it. He put the blood in his mouth as Mya was getting Luna out of the machine. Mya told Poison to grab a wheelchair for Luna and to get straps to tie her up so she wouldn't escape. When Mya got Luna out, her face looked terrified. Mya put on rubber gloves and took out all of the needles one by one.

"I lost a lot of blood because of you dimwits…" Luna sighed while crying.

"Good. We need it." Poison smiled

"I feel dizzy." Luna cried.

"It's probably from the blood loss." Mya smiled while taking the needles out of Luna.

"What is Poison pushing?" Luna asked.

"I'm pushing a wheelchair idiot." Poison said.

Mya picked up the container of the blood and put a lid on it while Poison grabbed Luna's arm. She tried to pull way but Poison was very strong. He sat Luna in the wheelchair and tied her arms and legs up. After they got Luna tied into the wheelchair, Mya told Poison to follow her and to take Luna with them. Luna tried to use her power but Mya had put an X stone collar on her so she couldn't fight back. Poison pushed Luna as he and Mya were walking down the hallway. As they were going down the hallway she testing rooms on both sides. Some of the testing rooms had blood all over the walls. Some had peoples body parts lying in the rooms. Mya was insane and she should be in jail for what she had done to innocent people. As they got to the last testing room on the right, Mya used her key card to open the door. Poison pushed Luna to a corner. She saw a man in a white testing outfit yelling for help. She asked who the man was. Mya sat the container of blood next to the man in the glass chamber. Mya explained that the man was named Bobby and that he would be the test subject. Poison added that her blood would be put into Boddy to see what the blood would do to the man. Luna cried and told them that it would kill the him. Mya laughed and told her that she didn't care. She just wanted to see what the blood would do to humans. She got a syringe from a white cabinet and walked over to Boddy. Poison turned on a speaker so Mya could talk to Boddy. She explained that he would be injected with green glowing blood. Bobby was scared and begged for her to let him out. Mya laughed and told him that he should have ran faster to escape her. Luna was screaming for Mya to not put her blood into the poor human. Poison hit Luna in the face to shut her up. Mya took the syringe and filled it up with Luna's blood. She opened the glass chamber and kicked Bobby in the crotch. He fell down in pain as Mya grabbed his arm. She jabbed him in the arm with the syringe. Mya quickly ran out and locked the chamber. Bobby stood up in fear. After five minutes of nothing, Mya started tog get angry. Before Mya could cuss up a storm, Boddy's hair started to fall out. My and Poison stared at him while he was getting sick. Bobby started to throw up blood. He fell to the floor as his guts were coming out of his mouth. Mya smiled and thought it was very fascinating. Luna cried to Mya that she shouldn't do what she was doing. Bobby died before Mya was about to kill him. She laughed and told poison that she didn't have to murder the guy. Luna was feeling bad about herself. She hated what her blood could do to people. Even to oni's that couldn't die. While Mya and Poison were testing Luna's blood on innocent people, Luna's friends were coming up with a plan to save her.

"Zane, Scarlet, and Savannah will go find Mya and distract her while Drake and I will try to find Luna." Aster smiled.

"Let's get going then." Zane said.

"I don't want to go back to the League of Science!" Savannah cried.

"Sis, we have God on our side so don't get upset. Luna needs us and we can do this in the name of the Lord." Drake smiled.

"I'm not scared!" Savannah smiled proudly.

"That's what I wanna here!" Drake smiled while giving her a fist bump

"I'll go get my extra teleporter gun." Aster said.

"Please keep my son safe guys. I hate him doing these types of things." Len sighed

"He'll be safe with us Len." Scarlet said.

"Don't worry." Aster added.

"I'll be ok mom." Zane said.

"I'm ready to teleporter. Are you guys?" Aster asked.

"Yep!" Drake smiled.

"I gotta pee first." Savannah cried.

"You have got to be kidding me." Zane sighed.

"Hold it!" Aster yelled.

As they teleported to the League of Science, there was a robot that was metal but looked like a human girl. Aster asked Scarlet if Mya had a robot as security. Scarlet answered that she didn't when she worked there but that it might have been a new touch to the hospital. When Drake ran to the entrance, the robot grabbed his arm and squeezed it tight. It was cutting off his circulation as he was trying to get free. He cried in pain that the robot must have been made out of X stone because he couldn't use his oni nor Simbyot power. Scarlet got her gun from her belt and shot the robot. The robot quickly turned its head to Scarlet and it glowed red eyes. It thew Drake into a mud puddle and started to walk towards Scarlet. She shot the robot in the eye but it kept moving towards her. Savannah blasted it with her darkness but it did nothing to it. As she tired to blast it again, the hospitals alarms went off. Aster helped Drake and he thought of an idea. While they were fighting the robot, Mya yelled for Poison to get Luna back into the machine. Poison asked why the alarms were going off. Mya explained that Luna's friends might be trying to get her back. Poison grabbed a sedative and jabbed the syringe into Luna's arm. She instantly fell asleep as Poison threw her over his shoulders. Mya knew that Luna's friends were at her hospital. She grabbed her gun from her belt and followed Poison.

Zane dodged the robot and it accidently hit the key pad. The key pad went up in flames. The doors immediately opened. Zane yelled that he got the door open. Aster blasted the robot with his water power. It started to spark and smoke up.

"Guys. The key pad is broken; we can get in now." Zane smiled.

"You and Scarlet go find Luna. We will take care of the robot." Aster said.

"Ok!" Zane said.

Scarlet and Zane ran into the hospital. Scarlet grabbed Zane's arm and lead him into the elevator. Zane asked which floor would Luna be on. Scarlet sighed that she didn't know so they had to guess. She pushed floor five because Mya would always use that floor for her evil testing. As they got to floor five, Poison was walking towards them. Scarlet pushed Zane into a bathroom and she ran inside. As Zane was looking around the bathroom, he saw pee cups and wipes near a little door. He opened the door out of curiosity. He was shocked at what he found. He tapped Scarlet's shoulder and told her that he found Aster's teleporter gun. Scarlet smiled and told him that Mya was trying to hide it but she didn't hide it that well. Zane grabbed the gun while Scarlet was checking to make sure the coast was clear. Zane suggested that they use Aster's teleporter gun to teleport to Luna. Scarlet thought that was a great idea as he was turning a switch to send them to Luna's location. When they got to Luna, they didn't know where she was. Zane was looking all over the room for her. Scarlet told Zane that she might be in the machine in the middle of the room. Zane didn't know what that machine was for so he asked what it was. Scarlet explained that it was kind of like an MRI scan but Mya must have added some different parts to it to alter it. Zane opened the machine up so find Luna breathing heavily and crying. Scarlet instantly pushed the gurney out from the machine. Luna begged for help. Scarlet took off all of the needles than Luna instantly hugged her. Zane asked if Luna was ok. Luna cried that Mya killed people with her blood. As Soon as the three were about to run to the others, Mya walked in with her gun and grabbed Zane and put it to his head. Scarlet grabbed her gun and pointed it at Mya.

"Don't you dare!" Scarlet yelled.

"Leave them out of this Mya!" Luna cried.

"Please Mya, he has a life ahead of him!" Scarlet cried.

"Like I care." Mya laughed.

"Let me go!" Zane cried.

Luna was searching for the X stone remote to take the collar off herself. As Scarlet begged and begged for Mya to not kill Zane, Luna unlocked the collar and blasted Mya in the face with black sticky goo. Mya dropped Zane to the floor and was trying to wipe the goo off her face. It got in her eyes and she yelled that she hated all of them. Scarlet kicked Mya to the floor and grabbed her gun and took the bullets out and thew them into a trash can next to her. Mya took off her glasses and spit out the goo that was dripping into her mouth. Scarlet helped Zane up and asked if he was ok. He nodded and thanked Luna and her for saving him.

"Scarlet. Help me now!" Mya yelled.

"No, I'm not your worker anymore." Scarlet said

"Scarlet, you are my best friend, come on." Mya laughed.

"Let's leave this heck." Luna said.

"It's so sticky and it smells bad!" Mya yelled.

Luna ran out to the hallway and fell to her knees. Zane and Scarlet walked up to her and asked if she needed anything. She cried that she wanted to be a normal Simbyot. Zane rubbed her back as Drake, Savannah, and Aster ran in to see the others. Mya was yelling that they wouldn't get away with what they did as she was trying to stand up. She wiped her face and stood up than Savannah blasted her all the way into a wall. She laughed and told Mya that, that's what she gets for abusing her in many ways.

"Did you destroy the robot?" Zane asked.

"Yep." Drake smiled.

"I'm going to take the robot to our lab and maybe add a thew things and make it our robot." Aster explained.

"I hate all of you brats…" Mya sighed while grimacing.

"Stop throwing a fit!" Scarlet yelled.

"Let's go home guys." Zane smiled.

"Luna?" Zane mumbled while Luna was sitting in a corner.

"Is she ok?" Savannah cried.

"I'll go see." Zane said.

I'm a monster. My blood killed that guy, Luna thought while crying.

"Hey." Zane smiled.

"Leave me alone human!" Luna yelled.

"Luna, tell me what's bothering you." Zane sighed.

"Sis, you good?" Drake asked.

"I'm a freak!" Luna yelled.

"You are not." Drake said.

"Why would you say that you are a freak?" Savannah asked.

"I want to be normal!"

"You are." Scarlet said.

"No, my blood killed a human man. Blood isn't supposed to kill people!"

"Listen Luna. We are all different in our own way. God made everyone different and special." Zane smiled.

"The devil makes oni's dummy!" Luna yelled.

"Therefore, if anyone is in Christ, he is a new creation, the old has passed away, behold the new has come, Zane said.

"You are not the same, Satan is not your maker." Aster smiled.

"God is your father now, and mine too." Savannah smiled.

"Thank you all for caring for me. I am so thankful for all of you."

"Let's get going before Mya gets out of Luna's goo." Scarlet explained

Aster used his teleporter gun to send the friends back to Scarlet's hospital. Kaden quickly ran to his mom and kissed her arm. Scarlet smiled and picked him up and asked Len why he wasn't in bed. Len sighed and told her that Kaden wanted to wait for her to come home to be sure she was going to be ok.

"I'm sorry, I should have put him to bed. "Len said.

"It's fine." Scarlet said.

"And by the way, what is the red X on the calendar?" Len asked.

"Crap, I forgot!" Scarlet yelled.

"What's wrong Scarlet?" Zane asked.

"The blood moon is this week." Scarlet sighed.

"Please tell me you're joking?" Luna cried.

"I'm sorry." Scarlet sighed.

"I hate my life!" Luna yelled while crying

"Isaiah 43:2 says, when you pass through the waters, I will be with you and when you pass through the rivers, they will not sweep over you, when you walk through the fire, you will not be burned, the flames will not set you ablaze." Zane said.

"Zane's right, God will be with you when you're the lunar destruction." Scarlet said.

"You promise?" Luna cried.

"We all promise." Savannah smiled.

"I love you all." Luna cried.

"Let's get some sleep, try not to think about it." Aster said.

"Drake, can I sleep with you?" Luna asked.

"Of course." Drake smiled.

"Me too?" Savannah asked.

"Ugh. Fine I guess but I'm a chunky oni so please leave me some room." Drake laughed.

"You're funny bro." Aster laughed.

"I like food." Drake smiled

"Hey Luna." Savannah smiled.

"What is it." Luna asked.

"It's ok to be scared of things. Mya always wanted to take me and when she did take me, she did really evil things to me. She mentally abused me by telling me that my oni body was ugly and also she sexually abused me and said that I was her toy. She physically abused me by doing evil experiments on me. You're not alone Luna, I had to go through lots of pain in my life. Like when Scarlet was evil and when my dad killed mom or when oni's wanted to keep selling me for oni money because I have no heartbeat, BUT!, when I met Zane and the others I had hope and I felt safe and I will help you to be safe." Savannah explained.

"I love you sis." Luna smiled while hugging her

"Cannon ball!" Drake smiled than jumped on top of both of them and they all fell down.

CHAPTER 12
BABY ONIES

Do you remember Arlo? He's been trying to find a way to go back into the human realm. After Scarlet used her gun to blow up his staff, he's been trying to fix it. He called an old friend because he had a great plan for his daughter and her half siblings. His name was Time Master, an oni who uses his evil power to make all beings become little or old, send people to the past and future, or just down right wipe them from existence. He wears a steam punk like outfit with a green top hat that has a clock on it. He wears gold rings on all of his fingers. He has the looks of an oni but one of his horns had been broken off and it never grew back. That's why he wears his hat out in public. As Time Master got to Arlo's mansion, Arlo welcomed him in. He got a wine glass and put some human blood in it for his guest. Time Master thanked him and they both sat down on a purple and black sofa. He asked Arlo what his plan was for his daughter. Arlo smiled and told him the plan. Arlo explained that Time Master had to use his power to turn his daughter and her dumb half brother into babies so Arlo could kidnap Savannah without any distractions or fighting. Arlo wanted to be the king of the oni so he needed Savannah's power in order to do this. Time Master laughed and asked why he wanted Luna to be a baby. He sighed and explained that when he finished making the human realm into darkness, Time Maser would turn Luna back to normal and make her become evil again. He loved Arlo's plan so he agreed to help. They both shook hands and Time Master used his oni staff to find the three dumb Christian oni's location.

In the human realm, Aster and Luna had their first date. It was Luna's first time not being promiscuous with a guy. When they got back, Zane asked how it went. Aster smiled that it went great and that Luna tried ice cream for the first time. Zane asked Luna if she liked it or not. Luna smiled that they needed to go again to the ice cream place. As Luna was talking all about her date with Aster, Drake came in yelling for Zane to help him. He asked Drake what the problem was. He explained that Scarlet was making him do laundry. While Drake was whining, Savannah asked Zane if he could tuck her in for a nap. Zane sighed and told her that he would be there in a minute. Savannah had gotten really attached to Zane. He couldn't even go into the bathroom without Savannah crying for him to come out. He loved her but people with autism don't understand about personal space. As he was about to take Savannah down for a nap, Drake warned that his sister shouldn't go into her room. She asked why as she was holding Zane's arm. Drake and Aster started to laugh at each other. Zane sighed and asked what they did do to Sav's room. Scarlet walked in to tell Savannah that there was a syringe with a note that says this is from Aster but Drake looked into her mind yelled for Scarlet not to tell what was in Savannah's room. Scarlet gave Drake a mean face and asked him to look into her mind. Drake smiled and looked into her mind than cried that she was mean. She grabbed Drake's arm and told him that he knows that Savannah hates syringes and anything that is involved with things that scientists use. He laughed and told her that he and Aster just like to prank. As Savannah heard the conversation between Drake and Scarlet, she blasted Drake with her darkness and he fell to the floor. He laughed and told her that he was sorry. Aster hid behind Luna as Savannah gave him *an I wanna kill you face*. Aster told Luna to protect him but you know how Luna is so she pushed Aster right in front of Savannah. Aster wined that Luna was cruel. Before Savannah could blast him, Scarlet grabbed Savannah's arm and told them that she needed to say something to them. Zane asked what she wanted to say as Savannah ran to hug him. Scarlet asked Aster about what they wanted to do with Mya's robot. Drake smiled and suggested that it could be used as a cookie maker. Luna slapped his shoulder and shook her head at him. As they were thinking what to do with it, Kaden ran in crying that he heard someone. Scarlet told him that they don't hear anything. Kaden kept poking his mom telling her that someone was in the hospital. She picked him up and asked if the voice was familiar. He shook his head as he was crying. He laid his head on her chest and told her that he was scared. Luna told Kaden that she would check it out. As Luna was about to head to the hallway, a tall oni that looks like a guy that was back in the steam punk days said hello to her. Luna yelled that Kaden was right. She backed up and went next to Savannah and Drake and asked him who he was. He laughed and told them that his name was Time Master, an oni who was the master of time. Drake asked what he wanted as he summoned his oni sword. Time Master summoned his staff and used it to teleport Drake, Luna, and Savannah to a deep cave in the oni realm. Scarlet grabbed her gun and shot Time Aster in the leg. He yelled that she was a brave human but she couldn't defeat an oni. He teleported to the cave as Aster was about to blast him with water but it was too late.

Savannah, Luna, and Drake were falling into a big pool area in a cave that had an orange liquid in it. Before Luna could fall into the liquid, she used her webs to swing to the top of the cave. She climbed up to a rock that was hanging above the liquid and yelled for Savannah and Drake. Drake used his webs to stick to the wall and onto Savannah's arm so they wouldn't fall. Drake told Luna that they were ok. Savannah cried that she couldn't hang on for much longer. Drake's webs were beginning to break as he was trying to hold Savannah's arm the best he could. As Luna was thinking of a way to get them away from the pool, Time Master pushed Luna to the hard ground on the big rock. She got up and summoned her Simbyot knife.

"Dang it. the wrong oni!" Time Master yelled.

"Huh?" Luna said.

"I can't hold on for much longer!" Savannah cried.

"Hang in there sis!" Drake yelled

"Do you really want to fight me? I'm the best fighter." Time Master laughed.

"Sure butt hole. You will pay for harming my siblings." Luna smiled.

"This will be easy. You're so skinny and short. You look rough but you aren't, little goth girl."

Time Master grabbed Luna's shirt and threw her down to the floor and she fell hard on her face. She got up and picked up her knife and she stabbed him in the chest. He kicked her down and pulled out the knife and thew it at her but she grabbed it before it hit her chest. Time Master was surprised at how good of a fighter she was.

"You're so skinny and weak." Time Master laughed as Luna stabbed him in the eye.

"Ok! You are not weak!"

"Listen, you will never hurt my siblings again and if you do, I will rip your guts out and skin you till your just bone. Do you understand?" Luna smiled.

"Geez, you're scary."

While Time Master and Luna were fighting, Savannah fell into the orange liquid. Drake cried Savannah's name as he tried to catch her but failed. Drake told Luna that their sister fell into the liquid. Luna dogged Time Master's oni blast and told Drake that she was trying to save him. Luna reached for his hands but before Drake could grab her hand, Time Master stabbed her in the hip. Luna pushed him away as blood starting to drip down her leg. Time Master was in shock. He had no idea Arlo's daughter had green glowing blood. He ran to Luna and touched it. Luna laughed and called him a dummy. As he was looking at Luna's blood on his finger, his skin started to burn off him. He screamed and yelled for help as Luna told him that he deserved it. He was so confused. He never felt pain like that in his life. As Luna was about to save Drake, he fell into the liquid. Luna sighed and thought to herself that she had failed. She walked to Time Master and watched him die as she was crying.

Arlo is gonna be mad at me. I messed up his plan...

"Welp. Sorry I killed you." Luna said as his eyes closed.

As Luna was sitting on the rock for about ten minutes. Aster finally found his teleporter gun. It had been charging so they couldn't use it but now it was finished. He quickly teleported the oni's back to the hospital. As the three oni got back. They all stared at Drake and Savannah.

"What the heck happened to them!" Scarlet yelled.

"Luna, what happened?" Aster asked.

"I don't really know but they fell into a big pool thingy that had orange water in it." Luna said.

"They are babies!" Zane cried.

"Well, Drake looks more like Kaden's size, so probably about five or six." Scarlet explained while Drake was picking his nose.

"Sav looks like about one or two." Aster added while Savannah was drooling on the floor.

"My dad is behind this…" Luna mumbled.

"Huh. What does he want?" Aster asked.

"I have no idea." Luna sighed.

Drake had a purple wizard hat on with just purple shorts with skulls on them. As they were looking at Drake he started to cry. He cried that humans were near him. He ran out of the living room and went down some stairs. Zane told Scarlet to check up on him. Scarlet nodded and went to find Drake. As Scarlet begin to look for little Drake, Savannah started to cry. They all looked at each other wondering what to do.

"Luna. It's your siblings. You deal with it." Aster smiled.

"Hey! I'm not doing this all by myself!" Luna yelled.

"I think Sav pooped her pants." Zane cried.

"Zane, you can change Savannah's diaper." Aster said.

"No, I can't. She is my girlfriend and my mom says it's inappropriate to see her girl things!" Zane yelled.

"She is a baby. It's different." Aster said.

"You smelled it first Zane. You do the job." Luna laughed.

"Sav is your sister. You do it!" Zane yelled.

Savannah was crying even louder and Luna stuck her tongue out at Zane then picked up Savannah. As Luna was holding Savannah. Scarlet was trying to find Drake. She checked the lab and the kitchen, and some of the testing rooms but couldn't find him. As she got to the bed rooms, she checked her room to see if he was hiding in one of the bed rooms. Drake started to cry for his mommy and daddy. He yelled for them so loud Scarlet heard him yelling underneath Scarlet's covers. His wizard hat was on the floor in her room so Drake must be in her bed. Scarlet walked up to her bed and lifted the covers and saw Drake crying and his nose running.

"Mommy! Daddy! Where are you. I need you." Drake cried.

Wait, I think they might have lost their memories. Scarlet thought.

"A human!" Drake yelled.

"Hey, its ok, I'm your friend."

"Back away or I'll eat you!"

"Yep, they lost their memories…"

"I want my mommy!"

"Drake, don't you remember me?"

"How do you know my name?"

"Because I'm one of your friends."

Scarlet picked up Drake's hat and he grabbed it and put in on. He stared at Scarlet for a second than ran off to the hallway. Scarlet followed behind him and picked him up. He was squirming and yelling for his mom. He bit Scarlet's arm then she let go. He ripped part of her lab coat and her arm started to bleed. She held pressure to her arm and told Drake to stay with her. Drake cried that he would never listen to a human. He ran away from Scarlet as she yelled for Drake to come back. As she was about to go look for Drake, Zane and Aster grabbed Drake's shirt to make him stop running.

"Gosh, Drake is a mess. He has snot and tears all over him." Zane sighed.

"I don't want to be a pet!" Drake cried and laid on the floor.

"We will never do that. You are not an animal." Zane said.

"Daddy says to never trust a human." Drake said while crying.

"He is a lair, don't trust your father." Aster said.

Luna gave Savannah to Zane than Luna went beside Drake. She smiled at him and he stared at her. As he looked at Zane, he saw that he was holding his little sister.

"Wait, my sister is taken too!" Drake gasped.

"We didn't take you guys. You live here." Luna said.

"Who are you?" Drake asked.

"I'm your other sister." Luna smiled.

"No, you're not!" Drake yelled.

"Hey Luna I have a good idea. Can you read his mind so we know what he is thinking? Maybe we can calm him about his bad thoughts?" Scarlet asked.

"Sure." Luna said while reading his mind.

"You can read minds too?" Drake smiled.

"Now there's a smile." Zane laughed while Savannah farted on him.

"Is she pooping again?" Aster laughed.

"I think so." Zane gaged.

"Luna, do you know what that orange stuff was?" Scarlet asked.

"I don't know what it is. All I know is that it turned them into babies. Savannah was in there the longest so that's probably why she is so young." Luna explained.

"I want to go home!" Drake cried.

"You are home dude." Aster said.

Drake ran to the kitchen and was hiding under a table. Kaden was in the kitchen and he saw Drake as a baby. Kaden was a little confused but he didn't like people to be sad. He put down his sippy cup and ate the last part of his cookie. He looked under the table seeing Drake upset.

"Why you sad?" Kaden asked.

"Humans got me." Drake cried.

"You want a hug? That makes you not sad." Kaden smiled.

"Yesh." Drake said and ran to Kaden than they both hugged.

"It ok to be sad" Kaden smiled.

"You a nice wolf boy." Drake smiled as he hugged even tighter.

"Thank you Drake." Kaden smiled and patted him on the head.

Scarlet and Zane ran into the kitchen seeing Kaden and Drake hugging. They both smiled at the little ones and Scarlet grabbed her phone from her lab coat and took a picture.

"Let's play tag." Kaden smiled.

"What tag?" Drake asked.

"It a game." Kaden said.

"Ok." Drake smiled and they ran out of the room.

"Kaden, you almost knock mommy over!" Scarlet said.

"Ha, those two are going to play well together." Zane smiled.

Luna was trying to change Savannah's diaper. It was very difficult for her because Savannah wouldn't stay still. She grabbed Luna's sunglass and began to chew on them. Luna told her to not break them as Savannah smiled at her. As she finished putting the diaper on for her sister. She was walking to the living room but Scarlet yelled that she couldn't find Kaden or Drake.

"We need to know what that orange stuff was." Aster sighed.

"Luna said the person who took them was named Time Master or something. That's all she knows." Zane said.

"I might have an idea." Aster said.

"What is it?" Zane asked.

"Scarlet and I will try to make an antidote to turn them back to themselves while you and Luna watch Drake and Savannah." Aster explained.

"Ok, sure, I love to play with babies." Zane smiled.

"Do you guys know where Drake is." Luna asked?

"We can't find him or Kaden." Scarlet said.

"I'll look at the cameras." Aster said and they walked to the security room.

"Let's hope Drake didn't eat Kaden." Luna said.

"Hurry up!" Scarlet yelled and ran to the room. As they got there, Aster sat down in a chair and looked at the cameras.

"Huh, I don't see them anywhere." Aster said.

"We need to find them!" Scarlet cried.

"Did you check the basement?" Zane asked.

"No, we didn't." Luna said.

"Wait, if they are in the basement, they might turn the robot on!" Aster gasped.

"Crap, let's go then." Scarlet said.

Kaden and Drake were walking around in the basement. As they were looking at boxes of old science equipment, Drake saw a robot in the corner. He ran to it and put his finger on the robot's leg. Kaden told Drake that Aster named the robot Clara. He smiled and told Kaden that the robot looks nice and that they could play with it. Kaden cried that his mommy said that it was dangerous. Drake smiled at Kaden and told him that it would hurt them because he has a power of darkness. He said oni's are powerful. He pushed a green button next to Clara. Kaden grabbed Drake's hand and told him that his mommy would be mad at them. While the robot was turning on. Everyone found Drake and Kaden next to Clara.

"Holy crap, did you guys turn the robot on!" Scarlet yelled.

"Human!" Drake yelled and hid behind the robot.

"Drake, that robot is dangerous." Scarlet said.

"Wait, I thought it was powered off." Zane said.

"Drake pushed a button than it turned on." Kaden smiled.

"Guys. Savannah is hungry. I just read her mind." Luna yelled.

"Sav bit me." Aster cried.

"It was funny." Luna laughed.

"We are coming to get you Drake. It's ok." Zane said.

"Kill all people who Mya hates!" Clara yelled than picked up Drake.

"I thought we were together; this relationship is over!" Drake yelled.

"Wow, he is in love with the robot." Zane laughed.

"Luna, we need some help!" Scarlet yelled.

"Hey dimwit, don't hurt my brother!" Luna yelled and used her webs and knock the robot down.

"I'm scared!" Drake cried and ran to Luna.

"It's ok little crazy head." Luna smiled.

"Aster, this is why we do not bring home any of Mya's things!" Scarlet yelled.

"Well, it looked cool." Aster whined.

"Hey water boy, try using your water power!" Luna yelled.

"Oh, right, robots hate water." Aster laughed and ran to the robot and blasted it.

Scarlet picked up Kaden and wiped his tears off his face. Kaden told his mom that he was sorry he brought Drake down to the basement. Savannah wanted her brother so Zane let her hold Drake's hand. She smiled at Drake and started to blabber. As they all got themselves together, Zane had an idea to get Drake and Savannah back to normal. Zane handed Savannah to Scarlet as he was about to tell his idea.

"We can call our old friend Talon and see if he knows what that orange stuff was." Zane explained

"So, we get the guy who was lazy and let Savannah get taken by Arlo." Aster said

"It's our only option." Zane said.

"I want down!" Drake yelled.

"Ok, relax,." Luna said and put him down.

Drake went up to Scarlet and was feeling her skin. He was hungry and he smelled Scarlet's blood. He thought her blood was the best blood because it smelled really sweet to him.

"Uh, whatcha doing?" Scarlet asked.

"No, no, no, you're not eating her!" Luna yelled and picked up Drake.

"I hungry!" Drake cried.

"I'll call Len to get us a pizza and some baby food." Scarlet said and got her phone as Savannah was drooling on her lab coat.

Drake got away from Luna and ran to Scarlet and was about to bite her leg.

"Drake, no!" Luna yelled.

"Drake, you love pizza. We can buy you a pizza." Zane said.

Drake bit Scarlet on the leg. She kicked Drake way from her and told them that she would be in her room hiding from the little demon child. She handed Savannah to Aster and took Kaden's hand and they walked to her room.

"Dang he has some sharp teeth." Scarlet cried as she was limping to her bed room.

"I like her blood. It's different than normal human blood. It has a hint of salt in it." Drake smiled.

"Drake, don't eat anyone that is in this room. ok dude." Aster sighed.

"But she isn't in the room anymore." Drake said and was running away.

"Ok, I meant no one in this hospital!" Aster yelled.

After ten minutes of settling everyone down. Aster called Talon as he gave Savannah to Zane. Talon answered the phone and asked who was calling him. Aster explained to him what happened to Drake and Savannah. Talon laughed and told him that they were doomed. Aster sighed and grunted that they needed his help.

"Is there any potions that turn people into babies?" Aster asked.

"Yeah, it's rare though." Talon said.

"Do you have any and can I have some." Aster asked.

"No, you can't just give a rare potion away like that!" Talon yelled.

"Savannah and Drake need it. Please." Aster said.

"Nope, sorry." Talon said.

"How about I give you five hundred dollars." Aster sighed.

"More than that!" Talon yelled.

"Five thousand?" Aster asked.

"Of course, I love rich people, I can buy lots of things with lots of money." Talon said.

"Take care of my money." Aster sighed.

"I'll be over." Talon smiled.

Welp, to get my money amount back to how it was, I need more of Savannah's blood to sell, Aster thought.

When Talon teleported to Scarlet's hospital. He saw Aster laying out on a chair in the sun outside of the hospital. He walked up to him showing him the potion. Aster was shocked at how awesome it looked. It was in a glass bottle. It had a golden chains tied onto it. He asked if it was real gold. Talon nodded and said that he needed the money. Aster sighed and handed him Five thousand dollars. Talon asked what he was going to do with the potion.

"Scarlet and I are going to make an antidote." Aster explained and he took the potion.

"Are they cute babies?" Talon laughed.

"Well, Drake is a handful and Sav is just a cute little thing." Aster said.

"So, don't get it on you or you'll turn into a baby." Talon said.

"I'll be careful." Aster said.

"See you later water dude." Talon said.

In Scarlet's room. Scarlet had gotten crazy. She didn't want to die from an oni toddler. She had her gun in her hand and was sitting on her bed. Kaden asked if his mommy got drunk again. Scarlet looked at Kaden and said proudly that she hadn't drank any alcohol in a month. Kaden clapped and hugged her and said good job to her. She asked Kaden if he locked her door. Kaden nodded and laid his head on her. As Scarlet was worried for her life, Aster knocked on her door. She asked who it was as she pointed the gun to the door. Aster told her that they needed to make an antidote fast so they could get drake and Savannah back before the blood moon tomorrow. She told Kaden to stay in her room as she opened her door. Aster He showed her the bottle of orange liquid. She asked if that what turned them into babies. He said yes and they both headed to the main lab on the ninth floor. Aster put on his lab coat and goggles and grabbed out two syringes, one for Drake and one for Savannah. After two hours of working, Scarlet put in one last chemical. They smiled at there success and Aster put the antidote into the syringes. Aster told Scarlet that they were lit and that they did an awesome job. Aster put his lab coat on in a closet in the lab as scarlet grabbed both of the syringes. They walked to the elevator to head to the living room on the second floor.

"I miss the real Savannah." Zane sighed.

"Sweetie, we will get them back to normal but science takes time. Scarlet and Aster are working on... I don't know what they are called but let God handle this. God says to be joyful in hope, patient in affliction, faithful in prayer." Len explained.

"Thanks mom, that really helped me." Zane smiled.

"Thanks Len, now I need a nap because that was too wise." Luna said.

"I know you miss your siblings being their normal age as well." Len smiled.

"Yeah…" Luna sighed.

"I think Luna just wants her sunglasses back." Zane laughed.

"Exactly! Savannah has been drooling on them all day!" Luna yelled.

"Ok, which one do we stick first?" Aster asked as he and Scarlet walked in.

"Did you get it done?" Zane asked.

"Yep, it took long but we did it." Scarlet smiled.

"The lab coat human." Drake said.

"No, no, no. I'm out!" Scarlet yelled.

"Where is Kaden?" Zane asked.

"He's In my room. I will not let him out till we get Drake back to himself because I don't want my son getting eaten." Scarlet explained.

"Wow, you need to relax." Aster laughed.

"I'll do Savannah because she will be easy." Scarlet smiled.

"Dang it, why do I get the hard one?" Aster whined.

"Because Drake wants to eat me!" Scarlet yelled.

Luna sat Savannah down on the couch and held her hand and told her that she had to be a brave little girl. She laughed at Luna and blabbered at her. She put her sister's sunglasses into her mouth as Scarlet went down on her knees in front of her. She smiled at Scarlet and put her hand on her lob coat. Zane was rubbing her leg as Scarlet was wiping a wet cleaning wipe on her arm. Scarlet got out the syringe and poked Savannah in the arm with it and she started to cry. Zane held Savannah as Scarlet put a band aid on her. They all prayed that it would work. It took Scarlet and Aster a long time. Aster walked up to Len having ahold of Drake. He was squirming and crying. Aster forcefully grabbed Drake's arm and poked him. Len kissed his forehead and told him that he was going to be ok. Aster gave Scarlet a fist bump and told her that he hoped it would work. After five minutes of waiting, Savannah yelled Zane's name and gave him a hug and asked why she had a headache. Zane smiled and kissed her on the lips and told her that he missed her. As they all ran to Savannah in joy, Drake asked why everyone was so happy. Aster shook Drake yelling that it worked. Savannah and Drake were confused. Luna explained everything as Scarlet showed a picture on her phone of Drake and Kaden hugging when he was a baby. Savannah laughed at Drake as Scarlet showed her a picture of Zane holding her as a baby. Drake laughed and told Savannah that she was such a cutie. As the two were picking on each other, Scarlet sighed and told them all that the blood moon was tomorrow so they needed to think of a plan at dinner that night.

CHAPTER 13
THE PACK

After the very long day of Drake and Savannah becoming babies. Aster had been working on Clara the robot. After three hours of working on her, he finally got her done. He put his welding torch down and put some clothes on Clara for some fashion. Aster was always into expensive fashion clothes so he put a five hundred dollar white and green tank top on her and some jean shorts. He put one of his rapper hats on her to give her a gangster look. He smiled and turned her on. Clara said hi to Aster and asked him what he needed. Aster was surprised that he had made good technology that can make a robot talk like a teenage girl. He told Clara that he was her new master. She asked why he changed her programming. Aster laughed and told her that she didn't need to be evil. While Aster was talking to Clara, Kaden was asking and asking questions about alphas all day. Scarlet didn't know what to say to him because she didn't know a lot about alphas. Seth never told her about his kind and how the culture was. All she knew was they were part wolf and part human. While everyone was in the living room, Aster introduced Clara to his friends. Zane asked if she was good now because they didn't want the robot to try and kill them. Before Aster was going to explain what Clara could do, Kaden asked her about alphas. She explained that alphas were evil beings that had the power to become any age they want for hiding and tricking other tribes of the alphas. They lived in a different realm from the human realm. They have a wolf tail and wolf ears. There were four different tribes. The bone tribe, the night tribe, the demon tribe, and the blood tribe. Scarlet stopped Clara's conversation and told her not to tell Kaden all about his kind because it would scare him. Aster explained that Clara could answer any question and he started to talk more and more about Clara. Scarlet yelled for everyone to stop talking because Luna was going to be the Lunar destruction soon and they needed a plan. Drake stopped eating his cookie and asked what she had in mind for a plan.

"Drake and I will sneak into the league of Science to take a type of power holder that Mya has." Scarlet explained.

"But X Stone can't hold me." Luna cried.

"It's more of a metal than a stone." Scarlet said.

"Huh, I don't get what you're trying to say here." Savannah said.

"What she is trying to say is that my creator Mya found a metal made by angels and the metal can hold any evil." Clara explained.

"Dang she's good." Scarlet smiled.

"Here is the teleporter gun." Aster said and handed Scarlet the gun.

Drake and Scarlet teleported to the lobby of League of Science. Drake asked where the metal would be while Scarlet was walking to the hallway. She told him to follow her and to be quiet. They got to the elevator and Scarlet pushed the third floor. When they reached the floor, they checked their surroundings to make sure Mya wasn't nearby. They ran to the last testing room on the third floor. Scarlet got out her key card and swiped it so the door could open. Drake saw black metal in a corner next to a hospital bed. Scarlet told him to grab all that he could. As Drake picked up a piece of the metal, Mya walked in not knowing Scarlet and Drake were in there. She looked at Drake and told them that they shouldn't take her things. They turned their heads towards Mya in fear. Mya got out her gun and asked why they were in her hospital. Drake dropped the metal and summoned his oni sword and pushed Scarlet behind him.

"So, where is Savannah?" Mya smiled.

"None of your business!" Scarlet yelled.

"Scarlet, I just wanna see her just at least one more time." Mya laughed.

"We would never let you get near her after the evil testing you did to her. You're disgusting and you make me sick!" Scarlet yelled.

Drake had enough of Mya harming his sister. Savannah doesn't even want to wear anything that shows her body, not even when they want to go swimming or a shorts that were really short, even she hates wearing a tank top and it's been really hot in Science City lately. Mya made her scared and his sister was ashamed of her body because Mya was an abuser towards her. He took a deep breath to calm down and blasted Mya with his power and she fell to the floor on her face. She looked at a Drake as her nose began to bleed. She yelled that she hated him and his two sisters. Scarlet grabbed Mya by the shirt and told Drake to take the metal. Mya gave Scarlet an ornery smile as Scarlet had ahold of her shirt.

"Do you remember back in the old days when you weren't a Christian? We would get drunk and I wanted to be your girlfriend.

"Quit talking about my old life!" Scarlet yelled."

"I thought you loved me. This Christian thing has really gotten into you."

"God forgave me so shut up!"

"Scarlet I have a ton of metal. Let's go." Drake smiled.

"In a minute Drake..." Scarlet cried.

"Are you ok?" Drake asked.

"I was young and gullible and didn't know right from wrong. You were the only friend I had so I let you lead me down the wrong path. God now has a good plan for my life. He brought Seth into my life opening my eyes to a healthy relationship. That proves that God was working in my life before I even knew it. Using Sam was part of God's plan for you. Hopefully you see that. God has shown me these things. Yeah! I can talk to God. Me. A scatterbrained scientist!" Scarlet explained.

"We need to go. Luna needs us." Drake said.

"I'm coming."

Scarlet and Drake teleported back to the hospital. Zane told them that Luna was getting out of control. She'd been crying and trying to fight the evil in her. Luna walked up to Drake and laid her head on his chest. Drake kissed her on the head and told her that they would help her. While Aster and Scarlet were going to set up a chamber in the basement with the metal, something evil was being planned in a different realm. It was three alphas named, Evan, Wayne, and Red. Evan had black hair and pale skin. He had brown eyes and had a big birthmark on his left eye. Wayne had brown hair with yellow highlights. He was every tall and had lots of muscle. His eyes were grey and he had a tattoo of a wolf on his neck. The last alpha was Red. He had red dreads and red eyes. He liked to wear no clothing because his tribe didn't wear clothes. He was part of the blood tribe and his friends were part of the night tribe. They all had wolf ears and a wolf tail just like Kaden. Two years ago, the night tribe leader died from an oni. It had been so long without a leader that the tribe was crazy and was not acting how a tribe should act. They were fighting and were not united. They needed a leader.

"We need our leader but he's been dead for a long time now." Wayne whined.

"I know, if only our leader had a kid." Evan sighed.

"He had a wife. They might have a kid. I don't know." Red said.

"Let's go find his wife and see if they had a kid and if not, we can take the wife." Wayne smiled.

"His wife is a human I think." Red cried.

"Let's just hope they have a kid then." Evan said.

"But his wife was a scientist, what if she does tests on us?" Red yelled.

"He's right." Wayne sighed.

"I don't care, we are alphas, we can handle a dumb scientist!" Evan yelled.

"Yeah, we can do this." Wayne smiled.

"I'm not going." Red cried.

"Yes, you are!" Evan yelled.

"Fine…" Red sighed.

"Let's use the holy staff to take us to the human realm." Wayne smiled.

"But it's the Leaders staff!" Red yelled.

"He is dead. You have to remember that." Evan said.

"Let's just make this quick." Red sighed.

Back at Scarlet's hospital, Aster just screwed the last bolt into the chamber. Scarlet told Aster that they did a great job. Savannah helped Luna down the stairs into the basement. Luna felt so weak that it was hard for her to move. Scarlet opened the door and explained that she put a bed and some things that she likes in the chamber so that it feels safe. Scarlet put in her star sunglasses, her purple blanket, a Tv, and Aster hung up her rock band poster for her. She thanked them for making it feel safe for her. Savannah gave Luana a hug and told her that she loved her so much. Luna smiled and told her that she loved her even more. Savannah looked at her and yelled that she loved her more. They both laughed and gave each other a fist bump. Luna jumped on the bed and told them that it was comfy. While Aster was shutting the door, Len ran down to the basement yelling that three weird people were in the lobby. "Is it a scientist?" Savannah asked.

"Mom, what did they look like?" Zane asked.

"Well, they kinda look like Kaden." Len said.

"Luna, stay here. We will be back." Aster smiled.

"I can't even get out if I wanted to." Luna sighed.

"I'll keep Luna company." Len smiled.

"Ok." Zane said.

"Zane, be careful sweetie." Len cried

"I will Mom."

While Kaden was washing his hands in the bathroom he heard his mom and her friends running by him. He dried his hands and went to see what was going on. He secretly followed behind Aster. When they got to the lobby, they were three wolf people looking around the place. Scarlet asked who they were and why they snuck into her home. Evan looked at Scarlet and smiled that they just wanted to meet someone. Zane looked at Red and asked him to please cover himself up. Red growled at him as Wayne calmed him down

"Mommy, who are they?" Kaden asked.

"Kaden, you were supposed to stay with Luna and Len." Scarlet said.

"Hey, that's an alpha!" Red smiled.

"Is Seth's wife here." Wayne asked.

"What if I say yes, will you kill me?" Scarlet asked.

"That has to be her." Evan laughed.

"What do you want with her!" Drake yelled and summoned his oni sword.

"Back off oni, we don't want a fight, we need one of your humans." Wayne said.

"Wow, they are like me." Kaden smiled.

"Miss Jones, do you have a kid?" Red asked.

"Why would I tell you!" Scarlet yelled.

"Yeah, I'm her kid." Kaden smiled.

'Kaden!" Aster yelled.

"Well, Wayne and Red, take that alpha kid." Even smiled.

"Yes sir." Wayne said.

"You are not going to touch my son!" Scarlet grunted.

"Haha, a human can't boss us around." Evan laughed.

"Leave my son alone!" Scarlet yelled than darkness started to surge in and out of her body.

"You will never take my son away from me!"

Scarlet had darkness forming around her body. Her eyes turned purple and she was spitting out darkness fog from her mouth.

"Scarlet, darkness is forming around you!" Savannah gasped.

"Huh, she can't be oni." Zane said.

"What...how, this is not real!" Scarlet yelled.

"Why didn't you tell us you were an oni." Aster asked.

"I never knew. I can't be an oni, I have human blood!" Scarlet yelled than she passed out.

"Wow, she scared herself that bad that she passed out." Drake laughed.

They all ran to Scarlet trying to wake her up. Savannah cried that she had all features of a human and that she had human blood. Zane calmed her down as Kaden was crying because his mom passed out. Before Kaden was about to run to his mom, Evan grabbed him and put tape on his mouth. Wayne picked up Kaden and they teleported back to the Alpha realm. Aster suggested that Drake should look into her mind so see if she was really an oni or not.

"I have a little of her old history. Her parents were Scientist and I see Scarlet getting tested on by her parents. I'll go back a little more." Drake explained.

"Why would she get tested on. She looks normal?" Zane asked.

"I'll try to go deeper into her mind." Drake said.

"Guys Kaden is gone and so are the three alphas!" Savannah yelled.

"While you're doing that Drake, we need to tell Luna and my mom that we might think Kaden got taken." Zane said.

"Ok, I'll be right here." Drake said.

"Come on guys!" Savannah cried.

All but Scarlet and Drake ran to the basement. Len saw that their faces were very worried. Luna asked why they looked upset. Zane sighed and told Len and Luna that Kaden had gotten kidnapped. Len cried that they needed to find the poor boy. Luna asked where Drake and Scarlet were and Zane told them the shocking news about Scarlet.

"Ha. You're teasing us." Luna laughed.

"It's true." Zane sighed.

"Guys. I have shocking news!" Drake yelled while coming down the stairs.

"Did you find more info?" Aster asked.

"Yes, a lot of it." Drake said.

"Tell us then." Savannah smiled.

"She is an oni. She was adopted by human parents when she was first born!" Drake yelled.

"What else?" Luna asked.

"Guys, where is Kaden!" Scarlet yelled as she tripped down the stairs worried.

"Scarlet, we have some news for you." Aster sighed.

"I said where is Kaden!" Scarlet yelled.

"He got taken by the bad alphas." Drake said.

"We need to save him!" Scarlet yelled.

"Calm down, we will." Zane smiled.

"Teehee, you are an oni by the way." Drake smiled.

"Quit lying." Scarlet said.

"Let us explain." Savannah sighed.

"I'm not in the mood for a prank!" Scarlet yelled.

"Scarlet, Drake looked in your mind and found some things." Aster said.

"Tell her Drake." Savannah cried.

"Your birth parents are oni's and you are too. You were adopted by humans. Your birth dad used a staff to make you look like a human than they sent you to the human realm because they didn't want a child. They were too young. I'm sorry you had to hear that but it's true." Drake explained.

"Is there anything else?" Scarlet mumbled while trying not to cry.

"That's all I can do. It hurts a little when I go too far back in someone's mind." Drake sighed.

"So, Kaden is an oni to right?" Len asked.

"I guess so." Zane said.

"I can't believe it. That's why when I was little I craved humans and I have sharp teeth." Scarlet cried.

"Huh, you don't have sharp teeth." Aster said.

"Mya made me fake teeth to put on so I wouldn't be bullied as a child!" Scarlet cried.

"Take off the fake teeth, I wanna see." Aster smiled.

"I'm floored…" Scarlet sighed than took the fake teeth off.

"Wow, you have teeth like me." Savannah smiled.

"I hate it." Scarlet sighed while crying.

"Don't hate who you are. It's kind of cool that you have different teeth." Luna said.

"Do you need information about oni's?" Clara asked.

"No thanks." Zane laughed.

"Hey Clara, when does a blood moon start?" Luna asked.

"Sun down to sun up." Clara smiled.

"Ok thanks, I have a little longer until the Lunar destruction thing starts." Luna smiled.

"About an hour till sun down, I think." Aster said.

"Actually, one hour and four minutes." Clara said.

"We need a plan to get my son back." Scarlet sighed.

"Hey Clara, do you know the location to where Kaden is? Aster told us that you have a GPS in your programing." Zane asked

"He's in the alpha realm. You guys should go to the alpha dungeon because that's where people get held captive." Clara explained.

"Luna has to stay here but Len and Clara can keep her company." Aster said.

"Ok, the rest of us will go into the alpha realm and find Kaden." Zane smiled.

In the Alpha realm, Kaden was scared. He was on the floor curled up in a ball. He wanted his mommy. Evan lifted his head and asked him what his name was. Kaden told him his name and asked him who he was. Evan laughed and introduced him and the other two.

"Where am I at?" Kaden asked.

"You're in the alpha realm kid." Evan said.

"This place scary." Kaden cried.

"Aww, you're so scared. Haha, deal with it little guy. This is your home now." Wayne laughed.

"Haha, crybaby!" Evan laughed

"Where my mommy at?" Kaden cried.

"Ha! You don't need your mom. You have us and the rest of the pack." Red laughed

"I need my mommy!" Kaden cried.

"Well, you will never see her again." Wayne said.

"This weak kid is not going to be our leader!" Evan yelled.

"But its Seth's son." Red sighed.

"God doesn't give me a spirt of fear but love power and a sound mind. God has my side and also, he helps me all the time, I not scared." Kaden smiled.

"Oh my gosh, you're a Christian?" Evan gasped.

"Yes." Kaden smiled.

"Haha, God is dumb kid, you need to know that." Wayne laughed.

"No, he not. He a good friend!" Kaden yelled.

"Listen kid, you are not acting like an alpha. Our kind is evil bud." Evan said.

"But I not evil, evil is bad." Kaden cried.

"We know evil is bad." Wayne laughed.

"I want to go home!" Kaden cried.

"This is your home now." Red smiled.

"No, I live in a hospital!" Kaden yelled.

"Ha, with a dumb scientist." Evan laughed.

"My mommy an awesome scientist!" Kaden yelled.

Kaden has been missing for an hour. The friends finally made up a plan to save Kaden. Luna's eyes turned red and she had red fog starting to from around her.

"Let me out you dumb idiots!" Luna yelled while banging the door.

"Welp, the blood moon is coming out..." Zane sighed.

"You sure you got her?" Scarlet asked.

"Yes." Len smiled.

"I will slaughter you to death than I will eat you than use your bones as a decoration." Luna laughed.

"Luna, that's not nice." Len said.

"I'm not nice!" Luna yelled.

"Nice try, you can't escape." Scarlet smiled.

"I will eat all of you!" Luna yelled.

"Yeah, yeah." Aster said.

"Not you dumbo. You're too cute to be eaten." Luna smiled.

"Let's go save Kaden." Drake said.

"I will hang Kaden by the head than rip out his guts." Luna smiled.

"Hush it!" Scarlet yelled.

Aster got his teleporter gun and sent them to the alpha realm. Len smiled at Luna hoping that she doesn't escape in some way. She prayed for Luna to stay calm.

"Ha, this place can't hold me forever!" Luna laughed.

"Let's hope Kaden is ok." Len sighed.

"Affirmative." Clara said.

"You humans make me sick!" Luna yelled.

"Sweetie, do you want a glass of ice tea?" Len smiled.

"Shut up." Luna grunted.

After twenty minutes of walking in the Alpha realm. Drake got a little over heated. It was like a desert in that realm. They stopped and sat down for a little rest. Aster sprayed Drake with his water power so Drake wouldn't pass out.

"Clara said that people get held captive at the alpha's dungeon." Aster said.

"Wow Scarlet, your husband was famous.." Drake smiled.

"What do you mean?" Scarlet asked.

"Look, they have a statue of him." Drake said.

"Can we just keep going?" Scarlet sighed.

"Sure, but are you ok?" Zane asked.

"Yeah, I'm fine…" Scarlet sighed.

"Hey Scarlet, how do you feel about being an oni?" Drake asked.

"I don't wanna talk right now. I don't have any sensory tools to keep me sane right now. My mind is a mess and my son needs me!" Scarlet yelled.

While Scarlet was having a meltdown, about ten alphas started to run around them. Scarlet stopped talking and asked what the heck was going on. Zane yelled for the alphas to stop. They stopped and stared at them. One alpha sniffed Zane's arm. He pulled his arm back and yelled at the guy to stop. Every alpha started to chant a song saying humans were evil spirits. Drake asked if they were going to eat them. A little girl alpha pointed a spear at him and laughed at him. Drake backed up and cried for mercy. They started to chant even louder. As they got closer to the friends, one of the alphas told his tribe to take the humans to the dungeon. Drake cried that he wasn't a human so he couldn't be sent there. The alpha just stared at him and told him that to was too bad. Three women that were alphas tied everyone up in chains. Drake was about to summon his oni sword but one of the women used her spear to stab him in the chest than put chains on him. Zane asked if Drake was ok. He cried that she looked cute but she was mean. The woman pulled out her spear from Drake's back. Savannah told the alphas to let them go. She explained that they didn't mean any harm to them. The alphas began to chant a song about victory as they walked the friends towards a big complex that looked scary. Savannah sighed and told Aster that she guessed the alphas didn't like them as she and Aster were walking beside each other.

Kaden was all alone. He didn't have his mommy or her friends. He didn't have Len. He had no one. Evan explained to him about how his father was the leader of the night tribe. Wayne added that they needed to teach Kaden about the ways of the pack. Kaden cried that his mommy could save him. The three laughed at him telling him that he would never see his mom again. Evan told Red and Wayne that they needed to give the kid the crown. Kaden asked why he needed a crown.

"You are our new leader bud." Red smiled

"Why?" Kaden asked.

"We told you this like seven times. Your dad was the leader of the alphas and when a leader dies his son or daughter gets to be the new leader." Evan explained.

"Follow us Kaden." Wayne said.

"Put this on." Red said.

"Why, it not my crown?" Kaden asked.

"It's yours dude." Wayne said as he put the crown on him.

"See, you look awesome in it." Red smiled.

"Now, we will show you to the leaders' throne chair." Wayne explained.

"What your guys names again?" Kaden asked.

"I'm Evan and your second in command."

"I'm Wayne and I'm your body guard."

"And I'm Red and I'm your butler."

"Butt!" Kaden laughed.

"Haha, he dissed you." Evan laughed.

"Let's just keep going..." Red sighed.

"I want uppy!" Kaden smiled

"Ok sir." Red said and picked up Kaden.

Ha, that stupid kid has no idea, Evan thought.

"The plan is going great so far." Wayne laughed.

"I know right." Evan smiled.

They took Kaden down the hallway and he asked where they were taking him. Red explained that they were taking him to his new throne chair. Kaden smiled and pointed to a red velvet chair and asked if that was it. Evan turned Kaden's face away from that room and laughed he was funny. Kaden was confused and asked where the chair was at if the chair in front of him was not it. Red laughed and thew him into a dark scary room. Red knelt down on his knees next to him.

"Ow, that hurt bad." Kaden cried.

"Poor thing." Evan laughed.

"Who that scary guy?" Kaden cried.

"That's Jack, he is going to kill you." Evan said and kicked Kaden.

"Why!" Kaden cried.

"Because your dad was nothing but trash and I want to be the leader and not you. You're just a little weak kid!" Evan yelled.

"But I don't want to die." Kaden said while crying.

"Put him in the chains." Wayne said.

"Ok." Jack said and took ahold of Kaden's hand.

"No please!" Kaden yelled.

"Shut up!" Red yelled.

Jack put Kaden in the chains as Evan walked up to Kaden and said "The only way that I can be the leader is if I kill you"

"Mommy, I need you!" Kaden yelled.

"She is not here!" Wayne yelled.

The friends were now in the dungeon and had no idea how to escape. It was made out of X stone so the oni's couldn't use their power.

"We are hopeless." Savannah cried.

"We can get through this Sav. God promises never to leave us or forsake us." Zane smiled.

"Kaden is probably so lonely and scared." Scarlet cried.

"I have an idea!" Aster smiled.

"It's not gonna work." Scarlet yelled.

"I didn't even say it yet." Aster sighed.

"Tell us Aster." Zane said.

"Watch this." Aster smiled than he hit his arm and a bracelet became visible.

"Wow, what's that?" Drake asked.

"It's a device. I can contact Clara in case something like this happens."

"Hurry, we need to get out of here." Scarlet said.

"Hello Aster." Clara said as Aster asked if she could hear him.

"We are captured in the alpha dungeon and its X stone so we can't use our power to escape." Aster explained.

"Do you know where the key is?" Clara asked.

"They destroyed it so we can never get out." Zane sighed.

"Guys!" Savannah cried.

"Are you ok Sav?" Zane asked.

"Luna is the only one who can break X stone."

"Dang it, you're right." Aster sighed.

"But she is the Lunar Destruction right now." Scarlet said

"I think letting her out is the only option. Sav is right. She can break X stone." Zane sighed.

"Clara, try to get Luna calmed down than let her out of the chamber." Aster said.

"But she is crazy right now!" Len cried.

"We need her." Drake sighed.

"We will be there when we get Luna calmed down." Clara said.

"Thanks." Savannah smiled.

"I'm here to help." Clara said as she was signing off.

"Luna, please calm down sweetie. We all love you so much." Len smiled.

"No, you're lying!" Luna yelled.

"Luna, your friends are in danger." Clara said.

"I have no friends!" Luna yelled.

"Yes, you do sweetheart." Len cried.

"No I don't!"

"You can fight it Luna." Clara said

"Don't let the devil mess with you because I know you can do this. We all love you so much." Len smiled.

"I need help!" Luna cried than went to her knees.

"You can fight it Luna." Len said and went and put her hand on the glass.

"I can't fight it!" Luna cried.

"Come on, you got this girl." Len smiled.

"We need to let you out." Clara sighed.

"No, don't." Luna cried.

"All of your friends are trapped." Len said.

"Len, take this sedative just in case she goes bad again." Clara said.

"OK, thank you." Len smiled.

"You can't stop me from being evil!"

"Just let her out Len."

"Yes, I can escapee this heck of a place!"

"Luna, if we let you out, don't eat me honey."

"It depends on how good your blood smells."

In the dungeon Savannah and Scarlet's autism wasn't making being trapped easy. Savannah was stressed wondering If the alphas were going to abuse her while Scarlet didn't have her calming medicine and was getting worried about Kaden. She was also thinking about Seth and how she really didn't like him.

"Guys, there is something I need to tell you." Scarlet sighed.

"Sure, tell away." Aster smiled.

"I really didn't love Seth that much." Scarlet said.

"What!" Zane asked

"You were so sad when he died." Savannah said.

"I just married him to get away from Mya. She wanted a relationship with me and I didn't want one with her. So when Seth came along I married him. His friends also encouraged him to marry a human. At least we all thought I was a human." she laughed.

"Wow. Didn't see that coming." Drake laughed.

"How did you guys even meet? Alphas don't live in the human realm." Aster asked.

"Mya captured him as a test subject so that I could test on him." Scarlet said.

"Yikes." Drake said.

"I started to fall in love with him but, he was being so demanding and mean." Scarlet sighed.

"Why did you have a kid then?" Zane asked.

"I wanted a kid but Seth only wanted one so that our kid could be the new alpha leader." Scarlet explained.

"I'm so sorry Scarlet." Savannah said.

"He was dying before Arlo killed him. An alpha named Evan put a spell on Seth that kills people. He did that so he could be the leader. Kaden is in real danger if Evan is still around." Scarlet explained.

"Remember that you have us." Zane smiled.

"I know." Scarlet said.

"Let's hope Luna can keep her cool." Aster sighed.

Len got Luna under control as Clara teleported the two of them to the Alpha realm. After just five minutes being in that realm, Luna had eaten six alphas. Len, trying not to puke, grabbed Luna's bloody hand and told her to calm down. As Luna was going to punch Len in the head, they heard Kaden crying and yelling for Scarlet.

"Oh my gosh. Kaden we are coming sweetie!" Len yelled.

"Len, is that you?" Kaden asked while yelling across the room.

"Yes baby, it's me and Luna." Len smiled.

"Help me!" Kaden cried.

Len followed the voice of Kaden and found him chained up. An alpha had an axe by his neck. Len cried for the alphas to stop. They all looked at Len wondering how a human go into the complex. Red got his spear and was about to stab Len in the chest with it but Luna ran up to him and stabbed him in the eye with a knife. He fell down as his eye was bleeding. He now didn't have a right eye. He screamed at the top of his lungs begging for help form the others. Wayne thew his spear at Luna but she grabbed it before it hit her. She thew his spear down and blasted him with a red blast. She walked up to him and skinned him to death. Len ran to Kaden and she kicked Jack in the crotch. Jack pushed Len way from him and yelled that he would kill her. Luna thew a knife at Jack's chest and he died. Len covered Kaden's face because Luna was getting very violent. Evan and Luna were fighting for ten minutes. He dogged Luna's knife and yelled that he would be the leader of the night tribe. Luna laughed and told him that he was no leader, just a weak doggy. She tackled him down but Evan had a dagger in his hand and stabbed her in the chest. She fell on top of him. The blood got on his body as Luna was getting up. Evan's body started to shake. Luna laughed and told him that he could never beat the Lunar Destruction. His mind stopped working as his heart was beating slow. Luna put some of her blood into his mouth as he died. After Luna ate Evan, Len uncovered Kaden's eyes and told him that they needed to save his mommy. Len got the key to the chains and took them off Kaden. She picked him up and gave him a kiss on the forehead. Luna explained that if she wanted to save his mom, they better do it soon before she changes her mind. After looking for about an hour, they finally found them in a dusty dungeon.

"Kaden, oh my gosh. You're ok." Scarlet smiled.

"Mommy, a guy tried to chop my head off!" Kaden yelled while crying.

"It's ok buddy, I'm here now." Scarlet smiled.

"They were mean!" Kaden cried.

"Kaden, look at me." Scarlet said.

"I scared!" Kaden cried.

"It's ok, no one can hurt you now." Scarlet said.

"Where is Luna? She is the only one who can get us out." Zane asked.

"Is she still… you know?" Savannah asked.

"Yes, she is." Len sighed.

"Did she give you a hard time?" Aster asked.

"A little but she was helpful in a way." Len said.

"Luna, can you let us out?" Aster smiled as Luna was walking into the room.

"Maybe or maybe not." Luna laughed.

"Luna come on. We love you. We are your friends." Zane said.

"Are you?" Luna laughed.

"Its four-o clock, the sun is rising soon." Scarlet said.

"Hurry Luna!" Savannah yelled.

"You're not in that form for much longer." Drake said.

"Ok fine." Luna sighed and put her hands on the bars and used a red fog to break the bars.

"Luna thank you." Zane smiled as they all ran out of the dungeon.

"Shut up!" Luna yelled.

"Hey! You in the sexy outfit and the crown. You will be put to death!" An alpha yelled. He ran up to Luna than she dogged the spear.

"Can't die dimwit." Luna smiled and thew a knife at his chest.

"I'll get ahold of Clara." Aster said and pushed the button on his bracelet.

"Hello Aster." Clara said.

"Take us home." Aster smiled.

"Sure thing." Clara said and teleported everyone to the hospital. When they got there Luna passed out and Zane caught her.

"Let's get Luna cleaned up and we can put her on her bed." Scarlet said.

After an hour, Luna woke up in her bed and everyone was there. Drake was holding her hand as she asked if it was over. They all smiled at her and Savannah explained that it was over and that she did great at controlling her evilness. Kaden thanked her for saving him. Luna patted him on the head and smiled at him. He handed her sunglasses to her. She smiled and everyone gave her some comfort. After five minutes of talking about how good Luna did, Aster asked for everyone to come to the living room. Savannah helped Luna out of her bed and they all gathered there.

"What is it?" Luna asked.

Aster went on his knees and smiled at her.

"Are you ok?" Luna asked.

"I think he needs to poop because he is on the floor." Drake said.

"This is not a bathroom!" Savannah yelled.

"No, that's not what I'm doing." Aster sighed.

"Then what are you doing?" Luna asked.

"Luna, I really think that you are beautiful and I really love your kisses and tickles. I need you forever and always, you are better than my money. I love you so much…. will you be my wife?" Aster asked and showed Luna the ring.

"Oh my lord." Scarlet said.

"Didn't see that coming." Savannah smiled.

"Yes!" Luna smiled.

"Wait, really?" Aster smiled.

"I said yes." Luna said. Aster got up and kissed her on the lips.

"Eww." Savannah cried..

"Luna, I need to be an uncle." Drake laughed.

"Not yet!" Luna yelled and used her webs to shut his mouth.

"Maybe someday." Aster smiled and kissed Luna.

"Congratulations." Zane said.

"This came out of nowhere Aster." Luna laughed.

Aster kissed Luna and they all got ready for bed.

CHAPTER 14
THE BIG PLAN

It's been a week since Kaden had gotten kidnapped. Savannah wanted to start to teach Scarlet about the oni ways because they found out she is one.

"Now, going into your oni form is a little hard but I believe you can do it. "Savannah explained.

"What if I look ugly?" Scarlet whined.

"All oni's look weird in their own way but it's just the way we are." Savannah smiled.

"Are you sure that black fog was an oni power?" Scarlet asked.

"Yes."

"What if I turn evil if I go in my oni form!"

"Well… You're a Christian so its fine. The evil in your oni form will not work because you have Jesus in your heart."

"Oh ok."

Savannah handed Scarlet a chi stick. She explained that oni's use it to get their oni energy level up. Scarlet asked if it was like smoking. Savannah sighed and told her that it wouldn't harm her. She went into her oni form as Scarlet turned on the chi stick. Scarlet put it in her mouth and blew oni fog out of her mouth. After she smoked the chi stick for five minutes, it was time for Scarlet to try and go into her oni form. Savannah put Scarlet's arms in a stance. She told Scarlet to stand up straight. She told her to think about power and being a powerful oni. Scarlet sighed and told her that she couldn't do it. Savannah went out of her oni form and walked up to her and lifted up Scarlet's arm a little bit. She asked for Scarlet to try again. After an hour of trying the ways of the oni, Scarlet only achieved to summon her oni sword for about five seconds but it vanished. Scarlet kicked the wall in stress and told Savannah that she couldn't do it. While Scarlet was having a meltdown, Zane was looking for her. He finally found her and Savannah in the basketball court room. He caught his breath and leaned his back on the wall. Savannah asked if he was ok. Zane explained that he was trying to look up a cookie recipe for his mom. When he opened up Scarlet's computer, it showed an email form the League of Science. Scarlet took a drink form her water bottle and asked if it is was from Mya. Zane told her that he didn't want to look at her personal things. The three walked to the elevator and Zane pushed the second floor.

"So much for my teaching." Savannah sighed as they ran to Scarlet's office.

"This better not be one of Mya's rude messages telling me mean things about all of us." Scarlet grunted and sat down in her chair.

"I don't want to be taken again! "Savannah cried.

"Sav, we have Clara as a security guard." Zane said.

"Let's hope she can defeat her if she comes." Savannah sighed.

"Wait, I think they forgot to take me fully out of the system,." Scarlet said.

"What does the email say?" Zane asked.

"It says, We need all of you guys to come to the lab for a really important meeting about oni's. We had an oni named Luna that you guys would love to meet but we need to find her again because some dumb idiots took her from me. I have a big plan for that oni and we need her as soon as possible. Plus my husband has to eat her blood to survive and that creeps me out a little... Just hurry and if you don't come today, I'll kill you and your family. Mya Gibbs out." Scarlet read.

"Oh no." Savannah cried.

"What big plan?" Zane asked.

"I don't know but we need to find out that big plan." Scarlet sighed.

"Let's get the others and tell them." Zane said.

Poor Luna. Scarlet thought.

When they got to the others, Drake asked Scarlet if she learned some oni skills. Scarlet sighed and told him that they had some bad news.

"What is it this time?" Drake asked.

"I got am email from the League of Science saying that Mya has a big plan for Luna." Scarlet explained.

"No, no, no! This better not be about my blood!" Luna yelled.

"It might, I don't know." Zane said.

"How did you get an email when you were fired." Aster asked.

"I guess they forget to put me out of their system." Scarlet said.

"It's a good thing they forgot because now we know what she's up to." Savannah smiled.

"Luna, why are you rolling on the floor?" Kaden asked.

"Because I can!" Luna cried.

"You not ok. I can tell," Kaden said.

"Mya is a poop head!" Luna yelled.

"I know right." Drake laughed.

"We need to know that plan. "Zane said.

"Yeah, if Mya wants all the members, something big is going to happen." Scarlet sighed.

"There are more scientists than Mya and her disgusting husband?" Luna asked.

"Yes, more than thousands." Scarlet sighed.

"Yikes, how can that many people stand Mya's bossiness." Drake said.

"And if you don't listen to her, she will kill you." Scarlet sighed.

"Dang, is she the boss?" Zane asked.

"Well, kinda because her parents were until they died so yes, she's the boss." Scarlet said.

"Mya is not going to take my sister!" Drake yelled.

"We need a good plan. Better than Mya's plan." Aster said.

"I actually might have one." Scarlet smiled.

"I have better plans." Drake laughed.

"Stress eating and blah. You think that's a good plan?" Aster asked.

"Yes, food helps." Drake smiled.

"Let Scarlet talk." Zane said.

"This plan will take Luna's good lying skills." Scarlet smiled.

"But I hate lying now." Luna cried.

"You can use lying for good for some things like, if you get taken by a killer you can say that your dad is part of the mafia and he will kill you If you don't let you go." Zane explained.

"Zane you kill me sometimes. "Aster sighed.

"The plan is that we make Luna go undercover as part of the League of Science and we will make her look like a scientist. I'll hook up a speaker so that we can all here what is going on." Scarlet explained.

"But she knows what I look like. I'm a skinny purple haired girl with black eyes and a raspy voice." Luna sighed.

"Sav and I will go to the mall to get some washout hair dye to put in your hair and get you some colored eye contacts." Scarlet smiled.

"Good idea,." Zane said.

"But my fangs." Luna said.

"Just don't smile that much." Aster said.

"Yeah, we can't do that much about that. I would let you use my fake human teeth but SOMEONE burned them!" Scarlet sighed.

"Teehee sorry. I just wanted to see if they were flammable." Drake laughed.

"Are you sure we can pull this off?" Luna asked.

"Yeah, we would let Savannah but she wouldn't emotionally handle it." Scarlet explained.

"Hey!" Savannah yelled.

"Do you want to see Mya?" Aster asked.

"No, please I don't want to!" Savannah cried.

"That's what we mean." Aster laughed.

"Savannah, let's go to the mall and get the thingies." Scarlet said

"Why do autistic people always say thingies instead of what its really called?" Aster asked.

"Because it's sometimes hard to talk and that's the only word that we would say at the time." Savannah explained.

"Luna, I have like nine other lab coats in my room so take one and use it." Scarlet said.

"Ok."

"Wait, nine more." Drake gasped.

"You can never have to many lab coats." Scarlet smiled.

"Take the teleporter gun so you don't have to drive." Aster said.

"Good idea water boy." Scarlet smiled.

Savannah and Scarlet teleported to the Science City mall. Savannah had never been to a human mall. She was excited to see what the mall has in store for her. Scarlet told her to hide her oni tail. She smiled and tucked it into her basketball shorts. Scarlet helped her curl up her tail in her shorts so the tail wouldn't stick out. While they were getting the supplies for the plan. Luna was having a very hard time.

"Luna, you can do this my love." Aster smiled.

"Yeah, we believe in you sis." Drake said.

"I'm a little scared doing this." Luna sighed.

"I would be too." Drake said.

"Life has some scary moments but God has your back. Thessalonians 3:3 says, But the Lord is faithful, and he will strengthen you and protect you from the evil one." Zane smiled.

"I know, but Poison scares me a lot." Luna sighed.

"Wow, I never knew you have fear." Drake said.

"Everyone does, even evil people." Zane said.

"Luna, are you crying?" Drake asked.

"Just leave me alone!" Luna yelled and ran to her room.

"Wait!" Drake said and followed her.

"Let's go, Zane." Aster said.

"Coming." Zane sighed.

"Whatcha looking at?" Drake asked.

"Nothing!" Luna yelled and she hid a picture.

"Come on sis. You can tell me anything." Drake smiled.

"Ugh… I'm just upset." Luna sighed while crying.

"Luna, we are siblings, you can tell me and Savannah anything." Drake said.

"My dad always gave me lots of comfort and would be with me when I need it but now, I can never see him because he hates me." Luna cried.

"Luna, you have all of us." Drake smiled.

"Is she ok?" Zane asked.

"Get out of my room!" Luna yelled.

"Hey guys we are back." Savannah smiled while carrying a shopping bag.

"Hi Sav…" Zane sighed.

"Why do you guys look upset?" Scarlet asked.

Drake took Scarlet's hand and took her to the hallway.

"What's wrong guys?" Scarlet asked.

"What's the matter?" Savannah asked and walked to Drake.

"Luna misses her dad. She says that he always helped her in scary and upset situations." Drake explained.

"I miss mine also!" Savannah cried.

"Don't cry sis, we have our friends." Drake smiled.

"I feel bad for you guys." Scarlet said.

"Yeah, we try to forget about our parents." Drake sighed

"Hey Luna, you have a soon to be husband. You don't need your dad. We can help you." Aster smiled.

"Thanks for being there for me." Luna smiled.

"No problem." Aster said.

"Is she doing ok?" Scarlet asked while she and Savannah walked in Luna's room.

"Yeah, she is feeling a little bit better." Aster smiled.

"I love you dumbo." Luna smiled.

"I love you too." Aster laughed.

"Hey Luna, I loved the mall!" Savannah smiled.

"I heard about the human malls. Are they cool?" Luna asked.

"Oh gosh, yes." Savannah smiled.

"All three of us have to go sometime soon." Scarlet smiled.

"Girls…" Aster sighed.

"Luna, let's head to a bathroom and put the black hair dye in your hair." Scarlet said.

"I have mine done blue." Savannah smiled.

"In the oni realm, my sis wanted blue hair so we asked our dad to kidnap a human who could dye her hair." Drake explained.

"Haha." Aster laughed.

"Ok, let's give it a try." Luna said.

After ten minutes of putting black hair color on Luna, she looked in the mirror. She yelled that she looked ugly. Scarlet turned Luna's face towards her. She put foundation on Luna's 777 mark and got out her lab coat. Luna put it on and said that it was too big. Drake laughed at she was an extra small so nothing of theirs would fit her. Luna punched Drake in the shoulder. Zane asked what were they going to do about Luna's fishnet tights. Luna looked her tights and yelled that they weren't going to change her clothes. Scarlet explained that Mya would know it was her if she would wear her normal clothes. Savannah let Luna wear her teal sweatpants and a black and blue t shirt of hers. After Luna got ready, she put on her ear com so that they others could hear what was going on.

"If you have a question. I'm here." Clara said.

"Kk, see ya." Luna smiled while saluting.

When she got to the League Of Science Lab, lot's of scientists were walking around the building.

I got this. Luna thought.

"This is Scarlet on the ear com. make sure to stay away from Sam as best as you can because we think that he can smell your blood."

"Ok." She said nervously.

"Hello, can I see your id card?" A man asked.

"Uh, I have one but my.…...my…uh…. I lost it." Luna stuttered.

"Do you know the id number?"

"I can steal someone's id number by hacking to the lab's system." Clara said.

"Yes, do that." Luna said.

"Huh, who are you talking to?"

"Say the numbers, 238694." Clara said.

"Uh, I remember my number its, 238694."

"Ok, so you are…. Molly?"

"Uh, yes, that is me."

"Ok, you may go find your seat in meeting room thirteen on the second floor."

"Ok, thanks." Luna said and ran up the stairs to the meeting room and sat down.

"I never seen you before. You must be new. My name is Bella."

"Hi." Luna smiled

"What is your name?"

"Its Lun… I mean Molly."

"Nice to meant you Molly."

"Hello peasants." Mya smiled.

"Hello, this is Molly, is this the new girl you were talking about?" Bella asked.

"I don't know and I don't care." Mya said while on her phone.

"I'll ask later then." Bella sighed.

"How do you put up with her?" Luna asked.

"She makes us put up with it but I love to do science so I love my job. I don't focus on Mya's temper and stuff. I just focus on my science."

"What do you do?"

"I help Mya with making these crazy vaccines to hurt her test subjects if they don't listen."

"That was one of my jobs!" Scarlet yelled.

"Ow, did you have to yell that?" Luna grunted.

"I'm sorry." Bella said.

"No, it's not you, my hearing is good and I can hear louder than others."

"Oh ok"

"She took my place." Scarlet whined while crossing her arms.

"We can get stared." Mya said and sat down in a chair.

"So, what's the big plan?" a girl asked.

"Shut up and I can tell you!" Mya yelled.

"Yes mam…"

"So, there is this oni named Luna and she has something that no other being in the world has."

"What is it?" a man asked.

"She has green glowing blood and it can kill anyone and any being, even oni's that can't die. My husband Sam got Luna's blood on him and now he is green and I'm glad he didn't die because everyone else that I put her blood into dies. Sam says that he can see the devil and he tells Sam that he is the only one who won't die from it because he was the first one to get the blood on him." Mya explained.

"Are you ok?" Bella asked.

"Yeah, it's just that my eyes water a lot." Luna sighed.

"They are black tears." Bella said.

"I have a bad infection that makes my tears black. I'm going to the doctor in two days." Luna said.

"I hope that will heal up."

"Thanks, Let's just listen to her speech." Luna said and wiped her tears

"Now for the big plan." Mya laughed.

"I hope it's awesome." a man smiled.

"Do you all remember Dr. Scarlet?" Mya asked.

"Yes, she was one of our best scientists." a girl said.

"I was the best. "Scarlet smiled.

"Shh, we need to hear this." Zane said.

"Bossy much." Scarlet sighed while holding her coffee cup and laying back into the chair.

"Well, Luna lives with Scarlet and not just Luna." Mya said.

"So, Scarlet betrayed us!" Bella yelled.

"Yes, she takes care of more than Luna, She lives with freaks. Three oni's, Luna, Savannah, and Drake and plus a boy made of water and Scarlet has a kid that is an alpha. Scarlet herself and another human are the only normal people." Mya explained.

"Wow, she has them all to herself." a man said.

"So, does the plan involve all of them?" Bella asked.

"Yes, we take all of them and test on the oni's, the water kid, and the little alpha and we will just torture the oni's. My husband will eat Luna's blood. We will force Scarlet to test on them and make the kid named Zane a slave." Mya explained.

"Wait, she wants all of us!" Aster yelled.

"Oh no." Scarlet said.

"Ha, no one will stand in my way if we have all of Luna's friends and the best thing I'm going to do is torture Scarlet." Mya laughed.

"This is bad." Zane sighed.

"I'm scared!" Savannah cried.

"Why do we need to do this?" Luna asked.

"Because I want to." Mya smiled.

"Hey Mya, what is that?" a man asked.

"Oh, this is an oni tracker, I'll show how it works." Mya said.

"Crap." Luna grunted.

"Luna, it would be a good idea to get out of there." Scarlet said.

"Go now!" Zane said.

"Ask to use the bathroom." Savannah said.

"I need to use the bathroom!" Luna yelled.

"Wait, wait, you will love this thing." Mya smiled.

"But I need to go." Luna said.

"Stay or I'll kill you!" Mya yelled and turned it on.

"Wait, why is the tracker beeping?" Mya yelled.

"Uh, I need to use the bathroom now." Luna said.

Mya got up and walked toward to Luna.

"See ya later!" Luna yelled and ran out of the room but Poison grabbed her.

"Luna, are you ok?" Savannah asked.

"Hey you, give me my knife!" Mya yelled.

"What are you doing?" Luna asked.

"Your body looks like hers." Mya laughed.

"Looks like who?" Luna asked.

"It's your voice and I smell your blood." Poison smiled.

"Ha, I don't know what you're talking about." Luna laughed.

"The tracker says that you are an oni!" Mya yelled.

"It must be broken." Luna sighed.

Mya used her knife to cut a little of Luna's face.

"Oh my gosh, it's you!" Poison yelled.

"Well, you ruined my plan so it's time for me to leave!" Luna yelled and put her webs on the wall and pulled herself out of Poison hold.

"Get her!" Mya yelled.

"Ha, I now know your plan and it will not work!" Luna yelled and used her webs to hang on the sealing.

"Luna, get out of there." Scarlet said.

"Wait, she is not a person named Molly?" Bella asked.

"Heck no!" Mya yelled.

"Bye." Luna smiled and swung on her webs out the door. As she was running she threw off the lab coat. Poison was running and Luna made him stick to the floor. Luna will be in so much danger if her friends don't save her in time.

"Teleport me!" Luna yelled.

"I'm on it." Aster said.

"Don't let her get away." Mya yelled and she shot Luna.

"Wait, my teleporter gun looks like it got burnt!" Aster yelled.

"That's odd." Savannah said.

"Hurry!" Luna yelled.

"Find the extra gun." Zane said.

Luna ran out of the lab than Poison grabbed her and pushed her on the sidewalk. Luna summoned her normal clothes back on and used her oni power to get her looks back.

"Ha, it is you." Poison laughed.

"Why do you want to do mean things to oni's?" Luna asked.

"Well, well, well, nice to see you again." Mya laughed and walked to Luna.

"What a beautiful night it is." Luna laughed as she was trying to change the subject. It was her best and only idea she had at the time.

"You can't fool me twit!" Mya yelled.

"I found the other teleporter gun." Aster smiled.

"I guess you know my plan." Mya smiled while holding Luna's shirt.

"Hurry Aster!" Luna yelled.

"What's that in your ear?" Mya asked.

"Nothing!" Luna yelled.

Mya took out the ear come and got up and smashed it. She laughed as Luna called her a dimwit.

"The teleporter gun seems weird." Aster said while it was turning black.

Scarlet suggested that Aster should do something fast or Luna would be in trouble. Aster sighed and used the teleporter gun to send Luna back. Luna stuck her tongue out at Mya as she was teleporting away. She thought she was going back to the hospital but instead Luna and her friends got teleported to Arlo's mansion. Luna open her eyes to see her dad with a shocked face.

"Well, I guess my plan kinda worked." Arlo mumbled.

"What plan!" Aster yelled.

"What is the deal with plans today?" Drake laughed.

"What is this place." Kaden asked.

"Shut up kid!" Arlo yelled.

"Why are we here!" Aster yelled.

"I'm not in the mood for you to talk crap about me." Luna cried.

Arlo used his staff to take them to Scarlet's hospital. Arlo thew his staff to the floor and let out some tears. The friends were back in the living room. They were all so confused. Luna's side was bleeding from Mya's bullet. She asked Aster to help her clean the blood off her. Aster got a wrap and lifted up her shirt and told her that he would not get any blood on him. He put gloves on and wrapped her side up. She thanked him as Kaden asked who was the black monster. Scarlet sighed and said that the name was Arlo and he was a very bad oni. Luna added that he was her father and she wishes he wasn't. As Scarlet was holding Kaden, he asked why someone was crying. Scarlet told him that no one was crying. Kaden insisted that he heard crying. She put him down and told him that she would check it out. She knew no one was crying so she walked to the hallway just to make Kaden stop worrying. As she looked to the right, she saw Arlo in the corner. She jumped and yelled asking how he was in the human realm. He smiled that he fixed his staff that she broke. She was about to grab her gun from her belt but before she could, he grabbed her and teleported them back to his mansion.

"What in the world!" Scarlet yelled.

"Let me talk." Arlo cried.

"What do you want!"

"I want to be loved!"

"Huh?"

"Uhhhh, forget what I just said…"

"What do you mean?"

"I've been watching you guys with my staff. I miss Luna and I looked up stuff about Christians and I read some things and I think that King Chen lied to us oni's."

"Are you crying?"

"No!"

"Luna misses you too."

"She does?"

"I don't get what's going on but yes, Luna misses you."

"Tell Luna I'm sorry…" Arlo sighed and got his staff.

"Wait, don't take me back yet, just tell me what's going on!"

"I'm trying for her!"

"What are you trying?"

"To be good… I hadn't eaten anything for a week now because I'm not killing humans and my heart feels weird. I'm scared of what I'm becoming!"

"Wait, so you trying to be a good person?"

"I want to be a good father to Luna and I hate to say this because King Chen will hate me but I want to learn about Jesus."

"Don't cry, that's a good thing."

"I'm trying so hard."

Is this really the guy who kidnaped Savannah and wants to make the world into darkness?

"I'm scared of God and the good world."

"You can't try to be good all by yourself but with God's help, you can be good."

"Ha, I can't believe I'm getting advice from a human."

"I'm not."

"Huh, but you look human."

"My birth parents are oni's but they didn't want a child so they used a staff to make me look human and I've been acting like one my whole life."

"Wow, ok, didn't see that coming."

"How about you come to my hospital and I'll let you see Luna. We can also teach you about God. My buddy Zane is good at that."

"I thought you good guys hate me."

"God says to love your enemies." Scarlet said trying to put her hand on Arlo's shoulder.

"I'm way taller than you." Arlo laughed.

"I can't reach your shoulder. Anyway, I don't mind you coming to my place."

Arlo patted Scarlet on the head telling her that she would never be able to reach his height. She asked how tall he was. He laughed and told her that he was seven foot fall. She said that she was five-six. They smiled at each other and he took them back to the hallway. Back at the hospital everyone was freaking out because they couldn't find Scarlet.

"What if she got taken by Mya!" Savannah yelled.

"I don't think that it would be that quick Sav." Zane said.

"Guys, I'm back." Scarlet smiled.

"Where in the heck have you been?" Aster asked.

"You went poof!" Drake yelled.

"Why is Arlo next to you?" Savannah cried.

"It was a bad idea brining me here." Arlo sighed.

"Guys, I got Luna cleaned up." Len smiled.

"Wait, why is my dad here?" Luna asked.

"Sweetie." Arlo smiled.

"Don't talk to me!" Luna yelled.

"Leave her alone Arlo." Drake grunted.

Luna was trying to hold back her tears. She yelled that she hated Arlo and ran to her room. He sighed and told her that he was sorry. She shut her room door and jumped on her purple bed that had skulls on it and started to cry. Savannah cried that she didn't want to make the human realm into darkness. She begged Arlo to not take her. Zane held her hand and told her that he wouldn't let him take her. Drake ran to find Luna as Aster was giving Arlo a mean face. Aster asked why he was in the human realm. Scarlet explained that he needed some help. Aster looked at Scarlet and yelled that he was an evil oni who wants to kill them. He explained that he shouldn't be there. He reminded her that he was the one who killed her husband. Scarlet sighed and looked at Arlo. He cried to Aster that he was sorry for what he did to them. He put his hand on Scarlet's shoulder and told her that he was sorry for killing her husband. Len tried to stop Aster and Scarlet from arguing. She grabbed Aster's arm and told him to relax. He sighed and mumbled that he shouldn't had yelled at Scarlet and that he was sorry. Len smiled and patted his back. She grabbed Kaden and told them that he wanted her to have a tea party so they would be in the toy room. Zane asked Arlo what he needed. He cried that he wanted his daughter to love him again that also he wanted to be a Christian. Savannah was shocked and yelled that he was lying to them. Scarlet explained that he wasn't. Savannah trusted Scarlet so she asked if he really wanted to be good. Scarlet nodded and smiled that they should help him. Zane smiled and told Arlo that he forgives him.

"Anyone can be forgiven." Savannah smiled.

"Yeah, leave the bad past behind you and start a new path in life." Zane said

"I can't believe you're trusting him!" Aster yelled.

"I don't want to make the human world into darkness anymore." Arlo sighed.

"It will be hard to forgive you because you killed my husband but I'll try. I did lots of evil things in the past and I was forgiven so you need a second chance too." Scarlet said.

"Ugh, he will have to earn my trust." Aster sighed.

"I just want to see Luna." Arlo sighed.

"No, you can't, you will hurt her!" Aster yelled.

"Aster, be nice." Zane said.

"No, I won't, I don't want my fiancé to get upset! "Aster yelled

"You're what?" Arlo asked.

"Ha, you haven't been around to know what's been happening!" Aster yelled

"I'll take you to Luna's room." Zane smiled.

"Are you kidding me!" Aster yelled.

"Don't listen to him. We will let you see Luna." Scarlet smiled.

"Scarlet, Arlo killed Seth for crying out loud!" Aster yelled.

"I know but I think the Holy Spirit is telling me to help him." Scarlet sighed.

Drake was calming Luna down. He made her laugh and he made her smile. She laid her head on his chest and told him that he was the best brother ever. Drake put on her sunglasses and asked her if he looked good in therm. She laughed and took them from him and put them on her head like she always does. While Drake was talking about food helping him when he is sad, Arlo knocked on her door. He explained that he was so sorry and that he loved her so much. Luna cried that he was lying.

"I'm sorry for the things I said to you. I was just mad. I didn't mean it." Arlo said.

"Luna, he isn't lying. I just looked into his mind." Drake said.

"He isn't?" Luna asked.

"I want to be a Christian but I need help and I love you Luna." Arlo sighed.

"You said you hated me and now you're saying that you love me!" Luna yelled.

"Can I come in." Arlo asked.

"Fine!" Luna yelled.

Arlo opened her door and asked why she was all beaten up. She yelled that he wouldn't even care if she told him. He told her that he missed her so much. He explained that he wanted to be a good dad. She yelled that he said if she was full blooded Simbyot, he would have killed her. Arlo cried that he was sorry and that he didn't mean it. He was just mad. She yelled that she hated him as Drake was trying to get her to stop yelling.

"Exodus 20:12 says to, honor your father and your mother, so that you may live long in the land the Lord your God is giving you." Drake explained.

"But what if you father doesn't love you!" Luna yelled.

"Colossians 3:13 says, Bear with each other and forgive one another if any of you has a grievance against someone, forgive as the Lord forgave you." Drake smiled

"Dad, do you really love me?" Luna cried.

"Yes, I'm sorry for the pain I caused you." Arlo said.

"I'll forgive you I guess but you will have to earn my trust." Luna said.

"Thank you, Luna." Arlo smiled.

"Guys, we need a plan to stop Mya's evil plan!" Aster yelled.

"Oh right." Drake sighed.

"Can we all stop saying the word plan!" Luna yelled.

"What's going on?" Arlo asked.

"Let us handle it. Just go back to your home. I'll talk to you later." Luna said.

"We need to hurry. We don't want Mya to win." Drake said.

"Can I help?" Arlo asked.

"Heck no!" Aster yelled.

"This girl is an oni obsessed creepy human. I would stay out of this If I were you." Drake said.

"Ha, I can kill a human easily, this will be nothing." Arlo laughed

"Sorry dad, maybe next time." Luna sighed.

Drake explained that Arlo could come back for dinner. He said that he would love pizza. Arlo thanked him for the invitation. He smiled that he would be back but he wasn't going to try any human pizza. He summoned his staff and teleported back to the oni realm.

Savannah ran into Luna's room and yelled that Mya was in the living room. Drake ran to Savannah and asked if she had a weapon. She nodded and cried that she wanted to be safe. Luna got out from her bed and summoned her knife. Drake asked where Scarlet and Zane were. Savannah cried that Mya already took them and put them into her van. Aster told everyone to be on guard. They walked to the living room seeing about one hundred scientists with guns. Savannah put her head on Aster's chest and started to cry. Drake used his webs to go onto the ceiling. He climbed to the middle of the living room. He summoned his sword and jumped down and stabbed a girl scientist in the back. Mya looked at Drake and yelled for the other scientists to shoot him. A tall scientist with black hair and glasses shot him in the chest. Drake ran up to him and blasted him with oni darkness. The guy passed out as Mya grabbed her gun. She shot Drake in the leg and he fell down. He picked up his sword but before he could get up Mya shot him in the head than he passed out. Luna thew a knife at Mya but Poison caught it before it hit her. Luna sighed and told him well played. Aster blasted Poison with his water. He fell down and coughed. He thew up some water and blasted Aster with his toxic power. Aster leaned his back on the wall in pain. He told Savannah to help them. Mya laughed and told Savannah that she was weak. She cried that she was not weak. Mya pointed her gun at her and told her that when she gets her, she would do very evil things to her. Savannah laughed at Mya and told her that she could try to abuse her and brainwash her but she told her that God was going to protect her. She went into her oni form and blasted Mya with her power. She fell to the floor and her glasses fell off her face. She walked up to Mya and told her that she would never harm her friends again. Mya put her glasses back on and yelled to Poison to help her. Poison kicked Luna to the wall and ran to Savannah and grabbed her. She kicked his foot and punched him in the nose. Luna ran to her and helped her out. She stabbed Poison in the arm. Mya got up and shot Savannah in the back. Savannah went on her knees and yelled for help. She went out of her oni form in pain and Luna walked up to her. She asked her if she was ok. Poison grabbed Luna's arm and put her in X stone bracelets. Three scientists grabbed Aster from the floor and put him in X stone too. Mya grabbed Savannah's shirt and said that she would always fail. She got out a sedative and jabbed it into Savannah's arm. A scientist put her in X stone and they all put them into the van.

After they got to the League of Science, they all woke up form the sedative. Savannah got up and was thinking back to when she was sent here before. She cried that she was scared. Drake was rubbing her back and calming her down. Aster asked where Scarlet was. They all had no idea of where she was. Mya was probably up to no good with her. Zane woke up his mom and helped her up. She asked where they were. He explained that they were trapped in a testing room in the League of Science hospital. Kaden asked where is mom was. Len sat down beside Kaden on the floor and told him that she was going to be ok. He went to sit on her lap and she gave him a kiss on the cheek. As they were trying to process what was going on, Poison opened the testing room and smiled at Luna. Luna took a step back and Drake put her behind him. He yelled that he wasn't going to hurt his sister. Poison laughed and blasted Drake with a green toxic substance. Luna caught Drake and asked If he was ok. Drake went on his knees in pain and yelled that he would pay for that. Poison kicked Drake in the crotch and went up to Luna. She tired to blast him with her power but she was in X stone. He took ahold of her arm and rolled up her sleeve and cut her arm open. She screamed as Poison was licking the blood off her. Len cried for Poison to stop. "You little green creep!" Aster yelled.

"Don't hurt her!" Drake yelled.

"Shut up! Get comfortable because tomorrow Mya is going to start testing on you guys." Poison yelled.

"Where is Scarlet?" Savannah asked.

"Oh, Mya is having as little talk with her." Poison laughed and walked out of the room.

Mya punched Scarlet in the nose and she fell to the floor. She yelled that she would obey her. Scarlet laughed and told her that would never happen as her nose was bleeding. Her blood got on her lab coat as Mya smiled at her. Scarlet gave her a mean face. She was wiping blood off her nose and asked what Mya wanted from her. Mya walked up to Scarlet and got up in her face. She traced her fingernails on Scarlet's thigh. Scarlet kicked Mya way from her and that made her mad. She got up and grabbed her gun from her belt and told her that if she wouldn't do as she asked, she would get killed.

"I will never obey you!" Scarlet yelled.

"You know I never hesitate shooting." Mya smiled and put the gun on Scarlet's head.

"You won't get away with this.." Scarlet yelled.

"I already have." Mya smiled and shot Scarlet in the head.

Scarlet was losing her breath. Blood was getting into her eyes. She looked up at Mya laughing at her. She laid her head on the floor in pain. She felt dizzy and her ears were ringing. She passed out while Mya was looking at her. About ten minutes later while Mya was on her phone sitting on the hospital bed next to Scarlet's dead body, Scarlet began to cough. Mya jumped and looked at her.

"You are supposed to be dead!" Mya yelled.

"I found out that I'm an oni." Scarlet sighed.

"What! all these years!" Mya yelled.

"Yeah, I was surprised myself." Scarlet sighed while blood was coming out of her mouth.

"You have human blood! It's not purple and you have no horns or tail." Mya said.

"This is just my full human form I guess." Scarlet said.

"Haha, I can do whatever I want with you now." Mya laughed.

"Where is my son?" Scarlet asked.

"Don't worry about him. Show me your oni form!" Mya yelled.

"I don't know how." Scarlet yelled than darkness was forming around her than she went into her oni form.

"Well, you just did!" Mya cried as she was in shock,

huh, how did I do that?

"Wow, I need to look at your oni body." Mya smiled.

"Don't you dare!"

Mya was staring at her oni body. It was weird to Mya that she was an oni. Her body looked so much different. The best part to Mya was that she barley had any clothes on. She had purple hair and black horns. Her eyes were exactly like Savannah's. She only had a loin cloth on and no top. She had three sevens on the left side of her nose and she had no shoes. Her tail made Mya laugh because of how dumb it looked. Scarlet took Mya's other lab coat that was hanging near her on a coat rack and put it on to cover herself up. Mya just laughed at Scarlet for two reasons. First reason because she looked weird and second was because she's secretly scared of her. She pinned Scarlet to the wall and just stared at her body. She told her that her outfit was something. She told her to shut up as Mya lifted up her arms. While things were happening in the League of Science, Arlo teleported to the living room of Scarlet's hospital. He wandered around the room trying to find someone. He couldn't find anyone. As he looked in a bed room, he saw a robot.

"Holy crap a robot!" I'm sorry what I meant to say was I'm Luna's dad."

"Well, your daughter and her friends are in trouble." Clara sighed.

"What happened to them?" Arlo asked while taking a step back away from Clara.

Mya took them all.."

"Who is Mya?"

"An evil scientist who studies oni's and she kidnaped Luna and her friends."

"I'll stop her." Arlo smiled and got his staff out.

"She is a really good fighter. Are you sure you can stop her?"

"Yes, I'm the best oni. I can kill a human in a second."

"They are at a big hospital called the League Of Science. It is about ten minutes away from here.

"Ok, I can do this. I want my daughter to love me. I will save them."

"I believe in you."

"Thanks weird robot that can talk."

Arlo summoned his staff and teleported to The League of Science. He teleported to a hallway with rooms in every direction. He yelled for Luna and started to walk down the hallway.

Scarlet went out of her oni form and told Mya that she wishes she never met her. She told her she was the biggest pervert she ever met and spit in her face. Mya laughed and walked away.

Arlo was yelling and yelling for Luna. He was looking in every room. As he was about to go into another testing room, Mya screamed and Arlo looked at her. Mya was in so much fear. A tall oni was in her hospital and he looked scary. She started to remember when her parents died from a tall scary oni. Arlo walked up to her and asked if she knew a person named Mya. She looked at him as she was backing up. He asked again as Mya shed a little tear. She asked who he was. He smiled and told her not to be afraid and that his name was Arlo Omagon. He explained that his daughter was here. Mya was confused and asked who his daughter was. As he was explaining that an evil scientist kidnaped his daughter Luna, Mya was thinking of how Luna could be related to a tall oni freak when she was so little.

"Wait, does Luna have glowing blood?" Mya asked.

"How do you know?" Arlo said.

Mya laughed at him and kicked him in the crotch. She explained that she was Mya and she had Luna. Arlo got up and blasted her all the way into a wall. She rubbed her head as he walked up to her. He lifted her up by the shirt. She begged for him not to kill her as he was giving her a mean look. He asked where Luna and her friends were. Mya cried that they were in testing room 434 on the fourth floor. Arlo thew her into the wall and started to run to the stairs. Mya was catching her breath as she was trying to get up.

"Dang, Sav is having a hard time." Aster sighed.

"I don't want to be an oni, humans hate oni's!" Savannah cried.

"Savannah, I don't hate you." Zane smiled.

"Aww, the little oni is upset. Suck it up oni." Poison laughed and thew Luna to the floor.

"Leave Savannah alone. Mya has already done evil and dirty things to her before. That's why she's upset!" Zane yelled.

"Who in the heck is knocking on the testing room door." Drake asked.

"Haha, it's probably Mya wanting to hurt you guys." Poison laughed and open the door. Arlo punched Poison and he got knocked out.

"I'm here to save you." Arlo smiled.

"Arlo, thank Jesus you are here." Zane smiled.

"Dad, I can't believe you're saving us." Luna laughed in an excited way.

"I want you to know that I love you and I really mean it." Arlo smiled.

"We need to find Scarlet." Aster said.

"Let's go." Drake said.

"Thank you, I couldn't take much more of this!" Savannah cried and gave Arlo a hug.

"Wow, it's surprising that you saved us." Aster said.

"I need my mommy!" Kaden cried.

"Who is this guy named Arlo?" Len asked.

"I'm Luna's dad." Arlo smiled.

"But Luna's dad is mean and evil." Len said.

"Mom, he wants to be good and be a Christian like us." Zane explained.

"Oh wow. That's good." Len smiled.

"Let's get out of here before Mya finds out!" Aster yelled.

They all walked out and found Mya lying on her back in pain. Arlo walked up to her and Mya yelled for him not to get close to her. She backed up as Arlo got up in her face. Aster blasted Mya with water and yelled that she would never win. She spit out water and gave him a mean face. Arlo put his arm on her shoulder and asked where Scarlet was. She smiled and told him that she would never tell them. Arlo kicked Mya in the ribs and asked again. She cried that she was down the hall. Arlo thew Mya to the other side of the room and they all ran to the last room on the floor they were on. Kaden waved bye to Mya as Len was picking him up. Len told him to not talk to Mya and they walked to the others. Savannah opened the testing room. They saw Scarlet on the floor bleeding everywhere. She had blood all over her lab coat and on her face.

"Scarlet are you ok!" Savannah cried.

"I think she is dead." Arlo sighed.

"She is an oni. She can't die!" Luna yelled.

"Then she is passed out. An oni passes out for about an hour or two when they so called get killed. She is fine if she is an oni." Arlo explained.

"Don't let Kaden see her like this." Drake sighed.

"I wanna see my mommy!" Kaden cried.

"How about you wait in the hallway." Len smiled.

"Ok, then can I see mommy?" Kaden asked.

"At home we will let you sweet heart." Len said.

Kaden went out in the hallway. He was walking around looking at they pictures on the wall. He thought it looked like his home. It had lots of rooms like Mya's place. He smiled and looked up at a big picture that was next to the stairs. It was his mom and Mya. Kaden thought they looked younger. He was confused why Mya and his mommy were together in a picture. He thought mommy hates her. Mya was walking around with her hand on her right rib. She saw Kaden and asked where her gun was. He smiled that her gun was on the floor and that she needed to keep it safe. He explained that she needed to take care of her things so that she won't lose things. Mya laughed and told him that he was funny. He asked why she was hurting. Mya sighed and asked him to grab her gun off the floor. He asked if it was hers. Mya nodded as Kaden grabbed it. Mya put her back against the wall in pain. He handed the gun to her and told her that he would pray for her to feel better. Mya walked away telling him that he was nothing like his mother. He laughed and told her that his mommy wasn't an alpha like him so they were different. Mya smiled as she was thinking that the little kid was so dumb. Mya ran to the last testing room and shot Arlo in the back. Luna yelled for her not to hurt her dad. Kaden heard the gun shot. He realized what he had done. He didn't know Mya was going to shoot someone. He just thought she lost it. Arlo blasted Mya and she fell to the floor. He kicked her and yelled that she would never be strong like an oni. Luna ran to Arlo and he picked her up. He cried that he loved her so much. Luna explained that she loved him and wants to be together again. He put her down and told her that he would love to be her dad again.

"I wanna go home." Savannah whined.

"We are but first we need to find my teleporter gun." Aster said.

"What do we do about Scarlet?" Zane asked.

"Arlo, do you have your staff with you?" Aster asked.

"Yep, all the time." Arlo smiled and summoned his staff.

"You take Scarlet and Kaden to the hospital and get Scarlet into a testing room with a hospital bed and take care of her and Kaden. The rest of us will find my teleporter gun and head home." Aster explained.

"And by the way can you bring me home a dead human to eat. I don't wanna eat this pizza thing." Arlo said.

"Killing isn't right." Len said.

"You are trying pizza." Luna smiled.

"Aww man." Arlo sighed and used his staff to take himself, Scarlet, and Kaden to the hospital.

"I think he will love pizza." Drake smiled.

"Let's go people!" Aster yelled impatiently.

They all walked out of the room and ran down the stairs to the next floor. Scientists surrounded them as they were about to go down more stairs.

"You have got to be kidding me!" Savannah yelled.

"You people are so cruel to these people and my son!" Len yelled.

"Aww, you think we care?" a female scientist laughed.

"Every bad guy has a reason why they are evil. Tell me your troubles." Len smiled.

"Mom, what the heck!" Zane yelled.

"Uh, you are a weird woman." a male scientist said.

"Lower that gun sweetie. Violence is never the answer. Len smiled as she walked up to the guy

"Len, get away from that dude!" Aster yelled.

"How about I make you scientists some cookies and have a chat about your troubles." Len smiled.

"Mom, come on." Zane sighed.

"Son, let me help these poor souls who have a broken heart and need Jesus." Len said.

"Who is Jesus?" another female scientist asked.

"See Zane, they need me right now, go find the gun thingy. I'll be fine." Len said.

"Uh ok?" Luna said.

"Let's just hurry." Zane said.

"So, is Len ok staying with the bad guys?" Savannah asked.

"Ha, I think so. We'll have to trust God will protect her." Aster laughed.

They left Len behind but quickly began looking for the teleporter gun so as to not leave her alone too long. They began searching rooms that contained several gross items. One room had shelves with teeth and fluids stacked up to five feet high. Drake wondered if some of those teeth were his and his sisters. Being onis, their teeth always came back quickly but the pain of having them jerked out was real. The next room was full of tubes of blood. Several were green and glowing which Luna knew was hers. They took a lot of it since Poison needed it to live. Drake commented that her blood was like a night light and if they ever got lost they could use her for a flashlight. Luna punched him in the arm. He was such an annoying brother, but she loved him. She was feeling pretty good right now about her family being all together. She never dreamed she would make up with her father and that he would love her enough to save her and accept her new way of life. They peeked in the next room and Savannah instantly shivered. This was the Punishment Room. There were many torture devices and this is where she experienced terror, pain, and humiliation at the hand of Mya. The teleporter gun was on the desk and Zane took a deep breath and quickly ran in to grab it. He didn't notice that someone was behind the door out of their sight. Drake recognized him as guard named Tike that Mya used to help control her subjects. They all ran into the room and Zane quickly teleported them back to their home. As they left they heard Tike shouting curse words at them.

"Hey, I was about to talk to those scientists about gun violence." Len sighed as they arrived at the lab.

"Sorry mom, we had to get out of there." Zane chuckled.

"I'm glad you guys are ok." Len smiled.

They quickly ran to find Scarlet. Arlo had settled her into a hospital room. They found Kaden and Arlo sitting by her bed and Arlo comforting Kaden that she would be ok. Aster hooked her up to an electrocardiographic heart monitor and answered Kaden's questions as to what he was doing and how the machine worked.

"Ugh, I'll say it so that you can understand. You go to the hospital and you see a thing next to the bed and the thing goes beep-beep." Aster said." This monitors someone's heart rate. Her heart beat is a little on the low end but she's alive."

"Come on Scarlet, wake up." Savannah cried.

After observing Scarlet for an hour she finally began stirring. She opened her eyes to a room full of eyes staring back at her. She was relieved to see their smiling faces.

"Ugh, what's going on?" Scarlet sighed.

They explained that they were back home and told her to rest. She had been hurt pretty badly and need time to recover.

As they all hung around talking Luna looked at Aster and said, "so who is going to tell them?"

"I guess I will. We are having a wedding tomorrow, but in an oni way so we don't need to dress fancy. "Aster explained.

"Wait, who is?" Arlo asked.

"Dad, I'm marrying Aster." Luna said.

"I can't believe my daughter is getting married!" Arlo yelled.

Even though this was a surprise announcement and maybe the timing was a little off, everyone was excited to celebrate with Luna and Aster. After all they have been through, a party would be good for all of them. An oni wedding is very simple so putting one together in one day would be easy.

Luna wished her mother could have been there to share this day with her but she had several people in her life now that loved her. She was grateful her dad was back in her life as well as her siblings.

"Mommy, can Arlo stay with us?" Kaden asked.

"Yeah, he is the one who saved us." Drake said.

"He did?" Scarlet asked

'I understand if you don't want me to stay after all I've done. Taking your husband's life was so wrong and I know it hurt you badly." Arlo said with tears in his eyes.

Scarlet remembered reading a scripture that said," Get rid of all bitterness, rage and anger, brawling and slander, along with every form of malice, be kind and compassionate to one another, forgiving each other, just as in Christ God forgave you."

"Wait, you forgive me?" Arlo asked.

"Yes, Savannah and the others forgave me when I was evil so I forgive you." Scarlet smiled.

"Thank you, Scarlet." Arlo smiled.

"Thanks for saving us." Scarlet said.

CHAPTER 15
IT TAKES COURAGE

It was a sunny morning in Science City. The friends were at church for Luna and Aster's wedding. Savannah was the flower girl. Well kinda, in a traditional oni wedding they throw human teeth on the floor. Kaden was the ringbearer and gave Aster the rings. In an oni wedding the bride and groom has to eat each other's blood. Arlo was in charge on the blood eating. Pastor Dan was the preacher for the wedding. He was a little freaked out about what you do in an oni wedding but he did it for Zane's friends. He said all the things he had to say and asked Aster if he agrees to marry Luna. He smiled and said I do. Luna said the same thing than they kissed. Arlo got a black dagger. Aster looked at it in fear. He asked if they had to do it. Len went in a panic mode and asked for them not to do the blood eating. Arlo explained that it was a thing they had to do. Scarlet asked why as he grabbed Aster's arm.

"How about we do it the human way!" Aster cried.

"Dad. He's a human. I don't think it's a good idea. I know you want this to be like the ones we have but he's not an oni nor a Simbyot." Luna sighed.

"Ok fine. Can we at least do the ritual." Arlo whined.

"We are Christians now Dad. We can't do any demonic things." Luna explained.

"This is dumb!" Arlo cried. He didn't get to do any of the oni traditions. It was going to take some getting used to when comes to humans and being a Christian.

Luna laughed at her dads whining. She said sorry as Aster put a ring on Luna. Arlo took off his black cloak with a red pentagon on the back of it.

Scarlet grabbed him by the hand and took him off the stage. She explained that what he wanted to do was demonic. Arlo mumbled that he wanted an oni wedding like he had. Pastor Dan told everyone to head down stairs for some cake and ice cream. Drake instantly ran down the stairs. They all walked to the lobby of the church for some food. An hour later, Drake had eaten six slices of cake.

"Did you know that a oni girl can have a baby in a week?" Arlo asked.

"Wow, that's fast." Len said.

"Is that why Kaden came early?" Scarlet yelled.

"Yeah, but not the growing into any age thing, that's an alpha thing." Arlo explained.

"I'm a mess right now." Scarlet cried.

"We told you not to bring any alcohol." Len sighed.

"I need it, especially after yesterday."

"Sweetie. How much did you drank today?" Len asked.

"This Christian thing is really hard!" Scarlet cried.

"But with the Holy Spirit in your heart it will get better. I'm proud of you for not going into any clubs like when we first met you." Len explained.

"I will keep trying to please Jesus the best I can." Scarlet smiled.

Savannah was not feeling well and asked to go home. Scarlet told Zane to teleport her back to the hospital. She apologized for not being able to help clean up after the reception. She felt fevered and chilled. Oni's rarely get sick but it does happen.

The rest of the group worked together and things were cleaned up fairly quickly. Drake made sure to bring home the extra cake. Pastor Dan's wife was an amazing cook. Zane called and asked if they'd stop and get tissues on the way home. Aster whispered in Luna's ear that he was looking forward to celebrating their wedding night. She grinned and gave him a wink. She had always been a bit wild. It felt good to know that now she was doing things God's way.

While they finishing up and getting ready to load up the car there was something stirring in another realm. A portal began forming in the parking lot and Luna asked her dad if he was creating it. He shook his head no and suddenly Baron stood before them sniffing the air. He smelled humans. He was a demon like creature with red skin, horns, tail, and long curly black hair. He demanded that they hand over the human named Len.

He had been searching for some powerful souls and saw in his spell book that Len had a pure soul which contained much energy and power. He realized onis were there and thought they might help him but instead they surrounded Len. He couldn't believe it. They were protecting a human!

So much for letting Kaden have a good sleep, Scarlet sighed as she was carrying him to the car. Kaden yawned and asked, who woke him up. Scarlet laid him in the back seat and shut the door before joining the group.

"You don't look oni. Arlo said.

"Because I'm not!" Baron yelled.

"Then what are you?" Drake asked.

"I am Baron the Master of Souls. I'm part demon and part warlock."

"Oni's are better than demons." Arlo smiled.

"Why do we fight over this?" Drake yelled.

"I had it with the arguing, just get along." Luna yelled.

"Uh, I don't get it." Len said.

"Oni's and demons don't like each other." Luna said." It's been that way forever."

"You are not taking Len!" Aster yelled.

"Yes, I am!" Baron yelled

Luna had enough. Yesterday they escaped from Mya and today this guy was ruining her perfect day. She summoned her oni knife and stared him down.

"You know what?" Baron smiled. "You're all coming with me!" He used his magic to send all of them to the soul realm.

It was 9:30 and they still weren't home yet. Zane was getting a little concerned. Savannah was on the couch eating chicken noodle soup for her sore throat. Clara was giving her all the facts about how chicken soup helps when you're sick. Zane tried to call them on their phones but did not get an answer.

"Where are we?" Aster asked.

"In the soul realm bluey." Baron smiled.

"Don't call me that." Aster yelled.

"Why are we here mommy?" Kaden asked.

"I don't know." Scarlet said.

"It's boring in this cage." Arlo sighed.

"That's what getting captured is. Its super boring," Luna said.

"At least it's not Mya." Scarlet said.

"I hope Zane and Savannah will find us." Len cried.

"They are probably worried about us." Scarlet sighed.

"I've never been captured before. This has to suck for you guys." Arlo said

"Arlo, we have a kid present." Scarlet grunted.

"Sorry Scarlet."

"Shut up all of you!" Baron yelled.

"Ok, chill,." Aster sighed.

"You chill! Baron yelled.

Drake and Baron kept arguing back and forth. Drake got much enjoyment out of annoying him. Baron had taken their phones so when one of them rang Scarlet begged for him to let them at least let Zane know they were ok. Baron looked at the phone and pressed the speaker button.

"I'm Baron and I have your friends." he smiled.

"What do you want with them?" Zane asked.

"Their souls. "Baron laughed.

"Guys where are you; we can save you?" Zane asked.

"We are in the sou…." Scarlet said.

Baron hung up the phone to prevent Scarlet from giving their location.

"Wait, they hung up." Zane said.

"I think I know what they were going to say." Savannah said.

"Tell me please."

"I think Scarlet was gonna say the Soul Realm."

"Clara, can you tell me some facts about the soul realm?" Zane asked.

"Yes, the soul realm is where human souls get taken when a soul master takes someone. If your friends are in that realm they are in danger. If a body has been there for twenty four hours their soul stays there and they are trapped forever." Clara explained.

"That means we have to find them fast." Savannah said.

"We have the teleporter gun. I hope I can figure out how to use it." Zane said.

"Zane, also a human will get weak in that realm. Be careful." Clara said.

"I have your back Zane." Savannah said.

Zane knew she didn't feel well and appreciated her going to help him. They just may need her oni powers if things got ugly. She grabbed a handful of tissues while he found the teleporter gun.

"What do you want with our souls?" Luna asked.

"Haha, like I'll tell you." Baron laughed.

"Tell me or when I'm the Lunar Destruction I will kill you." Luna smiled, hoping this threat would get him to spill his guts.

"Wait, you're the Lunar Destruction?" Baron yelled.

"Yeah, my daughter never hesitates when she wants to kill someone when she is in that state. She has zero self-control." Arlo said.

"Ugh, fine. I take all kinds of souls even oni's. Human souls like Len's, that are pure and perfect, are especially powerful. I will put the souls in me and when I get my energy up a have enough power I'll go to the human realm and make that world into my image." Baron explained.

"Bad guys always want to take over the world." Aster said.

"Yeah, I'm getting tired of it." Scarlet agreed.

"Not all." Arlo said, at least not anymore."

"I know but most of them." Aster said.

As usual Drake was concerned about being without food. His stomach grumbled reminding him that he may never eat pizza or cookies again. Luna told him to quit complaining and being so dramatic. The siblings bickered back and forth annoying Baron. They were distracting him from his plan. Baron decided to begin taking their souls and chose Kaden first. Everyone was of course trying to convince Baron that Kaden was too young and to spare him. Arlo was being very calm about the whole situation since onis couldn't die. Baron explained that they only had twenty four hours before they would be stuck there forever. He would take their souls and they could never leave.

"Sir, sorry I'm late." San said as he hurried through the door.

"San, what is it this time?" Baron sighed.

"I slept in. Sorry sir."

"That's it, go find something else to do. You are a bad assistant!" Baron yelled.

"But why?" San said.

"Now!" Baron yelled.

"Yes, sir."

"Anyway, in 24 hours I will first take that crybaby wolf boy's soul first." Baron said as he left the room.

Come on son, where are you? Len thought.

"I looked in your mind. I hope they will find us." Drake whispered.

San left wandering around outside in the wooded area in the dark. He really didn't know what to do since Baron didn't want him around. He though something caught his eye in the distance so he headed in that direction.

Zane and Savannah had been searching for an hour trying to find their friends. As they stepped out behind some trees they saw a guy coming their way. He spotted them at the same time. The two of them slipped inside a cave they had just passed and sat quietly in the dark. Savannah clung to Zane and then suddenly had to sneeze. She tried to hold it back but it was too late. San quickly entered the cave calling them trespassers. Savannah went into her oni form and summoned her oni sword. San was surprised to see that she was an oni. Savannah thought he was a scientist and was ready to let him have it good. Sam asked why an oni was in the Soul Realm. Savannah cried that a soul master took their friends. He laughed at her thinking that an oni was a powerful being and doesn't need any friends. Zane told San they had his mom and they really needed to find them. San started to think about what Baron had done today. He kidnaped lots of people to day and some of them were oni's. He smiled and had an idea to take Savannah and Zane to make his master proud of him. He used his power to draw Zane into his arms. Zane fell on the floor in front of San. Savannah went into her oni form and begged San not to hurt Zane. He just laughed at her and used his power to teleport he and Zane to Baron. Savannah ran to Zane but then he disappeared. She dropped to her knees and began to cry. She looked at the night sky while crying. She didn't know what to do at his point. She had no one to help her. She was all alone. *Jesus, help me find them please. You're my only hope. Zane says, God doesn't give me a spirt of fear but love, power, and a sound mind. I can find them. I got this.*

Savannah got up and picked up her oni sword from the ground. She prayed that she would find her friends. She took a deep breath and started to run towards a big castle. While Savannah was looking for them, Aster was yelling at Baron begging to let them out. Baron explained that if he kept talking, he would kill him. Len put her hands on Aster's shoulder to calm him down before he got himself killed. Luna told Aster to relax because Zane and Sav would save them. Right after she told him that, San came in the room with Zane in his hold. They looked at Zane and Len asked if he was alright. Aster looked at Luna telling her that they were doomed. Arlo asked where Savannah was as Baron walked up to Zane. Len cried for Baron not to hurt her son. He lifted up Zane's neck looking at his face. He told San to put him in the cage with the others. San nodded and thew him into the cage and locked the door. Len ran up to him and gave him a kiss on the head. She hugged him as she was crying. He smiled and told her that he was ok. San explained that an oni was with the guy that they just put in the cage. Baron looked at San and yelled for him to find the oni and bring her to them so that he would have more souls to steal. San smiled and told him that he would try his best.

"Where is my sis?" Drake asked.

"She's all alone. That guy caught me and Savannah was somewhere near a cave but I don't know now." Zane explained.

"Let's hope she's got the guts to not be scared." Arlo said.

"She is probably so scared." Scarlet sighed.

"I know but she is our only hope." Zane said.

"It ok guys. Savannah is a hero like all of us." Kaden smiled.

"Ha, love you Kaden." Scarlet laughed and kissed him on the forehead.

"You guys have 23 hours now." Zane cried.

"How did you know about the 24 hour thing? We just found out." Aster asked.

"Clara told us about this realm." Zane said.

"I'm just glad you're ok." Len smiled.

"Shut up! All of you!" Baron yelled.

"Listen, if you do anything to my daughter, you will pay!" Arlo grunted.

"Ha, you can't make me shut up." Luna laughed.

"Yes, I can shorty!" Baron yelled.

"Guys, next blood moon let me kill this guy!" Luna yelled.

"I might let you." Scarlet smiled.

"She can't be the Lunar Destruction!" Baron yelled.

"How did you know about me?" Luna asked.

"Every satanic being knows about her." Baron said.

"Well, you're looking at her butt face." Luna smiled.

"Just shut it!" Baron yelled.

Savannah was running to the castle and she finally made it. She opened the large wooden doors to find people in black ninja outfits with swords. She sighed as they all surrounded her. Savannah blasted a guy with her darkness and he fell to the floor covered in evil tentacles. He died as she cried that she wouldn't hurt anyone else if they let her in. A woman sliced her in the back. Savannah stabbed her in the chest with her sword. Three guys tried to stab her but she dogged all three of them. She had an idea put she didn't like it. Savannah closed her eyes and the satanic symbol was under her feet. She had darkness fog forming around her. She opened her eyes and made the room into darkness. Everyone one except her died from it. Her heart was broken but she needed to find her friends.

"You guys have 22 hours." Baron smiled.

"Mommy, I don't want to be here forever. I have the hospital as my home." Kaden cried.

"Savannah will find us." Scarlet sighed.

"Let's hope so." Aster said.

"Ok, if I give you a cookie. You can let us out?" Drake asked.

"No!" Baron yelled.

"Scarlet makes good cookies." Drake smiled.

"You are the most annoying oni in the world." Baron grunted.

"Hey you!" Savannah yelled as she was running in.

"Who are you?" Baron asked.

"Oh my gosh, Savannah." Zane smiled.

"You found us!" Drake said.

"Finally." Arlo laughed.

"You are not taking my prisoners!" Baron yelled.

"They are my family!" Savannah yelled.

"Fight him Sav!" Aster yelled.

"I'll try." Savannah cried.

"Don't be afraid sis. You got this." Drake smiled.

"Ha, she is hopeless." Baron laughed.

"No, she's not!" Luna yelled.

Baron ran to Savannah and kicked her down and called her a looser. She got up and summon her oni sword into her hands from the floor. He laughed and summoned his axe and swung it at her and she dodged it. He pushed her to the floor and called her a weak oni. Luna yelled that she wasn't weak. Savannah was about to stab him but he grabbed her arm and twisted it and threw her to the floor again. Her arm was broken and she started to cry. Her arm was purple and swollen. She used her oni power to turn her arm back to the way it was. She laughed and explained that oni's could regenerate any part of the body. He gave her a mean face and used his axe to slice her stomach open. She cried that God had her back. He explained that God hates people like her. Blood was coming out form her stomach. She tried to get up but she was too weak to move. He kicked her in the head making her not able to think straight. Drake yelled for Savannah to get up. Savannah got up and was dizzy. Her hands were shaking as she grabbed her oni sword. She fell down onto her back in pain. She cried that she couldn't defeat him.

"Come on Savannah. You can defeat him." Scarlet said.

"San, get me my magic bow staff, now!" Baron yelled.

"Ok. I'll grab it sir."

"I will take your soul, weak oni girl!" Baron yelled.

"Hurry Savannah! Get up!" Aster cried.

Baron used his axe to cut her stomach even more. The blood was going through her body and into her mouth. She coughed out some blood as he was laughing at her. San handed the staff to him and told him that he was awesome. Arlo yelled for Savannah to get up.

"Your soul will be mine." Baron said.

"No Savannah!" Get up!" Zane cried.

"With Jesus I'm not weak." Savannah grunted while blood was dripping out of her mouth.

"Haha, Jesus can't help you now!" Baron laughed while the staff had white flames that caused Savannah to go out of her oni form.

"Savannah!" Zane cried.

Savannah's skin was turning like a ghost. She closed her eyes while tears were coming out. Scarlet told Kaden to look away. He hugged him mom worried for Savannah. She wasn't moving while Baron had his staff to her chest.

"Savannah, please!" Drake cried.

This never takes this long., Baron thought.

"Please God, don't let her die!" Len cried.

"Oni's can't die! How are you doing that to Savannah?" Arlo yelled.

"Hahaha, Soul masters can take anyone's soul." Baron laughed.

"Is Savannah dying mommy." Kaden cried while hugging her.

"I don't know..." Scarlet sighed while crying.

"Savannah, get up. You are tough!" You're my tough little sister!" Luna cried.

"I think she is just passed out." Arlo sighed.

"It's like she's a ghost." Zane said.

"It's her soul..." Arlo said.

"Why is this taking so long?" Baron yelled than the white flames stopped.

"What the heck. Why isn't my staff working!"

Savannah's skin was turning back to normal. She was breathing again and moved her hand a little bit. She opened her eyes and looked around her seeing her friends crying and smiling at her.

"Does she have a soul sir?" San asked.

"You just saw it!" Baron yelled.

"Wait a sec." Luna said.

"What is it?" Scarlet asked.

"Maybe because she has no heartbeat, its messing up somehow." Luna explained.

"Oh yeah, I forgot about that." Zane said.

"Hey Baron, you can't take her soul." Drake smiled.

"Why!"

"She has no heartbeat. If she was a human, she would have been dead. It's like she is dead and her soul cannot be taken twice." Drake explained.

"She's a walking corpse Dude." Aster laughed.

"No, I need souls now." Baron yelled.

"We have the other prisoner's sir." San said.

"You're right San." Baron smiled.

"Savannah. Help us girl!" Aster yelled.

"We need you!" Zane yelled.

"Ha, she's hopeless." San laughed.

"Shut up, she is strong." Luna yelled.

"Well, today she is a weak little oni girl." Baron laughed.

"What's going on?" Savannah sighed.

"You're ok!" Len smiled.

"My head hurts." Savannah sighed.

"Help us." Scarlet said.

"Haha, she can't." Baron laughed and opened the cell door.

Arlo ran to the door than Baron tried to push him down. They all ran out as Baron was on the floor. Arlo thew Baron all the way across the other side of the room. Luna ran up to Arlo and gave him a hug saying good job.

"Yeet!" Aster smiled.

"Teens and their weird words." Len laughed.

"Help Savannah, I got the soul guy." Arlo smiled.

'I'm a young adult by the way. I'm twenty one." Aster smiled.

"Yes, we got out." Drake smiled.

"Savannah!" Zane cried and went next to her.

"Are you ok sis?" Drake asked.

"My chest hurts." Savannah sighed.

"It's ok, you're safe." Zane said.

"Hey Savannah, go get him." Aster smiled while Savannah went into her oni form.

"My oni form doesn't go on my command!" Scarlet yelled.

"It's ok mommy." Kaden smiled.

"You just need to practice." Arlo said.

"San, I want the oni girl! She will make a nice host." Baron smiled.

"Um. Why sir?"

"Because her soul makes me feel good. Its weak but I felt different getting close to it." Baron smiled.

"What do you mean?" Savannah asked.

"At night a soul master puts all his souls into one person because it's too much power for him to hold all the time and the host dies after a while. Because your soul is weak, we will use you as the new host." San explained.

"Your body can handle lots more souls and other people can't so they die after like there days but you, you could handle them for eternity." Baron smiled.

"You will never take my sister!" Drake yelled.

"Yeah, you can't have our sister. I love her so much and I don't want her to be in any more pain!" Luna cried.

"Well, I guess I have to fight to get her." Baron sighed.

Arlo sliced him on the back with his sword. While Arlo and Baron where fighting, San got his axe and sliced Savannah on the hip with it. She fell to her knees grimacing in pain. When she touched her hip she got blood all over her hand. She wiped the blood on her shirt and got up and prayed for God to help her win the fight. She blasted San with her darkness and he died. Baron was mad at her for killing his best henchmen. Before he could get to her, Arlo stabbed him in the chest with his oni sword. When a demon dies, he goes go hell but being a soul master as well, he would still get burned like humans. He fell down to the floor begged for Satan to help him. Arlo laughed and told him Satan couldn't help him. He summoned his oni staff. He threw it to Savannah and she asked what he wanted her to do with it.

"Now that I'm out of X stone I can use my staff and I want you to send him to the oni realm and let the other oni's have some slaughter time with Baron." Arlo smiled.

"No, I can't go to the oni realm. I can't breathe the oni fog!" Baron yelled.

"See ya never." Luna laughed.

"Do it Savannah." Scarlet smiled.

"Ok." Savannah smiled and used Arlo's staff to send Baron to the oni realm.

"Take us home please." Zane sighed.

As Savannah handed his staff to Arlo, Scarlet started to fall in love with him. She mumbled that he was cute. Aster laughed at her and asked fi she said what he thought she said. Scarlet looked the other way in embarrassment. When they got to the hospital. Aster laid on the couch glad to be back. Luna jumped on top of him and told him that she loved him.

"You guys made it. It's been 19 hours that you guys were there." Clara said.

Good to be back at the hospital." Zane smiled.

"Hey Savannah." Scarlet said.

"Yeah, what is it?" Savannah asked.

"You were really brave today." Scarlet smiled.

"Yeah, I've never seen you that brave before." Len said.

"Thanks." Savannah smiled

Zane ran to Savannah and Zane kissed her. They all went to bed and Luna and Aster hurried to their own room for the first time.

CHAPTER 16
MYA'S???

In the kitchen Arlo was making breakfast. Scarlet walked to the kitchen yawning. She went to grab a coffee cup but smelled something horrible. She looked at Arlo asking what that disgusting smell was. He told her good morning as he was stirring something in a pot. She explained that she smelled rotten flesh. He laughed and told her that he was making them all breakfast. Scarlet walked up to the pot and asked him what he was cooking for them. He told her that it was an oni food called human blood and teeth soup. Scarlet held her nose and told him that the humans probably wouldn't like what he was making. He explained that he was a great cook and that Luna loved the food he makes. She looked at the soup and gaged and said that she should cook. Arlo put his hands on her shoulder and told her that she would like it because she was an oni. She said to him that she lived like a human all of her life so she doesn't know if she would like oni food. She explained that she was taught how to not eat human blood as a child. She had a problem about eating other people's blood when she was little but her adopted parents had taught her how to eat human food. Arlo sighed as Luna ran up to give him a hug. He asked why she was so excited. She smiled at him and put on her sunglasses. All of the friends went into the kitchen for breakfast. Aster walked up to Luna and asked her if she could tell them. Zane asked why Luna looked happy and not her, trying to act tough self. She smiled and explained that she was pregnant. Everyone stared at Luna in shock. Aster gave her a kiss and Arlo ran up to her and picked her up and squeezed her tight. She laughed and told him to let her go. While everyone was talking, Scarlet walked to her room.

"I already feel like trash." Luna sighed.

"It's ok, Scarlet had the same problem." Zane said.

"We only have about a week before the baby comes." Drake smiled.

"A week!" Aster yelled.

"Yes, an oni baby comes within 7 days." Arlo smiled.

"Kaden, you slept in buddy." Zane laughed as he laid his head on Zane.

"Too tired." Kaden yawned.

"Do you know where your mom went?" Zane asked.

"No why?" Kaden asked.

"I wanted to see what's for breakfast." Zane said.

"I made breakfast for all of you." Arlo smiled.

"What did you make?" Aster asked.

"You don't wanna know." Luna said as she looked into the pot.

"Luna, you know I make good food." Arlo said.

"But some people in this hospital are humans Dad!" Luna yelled.

"And plus, I don't want to eat oni food because it's not ok to eat humans in this realm." Savannah said.

"Ugh, I'll just eat it I guess." Arlo grunted.

"I'll find Scarlet. I need food." Drake smiled and ran out of the kitchen.

Drake ran to Scarlet's room as Len went to grab Zane's laundry basket. He smiled that he was hungry and his tummy needed food. Scarlet yelled for him to go away. Len stopped walking and walked up to Scarlet's door and asked what was wrong. Drake opened up her door and asked her if she was falling back to sleep. Scarlet threw her lab coat on the floor and jumped on her bed. Len asked why she wasn't wearing her lab coat. She never takes it off, she even wears it to bed.

"Are you ok?" Drake asked.

"Just leave please." Scarlet sighed.

"I've never seen you without your lab coat." Drake said.

"Do you need anything." Len asked.

"No, I'm fine!" Scarlet cried.

"Are you sure?" Drake asked.

"Drake, do you like being an oni?" Scarlet asked.

"Yeah, I like my power and that I can't die. Why did you ask that?" Drake said.

"It's just that my whole life was fake." Scarlet sighed and laid her back on her bed.

"Why would you say that?" Len asked.

"All of my life I thought I was a human." Scarlet said and started to cry.

"That doesn't matter. You are who you are." Len said.

"Come on, put your lab coat on and let's have a good day." Drake smiled.

"Ha, I can't believe that I tested on oni's when I am one." Scarlet sighed.

"Mommy, wake up!" Kaden yelled and ran to her room and jumped on her.

"Ow." Scarlet cried.

"Don't sleep this long. We have all day to do fun things." Kaden smiled.

"Ok fine! I'll get up." Scarlet sighed.

"Where your lab coat?" Kaden asked.

"On my floor…" Scarlet sighed.

"I like when you wear it." Kaden smiled.

Drake picked up Scarlet's lab coat and handed her it. She sighed and got up and put it on. Kaden hugged her as she wiped her tears off her face. Drake explained that he was hungry. Scarlet fixed her glasses and asked what he wanted to eat. While Scarlet walked to the kitchen she saw Arlo whining about everyone not eating what he made. She laughed as she grabbed some pancake mix. Arlo looked at her whining that he wanted to make them food. She patted him on the back and told him maybe next time. Drake ran up to Luna saying teehee to her. Luna's face was pale and she explained that the pregnancy hormones were kicking in. Savannah gave Luna a trash can and gave her hug as she threw up in it. Zane looked at her puking and his face got pale. Len ran to him telling him that he should go to the living room and she would bring him his food. Zane gaged as he walked to the couch. Savannah followed behind him asking what was wrong. Len explained to her that Zane couldn't handle the sight of blood, puke, pee, or poop. She laughed and explained that oni's love those kind of things.

"Guys, it feels like I'm getting shocked my something." Clara explained.

"It might be a malfunction. Don't worry." Aster smiled.

"Her eyes are a little glitchy." Len said as she walked in.

"I'll see what the problem is." Aster mumbled and got up and walked to her.

"I don't think this Is a malfunction Aster." Clara said.

"Let's go to my study room." Aster smiled.

"Hey Aster, she's sparking really bad." Scarlet said.

"Let's go Clara, let's see what's going on with you." Aster said.

At the League of Science, Poison and Mya was doing something evil. Poison was typing on his computer as Mya was watching him. He explained to Mya that it was hard to hack into the robot's system because the water boy changed the programing. Mya yelled for him to hack her so they could see what was happening at Scarlet's hospital. He sighed and mumbled that he was trying his best. Mya told him to keep trying.

"It's going to be ok Clara." Aster smiled while looking at her wires.

"Are you sure?" Clara asked.

"I hope." Aster said.

"Is everything ok?" Luna asked as she was walking in holding her stomach.

"I'm not sure why she is messing up." Aster sighed.

"Did she get water on her somehow?" Luna asked.

"I wasn't around water." Clara said.

"Well... Aster kinda is water." Luna laughed.

"Time to control!" Poison laughed as he hit a button on his keyboard.

Clara started to walk to the hallway. Aster asked where she was going. She explained that she didn't know and she wasn't trying to walk. Luna asked what she meant by that. She ran out of the study room and ran down the stairs. Luna and Aster looked at each other and ran to find Clara. Poison was controlling Clara so he could grab the teleporter gun so they could get Scarlet and her friends. As Clara was walking to Aster's bed room, Mya thought that it would be best to just kidnap Scarlet for now. He asked why as he was typing on his computer.

"Where are you going?" Savannah asked.

"Just to my room for a little bit." Scarlet said.

"I looked in your mind. You're upset because you think your life was a lie." Drake said.

"Just leave me alone!" Scarlet cried and walked to her room.

"I don't wanna be an oni!" Scarlet yelled and opened her door and slammed it shut.

What is going on with me? I don't want to hold Aster's teleporter gun. Clara thought than she started to walk to Scarlet's room. "Let me walk on my own you hacker!" Clara yelled.

Clara opened Scarlet's door and walked right in. Scarlet was surprised to see her standing there with a teleporter gun. Clara warned her that she did not know what she was doing and that she felt like she was being hacked. Before Scarlet could yell for Aster, Clara pushed and button and teleported Scarlet to Mya. Arlo walked in finding Clara holding the teleporter gun and saying "powering down."

"Ugh, what happened?" Scarlet sighed while on the floor.

"Hello." Poison smiled

"Wait, why am I here?" Scarlet yelled.

Mya welcomed her back with a hard kick to the ribs. She told her husband to put Scarlet in x stone. Scarlet got up and tried to run. Mya got a sedative and gave it to Poison to inject in Scarlet when he caught her. She ran out the door but ran into three scientists. Poison yelled for them to stop her. One tackled her down holding her there until Poison caught up. Scarlet couldn't believe this was happening again. She had enough of Mya she thought as she drifted off to sleep. One hour later Scarlet woke to an electrical feeling going through her body. Mya was shocking her awake.

"What do you want with me Mya?" Scarlet asked.

"Oh, just what I want with all oni's, that's all." Mya laughed.

"Crap, you found out about that." Scarlet sighed.

"I hate you even more because you're an oni." Mya said.

"I can't even control my oni form. I don't know how to even go part oni form.' Scarlet yelled.

Sam put Scarlet onto a hospital bed. She tried to reason with Mya which was almost impossible because she had such an evil mind. She was obsessed with hurting onis to get revenge for her parents death so even an old friend couldn't get through. She told her that God loved her even though she did the things she did. She quoted 1 Peter 4:8 which says "above all, love each other deeply, because love covers a multitude of sins." The more she talked about God the madder Mya got. She yelled hateful words at Scarlet. She didn't want to hear it.

Realizing that Clara was hacked alarmed the friends that possibly Scarlet had been taken. They looked everywhere they could in the hospital facility and she was no where to be found. After examining the teleporter gun Aster realized Scarlet was sent to the League of Science. They all understood that Scarlet was in danger, especially if Mya had figured out that she was an oni too. The fact that Scarlet didn't die when shot may have given it away. Once again they need to come up with a plan. It was going to get harder to break into the League of Science because they will be expecting a rescue attempt. While they were brainstorming, Scarlet was silently praying.

Mya demanded that Scarlet go into her oni form so she could take some of her blood. Scarlet could not make herself transform at will. She tried and Mya threatened her with the Punishment Room. Scarlet knew exactly what that meant. Mya got up in her personal space and took her lab coat off her making her feel very threatened. Her lab coat was her security. Poison told her to lean against the wall. Mya got a knife and began teasing her with it. Mya traced her fingernails on Scarlets back and sliced her back pushing her to the floor and yelled that she hated her. A familiar voice broke through her hateful words.

"Mommy?" Zach questioned.

"Crap." Mya sighed.

"What are you doing to dis lady? Zach asked.

"You have a son?" Scarlet asked

"Why you got a knife?"

"Uh, you're not supposed to be at this part of my lab." Mya scolded.

"Why dat lady bleeding?"

Poison ran into the room quickly snatching Zach up in his arms. Zach was very confused why his mommy had blood on her hands and was hurting that lady. He tried to explain that she was an oni in human form and onis are bad. She didn't listen so she was being punished. Zach got scared that if he didn't listen his mom would hurt him. Poison assured him she would never do that. Zach wasn't so sure.

Aster reassured Kaden for the tenth time that they would get his mom back. Luna was in the bathroom puking while the rest of them were planning in the living room. Arlo's grand plan was for he and Savannah to go to the League of Science and quickly kill Mya and Poison and never have to worry about them again.

"That would work except that God doesn't like killing. He actually hates it. Listen to this from the bible. The Bible says there are six things the LORD hates, seven that are detestable to him, haughty eyes, a lying tongue, hands that shed innocent blood, a heart that devises wicked schemes, feet that are quick to rush into evil, a false witness who pours out lies and a person who stirs up conflict in the community." Zane explained.

"Mya is doing all those things. She should pay." Arlo grunted.

"I know but she will answer to God one day. Right now we just need to save Scarlet." Len said.

"Arlo, my mommy says you are cute." Kaden smiled.

"She what?" Arlo yelled.

"That's funny." Drake laughed.

Savannah, having gotten much braver since the ordeal with Baron, came up with the idea to have Arlo distract Mya, without killing her of course, while the rest searched for Scarlet. Hopefully they didn't get caught because she didn't have a plan for that.

Since Aster fixed Clara she was following Luna everywhere concerned about her pregnancy. She followed her into the bathroom and examined her vomit saying it shouldn't be black cause that could mean there's bleeding. Luna got scared and yelled for her dad. He explained that Simbyot vomit was black. She was relieved. She may have to power down Clara if she didn't back off.

Mya was very upset that Zach saw her hurting Scarlet. She never wanted him to know about her job and her dark side. She hid her pregnancy from everyone, even Scarlet when they worked together. She always wore baggy clothing with a lab coat over top. She was very protective and never wanted anyone to hurt Zach. Her parents brutal death really messed with her head. The pain of their deaths and the revenge in her heart caused a darkness she couldn't escape. All she knew was that she was very angry and didn't care if she hurt others.

"I need to let my anger out on you. "Mya said. Mya hit Scarlet in the face and made her mouth and nose bleed and said," you dumb oni's will never get close my son."

"Is this why you hid him; because of what happened to you as a kid?" Scarlet asked.

"Yes!" Mya yelled and hit her again.

"Please stop hurting me." Scarlet cried.

Mya began threatening to hurt Kaden saying that Scarlet would not be able to save him. Scarlet got so mad that darkness formed around her and she went into her oni form. Mya was glad to see that Scarlet's anger triggered her power. She wanted to examine her oni body and just as she was about to Zach walked in saying he wanted to watch. He wanted to be a scientist one day. He was much too young to see what Mya was doing so Mya took a break from her test subject and took him to a lab room and showed him some cool experiments with chemicals that kids could do.

Aster made some more adjustments on Clara and pushed a button on her face." Hello Aster." Clara said.

"So, we are pretty sure Mya hacked your system. We will see if it was her." Aster said.

"I'm sorry Aster." Clara said.

"It's not your fault." Aster smiled.

"Yeah, you can't help If someone is hacking you. "Savannah said.

Arlo and Zane were ready to roll and go save Scarlet. Luna decided to stay behind as she was gaging and running toward the bathroom. Len and Kaden stayed behind as well. Clara of course would be there to help anyone who asked.

"So, why do you want to be a scientist?" Mya asked.

"I want to be just like you." Zach smiled.

"That's cute. I'll show you my stash of oni blood." Mya said.

"What is oni blood?" Zach asked.

Mya smiled and held his hand and lead him to a room filled with, oni blood, fluids, teeth, and little pieces of hair. Zach got really excited and looked at some oni teeth that were in a big jar. He smiled and told his mom that he wanted to be just like her. Mya sighed and looked away as he was putting his hands on jar of oni blood. He asked why she hurt oni's as Mya shed a little tear. She wiped her face and fixed her glasses.

"I don't want to talk about it." Mya sighed.

"But I wanna know badly." Zach whined.

"Just shut your little mouth and don't ask again!" Mya yelled.

"Ok mommy, I sorry!" Zach cried.

"It's compilated Zach…" Mya sighed.

"I want to see a oni."

"Scarlet is in her oni form, so why not."

"Yay! Thank you mommy."

Poison laughed at Scarlet's oni clothing. Scarlet didn't like being without her lab coat. She didn't like the oni look at all. She didn't even have a shirt nor a bra on and that made her embarrassed. Poison kept saying that her clothes made her look so dumb. She agreed with Poison on that one as Mya came in with Zach. He ran up to Scarlet begging his mom if he could pet her. Poison made Scarlet fall to her knees as Zach smiled at her. Mya laughed and told him that he could go ahead. Scarlet gave her a mean face as Zach petted her arm. She yelled that she wasn't an animal.

"Daddy, she looks scary! I changed my mind!" Zach cried than hugged Poison.

"Ha, Sam is the scary one." Scarlet mumbled.

"What did you say?" Poison asked.

"Uh, nothing." Scarlet laughed.

"This is your little Simbyot friend's fault I look like this!" Poison yelled and kicked Scarlet.

"It was not her fault!" Scarlet yelled than got up and punched Poison in the nose.

Mya got her gun and shot Scarlet than she fell down. Scarlet went out of her oni form while Mya called her an idiot as Zach began to cry. He yelled that he wanted to go out of the testing room because he was scared. Mya pointed the gun at Zach and yelled for him to go to his room. He cried that he was sorry and ran to the hallway and went to his bed room. She sighed and told Poison to take Scarlet to a tube and she would test on her tomorrow. He smiled and told her that he would do anything for her.

Back at the hospital, Arlo asked if everyone was ready to save Scarlet. Savannah explained that she needed her friend back. Aster patted her on the back and told her that they would get her back in no time. Luna explained that she should stay because she has been puking all day. Len smiled and told her that she would take care of Luna and Kaden for them. Arlo nodded and summoned his oni staff and teleported everyone else to the League of Science. Arlo explained that everyone will go find Scarlet while he would handle Mya. They agreed and Arlo went left and the rest went the other way to the stairs. Arlo found Mya walking in the hallway. He smiled and ran to her and grabbed her. She was in shock as he threw her into the wall. He walked up to Mya while she was shaking. He asked where Scarlet was. Mya laughed and told him that she would never tell him.

"Do you want to die?" Arlo asked.

"No!" Mya cried.

"Then tell me little weak human!"

"Ok, ok, ok, in a tube third floor! Just leave me be!"

"Good human."

"I hate you twit!"

"You're lucky my friends don't want to kill you because God doesn't like killing."

"Haha, God is so dumb."

"If he is dumb, tell me how be made the world in one breath?"

"Shut up, God is not real and you are an oni and shouldn't be into Christian things!"

"Whatever you say human."

"You're felling Froggie... Leap." Mya smiled.

"You really wanna go there?" Arlo laughed.

As he said that to her, she realized she shouldn't have said that. He grabbed her up by the shirt. She laughed that she was sorry as Arlo smiled at her. While Arlo was making Mya scared, the others had looked on the first floor. They got off the elevator to the second floor. They all herd a tv playing. It was playing a little kids show. They all thought that was a little odd. They walked in the room seeing a kitchen, living room, and two bed rooms. One of the rooms was a blue door with the name Zach on it. They were confused and heard a little boy crying. Zane suggested that Savannah and Drake should summon their swords. They both summoned their swords while Aster opened the door. They were in shock. It was a little boy with dirty blond curly long hair and blue glasses. He had a blue puppy dog shirt on and green dinosaur socks on his feet. He was crying as the friends stared at him wondering who the child was.

"That's a little human kid, not a scientist." Savannah explained.

"Hi, I'm Zach."

"Uh, sup dude." Aster laughed in a confused way.

"I like your swords." Zach smiled.

"Thank you." Savannah smiled back.

"Wait, who is this kid?" Zane asked.

"Oh no! Is Mya testing on kids now?" Drake yelled.

"That would be bad if she did." Aster said.

"Should we take him to the hospital?" Zane asked.

"I'll contact Clara to take him." Aster said, then tapped his hand and a bracelet appeared.

Aster explained that Mya had kidnapped a little boy and they wanted to save him. Clara smiled and told him that she would teleport him to the living room so Len could calm him down. He thanked her as Zach asked Zane if he could play dinosaurs with him. Zane smiled and went on his knees next to him. He asked what the dinosaurs name was. While Zach and Zane were playing, Savannah explained that she knew this place all to well so she might know where Scarlet was. Zane told Zach that he was going to get teleported to a safe place. He cried that this was his home. The friends looked at each other upset. Aster explained to Zach that Mya was not a good person and that a nice lady named Len would play with him. Zach cried that he needed his mommy. Savannah smiled that they would find her for him. Clara teleported Zach to the living room and Len walked up to him wiping his tears off his face. They all followed Savannah to the elevator. She pushed the third floor button. When they got to the third floor, she started to remember the bad times at this part of the hospital. Zane explained that they needed to keep going. They all walked to the end of the hallway and Savannah's face looked traumatized. Aster asked why they stopped. Savannah cried saying that was her testing room. She hugged Zane while crying and thinking about when Mya did inappropriate things to her. Zane explained that the testing room after hers was the last one on that floor. He wiped her tears off her face and told her that they would save Scarlet. When they opened the door they saw Scarlet in a tube crying. They ran up to her thanking God they found her. Aster opened the tube and Scarlet fell into his arms. She pointed at her lab coat that was sitting on the floor. Drake handed it to her as she put it on and thanked them for saving her. Savannah asked if Mya touched her. She walked up to Savannah and explained that Mya did nothing like that to her. Savannah was happy she was ok. Arlo was looking for the others. He made Mya pass out so she wouldn't be looking for them. He heard Savannah's voice and followed it. He found them all hugging Scarlet. Arlo explained that they needed to get out of there before Mya or Poison woke up. Scarlet asked what he did do them. Arlo smiled and told her that he didn't kill them. He made them pass out. He laughed that to make Mya pass out was to just smile at her in your oni form while having a knife to her face. He summoned his staff and teleported them all home.

"Guys, why do you have Mya's kid?" Scarlet asked.

"Wait, that's Mya's son!" Savannah cried.

"Yeah, why is he here? She is going to freak if she finds out he is gone!" Scarlet yelled.

"We thought Mya was testing on kids so we wanted him to be safe." Zane said.

"This is bad." Drake sighed.

"Mommy!" Kaden smiled than ran and hugged Scarlet.

"Be careful Kaden. Mommy is hurting." Scarlet sighed.

"Who is dat?" Zach asked.

"That's Kaden." Len smiled.

"Is that the oni who my mommy was hurting?" Zach asked

"Bad parenting, that's all I'm gonna say." Aster sighed.

"I'm going to see how my daughter is doing." Arlo said.

"An oni!" Zach cried than hid behind Len.

"Arlo I would go into your human form." Savannah said.

"He has a human form?" Scarlet asked.

"Yes, I do." Arlo smiled than went into the human form.

When Arlo went into his human form, Luna said hello as Drake smelled her. He explained that she smelled like puke. She asked why her dad was in his human form. Arlo pointed to Zach and Luna was confused. Aster explained the kid was Mya's son. Luna looked at Zach thinking that they did look alike. They have the same hair and face. Zane explained that they wanted to save Zach but now knowing that it's Mya's son, they needed to give him back to his mom. Zach asked Kaden why he has doggie ears. He smiled that he was an alpha. Arlo told them that he would take Zach to his mom. Len thanked him as Zach asked what Arlo's name was. He smiled and told him his name as he summoned his oni staff. At the League of Science, Mya was looking for Zach. She couldn't find him anywhere.

As she was looking in the living room, she saw Arlo with Zach. She cried for Arlo not to kill him. Arlo let Zach run to his mom. She grabbed him tight crying. Arlo was shocked that Mya cared about her kid. Zach said goodbye to Arlo as he teleported back to Scarlet's hospital.

"What did they do to you?" Mya cried.

"Nothing, the oni's at the place I was at were nice." Zach smiled.

Oh gosh, they brainwashed him. Mya thought while feeling his head.

CHAPTER 17
KADEN'S NEW FRIEND

It's been a week since Mya had kidnaped Scarlet. While Luna was sitting on her bed watching a movie, her water broke. She yelled for Aster while crying. Aster heard Luna yelling so he got up from his gaming chair and put down his controller. He quickly ran to Luna's room. He asked what was wrong as Luna was holding her stomach. She explained that her water broke. Aster yelled for Scarlet as he held Luna's hand. Scarlet was in the other room reading her book and holding a wine glass. She got up and set her glass and book down. She ran to Luna's room and asked why he was yelling. Luna cried that her water broke. Scarlet told him to carry Luna to a hospital bed. He picked her up. She was breathing heavily as he kissed her head. After five minutes of getting Luna calmed down in the hospital bed, Savannah and Drake ran in to see what was going on. Scarlet told Savannah to tell everyone that Luna's is in labor. Drake walked up to Luna and told her that she could do it. Everyone came in asked what was going on. Scarlet explained everything as she was grabbing an Iv for Luna. Arlo smiled at his daughter. He was so happy for her. While everyone was talking about Luna, Len explained that Luna had blood that could kill anyone. Scarlet forgot about that. Savannah cried that she couldn't be sent to a human hospital.

"I can deliver her." Scarlet smiled.

"Wait, you know how to?" Zane asked.

"Mya had taught me about this kind of stuff. I've never did it but I watched her do it. "Scarlet smiled.

"Did you learn anything in college Scarlet?" Len asked.

"I really didn't study it but Mya is a Gynecologist and she taught me things."

"Scarlet is our only option guys. Trust in the Lord to help her." Zane explained.

Drake asked if her blood had killed the baby as he was worried for Luna. Scarlet explained that she did an ultra sound yesterday and that he or she was still moving. Aster kissed Luna and was playing with her hair. She laid her head on his arm as she was grimacing. Drake whined that Scarlet should have checked to see if the baby had a wiener. Savannah smacked Drake on the head. He said teehee and shook his butt at her. While Drake and Savannah were fighting, Luna screamed that the baby was coming. Scarlet told everyone but Aster to get out so she could start the process. She sighed and put gloves on. She was a little scared of delivering her because of her blood. She prayed for God to help her as she walked up to Luna and put an Iv in her arm. She put medicine to help with the pain. After two hours, Luna had a baby girl. Scarlet handed the baby to Luna. Aster smiled at his daughter while the baby was crying. He told Scarlet that she should take off the bloody gloves before she got any blood on her. She put the gloves in an orange biohazard bag. Luna looked at the baby. She was a mixed child with a blue mark on her life eye just like Aster's. She had some hair that was the color purple. It had some light bule highlights in the hair. The baby latched her mouth on Luna and began nursing. Aster laughed that she was hungry. He asked what her name would be. Luna really liked the name Eclipse. He smiled and said he liked that name as well. Eclipse's eyes were opening. Her eyes looked like Luna's.

"Wait, already?" Aster asked.

"Oni baby's eyes come really sooner than a human and her hair will start to grow more by tomorrow." Luna explained.

"Her eyes are like yours." Aster smiled.

"She has the same face as you." Luna smiled.

Scarlet opened the door and everyone ran inside and almost pushed her over. Arlo ran up to Luna and asked the name. She said that her name was Eclipse. Savannah smiled at Eclipse and rubbed her head. Scarlet asked Luna if she could test on Eclipse because she didn't die from being exposed to Luna's blood. Aster and Luna looked at each other and Luna told her yes she could. They both want to know how she didn't die. Arlo asked Scarlet if she had any oni baby food for his granddaughter. She said she didn't have anything. Aster asked why she needed oni food if she was half human. Arlo explained that she was also part oni and part Simbyot. Eclipse needed oni blood to be a healthy baby as well as breast milk like a human. Drake added that if an oni baby doesn't get any human blood, she would get very sick. Luna asked her dad if he could go into the oni realm to get some oni food for her baby. Len suggested that they should try animal blood instead. Savannah sighed and told her that she wishes that would work but the baby needed human blood to be healthy. Zane explained to his mom that Eclipse isn't full human like they were. Arlo summoned his staff and teleported to the oni realm. He teleported into an oni food store. While he was getting food, Luna let Savannah hold Eclipse. She smiled at the baby and told Luna that her baby was really cute. Scarlet took the Iv out of Luna's arm and she helped Luna off the bed. Luna summoned her normal clothing back on and put her sunglasses on her face. Drake gave her a high five for getting it done. Eclipse grabbed Savannah's hair and she asked for some help. Luna ran up to her and grabbed Eclipse. She blabbered at her mom.. Len asked Aster if they needed to get some baby girl clothes for the baby. Aster said that was a great idea. He gave Len some money. Len told Zane to hop in the car so they could go to the mall. Zane always loved shopping with his mom. Before Savannah arrived to the human realm, he and Len always would go shopping. Zane explained to Savannah that he would be back in an hour. Savannah cried that she wanted to go with him. Luna told Savannah that Eclipse needed her aunt to play with her. Zane thanked Luna as he went to get his shoes on. He loved Savannah but sometimes needed a little space. While Len and Zane were heading to the car to go shopping, Arlo came back with a black shopping bag full of oni food and drinks. Luna asked why he got a ton. Arlo laughed as she gave him a look. Luna explained that she looked into his mind. Arlo laughed that he just wanted a treat for himself. Aster put his big iced out chain on Eclipse while Luna was distracted. Drake and Aster smiled at each other thinking the same thing, The baby was gonna be a rapper one day. Luna looked at Aster saying that she looked in his mind. Eclipse was chewing on the big chain while Savannah asked Luna if she could help with the bottle. Luna picked up Eclipse and told her that Arlo could help Savannah while she went and put her baby down for a nap. Arlo and Savannah ran to the kitchen. While Arlo and Savannah were making the bottle of human blood mixed with breast milk, Kaden asked his mom if she could play with him. Scarlet patted him on the head and explained that she had some work to get done. She told him to ask Sav. He smiled and told her that Savannah and him could play dragons and fairies. She laughed as Kaden ran to the hallway. Aster wanted Scarlet to safely put the orange liquid that turned Savannah and Drake into babies into a safe container so that the kids or a bad guy would not mess with it. Kaden asked if Savannah would play with him. Savannah explained that she was helping with Eclipse's bottle. She said that she was sorry as she picked up a packet of human blood. He sighed and walked to the living room. He sat on the couch upset. No one had been playing with him the past week. He wanted to play with someone his age. He could turn to a young adult like his mommy, but she would get mad at him. He remembered when Zach was at his home. He looked friendly. Kaden really wanted to play with him but his mommy was Mya. While Kaden was about to turn on the tv, he saw Aster's teleporter gun on the love seat. He walked up to it and thought of an idea. *Maybe I can send me to Zach so we can play.*

Luna was walking to the living room to let Eclipse eat in her arms. Drake followed Luna asking if he could put on some football. Luna didn't care but he had to be quiet. Drake smiled and gave her a thumbs up. Before Luna sat down, she saw Kaden with Aster's teleporter gun. She asked why he was holding it. Drake told Kaden to put it down because he didn't need to be messing with it. Kaden teleported to the League of Science as Drake asked for him not to use it. Luna and Drake looked at each other. He handed the bottle to Luna and ran to find Scarlet. He yelled for everyone to come to the living room. Scarlet was walking to get a cup of coffee as Drake was screaming her name. She ran to Drake and asked what happened. While everyone was coming to him, he explained that Kaden used the teleporter gun to send himself to Zach. Scarlet laughed at him telling him that was a great prank.

"You almost had me there." Scarlet laughed.

"It's not a prank…" Luna sighed as she walked to Scarlet.

"How did he get my gun?" Aster asked.

"I think you left it in the living room after you and Clara were working on giving it an upgrade." Drake explained.

"He should have known better." Scarlet sighed.

"I'm sorry I didn't put it away." Aster said.

"Its fine but we need to find him before Mya does." Scarlet said.

"Why would he teleport without saying anything?" Savannah asked.

"Didn't Kaden say he wanted to play with someone." Arlo said.

"Yeah, I told him I would play with him later!" Scarlet cried.

"I think Kaden wants to play with Zach." Arlo said.

"Dang it, I wish he had someone his age to play with!" Scarlet cried.

"Relax Scarlet, we will get him." Savannah smiled.

"Sometimes it's hard being a single mom." Scarlet sighed.

"It's hard being a single dad and Luna was a rough kid to handle." Arlo laughed.

"Aster, call Zane to tell him what happened." Scarlet said while crying.

"I'm on it." Aster said.

Kaden had teleported to the League of Science. He was in front of a door that had the name Zach on it. He smiled and opened the door. Zach was playing with his dinosaurs as he walked in. Kaden said hello to him and he looked up and smiled. He asked why Kaden was at his place. He explained to Zach that he wanted to play with him. He told him that he could play with him if he wanted. Kaden sat down on the floor on Zach's green rug. He explained that his mommy can't find out that he was in his place. Zach told him that he wouldn't tell his mommy or daddy. Kaden told him that he loved his room. He thanked him and asked if he wanted a snack. He nodded saying that he would love a snack. Zach got up and told Kaden to stay in his room. He walked out to the kitchen seeing his mommy upset.

"I'm running out of plans!" Mya yelled.

"Calm down Hun. Give me a break with the yelling." Poison sighed.

"Hi mommy." Zach smiled.

"What?" Mya asked.

"Can I get a snack?" Zach asked.

"I don't care, go ahead." Mya sighed.

"Can I have an extra snack please?" Zach asked.

"Why?" Poison asked.

"Uh, I'm extra hungry." Zach stuttered.

"Sure, but don't eat too much because your mom is gonna make dinner." Poison said.

"Ok." Zach smiled.

"I'm not making dinner!" Mya yelled.

"Then who is?" Poison asked.

"You." Mya smiled.

"No, I made something last night!" Poison yelled.

"It was disgusting by the way." Mya smiled.

"Wow, that's mean." Poison whined.

"Anyway, do you have any more tubes of Luna's blood?" Mya asked.

"I only have two more…" Poison sighed

"Think of plans Sam! I want the dang oni's!" Mya yelled while walking away.

Zach handed Kaden a cookie with icing on it. Kaden thanked him as they both smiled at each other. Zach asked what they wanted to do as he took a bite of his cookie. Kaden suggested that they watch a movie. Zach told him that was a great idea. He looked out of his door to make sure his mommy or daddy wasn't in the hallway. He told him to follow him. They both ran to up the stairs to Poison's man cave. Zach opened the door and let Kaden in. He locked the door so his daddy or mommy couldn't find Kaden.

While Kaden and Zach were finding a good movie, Scarlet was super stressed. She was pacing around her office wondering what to do. Arlo walked into her office asking if she was alright. She cried that she wanted her son back. Arlo put his hands on her shoulder telling her that they would get him back before Mya did anything to him. Scarlet surprisingly hugged Arlo. She was crying on his chest. Arlo didn't know what to think about the hug. He told her everything would be ok.

Back at the League of Science, Mya was knocking on the man cave door yelling for Zach. Kaden cried that he didn't want to see Mya. Zach didn't know what to do. He had to listen to his mom or else something bad would happen to him. Zach walked up to his door crying and opened the door. Mya asked why he was crying. She looked over Zach's head seeing Kaden shaking in fear.

"Why in the freaking heck is Scarlet's little bratty son here?" Mya asked.

"I just wanted to play." Kaden cried.

"You will never play with Zach!" Mya yelled.

"Mya, is everything ok in here?" Poison asked.

"How did you get here?" Mya yelled.

"I used a teleporter gun." Kaden said.

"Wow, didn't know that kid was in the man cave." Poison said.

"Don't hurt him mommy." Zach cried.

"Sam, take the alpha kid. I'll be there in a second." Mya smiled.

"But I want him to be my friend!" Zach said while crying.

Poison grabbed Kaden's arm tight. He cried for him to let him go. Zach was crying and begged for his daddy not to take his new friend. Mya walked up to Zach and grabbed his shirt. He cried that he was sorry. Mya pushed him to the floor and yelled for him to get up and go to his room. Poison put Kaden onto a hospital bed and chained his arms onto it. He cried for his mom as Poison shut the door.

After Arlo calmed down Scarlet, he explained his plan to everyone. Luna sighed and told her dad that going in and just winging it was not a good plan. Scarlet cried that Kaden was in danger so she didn't care about a dang plan. Arlo summoned his oni staff and teleported he and Scarlet to the League of Science. When they got there, Scarlet instantly started to run to the elevator. Arlo followed behind her and told her to relax. Scarlet explained that she needed a margarita before she would lose her sanity. Arlo patted her on the head telling her that God was protecting Kaden. As the elevator stopped, Scarlet and Arlo walked out of it wondering where to go next. While they were walking, Arlo explained that he was sorry for eating her husband. She sighed that it was fine and that she didn't want to talk about him.

"So, Luna says that a guy who lives here eats her blood." Arlo said.

"Yeah, his name is Sam Gibbs or now known as Poison." Scarlet answered.

"Like how does her blood not kill that human?" Arlo asked.

"I think because Sam was the first one to get her blood on him, it didn't react to his body somehow." Scarlet explained.

"Wow, you're smart." Arlo smiled than started to blush.

"Um, thank you." Scarlet laughed.

Mya opened the door seeing Kaden crying. She laughed and walked up to him with a knife. He begged for him to let her go. Mya traced her fingernails on Kaden's arm as he was breathing heavily. She wiped his tears off his face and told him Zach would never be his friend. Mya sliced a little piece of skin off Kaden's cheek. He screamed and yelling for his mommy. "Psalm 121:1-2, "I lift up my eyes to the mountains, where does my help come from, my help comes from the Lord, the Maker of heaven and earth." Kaden cried.

Mya sighed and suggested that he shut up before she got mad. She looked at her knife thinking about what to do with Kaden. She felt his ears telling him that he was ugly. *Isaiah 41:10 says, "So do not fear, for I am with you, do not be dismayed, for I am your God, I will strengthen you and help you, I will uphold you with my righteous right hand.* Kaden thought while crying. Mya asked if Kaden was an oni like his mother or if he was full alpha. He cried that he didn't know as Mya lifted up his shirt. She felt his ribs knowing that Savannah' s and Scarlet's felt different from a human. He cried for Mya to stop touching him. While Mya was examining Kaden's body to see if he was an oni like Scarlet, Savannah's oni sense was out of control. Zane asked why she was shaking in fear. She was such in fear she could barely speak. He put his hands on her shoulder and asked what was bothering her. She cried that her oni sense was acting up. He asked what that meant as he wiped her tears off her face. Luna explained that an oni sense is when an oni feels something bad is going to happen or that evil is nearby.

"I don't know who or what is coming soon but we need to prepare." Savannah sighed.

Arlo and Scarlet were walking in the hallway on floor five. While Arlo was looking at a bloody hospital bed outside of a testing room, Scarlet yelled that Poison found them.

"What do you want Gibbs?" Scarlet grunted.

"We have your son." Poison smiled.

"We know that." Arlo said.

"You better not torture him!" Scarlet yelled.

"Ha, I don't know what Mya has in store for him but I know it's gonna be bloody." Poison laughed.

Poison summoned a green emerald dagger than thew it at Scarlet's chest. Scarlet fell to her knees and pulled it out while grimacing. Poison laughed and showed them Aster's teleporter gun that Kaden used to get to the League of Science. Scarlet sighed as Arlo helped her up. She held her hand on her bloody chest while Arlo walked up to Poison. He was about to kicked Poison to the floor but he used the teleporter gun to grab a hold of Scarlet. She yelled for him to let her go. As Arlo was running to Scarlet, Poison used the gun to send himself and Scarlet to Mya. Arlo got really angry at this green dumb butt human. He now needed to think of a plan to save Kaden and Scarlet all by himself. He summoned his oni sword and began to walk upstairs to the next floor.

Poison threw Scarlet in front of Mya. Scarlet looked up seeing Mya smiling at her. She grabbed her shirt and told her that her son would die if she didn't listen to what she said. Scarlet asked where her son was. Mya pushed her next to a hospital bed saying that she just had put a sedative into Kaden. She got up and begged for her son to wake up. Mya put her hands on Scarlet's shoulder saying that she came just in time. Scarlet yelled at her asking what she was going to do with Kaden. She explained that Kaden had only 10% oni in him so she didn't want to test on him. Poison added that Mya was going to see if he could die because he barely had oni in him. Scarlet cried for Mya to not kill him. Mya pinned her to the wall touching her hair. Scarlet yanked her head away begging for her to let Kaden go. She yelled that she didn't even want Kaden, she wanted her. While Scarlet and Mya were yelling at each other, Kaden yelled mommy. Scarlet smiled at him saying that she was ok. Poison whined to Mya that he needed more of Luna's blood. Kaden laughed and told him that Luna can't because she needed to rest because she had a baby girl today. Mya and Poison looked at each other while Scarlet took a deep breath trying not to lose it.

"So, Luna has a child now." Poison laughed.

"You will never take her baby!" Scarlet yelled.

Before Mya could ask questions about Luna's baby, her walkie talkie beeped and she grabbed it. It was one of the workers saying that one of her test subjects got out and he's threatening to kill them if he doesn't find Scarlet and Kaden. She was confused and told her worker that all the test subjects were with her at this time. Before she could ask what was going on, the worker screamed and she heard his bone break. She dropped her walkie talkie in shock. Poison grabbed it and asked if he was alright. The worker screamed that a very tall oni was heading their way. As Arlo was running trying to find his way in the lab, Zach was crying. Arlo walked up to him asking if he was ok. Zach cried that his mommy and daddy were hurting his new friend. He asked if his new friend was Kaden. Zach nodded and cried that his mommy was going to kill him. Arlo told Zach that he would stop his mom from hurting his buddy. He thanked him as Arlo walked to the next floor. As he got to the hallway on the next floor, he heard Scarlet yelling. He followed her voice seeing Mya having a knife into Scarlet's chest. She looked at Arlo in fear. She took out the knife and back away. Before Poison could blast him with his toxic power, Arlo lifted him up and threw him all the way out of the testing room into a wall in the hallway. He hit his head than he passed out on the floor. Mya got her gun from her belt as Arlo was walking up to her. He punched her in the ribs and kneed her in the stomach. He grabbed the gun away from her and threw it to the other side of the room. Kaden cried that he wanted to go home as Arlo pushed Mya to the floor. Mya couldn't move because Arlo hit her good. He ran to Scarlet and gave her a big hug.

"Thanks for saving me and Kaden." Scarlet smiled.

"No problem.." Arlo said.

"Wow, you're close." Scarlet mumbled.

"I hope Mya didn't hurt you that bad." Arlo cried.

"She only stabbed me a few times." Scarlet sighed.

"Scarlet, I don't know if I should say this yet but, I really think you're pretty." Arlo smiled while blushing.

"Thanks." Scarlet laughed.

Arlo grabbed Scarlet closer to him. Kaden asked if they could kiss. Scarlet got embarrassed as Arlo pulled her hair out of her face. "Scarlet, will you please be my girlfriend? I know it's a lot to think about because I killed your husband. I just don't want to be alone anymore." Arlo asked.

"I don't know…" Scarlet sighed.

"Its fine if you don't like me." Arlo said.

"Mommy, say yes!" Kaden smiled.

"Fine, I do like you and I've been hiding it but I don't know if I should because you did kill Seth and all. I talked to God about it and I think I can trust you." Scarlet cried.

"Mommy, are you crying?" Kaden asked.

Arlo kissed Scarlet on the lips. Mya looked up at Arlo and Scarlet. *What the heck,* Mya thought.

Mya got up and laughed at them. Scarlet gave her a mean face. She laughed that she had to be joking. Arlo summoned his staff hit Mya in the head with it than she passed out to the floor. Scarlet unlocked Kaden's X stone. She picked him up as he was crying. He was sorry for using the teleporter gun. She told him that she forgave him but the next time he uses it, he would get a punishment. He said sorry as Arlo picked up the teleporter gun. He gave it to Scarlet as he used his staff to take them to the hospital. When they got back, they saw Eclipse laughing at Drake being silly. Savannah ran up to give Scarlet a hug and crying that she was having a hard time. She put Kaden down and he ran to Drake asking him to hold him. Scarlet asked her what the problem was. Arlo sighed and told her that he thinks her oni sense is bothering her because his was acting up as well. Len explained that she cooked a nice dinner for them and that it was her homemade mac and cheese. They all ate than after that they all settled down for the night.

CHAPTER 18
THE BATTLE

It was the next morning after the long day trying to get Kaden back. Luna picked up Eclipse and walked out to the kitchen. Scarlet was making breakfast pizza and fresh brewed sweet tea for breakfast. Luna asked where Savannah was as Eclipse was sucking on her binky. Zane sighed and told her that Sav wasn't feeling herself. She asked what was wrong with her. Drake explained that she was up almost all night crying in fear. She asked where she was now. Zane told her that she was outside looking up at the sky. He explained that he tried to get her to come in but she said she wanted some alone time. Luna smiled and told Zane that she'll check up on her for them. She gave Eclipse to Aster and walked to the lobby. She went out of the door seeing Savannah holding her hands on the railing outside of the hospital. Luna walked up to her asking if she was alight. She looked at Luna and sighed that evil was coming soon. Luna was rubbing her back while asking what kind of evil. Before she could say anything, black darkness fog formed up in the sky. Luna shook her to get her attention. She asked why she looked traumatized. She pointed to the sky and Savannah's heart dropped. Before she could pass out from shock, the black fog disappeared. They both looked at each other confused.

"What just happened?" Luna asked.

"We need to tell the others!" Savannah cried.

While Aster was holding Eclipse, Scarlet was playing with her fluffy blue and purple hair. She smiled at Scarlet than blabbered at her. She was kicking her legs happy and just kept smiling at everyone. She grabbed Aster's diamond chain and put it in her mouth. Arlo smiled at his granddaughter as Savannah and Luna ran in. Drake asked why they looked scared.

"Hey Savannah, my oni senses bothered me all night too. It's really weird." Arlo said.

"Crap, that means something bad is going to happen. Luna and I just saw darkness fog." Savannah cried.

"What!" Zane yelled.

"We need to tell other humans, especially if the oni fog spreads into the city!" Drake yelled.

"Scarlet and Clara, you two hack people's phone and radios and tell them about the fog." Aster said.

"Ok. We can do that." Scarlet smiled.

"Sis, what if our Dad is behind this?" Drake asked.

"That would be the worst thing in the world!" Savannah cried.

"King Chen will want you if he wants the human realm into darkness." Arlo said.

"Yeah, that's probably why the fog disappeared. I'm the only one who has the power to do it." Savannah explained.

While they were all wondering what to do, an oni portal came into the room. Luna asked for her dad to stop it. He explained that he could try as he had purple fog around his hands. He tried but the portal got bigger and bigger. He fell to the floor because he used to much of his strength. Scarlet helped him up as they heard a creepy voice laughing. Savannah and Drake knew that laugh really well. A guy that had black and purple long hair and a crown on made out of human jaws and teeth appeared. He had half of his face ripped off and you could see his skull and bones. He had black horns in his head and a black tail. His shoes had spikes on the bottom of them. Savannah was in so much fear. She cried that she didn't want to make human realm into darkness. She ran to Zane hugging him tight. Zane looked at the freaky oni in fear. Arlo sighed and said hello to King Chen. He summoned his sword as King Chen gave him a mean face. Chen blasted Arlo to the floor as Aster gave Eclipse to Len. He told her to protect Kaden and Eclipse. She nodded and ran to Kaden's room and locked the door. Kaden asked why she was scared. She told him to be quiet as she put Eclipse next to Kaden on his bed. Chen looked at Savannah telling her she had changed. He told her she was just like her mother, a demonic woman who wanted to be friends with humans.

"Wipe that smirk off your face!" Drake yelled.

"So, he's the one that killed Lilly?" Arlo asked.

"Yes." Savannah cried.

"Wait, how do you know her?" King Chen asked.

"She was my wife before yours!" Arlo yelled

Luna summoned her Simbyot knife and threw it at King Chen's chest. He pulled it out as Luna called him a dimwit.

"I see you're not human." King Chen laughed.

"You freaking dimwit killed my mom!" Luna cried.

"Huh? I don't even know who you are!" King chen yelled.

Arlo ran to Chen and sliced his arm with his sword. While Clara and Scarlet were hacking people's phones telling them about the darkness fog, they heard Arlo screaming in pain. Scarlet ran to see what was going on. She ran to the living room seeing Arlo's arm bleeding badly. Aster blasted King Chen with his water. Chen laughed at him telling him that his power was stupid than he used his darkness on him. Luna begged for Chen not to kill him. Aster got really dizzy and fell to his knees in pain. His ears were ringing as Scarlet ran up to him. She asked if he was ok. Aster fell to the floor and passed out. Luna cried that King Chen would pay for that. He walked up to Luna and lifted her up by the shirt. Luna put her webs on a wall than pulled herself out of his hold. He asked if she was a Simbyot. Arlo was grimacing and begged Chen not to hurt his daughter. Scarlet ran to Arlo looking at his arm. She explained that it was a big gash in his arm. King Chen had the satanic symbol circling around him and he yelled that evil is more powerful than good. Zane yelled that he was wrong. He laughed at Zane and used his power to make the room into darkness. Savannah cried for Zane to get out of the living room. Drake pushed Zane to the hallway before Zane got frozen into darkness. Zane asked if he could help them. Arlo yelled that he would end up like Aster if he came into the living room. Savannah begged him not to come in. Chen asked Savannah how the woman in the lab coat could breathe the darkness fog. Scarlet explained that she was an oni. King Chen was in shock so he ran up to her and was going to kill her but Arlo stabbed him before he could get to her. King Chen ran up to Drake and told him that he wishes that he was never born. Drake tired not to cry as King Chen walked up to him. Drake got his sword telling him that God was his father, not him. Chen King got mad at what he said so he stabbed him in the chest and threw him into the wall. Savannah cried that her dad was too strong. Scarlet told Luna to put her blood on Chen. Arlo told Luna that she could do it. Luna summoned her knife and rolled up her sleeve. Chen laughed at her telling her that blood couldn't kill an oni. She smiled and sliced a little bit of her arm open. Chen was confused while Luna walked up to him. Before she could put her blood onto his arm, he pushed her to the floor and punched her stomach and she passed out. Arlo got angry and ran up to him but Chen cut his face open with his sword. Arlo fell to the floor as Scarlet ran up to him. King Chen made a oni portal next to Savannah than ran to her and pushed her in. Drake cried for Savannah but she was gone. King Chen went into the portal saying that they lost. The portal closed before Drake could get to it. Darkness went out of the living room and Zane went in asking if everyone was ok. Scarlet explained that Chen got Savannah. She told Zane to help her get Aster, Luna, Drake, and Arlo to a hospital bed so she could help them.

In the oni realm Savannah fell from the ceiling onto the floor. She got up and put her hat back on her head. She was at her old home in the oni realm. She was scared for her life. She thought of a good bible verse to help her relax. *Isaiah 35:4 says that, Be strong, do not fear, your God will come, he will come with vengeance, with divine retribution he will come to save you.* Savannah thought while crying.

King Chen walked into the room seeing Savannah in fear. She looked at him in terror as he walked to her. She cried for him not to hurt her as he took her hat off. He yelled for her to go into her oni form. She was in so much fear that she listened to him and obeyed. He grabbed her arm tight and walked her into the basement. He threw her to the floor in front of the machine that Arlo used to make the human realm into darkness.

"No one is going to save you Savannah. I am the strongest oni in the universe." King Chen laughed.

"I don't want to do this Dad. I'm not evil anymore and you can't make me do anything bad!" Savannah yelled.

"You are a disgrace to me and the other oni's. We are evil powerful beings and kill humans!" King Chen yelled.

"I'm not like that!" Savannah cried.

"I wish I never had kids. I hate you and Drake because you guys have crossed over to the light!" King Chen yelled.

"Mom loved us." Savannah said while crying

"I don't care about Lilly!"

"Humans are so nice and all you want to do is kill them and eat them!"

"I had it with the good oni thing. You are going to make the human realm into darkness if you like it or not!"

Scarlet was tying to wake up Aster. She had an idea. She was going to shock him awake. She grabbed the heart defibrillator and put it onto Aster's chest. She turned the shock level high and pushed a button and it shocked him awake. He screamed and sat up on the hospital bed. He asked what happened as Luna was on the other bed nursing Eclipse. She sighed and told him that Chen took Savannah. She cried that she almost had him, she felt dumb for not putting her blood on Chen in time. Drake held the baby so Luna could rest. She was so disappointed that she failed Savannah and cried in her pillow.

"What are we going to do?" Scarlet mumbled while pacing around and having a pen to her teeth.

"King Chen is way too strong." Aster said.

"Arlo is strong." Len smiled.

"I tried. King Chen is way too hard to beat. Scarlet has to stitch my face up because he ripped some of it off." Arlo sighed.

"Luna has blood that can kill any being. We can use that in a way." Drake said while Eclipse was playing with his hood.

"We need to be sneaky though because Chen knocked Luna out when she tried to put her blood on him." Scarlet explained.

King Chen had Savannah onto the machine and he turned it on. She was trying not to puke from the needles in her arms. She cried that his plan would fail because God was more powerful than him. He just laughed at her while drinking human blood out of a stone cup. He smiled that he loved to see his daughter in pain. *God says, Be strong and courageous; do not be frightened and do not be dismayed, for the Lord your God is with you wherever you go.* Savannah thought.

"I think I might have a plan but it's really risky." Aster sighed.

"We need all the ideas we can get." Zane said.

"Maybe we can somehow get Luna to go into the Lunar Destruction mode and let her fight King Chen." Aster explained.

"The blood moon is the only way I can go into the Lunar Destruction." Luna sighed while Eclipse was holding her sunglasses.

"It's a Friday and the blood moon is next Friday." Scarlet said while looking at a calendar.

"This is so stressful." Drake sighed.

"What's that sound?" Arlo asked.

"It's so loud. It hurts my ears!" Kaden cried.

"It's the news." Aster said while looking at the tv.

The Tv man said that there was Important news. "Black fog is going around Science City and it's turning people pitch black and they can't move. We think they might be dead, all of you need to stay indoors. We don't know what this terrifying fog is but it's dangerous and you need to be safe. Don't let your kids or pets outside until it goes away. We will be back when we get more information."

"Luna is the only one who can kill King Chen and we found out if talk be sweet and kind to Luna when she is the Lunar Destruction she will calm down. When we use hate, it makes her even more evil. If we make Luna mad, she might trigger her Lunar form." Zane explained.

"You have got to be kidding me." Luna sighed.

"We need to try." Zane said.

"I'm sorry Luna but your outfit sucks today." Aster smiled.

Luna crossed her arms as Aster was laughing at her. Aster laughed that Luna was a weak idiot. She gave him a mean face while growling at him. Arlo grabbed Eclipse as Luna was getting a little mad. Drake smiled that she was skinny and wasn't tough. Luna yelled that he was a dimwit. Arlo told her that she was bad at being good. Luna yelled for them to shut up as her eyes turned red. Zane smiled that it was working.

"Weak little poop head." Aster laughed.

"Shut the heck up before I rip your guts out!" Luna yelled.

"I think it's working." Len said.

"Yeah, it is." Scarlet smiled.

"I'm embarrassed being around you." Arlo laughed.

"Shut up!" Luna yelled than red fog was circling around her.

This might have been a bad idea. Zane thought.

"She is gonna hate this one." Drake smiled.

"Do it bro." Aster smiled.

"I want to break your sunglasses and I'll will let Poison have you because you hate us all." Drake laughed.

Luna's anger had risen to the roof. She used her evil red power to blasted Drake. He fell down saying sorry to her. Luna laughed that she would kill them all. Aster looked at Zane saying that it was his plan, so now what? Zane explained that he didn't know what to do now, all he knew was how to trigger it. Aster cried for Luna not to eat them. Eclipse was waving at her mommy so Arlo put her hand down telling her that she shouldn't wave at her mommy right now. She laughed and smiled at him. He gave her to Len and told her to take Eclipse and Kaden to the toy room so Luna wouldn't try to kill them.

"Drake, why don't you come here and have some fun." Luna laughed.

"Uh, no thanks." Drake cried.

"Don't you want to feel your blood dripping off your face?" Luna asked.

"I got this." Aster smiled.

"What now." Scarlet sighed.

"Listen Luna. King Chen has your sister and he is hurting her." Aster said.

"Like I care." Luna laughed.

"Did you know King Chen killed your mom?" Arlo asked.

"He what?" Luna asked.

"I would get revenge on Chen for that if I were you." Scarlet said.

"You guys just don't want to die so you're wanting me to put my blood on someone else." Luna grunted.

"King Chen wants to be more powerful than you. Go and kill him so you can be the best." Zane smiled

"Ha, no one is more powerful than me." Luna laughed.

"Chen will not be powerful If you get rid of him." Drake said.

"Chen killed Lilly. She would still be here if Chen wouldn't have killed her. Lilly would have seen her granddaughter." Arlo sighed.

"Come on Luna. We know you wanna kill everyone in the world so why don't you kill the oni king and get him over with?" Scarlet asked.

"That would be nice getting rid of the oni king." Luna said.

Arlo used his staff to send Luna to the oni realm to kill Chen. When she got there she heard Savannah yelling in pain. She followed the voice seeing Savannah in a machine and King Chen laughing at her. Savannah looked up at Luna yelling for her to help her. Luna walked up to King Chen giving him a mean face. He asked who she was as he summoned his oni sword.

"God says killing is wrong but, my Dad is the brother of Satan and he's the only person who Jesus hates. Luna you can defeat him." Savannah said.

Luna blasted him with red fog. He coughed and asked who she was. She smiled and told him that she was the Lunar Destruction. Chen was in shock. He never had thought he would ever meet the Lunar Destruction. He yelled that he would never bow down to her because he was a king. She laughed and used her power to make him fall to the floor. She used the Lunar power to make his body hurt. He felt burning in his skin and his bones felt like they were going to break. He screamed at the top of his lungs in pain. She stooped and walked up to him. He begged for Luna to kill Savannah instead. She smiled and told him that she wanted to kill him first because he killed her mother. He got up and stabbed her with his sword. He pulled out the sword and she fell to her knees. Savannah cried for her to get up as Chen was about to stab her again. She dodged the sword and told him that he shouldn't have done that. She yelled that she was darkness in the flesh and that she would rip him into pieces. Before King Chen could stab her again, she put some of the blood on her chest onto her hands and ran up to him and wiped it on Chen's arm. He fell to the floor screaming that it hurts. She put her blood on his face and he yelled that he would still beat her. His face and arm were burning off. His eyes fell out and his teeth as well. His body was shaking. She smiled as he died in front of her.

"Luna, it's not even the blood moon. How are you the Lunar Destruction?" Savannah asked.

Arlo opened King Chen's door and ran inside. He wanted to make sure everything was going as planned. He saw Chen dead on the floor. He smiled and ran to Luna as she was about to eat him. He grabbed her hand and knocked her out before she could kill anyone else. He sat Luna nicely on the floor and walked up to Savannah. He helped her out and she hugged him tight. She thanked him as he smiled at her.

When they got back they put Luna on her bed and waited for her to wake up. After an hour of waiting she asked what happened. Aster kissed her on the head telling her that she did a great job. Savannah explained that she killed her dad and she was happy that she did it. Drake sighed that they didn't have a dad or a mom now. Scarlet and Arlo smiled at each other. Arlo walked up to them smiling at them. Luna asked why he looked so happy.

"Scarlet took me to a place called a court house and I signed some papers and now you two are my kids." Arlo smiled.

"Wait what!" Savannah yelled.

"You guys are mine now. You are adopted." Arlo smiled.

"Thank you!" Drake smiled.

Savannah and Drake ran to Arlo and gave him a hug. Luna ran in to get a hug too. Everyone was so happy for them. Savannah cried that he loved Arlo so much. Luna thanked her dad for letting Savannah and Drake be her siblings.

So, now that the battle with Chen is over it's time for them to relax and enjoy Eclipse. As Luna looks at her daughter she wonders; *is her blood like mine? Will it kill people? Will she be cursed to be the Lunar Destruction? One day we will know but maybe I don't want to know.*

Made in the USA
Coppell, TX
31 July 2024

35417689R00167